The Bookseller's Sonnets

The Bookseller's
Sonnets

Andi Rosenthal

BOOKS

Winchester, UK
Washington, USA

First published by O-Books, 2010
O Books is an imprint of John Hunt Publishing Ltd., The Bothy, Deershot Lodge, Park Lane, Ropley,
Hants, SO24 0BE, UK
office1@o-books.net
www.o-books.com

For distributor details and how to order please visit the 'Ordering' section on our website.

Text copyright Andi Rosenthal 2009

ISBN: 978 1 84694 342 3

A CIP catalogue record for this book is available from the British Library.

Design: Stuart Davies
Front cover design by Howard Levine

Printed in the UK by CPI Antony Rowe
Printed in the USA by Offset Paperback Mfrs, Inc

We operate a distinctive and ethical publishing philosophy in all
areas of its business, from its global network of authors to
production and worldwide distribution.

This book is dedicated
to my family, and to my teachers.
And to my father, Leo C. Rosenthal (z"l)
who was both.

In the things of the soul, remembrance without knowledge
profits little.
— St. Thomas More, 1522

Time trieth truth.
— St. Thomas More, 1529

Prologue

Dust filled her throat as the shovel pierced the dry earth. The bones of her hands ached as she awkwardly lifted another load of crumbling dirt. She looked over her shoulder, making sure no one saw or heard her. As the dirt slid unsteadily from the shovel to the ground, it made a sound like rain. She held her breath. Even that was too loud.

Aware of her solitude, she listened. These sounds were not new to her; the ringing of metal against the ground, the ragged descending clatter of earth in motion, the echoing-after silence. But then she had been surrounded by others; those whom she loved, those who also mourned. Now she was alone, attending this burial without witnesses. *Perhaps, she thought, this is the sound of my own funeral.*

She pressed the shovel close to her body and listened. A hot, unexpected breeze suddenly emerged from the grove of trees behind her. She felt it roam over her face, her arms, the cool cotton of the skirt that clung to her hips.

Her limbs tightened against the wind's appraisal of her body; the dead, dry grasses waved, whispered, and were stilled again. Her eyes followed the line of dark trees to the horizon. There was silence and there was sunlight. And yet, she felt a tiny sensation of movement beneath her feet, something coming from the earth itself, a tremor of something about to be born.

Looking around again, she felt every nerve in her body intent upon the sounds as they vibrated up from the earth. The smooth metal handle of the shovel felt as heavy and solid as bone in her hands. Her eyes flickered from one end of the field to another and back again, a blur of golden wheat, red poppies and cerulean sky. The palms of her hands gripped the metal shaft, poised to dig. The soles of her feet gripped the earth, poised to flee.

She heard the trucks before she saw them. The sound came out of the distance, muffled by the trees. There was a distant squeal of brakes, a rumble of tires. She silently laid the shovel on the ground and picked up the box, holding it in her arms. For a brief moment she thought about running, but it was already too late. She crouched on the ground, surrounded by the thick stalks, and forced herself to quiet her breathing. The trucks, roaring, came closer; the sounds grew louder, then stopped.

"Aus! Aus!"

There was a babble of voices, and then the clipped German orders ringing out above them. She tried to judge how far away they were - *A hundred meters? Two hundred?* But she knew there was no way of knowing unless she looked, and she knew she could not.

"Jetzt! Aus! Jetzt!"

The babble dissipated into a murmur as she listened, feeling the sharp angles of metal digging into her arms, the clasp of the box smooth as silver beneath her fingertips. There was the sound of feet on gravel, punctuated every few seconds by a cry of pain.

"Anordnung! Jetzt!"

She closed her eyes and opened them again, but all she could see around her was the golden grass, the earth below, the soft warm blue above. Her mouth was dry, the edges of her lips caked with dust.

"Anordnung!"

She heard the feet begin to move, shuffling over the dry ground. A child's quiet voice, pleading *Wo sind wir, Papa?* fluttered toward her through the air like birdsong.

"Nehmen Sie dieses. Grabung." A single voice, knifelike, repeated the command, over and over like a chant. The only other sound was the sharp bite of metal in the earth, first one and then others, and more shovels joining in like a chorus. She looked over at her own shovel lying on the ground, useless.

The sound of digging continued for another eternity. Sunlight slanted against the horizon. The metal grew cold in her aching arms. She longed to put the box on the ground. But she did not move.

"Entfernen sie ihre Kleidung!" The digging stopped, and she heard the murmur of voices rise again. The German voices rang out in the gathering dusk. *"Ruhe! Ruhe!"* And then a lower, insidious growl. *"Verachter Juden!"*

2

So it is true, she thought. *Everything that he said, everything he told me before they took him away.* She heard the sound of women crying, the sound of German jeers and laughter. Another thought flashed into her mind: *Is he there with them? What if this is his transport? Is he with those people, naked and waiting to die?* The sun slipped from her line of vision. Her skin grew colder; the box lay like a small dead thing in her arms. She knew there was not much time left.

Everything inside her told her to look, to raise her dark head above the golden wheat, to search the faceless forms until she saw his lean, familiar body, to listen among the incoherent cries and pleas for the sweetness of his voice.

I cannot, she told herself. *I have to think of my daughter. I cannot risk —*

The shots echoed through the still air. Screams rose into the sky like fire; voices merged into one cry so she could not separate them from one another; and all through the chaos the gunshots, as calm and orderly as marching feet.

She flinched over and over with the fiery burst of each volley; there was the sudden metallic taste of blood in her mouth where she had bitten her tongue to keep from crying out.

The sounds continued and then, without warning, grew quieter; now there were fewer voices; now even fewer. She could distinguish them now, one from another. The quiet drone of men's praying voices was drowned in a storm of bullets. A child, boy or girl, impossible to know, crying for its mother. A young man cursing the Fürher, cursing them all, whose false bravery ended with his crying "*Nein, bitte, nein.*" Until finally, a singular voice, female, pleading, weeping, was silenced with a blast of gunfire.

Now she heard the soldiers' voices, talking quietly at first, then more boisterously. She heard the ringing iron sound of shovels, the soft raining sound of the earth being resettled, and then a quiet hissing sound that she could not identify. After a few moments, a carbolic smell of acid drifted through the grass and into her nostrils. She tasted a

3

burning at the back of her throat; and silently bit down on her fingertips, trying to stop the lurching of her stomach as she fought down the urge to vomit.

The voices talked easily as they completed their task. Soon she heard the sound of their boots as they walked briskly back to their trucks, and the grind and shift of gears as they drove away into the dusk.

Light seeped from the sky as she moved, gingerly, her cramped and aching arms finally placing the weight of the box on the cold ground. For a moment she wrapped her arms around her body, holding herself tightly. Her hands gripped her shoulders; she tried to rock herself slightly as if she were a child who had awakened from a nightmare.

She listened to the sounds of the night. Suddenly out of the silence and distance she thought she could hear a tiny cry, barely audible. With her body she listened for the sound of a human voice, but there was silence.

Alone in the field of wheat, with the sounds of the summer evening beginning to whisper through the grass, she pushed herself up, feeling the burning ache in her cold legs and the dank souvenir of sweat sticking to her back. She picked up the shovel and started to dig again, quickly and carelessly, her eyes barely able to see in the gathering darkness.

Finally, the hole was large enough. She fell to her knees, scrabbling for the box with her hands, feeling around in the dirt and darkness. She placed it into the hole, into the moist dirt that lay below the dry surface of the summer field. The deep, wet earth clung to her hands; in the rising moonlight it looked like blood.

She stood, picked up the shovel and began to fill in the hole, working as quickly as she could. The moon rose white and cold in the sky. The birds were gone. The wheat stalks scratched at her bare arms and legs.

When she was finished, she walked back toward the road, the shovel heavy and dull in her tired hands. Just as she reached the edge of the field, she thought she heard the sound again, the barely human cry from the bottom of the pit.

She told herself was hearing things, that it might even be one of her own cries trapped inside her. The sounds had formed a stone of silence in her mouth. She wondered where he was....if he was; but she could not think of him, she would not let herself think of him. She hurried back toward home, letting herself think of nothing but the sound of the living earth falling quietly upon the gray metal box.

1

The apartment was just like dozens, perhaps a hundred other apartments I had visited before, and it was what I had come to expect from the home of a ninety-year-old Holocaust survivor.

We sat, perched on the rose-patterned linen cushions of an aging sofa, and sipped tea from cups so delicate that I was afraid that mine would disintegrate in my fingertips. Across from me, Mrs. Esther Feinberg, her white curls perfectly set and waved, her blue eyes sparkling with the delight of entertaining a visitor - clutched the small silver spoon in her arthritic fingers.

"My mother was a strong woman. She had endless energy, even after giving birth to six children. My father was a lawyer, and my mother was what you would refer to in America as a housewife, even though we always had a girl helping us in the house. But my mother was never idle. She was raised to be a good wife, and she always treasured all of the beautiful things in our home."

"And this little baby spoon," she said, the words curling lovingly around the vowels of her slight German accent, "is all that is left. It was the only thing she brought with her into the camps. When we got there the guards took our suitcases, and put them off to the side of the train yard. Then they told us to get in line. My three brothers and two sisters went in one line, my mother and I went in the other. My youngest brother, Motti, he was only three years old. He went holding the hand of my sister Gretel, who was seven. They were so brave. They never even cried. I was fourteen, the oldest. They knew that my mother and I were strong enough to work. And we had worked very hard in those three months since my father had been taken away in a convoy. Because we knew after they came for the men that we didn't have much time."

The pleasantries were over, I thought. It was time to listen to the story that I had come prepared to hear. I placed my teacup in the center of the tiny saucer and rested them on her coffee table, and reached for my notebook, prepared to ask the questions that all of our museum's curators were trained to ask.

"Mrs. Feinberg, would you mind terribly if I took some notes on your story? It's very important to us to know where your artifact comes from and its history."

"Of course not." She smiled warmly.

I adjusted my glasses, removed the cap from my pen, opened to the next blank page in my notebook. "What was your mother's name?" I asked, trying to make my voice sound as calming and professional as I could.

"Miriam," she replied. "And my father was Chaim, but everyone called him Henry. You see, after a certain time, in the thirties, it was dangerous to be called by a Jewish name. My father wanted my mother to shorten her name to Mary, but of course she refused."

I wrote the names in my book. This was something of a slightly unusual story. I had interviewed many survivors who came from Jewish families that had changed their names, either by choice or by force. I loved hearing stories where people had refused to give in.

"Where in Germany did you live?"

"We lived in Nuremberg," she sighed. "We couldn't have been in a worse place. They made an example of our city. Everything they could do to maintain their laws, their idea of *Judenraus* – a city that was free of Jews - they did.

"In the early thirties my mother used to take us to the park, wheeling the youngest baby in the carriage. It was a beautiful English carriage that her parents had given her when I was born." As she spoke, her eyes seemed to look at something in the distance, far beyond the dining room.

"There was a day in 1934. It was May, a beautiful spring day. An officer in uniform, wearing the swastika armband, arrested us in the park. He said that my sister Ruthie had stepped on the grass. We were brought to the city jail and held there. I can still remember how the cherry blossoms fluttered from the trees, as my mother was led away in handcuffs, with us children following behind her like ducklings.

7

"The magistrate knew us – I told you already that my father was a lawyer, and at that time such things still mattered – so we were allowed to leave after a few hours. But I still remember my mother sitting in the cell, holding the baby, while my sisters and my brother and I sat on benches with real criminals looking at us, watching us. We were so glad to leave. But they never gave back the baby carriage.

"One day, we were riding in the city trolley – one of the last times we were allowed to do so, before Jews were forbidden to use public transportation. We looked out of the window and saw one of the officers' wives wheeling her baby in the carriage. It was one of the only times I ever saw my mother cry."

She fell silent for a long moment. I cleared my throat a little bit, hating myself for interrupting her memory. "Your spoon," I said, gesturing to the little piece of silver in her hands. "Your mother was able to smuggle it into the camps?"

"Yes," she said, looking down at it. "When we arrived at Dachau, after five days on the train without food, without water, without air or light or space, it became clear that the people who had gotten off the train first were being ordered to leave their suitcases in the trainyard. She took the spoon out of her suitcase pocket and slipped it into the ripped seam of her skirt.

"It was a miracle that she managed to hold on to it. She told me that it was small enough to hide in her clothes, that she had torn the hem at the bottom of her uniform shirt and hidden it there. She said that during more than one inspection, she would tuck it right under her arm and hold it to her side, praying that she would not be ordered to move and that it would drop to the ground. She saved it because she had fed each of us, for the first time, with this spoon. Each of us had touched it with our lips. She said it was the only thing left of her children's kisses."

I scrawled furiously in my notebook, wishing I had taken my tiny cassette recorder with me instead. "Did your mother survive the war?"

"For a little while," she answered. "After the war we went back to Nuremberg, to our old house, which, we realized soon enough, wasn't our house anymore. We lived in a shelter for a while with twenty or

8

thirty other people who had also returned from the camps. Eventually we got some help from an American organization that was helping survivors to relocate. They said that we could go to Israel or to America. Those same people helped us to find the records of my father, my sisters and brothers.

"It was two years later when we found out that they were gone. My mother always knew that they were dead. But when we got the letter saying how and when and where they died, something in her seemed to die as well. A few months later, she went to sleep one night and never woke up. She was only forty-eight years old."

I continued writing without looking up. "And you came to America after that," I concluded, filling the silence. I didn't want to rush her, but in the tiny, claustrophobic space of that apartment, I suddenly became aware of the sun sinking low in the sky, of the long subway trip back to the museum, of the pain in Esther Feinberg's voice. I needed only a little more information and hoped that somehow I could get it without launching her into another story. "What year did you arrive?"

"I came in 1946. Some friends and I made the journey together. We all settled in this neighborhood. I met my husband at the congregation around the corner. He had come from Germany as well, had lost his wife and two sisters and his parents. Only he and his brother survived."

She surveyed the room, nodding towards the cabinet in the dining room. "After the war I tried to find what I remembered of our lives in Germany. We traveled all over the world, to auction houses, sale rooms, antique stores, looking for things that I remembered, or thought that I remembered, from our home. The silver, the porcelain, the dishes. All of the things that we were taught to treasure, we taught our children and grandchildren to treasure. I don't know if any of these things belonged to us, or even if I remember, really, what my mother's and father's and grandparents' beautiful things looked like.

"But I pretend that they are our family heirlooms, because I am sure that they belonged to someone. Maybe even someone like us, who wasn't fortunate enough to survive. But for me, I have this spoon," her voice softened. "Only this spoon." She smiled, her eyes tired with emotion. "And now it will belong to the museum."

I made some final notes, smiled and patted her hand reassuringly. "I promise you, we will take very good care of it. And generations of children will learn from your story. Sometimes children learn more when we let them see, or hold, or touch an object that tells a story, instead of just hearing it by itself."

She nodded. "Yes, when I visited your museum a few months ago with my daughter, we saw a group of young children gathered around one of your docents, as she showed them a pair of Shabbos candlesticks. As she talked, I could almost hear my mother's voice whispering the blessings. That was when I decided to call you."

She carefully laid the spoon in front of my teacup, her aged hands shaking slightly. I took a pair of white cotton gloves from my bag, put them on, and tenderly picked up the spoon and turned it over. On the back of the tiny bowl, I noted the infinitesimal marks that had become so familiar to me after five years at the museum – the state crown and crescent of Germany that was imprinted on all silver pieces created after 1884 – the number .835, denoting the purity of the silver content, and the tiny, almost unreadable six-pointed star of the maker's mark.

In all likelihood, I thought, this had been made by Lucas Posen, a German-Jewish silversmith who had - not inexplicably - stopped production right around the end of the 1930s, when Jewish businesses, by law, were forbidden to exist, and Jewish merchants found themselves arriving at ruined and burned shops, and they and their livelihoods suddenly began to disappear.

The silver mark reminded me of a briefing I had read in a recent circular from the Stolen Art commission of the Holocaust Claims Conference. Several of Posen's most beautiful and elaborate Judaica pieces were currently under investigation as being stolen property in a suit brought by the grandchildren of a survivor.

The circulars came to us regularly, since we were asked to be on the lookout for people who might try to sell us stolen items. In fairness, however, many people – generations later - didn't even realize that the treasures that they wished to sell, loan, or simply have appraised had been taken from interned and deported Jewish families in the certainty that no one would ever return to claim them.

Mrs. Feinberg's spoon couldn't have weighed more than an ounce, and it was scarred and tarnished, as if its very history had become ingrained within. I gently placed it in a sleeve of lamb's wool, and then tucked it into a small protective case that I had also brought with me. I didn't speak, and Mrs. Feinberg watched me in silence.

Years of curatorial work meant that I was used to such scrutiny. Artifact donors wanted to know – wanted to trust – that you would care for their item with the reverence it deserved, and after hearing her story, I did not want to disappoint her. Placing an artifact in a case, for some, was not unlike closing the coffin over the face of a loved one and I had learned to treat the moment with silence and respect. We always wore white cotton gloves when handling artifacts, to keep them safe from the oils that occur in our skin. Many people, however, seemed to interpret this gesture with almost the same respect accorded to an honor guard.

Removing the gloves, I shut the case with a soft click, gently placed all of the items in my bag, and started to gather my things.

Outside the window, the winter sky was darkening to a shade of smoky gray tinged by the pink glow of the neon signs that lined upper Broadway.

"That's all of the information I need," I said. "I'll bring your spoon back to the museum, where we'll take a closer look at it, and as soon as the registrar has a chance to look it over and assign it an accession number, I'll send the deed of transfer for you to sign, and the rest of the ownership agreement paperwork."

She nodded. I felt a tickle of sadness in my throat as I rose from the sofa, put on my coat, and extended my hand to her.

"Thank you so much for trusting us with your story, Mrs. Feinberg."

I wanted to hold on to the elderly, age-spotted hand that she placed in mine, instead of simply shaking it cordially and walking away. The end of an artifact donation visit was always a moment when I disliked myself for my professionalism, even though I knew, from years of training, that such professionalism was there to make the moment easier for us both. I didn't want her to feel as if she was saying goodbye to her past, or to her mother, simply because I was walking out the door with a tiny silver spoon. But I saw a brightness in her eyes as she held my hand for a just a moment longer than was necessary, and then, together, we walked haltingly to the door.

"Thank you for listening, Miss Levin," she said, her voice strong and clear, as she undid the locks from top to bottom. "It is not an easy story to tell, nor to hear. And I imagine that after a while, in your line of work, all of these stories must sound the same to you."

I didn't know what to say. She had, unerringly, identified the things I loved and hated and feared the most about my job. I had heard so many stories of survival, of terror, of murdered mothers and fathers and children, and horrors and sadnesses so great that I could hardly bear to listen, much less record them for posterity. And when the nightmares came, as they inevitably did, I sometimes didn't recognize the specific stories that gave rise to the terrifying moments of my dreams.

I walked out of the building towards the subway, marveling at the few old shops that peacefully coexisted with the bright bodegas and *taquerias* of Washington Heights. Long ago, this place had been a German-Jewish survivor community. Now as the stories faded from memory, and the children had created their own Diaspora of wealthy towns north and west of the city, it was home – again - to new immigrants.

My grandmother still lived a couple of subway stops north, in Riverdale, in the apartment she had lived in ever since her arrival with my grandfather from a Displaced Persons camp after the war. My mother was the person in the family who talked – incessantly -about my grandparents and what they had endured, but I had never heard much about the war from either of them. It was a subject about which they preferred to remain silent, even when I had asked them directly about their experiences. Ironically, even though I had heard so many survivors speak, I actually knew very little about their lives in Germany before the war. No matter how many times I asked about what had happened to them, my questions were met with a shake of the head, with a small, sad smile, with silence.

12

In the years that had passed since my grandfather's death ten years ago, my grandmother started to talk to me a little about what had happened to some of her friends in the years leading up to the war, but unlike many survivors, she never expressed an interest in formally sharing the story of what had actually happened to her and her family following their deportation. And even though my grandmother refused to sit in a brightly lit room and give testimony to the cold metal and plastic and glass of a video camera, I was sure, in some oblique way, that among the ghosts of the six million were members of my own family. The truth of the Holocaust was something I had lived with ever since I could remember; in the way that the play of darkness and sunlight can change the color of the walls in a room, a shadow of fear and loss tinged the very air that I breathed in my grandparents' home.

Now, nearly every other day, Monday to Friday, between the hours of nine and five, while other people worked for banks or marketing firms or law offices, I went to the home of a survivor, or a survivor's child, and took gentle custody of another symbol of their history and of their loss. I knew that I was good at my job because I could balance on the tightrope between professional empathy and personal involvement. But sometimes I was afraid that without my carefully recorded notes, I would confuse one story with another. It wasn't so much that they sounded the same; it was just that - all too often - they had the same ending.

Once I got back to the office, it took some juggling to unearth the heavy package from under the pile of mail, which in my absence had grown like a recriminatory stack of dirty dishes, now perched precariously on the corner of my desk. Envelopes, memos, junk mail and small parcels were jumbled one on top of another like a haystack. The rectangular package wrapped in plain brown paper was the only obviously interesting item.

I put it on my lap and postponed the pleasure of opening it while I did a quick sort-through. Invoices to one side, waste-of-time brochures and outdated memos in the trash, letters that required a reply to the other side. What I really wanted to do was plug in my camera to the office computer and upload last week's vacation photos so I could email them to Michael. After that, I wanted to spend the rest of the afternoon remembering the two of us wandering barefoot down that pink sand beach.

A drifting smudge of frozen clouds outside the window brought me back, with a sigh, to the task at hand. January, with its inherent darkness and cold, is traditionally a bad month for museums. Despite the city's pride at being one of the most cultured places in the world, anyone who works in a museum can tell you that a lot of people won't bother to brave bad weather just so they can stare at art for a couple of hours. And in our case, I couldn't think of a single person who would venture all the way downtown to the damp, windy edge of Manhattan to spend a depressingly dark and icy afternoon being reminded of the Holocaust.

Settling into my chair, I looked around at the office I had shared for more than three years with Aviva, the senior registrar in our department, my closest colleague. On shelves surrounding the room were dozens of objects waiting to be catalogued: ragged canvas shoes and silver synagogue candlesticks, fragments of photographs and delicate china plates, faded books, tarnished silver, bits of blankets. Each belonged to a victim or survivor; each represented a remnant of an interrupted life, and each came with its own story. The question I often asked myself was whether I could bear to listen to yet one more testimony, one more unimaginable narrative of death and loss.

During the ten years I had worked as a curator, the thrill of examining newly donated artifacts had long ago worn off. Enthusiasm for my job waned as the past, on many days, seemed to overwhelm the present. Often, I wondered if my family, my friends, and my relationship with Michael were enough to balance the living side of the equation. But whenever I contemplated leaving, maybe even someday soon, the guilty thoughts reared up again. *"What about your family, your heritage? Doesn't that mean anything to you anymore?"* My grandmother's voice again: *"Or has that goyische boyfriend of yours made you forget who you are?"*

In truth, Michael was all for telling my family how serious our relationship was, but I knew what we'd be in for if they learned the truth. Even going on vacation required a complicated and wearying set of lies. I told my parents I was going away with a group of girlfriends. Now, I'd have to edit the photos I showed them so the guy with the fair skin and freckles would not be seen standing next to me. It was a ruse I had kept for three years, needless to say at great expense of our relationship. I knew that I didn't want to do it anymore. But I couldn't figure a way without hurting someone. I just wasn't sure who it was going to be.

I lifted the parcel and turned it over in my hands. It weighed more than it appeared to; I could feel padded layers of wrapping cushioning the thick brown paper. Probably another photo album full of dead people, I thought, or a memorial book from a destroyed synagogue. I had seen so many of them. I sighed, scanning the disarray on my desk. If I wanted to fix things, I'd have to get to the bottom of the mess on my desk before I did anything else. I put the package down on Aviva's chair and tore into the mountain of mail.

"Don't even think about it," Aviva said, waddling into the office, hands clasped over her pregnant belly.

"What?"

"The package," she said, gesturing to where it lay on her seat "Don't dump it on me. Either deal with it or pass it on. The senior registrar has enough to do." Her smile erased the harshness of her words.

"I wasn't leaving it there for you. I'm just trying to clear off my desk."

"Serves you right for being out for a week. I'm still jealous," she grinned.

Aviva's green eyes sparkled from beneath the bangs of the auburn wig – she called it a *sheitl*. I still marveled that this lovely young woman willingly covered her hair every morning, unable to imagine a life when I would actually have to do more in the morning than pull my hair up in a ponytail and run for the subway. But Aviva was meticulous in her religious observance, taking a rigorous approach to her modesty and dress. Once she was married, her beautiful blonde curls disappeared from view. And I had never seen her in a skirt with a hemline higher than the top of her ankle, or a blouse with a neckline lower than her collarbone.

Given our religious differences – her orthodoxy, and my tradition of going to synagogue twice a year – I hadn't expected us to get along so well. And in the beginning, when we had both been promoted as a team to senior curator and registrar positions, our relationship was cordial, but purely professional.

That all changed on the morning of September 11 – when from our office window four blocks south of the World Trade Center, we saw the two planes strike the two towers, and then watched the buildings as they fell, one by one. Terrified, and unable to handle the long walk home to Queens, Aviva came back with me to my apartment on the Upper West Side.

That was the first time she met Michael. Our dating was still a secret to everyone but a small circle of my closest friends.

Aviva was nervous about staying with us. We didn't keep even remotely kosher, and I assumed she was anxious about the possibility of sharing a space, even for a night, with a colleague who was in an intimate relationship with a man to whom she was not married. My life must have seemed like a different planet to her; she had never even so much as shaken the hand of a man who was not a family member. But I pleaded with her to join us. And when Michael returned from the store with paper plates, plastic utensils, and ready-made food from the strictest kosher supermarket on the West Side, a real friendship emerged.

Aviva became one of the very few people in my life who knew of Michael's existence – that we lived together, that sometimes we talked about getting married, and that he wasn't Jewish. Even though by her religious standards she couldn't possibly approve of our relationship, it was obvious she genuinely liked him.

A little more than a year ago, at the age of twenty-nine – an old maid by Orthodox standards - Aviva married her husband, Jacob, after an intense, abrupt courtship of eight weeks. I counseled and soothed her after every call from the matchmaker, a pushy, exhausting woman who was known to have an unblemished record of success in finding mates for even the most stubbornly unmatchable candidates. Aviva's mother was clearly placing what remained of her hopes on this *shadchan*, after her daughter's rejection of all previous suitors.

With every call, and each date, the stakes had grown more significant for both families, until finally the terms of the engagement were agreed upon. The wedding was unlike any I had ever attended – four hundred guests at a catering hall in Borough Park, separate seating and dancing for the men and women, and no less than seven elderly, white-bearded rabbis present to bless the union.

I'd had my doubts about Aviva marrying someone she had known for such a short time, but she seemed happy. At times I found myself missing the tangle of her blond curls over the low wall of my cubicle, and I wondered how she felt about hiding her true self from the world. In spite of our friendship, the religious barriers between us made such questions too intimate to ask.

She was certainly a refreshing change from most of the junior-level curators and registrars who came and went with alarming speed in our department. Usually they were vehemently secular art history graduates who lived in Brooklyn or the Lower East Side, with dyed hair, black clothes, and an array of body piercings. But Aviva had a sweet and unassuming way, without ever really saying a word, of teaching them how to curb the worst of their bad language, show appropriate respect in the galleries, and treat the artifacts with care and reverence. It was a quality I hoped to emulate during her impending absence.

"Here," she picked up the package from her chair. "I'll open it."

"Gee, how awfully nice of you."

"Well, I do need somewhere to sit."

I continued to go through the mail as she slit the package open. The outer paper rustled as she removed an object encased in bubble wrap and tape. "Looks like another book," Aviva said, reaching for her scissors.

"That's what I thought."

I turned in my chair and watched as she carefully cut through the wrappings and unfurled them to reveal an ancient-looking, battered album.

"This one's in worse shape than usual," she remarked.

"And it's getting dust all over you."

"Ugh, gross." She swiped at the fabric of her long skirt.

"Here, let me take it."

I carried the book over to the conservation area counter, set it down and looked at it more closely. The cover was scratched and worn, the spine in thready tatters, as if it had been opened and closed countless times. The corners of the binding appeared to be separating, and from what I could see, the edges of the paper inside looked as if they had yellowed with age.

Tucked inside the cover was a sheet of white paper folded in thirds, its edges crisp and neat. I unfolded it and saw that it had been produced on what appeared to be a very old typewriter with uneven keys. Some of the letters were heavily inked while others were only half-visible.

I smoothed out the paper and began to read.

2

Miss Jill Levin, Senior Curator
Museum of Jewish Heritage
36 Battery Place
New York, NY 10280

Dear Miss Levin:
I have had the pleasure of meeting you on several occasions during your time with the Museum. In recent years, I have donated several of my family's artifacts to the museum's collection, and you have visited my home a number of times.

During one of your visits some years ago, you told me that you were the grandchild of a Holocaust survivor. It made me very happy to see that such a vibrant young person had committed herself to remembering what we endured, and it gave me hope that my story would continue to be told to future generations.

I am enclosing a book that has been in my family for some years. I am giving it to you because it is very important to me that it continues to be cared for, as I have taken care of it for many years.

It is difficult for me to type so I will end this letter. However, I will write to you more about this book until such a time as I am no longer able. My memory is fading, and I am afraid that I will soon forget what happened. But you are young, and you will not forget.

I hope you will also continue to make sure that
the world never forgets.

"Unbelievable," I murmured.

"What did I tell you?"

"This letter. It's so strange," I said. "From someone who says they've met me before, but doesn't say who they are. No name, no address, nothing."

We both looked down at the scarred volume. Together, we gingerly turned the pages to reveal whatever was inside, afraid to do even more damage to the fragile structure of spine and binding. A soft smell of dust and mold rose from the parchment. Delicately, we turned a few blank pages, and then suddenly the words lay before us, vulnerable, amazingly, in English – in spidery, elaborate lettering that had been so intricately inscribed, the text seemed to float upon the page.

The rose that sleeps within this woman's eyes
unfolds at last. My mind, an unsealed tomb
What mystery sleeps low within that bloom!
This ruby red remembrance of device.
These fainting lovers with their clustered sighs
Forsake me not. Upon the fading moon
Whose light illuminates this sacred room,
She entertains that honeybee and dies.
This posy laced with sweet vermillion flame
Such potent nectar never shall be shared
By one who calls me 'wife.' The insect turns
Beneath the wrath of artful woman's game
And there is crush'd. All those who sue, beware
My arms, Athene's; my love is love that learns.

London, England

The Sixth day of September
In the Year of Our Lord, One thousand Five Hundred Thirty Six

Here are the words of a bride double-bound: first, by the amity of a father and second, by the enmity of a husband. These men — whether the word is inscribed by the holy hand of my precious father or scrawled upon the witless page by the unjust husband, tho' mortals both, they shall write what they will, and it shall live, for men's words are turned towards eternity as the bird's melody is turned eternally against silence.

Yet these words, a woman's words in which no God, nor Bishop nor Sovereign believes, are unfit for mortals when inscribed by those creatures whose duties extend no further than marketplace, marriage and motherhood, and thus, fall short of the blessings of Heaven; these very words are a sin of Pride; and my punishment shall be that no mortal shall accept nor remember them.

My Father, the blessed Instructor, with such love and genuine humility taught his daughters, tho' cursed by their very sex, to learn and yet fear Wisdom. Yet there are those of the other persuasion — those men — who are taught that they alone are the keepers of Wisdom, who are proud, unseemly, and forgetful of the essential godliness of Humility.

It is thus, the misnamed wisdom of mortal men that taints Humility, and forces her most modest scholars behind demure veils, her most ardent poets to the childbed, untried.

Over the parchment page, Aviva's eyes met mine.

"1536?" I asked, incredulous. "I've never seen anything so old, except for that document from King Ferdinand and Queen Isabella that was donated to the collection a few years ago."

21

"That's exactly what I was thinking," Aviva murmured softly. "The proclamation from Ferdinand and Isabella, expelling the Jews of Spain. This made me think of it. Certainly, the paper looks similar. The handwriting has the same characteristics, the same look from that period of history."

Even as I heard the excitement in her voice, I saw her drawing back, both physically and professionally. "But I'm getting ahead of myself," she said. "We can't even let ourselves think that this might actually be authentic. Not without reading further. And definitely not without having the paper tested in a lab."

"I know," I reluctantly agreed. "When we got the proclamation, it came with paperwork and provenance and documentation from Spain's royal archives. This," I nodded toward the book, "came with nothing. Well, that's not completely true. We have a date – 1536. And it's in English, written in London – so we have a location. And a gender – we can assume this was written by a woman."

I started thinking about content, context, meaning, history. "The words sound as if she is writing about her father, and raging against men in general. Could she be an early feminist?" I asked. I was thinking about the female religious mystics of the medieval period, like Julian of Norwich and Margery Kemp.

"I don't know. Maybe." Her face appeared distracted. "What about the letter?" she asked suddenly. "Can I see it?"

I passed the paper to Aviva. "Well," she finally said, "it looks like it's from someone who knows you."

"That's the weird thing – it's been a long time, probably a couple of years, since I mentioned to an artifact donor that I am a grandchild of a survivor. I finally realized after so many survivors had asked me questions about where they were taken from and what camps they were in, that I didn't have enough information from my grandparents to really be able to talk about it in detail."

"So, does that narrow the possibilities of who this mystery donor could be?"

I thought for a moment. "Not really. I mean, how many interviews have I conducted in five years? Four hundred? Four fifty?"

"Probably more than that."

"Let's say I told two hundred artifact donors in three years. How could I possibly narrow that down?"

"You could always go through the database," Aviva said, in her ever-practical way, "and see who's still alive."

"Oh, sure. Because this job isn't depressing enough."

She laughed. "Good point. I didn't see any clues in the packing material. Did you?"

I knew where she was going with the question. A few years back we managed to locate an elderly artifact donor who had forgotten to include his name and return address with his donation. We had received a box containing an album filled with photographs of the liberation of Auschwitz, pictures he had taken as a young Army photographer in the closing days of the war. The photo album came to us wrapped in yellowing sheets of his local newspaper, which fortuitously included the cover page and the mailing label. But here, there were no clues. I shook my head.

The sky had darkened outside our office window. All along Battery Place, the lights burned cold and clear in the winter air. "Listen," I said to Aviva, "It's been a long day. If we're going to keep reading this, I need a cup of coffee. Do you want one?"

"I can't, remember?" She patted her big belly. "Wish I could."

I glanced at my watch. I knew Aviva would tough it out no matter how tired she was, and I had my own reasons for calling it a day. "On second thought, it's almost six thirty." I feigned a yawn. "I promised Michael I'd be home at a decent hour. Do you mind if we pick this up in the morning?"

Aviva stood and stretched, then rubbed the small of her back. I could see the relief in her eyes.

"Great, Jill. But let's get started early. We might have something really amazing on our hands, but, of course, we've got to read further and examine this more closely before we can decide to do with it. Why don't you put it back in the vault?"

She handed the letter back to me. I folded it back in thirds and taped it to the top of the package. Then I walked back to the vault and carefully placed the wrapped package at the back of the bottom shelf, where it would receive the least exposure to light, or to prying eyes.

I hated putting it away. I watched as Aviva pulled on her coat, buttoning it up tightly against the bulk of her belly. "Don't stay too much longer."

"I won't," I said.

"Good." She tied her scarf around her neck. "Say hi to Michael for me."

"Sure."

She paused, and then spoke again. "Things okay there?"

I looked down at my hands as she hoisted her bag over her shoulder and pressed the elevator button. I could hear the muffled sound of the motor starting up. "You know," I shrugged. "The same."

"Your family still giving you problems?"

I didn't answer.

"I don't mean to pry."

"That's one of the things I love about you, Aviva. You never make me feel like I'm being evasive."

She grinned as the elevator doors opened. "Get home safe."

Later, after I stopped myself half a dozen times from returning to the vault, I pushed the heavy glass doors open and walked outside into the blustery winter night. The lights of the skyline gleamed in the clear cold air and I could feel the skin of my face turning rosy from the chill. I knew Michael would be at home waiting for me. By now he would have opened a bottle of wine, the pasta water would be boiling on the stove, and classic rock would be playing on the radio in the kitchen. I wondered how much longer I would be able to go on lying to my family, to him, and to myself.

3

As I opened the door to the fourth floor walk-up Michael and I shared a jolt of the Rolling Stones' *Sympathy for the Devil* came booming from the kitchen. The apartment was warm, and I could smell sautéed garlic and chopped basil. "Hey there," I heard a voice from somewhere in the vicinity of the bedroom. "Just in time. I was about to put the spaghetti in the pot." "Great," I replied. "Sorry I'm a little late." I heard his light step in the hallway. "No problem." He emerged from the doorway and I smiled at his tousled shock of dark curls. His nose was peeling where a rosy sunburn had been just a few days earlier, a remnant of our week at the beach. "I just got home about half an hour ago. That's the problem when you have a conference call with clients in California."

I took off my coat and hung it on the rack in the hallway. "Thanks for starting dinner," I told him. "Do I smell garlic bread?"

"Of course. You're freezing," he said, touching the tip of my nose. "How was your day?"

"All right, for the first day back after vacation," I replied. "I had an artifact donation house call that ran late. Then I went back to the office for a while. We received a really strange package today, and looking at it took up a lot of time this afternoon, so I ended up staying later than I should have."

"What do you mean 'strange package'? Strange in the Department of Homeland Security sense of the word?"

Michael was now an attorney for what he frequently referred to as a "do-gooder" organization. Originally, he specialized in dealing with unfair housing and labor issues, but these days he was often called in to consult on immigration and deportation cases, which meant dealing with the terms of the Joint Terrorism Task force, and the ever-widening parameters of the Patriot Act.

I was touched by the concerned look on his face. "No," I hastened to reassure him. "That's not what I mean."

"Well, you know how I worry." He smiled. "And don't tell me that I shouldn't. Because you know that if there weren't anything to worry about, you wouldn't have NYPD Special Ops paying surprise visits to your office."

He was right. Ever since 9/11, the museum, like many synagogues, Jewish community centers, and other cultural and religious institutions around the city, had been designated one of the city's "sensitive locations." This distinction earned us the privilege of having concrete barriers installed in front of our doors, and unannounced, on-again off-again periods of protection by special police teams with names like Atlas and Hercules, who came complete with body armor and bomb-sniffing dogs.

"No, nothing like that," I continued. "It was a book. Actually, a book that looks as if it's a few hundred years old. It arrived in a package addressed to me and contained a letter from someone who says that they've met me, that they've donated other artifacts to the museum. But no name, no return address, nothing about who they are or what the book is about."

"But it was addressed to you. Was there anything about it that seemed familiar, like the handwriting? Do you have any ideas at all about who it might be from?"

"No," I paused for a moment. "I think it might be from a survivor. It's definitely from someone elderly. And the letter talked a lot about the Holocaust, making sure that the world never forgets. It was also typed out on an old typewriter; it obviously didn't come from a computer."

"That's weird. I mean, even my parents are online these days. And they couldn't even work the DVD player a couple of years ago."

"Well, a lot of survivors are on fixed incomes. Not every child is good enough – like you – to buy a computer for their aging parents."

"Don't give me too much credit for giving them the desktop when I bought the laptop." He paused for a moment before continuing. "But speaking of the elderly, your grandmother called."

I felt my shoulders tense. "You didn't pick up the phone, did you?"

"Of course, I didn't pick it up. She left a message asking if you wanted to visit her this Saturday."

"Oh, no, I think Saturday is Bill's dinner party." Michael followed me into the kitchen and together we looked at the calendar on the refrigerator. "Yeah, it is. Maybe I can go see her and then meet you there. But she'll want me to stay for dinner. I just know it." I sighed. Suddenly, the day felt even longer. "I don't want to miss the party. But I haven't seen her in a couple of months. I really ought to go."

"Yeah, you should." I felt his hand making soothing little circles on my back. "But don't you think it would be easier," he said quietly, "if I went with you?"

I looked at him. "You know what would happen."

"Do I?"

"Haven't we been through this enough times?"

"I still don't understand." His voice was low and sad. "We found each other. I love you. We have a great life together. Why wouldn't she be happy about that?"

"Do we have to talk about this tonight?"

"No." He turned away from me and lowered the flame under the pot of boiling water, opened the box of spaghetti and emptied it into the pot. "But we have to talk about it sometime. It's not like anyone else cares. My parents don't care that we're not the same religion, and if my grandparents were still alive, I'm sure they wouldn't care either. I mean, I understand she's been through hell. But I don't want us to have to put off getting married," his voice softened to a murmur. "Until, well...you know."

I opened the refrigerator door and busied myself, shuffling through the crisper drawer. I didn't want him to see the tears starting in my eyes, or hear the catch in my voice, so I buried my head in the fridge and didn't say anything.

He seemed to be waiting for me to speak. When I didn't, he said, "It just seems like a bad way to start a life together, waiting for someone you love to die."

I put the lettuce and tomatoes on the tiny kitchen counter and gently

27

kicked the refrigerator door shut.

"Look, I agree with you. I'm just not sure what the best thing to do is. And it's not like we're waiting for something terrible to happen. Even if some miracle happened – and it won't, trust me – and she changed her mind and approved of this, we would still have my parents to deal with. And you've already seen them in action."

He nodded. "I know. But avoiding the discussion isn't going to give anyone a chance to change their minds."

"You're being optimistic. But I know them, and I just don't think it's possible for them to even acknowledge this relationship, much less accept it. I mean, I've thought about starting the conversation with them, about how serious we are, many times, but then I can't bear how I know it will end."

He turned from the stove to look at me as I continued talking. "Always, *always*, one of them — my mother, or my grandmother— manages to come out with a story about some child or grandchild of one of their friends, who married someone 'inappropriate' – that's always the word they use – and how it was such a *shanda*, a shame, a scandal. And I don't know how much of it is my mother's fault. It's also my grandmother, it's what she went through, it's all about what she suffered. To her, she'll always think that anyone who isn't Jewish is the enemy."

"But I'm not," Michael said. "And you're her granddaughter, her only grandchild. She loves you. She wants you to be happy."

"Yes," I replied. "And all she ever talks about is how her life will be complete when I marry a nice Jewish boy. You know, when she says things like 'This is why I survived Hitler. This is what it's all about – my grandchild's future.' How am I supposed to answer that?"

"I gotta hand it to her. When in doubt, mention Hitler."

"Yeah, tell me about it. I've been hearing it all my life."

"But that's exactly my point. You're your own person, with your own life. You can't just live a certain way because it's what your mother or your grandmother expects you to do."

"I know that." I took a small serrated knife from the drawer, sliced

28

into a ripe red tomato. "But every day at the museum, we talk about 'the legacy, the generations' – all of these beautiful poetic words that are meant to underscore the fact that we are losing the survivors. When they're gone, only the children and grandchildren can keep that legacy going. I know that's what she wants me to do. She thinks that I should live a certain way. For her, for my mother, there was no other choice – and they think I need to abide by the same rules."

"And this certain way, by her definition, means marrying a Jewish guy."

I nodded.

"I know I've asked you this before, but is that what you think, too? Is that how you really feel, and you're just not telling me?"

"No." I said. "You know that's not what I think. Would I even be here," I wiped my hands on a dishtowel, "if that were the case?"

He sighed as he lifted the heavy pot from the burner and drained the pasta into a colander in the sink. A damp cloud of steam rose into the air. "Probably not. But it seems as if you get it from all sides – your mother, your grandmother, your job, even the survivors that you visit every week. Sometimes I feel like I can't convince you to talk to her," he seemed to be choosing his words with some care, "not so much because of what she thinks, but because you're so steeped in these ideas yourself. And there are times when I wonder if you didn't have this job, would it be easier for you?"

"I don't know. I have no way of knowing. I mean, this is what I do." I gathered up the sliced tomatoes and tossed them in the bowl with the lettuce. "Why? Do you think I should give up my job?"

He didn't answer for a moment. Then he said, "There are hundreds of museums in New York City."

"And only one," I said, "where I was lucky enough to find a job in an area of expertise that actually means something to me."

"I know. But face it, Jill, you're getting burned out listening to these stories all day. You're burned out now. On vacation, you were a different person. You were happy. You weren't tired all the time. There was light in your eyes. And it wasn't just that you were

29

happy. *We* were happy."

I stopped fixing the salad for a moment and considered what he was saying. All at once, I felt a shiver come over my body, remembering the nights in the little hotel at the beach, the sweet touch of his fingertips on my skin, his deep voice whispering, making irresistible pictures in my head, his contented smile in the darkness, the feel of his body curled against mine.

His next words brought me back to the kitchen.

"Now you're back at work, just one day, and you have this shadow on you all over again. Don't get me wrong, I think it's great that you came home tonight and started telling me about an artifact that sounds as if it might have an interesting story. But to be honest, I haven't seen you excited about your job in months. You're just sadness and shadow all the time. And you just don't want to face it."

I didn't say anything. I knew he was right. He knew he was right. But I didn't feel like talking about it anymore. I didn't want to ruin the evening by escalating a conversation into a fight. After a moment or two, I looked up from the salad bowl and tried to smile.

"Come on," he said, as he tossed the cooked pasta in the sauce. "Why don't you bring in the wine, and I'll take the dishes inside." He took two plates from the cabinet, expertly piled them with pasta, and removed the garlic bread from the oven. "We can figure this out some other night."

"Thanks, Michael."

"Don't thank me," he said, cutting the bread with a stabbing motion. "This is only another postponement. You know that we'll have to talk about it sometime."

"I know," I murmured. "I just wish we didn't have to."

"Me either. Because maybe we both already know how this is going to end – and all of these conversations are just a polite way of telling us that we're only putting off the inevitable."

4

I loved the quiet peace of the museum early in the morning, before the other staffers – and the visitors – arrived, the way the early sunlight sparkled on the water of the harbor and the icy bare trees in the park as I walked from the subway. Getting in at 8:30 also meant I had a chance to get out of the house without resuming the conversation of the night before.

Sometimes I used early mornings to check over the assignment lists before the junior staffers arrived. To my surprise, Aviva was already at her desk, talking on the phone in a voice too low for me to hear what she was saying. After a few more minutes, I finally heard the plastic click of the receiver being replaced in the cradle.

I settled into my chair. "You're obviously trying to make me look bad, getting in so early."

"I have a lot to do," she replied quietly.

I peered around the wall. Violet shadows clouded the skin under her eyes. The rest of her face had a translucent pallor.

"Aviva, are you all right?"

"I'm fine," she said dismissively. "You know what they say about the bloom of pregnancy? It's all lies."

"Didn't you get any sleep?"

"Not a lot." She cradled her belly. "I just can't get comfortable. The baby kept kicking every time I closed my eyes."

"I'm so sorry. You look exhausted."

"I am exhausted," she said. "But I wanted to talk to you before the meeting. I've been thinking about how we might use the artifact donor database to find out who sent the book."

"You're far along enough in your day to think about going through the database?" I shook my head incredulously. "How early did you get here?"

"Early enough."

"But we haven't even had a chance to really take a look it," I said.

"Maybe we should do that before anything else. Let's keep reading. There might be some clues in the text."

She nodded. I walked across to the vault, retrieved the book and settled it on top of the counter in our conservation area. Then I pulled up two chairs and motioned for Aviva to join me. I noticed how heavily she seemed to carry herself, even across the short distance. She brought over two pairs of white cotton gloves that she had picked up from the basket between our desks.

As she approached, I noticed a couple of stray blonde ringlets unfurling from beneath the edge of her crimson wool beret, a tiny careless sign that something was bothering her. I had a feeling it went deeper than lack of sleep.

I put on the gloves and positioned the book carefully upon the paper-covered counter. Even those small motions gave me pause to worry about whether the worn covers would begin to crumble in my hands. "Well, at least we know that this is definitely pre-World War II."

Aviva laughed. "Of course it is! Even if we hadn't seen the date on the inside, this doesn't even look like a twentieth-century object. You expect everything that comes in to be from the 1930s and 40s."

"Sometimes that's how I feel, given the sorts of artifacts we usually deal with."

"I know, it feels like a lot of the objects we've been seeing lately are coming from people who hid things during the war, but remember, there were more than three thousand years of Jewish history before the Holocaust."

Aviva and I surveyed the book with practiced eyes. Then she reached into a box for a small white surgical mask to cover her nose and mouth. Placing a magnifying loop over her eye, she drew closer to the book, the thick glass mere inches from the dark brown binding.

"It's not from this century, that much is certain. And it was definitely bound by hand. See the imperfections right there, in the spine?" she asked, pointing.

I nodded.

"Those didn't come from a machine," she continued. "Also, there's a lot of dust in the spine, but it doesn't look like regular house dust to me. Actually," she peered closer, "it looks more like dirt. I'd guess the book was exposed to the elements at some point. We should look at it under the high-powered light."

"Well, the binding looks tough, but I don't know if I'd expose the interior pages."

We carefully opened the book again and turned to the page where we had left off reading the night before. "See how fragile they are?"

Oh, that the days when I learned my lessons could be restored to me, for I am sick with betrayal and with grief. I record the poetry of these lines, this first gentle sonnet written in my days as a schoolgirl, as proof of what I once was. For the arrogance of youth believes that each day and each unthinking act will not alter the immortal soul. Of all the lessons I have learned, this is the most bitter. I am no longer the thing that I was; for as the verses tell: This is as I was.

It is vanity; proud arrogance, and perhaps – though I can hardly bear to write it nor think it - the betrayal of the very learning that defines me that has led to my fall. I am defeated. My life's unborn purpose has been torn from me, as a child is torn from the womb in which it is nourished until such time as it can draw its first breath from the world.

Now it is mere months since my dearest father was lost to me, and I fear that he, who loved me so well, would not know the daughter's face he looked upon with such fatherly pride and gentleness.

When I was a child, the eldest child of four not unintelligent creatures, my father said to me, on the passing of my mother: Dearest Margaret, assuage thy grief in study, for in these books and these languages, thou shalt learn that there is real solace in the mastery of skills, so thou mayest arm thyself against further griefs, and instruct thyself to be aware of truths greater than one's own.

Haply I immersed myself in languages and learning until that sore day; oh, that day wrought with grief and sorrow, when the serpent entered the garden - the garden that my father had prepared for me, so that I might later enjoy the sweet and mellow fruit borne from my youth; alas. Now that it is ripe, there shall be no gathering. For the serpent hath destroyed the best of the harvest; and hath laid the blossoms to waste.

I looked up from the page and saw Aviva's face suddenly turn even paler under the white cover of the mask. "Are you all right?" I asked. "Is it the baby?"

"Just some kicking." She tore the mask from her mouth. "And punching. And any other forms of pre-natal violence that this kid can dream up."

"Do you want me to run the staff meeting today? It's not a problem."

She shook her head. "No, let me take care of it. I have a ton of database and exhibition catalog items to assign." She gazed at the book. "Stay here with this," she said, and heaved herself up from the low chair. "It had your name on it. And I think it's going to take more than the usual workup to figure out what we've got here."

"I agree. And I don't know if anyone else in the department should see it yet."

As with any museum dealing in the currency of historical artifacts, we both intimately knew the process by which an artifact's actual date and origin had to be proven, and then authenticated – a lengthy, detailed process that involved a combination of scholarship and science. And thus, we knew from experience to keep quiet about an object – no matter how potentially significant — until we knew exactly what we were dealing with.

Much of the time it was easy for us to prove an artifact's legitimacy. In our museum, objects tended to occur in multiples, and it was easy for us to compare potential new acquisitions with existing items in the collection. For instance, when a yellow fabric star – used to designate Jews from Gentiles in many European cities during the war - once arrived from a potential donor who had in turn purchased it from a seller on eBay, we knew by means of comparison that it was not an item that came from a ghetto, but probably from the set of a Holocaust film.

After so many years of examining artifacts, Aviva and I intimately knew the hallmarks of genuine objects; the color and shape of the coins and bills that had been exchanged as currency in various ghettos; the particular weave of the uniforms worn at Auschwitz, the composition of metals in a labor camp's fencepost, painstakingly chipped away and melted down in hiding to make a ring for a secret marriage.

For the most part, many of the people who came to us with their "one of a kind" objects weren't looking to scam us. More often than not, the most heartbreaking part of our job was when we had to tell someone they didn't possess the symbol of a story they had heard their whole lives.

It was unutterably sad when we had to tell an elderly person that the translation of the inscription on the title page of an ancient book revealed no connection to a long-lost relative; or that a cherished, priceless silver *yad* – a pointer used to read the Torah, believed to have been rescued from a destroyed synagogue, was actually made of pewter or tin, and virtually valueless except for its historic significance. It was just as painful to see the reaction of a survivor's child upon hearing the crumbling, yellowed postcard from Germany was not from a long-dead relative writing in the early 1930s, as the inks used to create the illustration were chemical-based, and unavailable for use until the mid-1950s.

So far, our museum had been able to avoid being duped, but we had seen others in our field humiliated both publicly and professionally when they had gotten overexcited about an artifact before proving the truth of its origins.

35

And everyone in the very small museum community knew about the scandals that had taken place behind closed board room doors, away from the eyes of deep-pocketed donors and loyal supporters, when certain curators and executive directors had been forced to admit that their so-called cultural institution had actually been dealing in stolen goods.

In recent months, the newspapers had been full of stories about stolen art, falsified records, and under-the-table deals, which had deposited significant amounts of cash in the pockets of certain high-level, internationally known museum officials. In my department, we followed those stories the way that most New Yorkers follow the Yankees or the Giants.

From the hallway we heard the usual commotion of our staff arriving. "Let me go take care of the meeting," Aviva said, "and then we'll keep going."

I turned back to the parchment page that lay open before me. Softly, I touched the paper with a gloved fingertip; carefully, I turned the pages back to examine the book's endpaper. It was patterned in a beautiful design, swirling, almost Florentine-looking blues and greens and golds, nearly unfaded except for about quarter-inch of what appeared to be water damage along the outer edges, where the endpapers had once been glued to the binding.

I saw that along the edges, the intricate designs were blurred, creating a muddy, faded stain of the once-colorful inks. As I examined underneath the unglued sections of the inside cover, I marveled at how the rich quality of the endpapers and the fine, delicate parchment were at odds with the thick, rough-beaten binding. It made me wonder, again, who had sent us such an object, and where it came from.

I waited impatiently for Aviva, listening to the muffled tones of her voice from the conference room as she gave the junior curators their assignments for the day. When she returned, her color was a little better, and she looked less tired.

"Find anything interesting?" she asked.

"I waited for you," I replied. "But this looks very promising," I said, revealing the endpapers. "This green and the gilt trim this looks almost Florentine. So I would think the construction was somehow linked to Italy. And over here," I pointed to the edges, "this looks like water damage."

Aviva nodded. "I'd say so. Look at the way the inks have blended together. You're right, it does look Italian, but it could have been created by someone who knew that style, or who was familiar with different types of paper and bindings."

"Like who?"

"I don't know, maybe it was someone who published books for the wealthy. Or it could have come from a monastery. Think about all of those beautiful illuminated manuscripts from the middle ages. This paper looks hand-painted."

"What do you think the chances are that it's authentic?" I asked.

"I don't know enough about the sixteenth century, or about bookbinding styles, or paper and ink and illuminations from that time, to be able to answer. But whether it's the real thing or not, whatever time period it comes from, this book looks as if it's had a hard life."

We turned the page and continued reading.

It was thus, in happy, happy childhood: I remember so clearly the long, misty days spent in the nursery, or the bright days of the garden in sunlight. In my memory there are books, always books; as if there were no end to the glorious possibilities of men and their ideas. The touch of soft vellum pages, the sharp deep odour of ink; the letters upon the page so clear as to nearly be breathed in, the words becoming part of my breath and blood and bone, their taste nearly as sweet as fruit of knowledge itself.

How dearly I remember the patience and wisdom of my dearest governess, as she sat for hour upon hour with me, learning the mysteries at the heart of some ancient text, her face pale in the light from the leaded window, the candlelit shadows of afternoon and evening falling upon the antique drape of her modest gown, her sweet soft voice gentle with praise or reproof ; O sweet lady, that thy most devoted student should have come to this end; locked in a stone tower room like her father before her; but the keeper this time is no King - though joined to me as subject to sire - he is the man I call husband.

And I am here now, among these distrait, half-writ thoughts; under lock and key, by light of a thin taper, under cloak and secrecy; for if the man knew of my deeds, I should suffer punishment at his hand; untempered by justice or mercy.

"She was a prisoner of some sort," I said. "In London, in 1536."

"That was during the reign of Henry VIII," Aviva mused. "She could have been in the Tower of London."

I glanced at her, surprised. "They taught you about the Tudors in that yeshiva of yours?"

"Ever heard of the Inquisition?" She raised her eyebrows. "Henry's first wife was Katherine of Aragon. A fervently Catholic Spanish princess."

"Let me guess. Bad for the Jews?"

"Sure, she would have been, if there had been any Jews left in England. They were expelled from England some years before, almost concurrently with the Spanish Inquisition, which as you know was brought about by Katherine's parents, Ferdinand and Isabella. And our museum has the papers to prove it."

"Which somewhat resemble the papers we're looking at right now," I pointed out. "As you said last night."

"And I also said we shouldn't get ahead of ourselves, if I remember correctly."

"You remember correctly," I murmured. "Let's keep reading."

Were I to question the will of the Lord, I should fall upon my knees and ask of Him: what in His wisdom would sever such a gentle connexion between father and child; leaving that child to the care of a servant of cruelty and darkness? Is it in the realm of His wisdom to consider my sin so grievous, that all I hath been given should be taken from me, as the earth hath demanded rain from the heavens to nourish its starving soil after the hot suns?

Perhaps it is as the husband says; it is dangerous for a woman to know too much; and those who invite danger in the form of knowledge, who succumb to temptation of thought and will as in the time of Eden, must be punished. It is thus that he binds me in this way; I am confined here with no light; no books; no reason; as was my father in his last days, with only my faith in God and the memory of my sweet father to sustain me.

There is nothing left for me without my studies; without them I am denied all former pleasures. I have purchased the precious paper on which I write these thoughts from my dearest friend; I hath been forced to hide the pages within the folds of my sleeves as I move through the house, and it is upon this parchment that I mark my thoughts until the time when the husband arrives; and it is then that I must again hide them away from his sight. For if he knew that I indulged the reason of my thoughts...if he knew the source of the papers, he would surely destroy them both as he endeavors to destroy my very soul.

This is a tale I must confess - tho' there is no confessor but this gentle paper and this sacred ink; but perhaps the finder of these pages will learn and tell all who cherish the memory of the Margaret More who lived; lived, yes, and died with her father; in spirit and following the hand of her ruler, for her God.

The words on the page came to an abrupt end, the deep black color of the ink like a wound upon the aged parchment.

I looked up from the book. The dark hands of the clock upon the wall told me it was 10:00. All around us, we could hear the rush and bustle of the building coming to life as it opened to the public. Outside the tall, light-filled windows that overlooked the front door, we heard the energetic babble of dozens of schoolchildren as they emerged from long yellow buses to be met in the courtyard by volunteer docents.

More pages beckoned. I looked over at Aviva, whose face seemed solemn, lost in thought.

"What are you thinking?" I asked.

A long silence. And then: "Do you know who she is?"

"Who? Margaret More?"

"Yes." Aviva distractedly felt for the strands of curling hair on the back of her neck, found them and tucked them back under her hat. "If I've got my history straight, then I'm pretty sure that she was the daughter of Thomas More. He was an advisor to Henry VIII, but he fell out of favor because of his refusal to accept Henry's marriage to Anne Boleyn. He was eventually beheaded. More was one of the king's chief counselors, but he disagreed with Henry's break with the Catholic Church and the establishment of the Church of England. Eventually, his death was considered to be a holy martyrdom to the Church and he was granted sainthood."

I leaned back, impressed, as always, with her secular knowledge. "I think I knew that. *A Man for All Seasons*, right? Wasn't that the film?"

"Actually, it was a play first. But yes, it was also a film," she said.

I made a mental note to rent the DVD as soon as possible. "So there's a chance that this could be authentic."

"And there's a good chance that it may not."

"Why do you say that?" I asked. "It certainly looks old enough. Obviously we need to get it examined by a lab, someone who could date the paper with certainty. If Dr. Schiffman approves the budget to have it done. You know how expensive the process is."

"I wouldn't say anything about it to anyone yet. Because in all honesty, I'm wondering why anyone would send this to us. So far, it doesn't have anything to do with Jewish heritage, or the Holocaust." Her eyes narrowed. "I mean, is this some sort of sick joke? Another means of telling us about the 'true faith?'"

I knew Aviva was particularly sensitive to attempts, on the part of well-meaning Christians – and some not so well-meaning– who sent dire warnings both through the mail and through the email addresses on the museum website to those of us who hadn't "heard the Good News." It was always jarring and sometimes frightening to hear, in painful detail, exactly what would happen to those of us who failed to heed the call of the Gospel.

But I didn't know what to think.

"You have to admit, this would be someone going to a lot of trouble to send us that message," I replied.

"Or whoever the message is meant for."

"What do you mean by that?" I asked. "It came to the museum."

"Very true," Aviva said. "But don't forget, even though it was sent to the museum, it had your name on it."

5

For the next few days, the manuscript and its mystery were all I could think about. But it was impossible to take the time to read further. Due to a series of immovable deadlines and intensive special exhibition meetings with the team of fabricators, curators, registrars and historians with whom I would be working as soon as Aviva went out on maternity leave, the manuscript remained safely stored in the very back of the vault, where I fervently hoped no one would stumble upon it by accident.

I could hardly stand knowing it was there and not having the time or privacy to look at it again. By Thursday, I was trying to figure out how to get back to reading it without having to bring it home with me.

Removing the book from the safe confines of our conservation area could be a big mistake, especially if it turned out to be as old as I thought it to be. Because it was in such delicate condition already, exposing it to the winter elements would be risky. So I figured I would be staying late again, instead of going to the gym, or more importantly, spending time with Michael.

I was trying to mentally juggle my work for the afternoon and that evening's obligations when another letter landed on my desk. Again, no return address. The same inconsistent ink patterns as on the letter tucked inside the book. What would the mystery survivor have to say to me today? I hoped that whatever lay inside the envelope would prove the manuscript's authenticity.

Miss Jill Levin, Senior Curator
Museum of Jewish Heritage
36 Battery Place
New York, NY 10036

Dear Miss Levin:
By now I hope you have received the book which I

sent to your care about a week ago. The book was passed down through my family for many generations. It was given into my care by my mother in late 1937. As a child, I always thought of it as only one of many books in our family's library, but for my mother, and her mother before her, this book always held special significance.

A few hours before the signing of the ketubah, on the morning of my wedding, my mother, with great ceremony, gave me this book and instructed me that it had been passed down to the firstborn daughter in every generation on her wedding day, and that it was up to me to keep that tradition.

As you read in my last letter, I wish to keep this donation private, and my identity a secret, I do not wish for you to have too many details of my life. But because there are certain things I must disclose to you which are important to how this book survived the war, I will tell you that I was born in a small town in Germany, just outside of the city of Berlin.

My parents were not German but Austrian and Polish. My mother still had family living in Poland in the late 1930s. And because of this, we found out what was happening in the Warsaw Ghetto. In the end, this information saved the life of this book. Because our cousins could still get letters to us, written in code, to tell us what was happening in the ghetto, this gave me just enough time to see that this book would be safe before we were deported.

I will write more to you as soon as I find

the strength to do so.

I sat back in my chair and leaned around the wall of the cubicle. "The book's not from an evangelist," I said to Aviva, as I folded up the letter and placed it carefully back into the brittle envelope.

"That's good to hear." She leaned around the edge of the cubicle. "How do you know?"

"I just got another letter from the mystery survivor."

"Can I see it?"

I passed the typed pages over and watched her read them.

"What are you frowning at?" I asked. "This certainly sounds like it's from a survivor."

"I don't know," she sighed. "There's no detail here. It could be anyone's story."

"There are plenty of details," I argued. "We know she's a woman. We know she was born in Germany."

"You call those details?"

"It's a lot of people's stories

"Well, at least it sounds like she's Jewish."

"What do you mean by that?" I said, a little annoyed. "It *sounds* like she's Jewish? What exactly does being Jewish sound like?"

"Okay, so that was the wrong way of putting it. But there's not a lot of information here. I'm always afraid of being taken in by another Benjamin Wilkowski."

"Come on. One person faking a survivor's story has jaded you to the point of not believing anyone?"

"I'm just saying that I'd feel better if we had some specifics to go on."

"So what you're telling me," I said in a low voice, "is that you'd be reassured of her ability to tell the truth if you saw the numbers on her forearm?"

"That," Aviva said quietly, "was totally unnecessary."

"Okay, I was out of line. But what are you really trying to say?"

She was silent for a moment. "Jill," she said, "something makes me think that you want this artifact to be authentic because it was addressed to you. But you know as well as I do that we have to think about it in a smart way. It could be a fake. Her story – if she's real – could simply be fiction. I'm not saying that's the case, but I am saying that we don't know. We simply don't yet have enough information. You have to consider the kinds of people who try to use us in order to tell their own story, who even lie to gain a platform that gives them credibility when they don't deserve it."

"It just feels like you're being overly cautious. Is your way of thinking even realistic?"

"Of course it is. We've seen it before. And right now it's all over the papers, what some other institutions are going through. Mostly because they didn't really care whether something was a fake, because all they could see was the money."

"You're talking about antiquities. I'm talking about survivor testimony. There's a huge difference."

"Maybe. But maybe not. Listen, I know it's tempting to take this at face value, but you have to remember what those other museums and synagogues went through when they found out that Wilkowski's book wasn't even true. It was just a bunch of facts, cobbled together to make it sound as if he had lived the life of a survivor. And when he was caught, they realized they had invited someone in to tell – and then sell – their story. Ultimately it came out; they had been used to perpetrate a lie. And not just any lie, but a lie which gave people like David Irving and his Holocaust-denier friends the kind of ammunition that keeps them going. Imagine finding out we had contributed to the problem. Imagine it happening here."

"But she's not trying to sell anything," I replied.

"You don't know that yet. You don't know where this is going."

"I don't understand why you don't want to believe her."

"And I don't understand why you do."

We glared at one another. It was the first time in years we had clashed over the legitimacy of an artifact.

"Look," Aviva said, "I don't want to fight about this. But you need

45

to be professional about this. It doesn't matter that your name was on the label. We've still got to examine it carefully."

I nodded.

"Good. You keep going. I'll take care of the rotation schedule. And if anyone comes looking for the new timelines, I'll say you're working on them. Don't worry. I'll cover for you," she said.

"Thank you so much, Aviva."

She smiled. "Don't thank me, Jill. If your hunch is right, we'll both get our names in *Art News*, and then we'll see who gets a bigger bonus."

I turned back to the parchment and turned the page.

He looks upon her, yet is bound to me
The words unto his master, but a lie;
Who takes upon himself a blinded eye
To poses of deceit and trickery.
One sister, loved by wit and modesty
is fain to let the devious serpent by;
The other, with a meek, insipid sigh
Inspires his art to heights of treachery.
The cruel Apprentice severs family peace
with one turn of his tongue, one twist of speech
One sister loved; the other is betrothed
In duty. How his honor doth appease
The father, who in love, hath loved each;
and choosing, chooses him that I hath loathed.

The darkest of days that I recall, save for the death of my father, are those in that most tragic spring of 1518, when William Roper first invaded our house, and from within our house, our lives.

When I first learned that he was to be a member of our household, as apprentice to my father, I rejoiced for a man whom I believed could be of help to that most noble soul in the offices of his profession. Roper had also been promised to us as a companion in our learning; in the hope that perhaps this well-traveled man could bring to us new insights and ideas from the bright worlds he had explored as a young man.

Yet the moment that he stepped over the threshold and into our house and I saw his face in the light for the first time, I could not understand how he could be a man of my father's choosing. From the first hour, I could not endure his company. It was not that he was not pleasing to the eyes; indeed, he was a fine looking young man; yet something in him remained a mystery, something deliberately hidden from sight, a defect of the soul, perhaps; for his manner was as coy and evasive as if he was loath to have some detestable trait brought to light.

My father brought him to me and said to him, This is my jewel, my own dearest child Margaret, whom I call my dearest Meg. Hearing my father's sweet words, I dropped a careful and modest curtsy, as my lady governess had taught me, but from beneath my downcast eyes I could see that the stranger looked upon me as if my respect for him were no more than his due. Enraged, I defiantly lifted my countenance unto his. And in that first glance, he cowered beneath my scrutiny as if his very soul was being called before the holy God on the day of his Judgment.

I disliked him from the very first; yet felt it my duty to conceal this from my father, for being a man of such honor and justice, I believed his choice to be sound, and my first dislike of this apprentice perhaps a passing whim of distrust, to be remedied in the future by this man's service to my father.

Indeed, my sisters took a liking to the stranger with apparent ease of mind and treated him with great kindness and gentle hospitality. Cecily, in particular, took note of his learning and wit, and enjoyed his fair and constant companionship to her in his idle hours.

He was our tutor to begin with, though by this time I was nearly thirteen years of age, and no longer in need of a tutor or a governess. Before William's arrival, I studied each day for an hour in the company of my father, who believed that I hath gained a level of intellect far beyond the tutors and governesses who hath been my instructors in my youth. Indeed, my own work as a scholar was greatly esteemed by my father, and it was by his grace that I had continued my studies with him. Yet for some reason, perhaps goaded by his new responsibilities sating the relentless demands of the Throne, the Law, or the Holy Church of Rome, my father deemed it his new wish that William and I should be companions in study as well as leisure. At first, I told my father of my desire to continue my work in solitude, as I always had; but my father entreated me to befriend his apprentice. I had not the heart to deny him his wish.

When first I encountered William, it was clear that he desired my companionship no more than I desired his. William distracted me from my studies, and worst of all, he represented the work of my mind and hands as his own, so that he might gain in the confidence and esteem of my father. It was a mark of evil; but that my good father did not recognize the fruits of his own child's labor - this cast me into depths of the greatest sadness. I felt I had lost the esteem of a worthy man to the deceit of a lesser one.

From that moment, William's inconstancy, by word as well as deed, became my constant sorrow. My eyes that bore witness to the ill-conceived works of his hands, my ears that bore witness to his lies. His devious and ill-made soul cast him to the depths of my esteem, and I knew I could not befriend such a man, who seemed to revere my father to his countenance; but once leaving his sight, spoke of his teachings as suspect, and his word as traitorous.

For William spoke as a traitor to the one beneath whose roof he dwelt. It was William, I believe, who was in service of that godless Monarch, the adulterer Henry, whose ill-treatment of his good and godly wife is a mark of sin upon his soul, and as the angels of heaven dwell with the Holy One upon the Throne of Judgment, he shall learn that such a throne is not his, and woe unto this king whose sin pervades the throne and pollutes the honor of his subjects!

It was not long before I realized William's cruel intention - to marry into my father's house and inherit the honors and offices of my father's affairs, rather than work to earn his own place in the world. It was then I realized it was my fair sister Cecily whom he desired as wife, a choice which I abhorred, for I cherished my dear sister and wished for her happiness to be completed by a worthy mate.

I hath no such desires for myself. I believed that my fair sisters would marry, and I should be left in peace as a happy spinster, desiring no other mate save for my beloved books and quill. Alas, it was not to be; for my dear father, so perfect in all things, forced the fate upon me that forever altered my happy course, as the gentle wind tenderly caresses the blossoms, yet in one breath, strips them from their stems with savage ferocity.

It is late, and my taper burns low. I must conceal this story in its usual place, and be silenced until the next solitary hour.

6

The week finally ended. It was Saturday afternoon. Alone on the subway, headed uptown, I realized it was taking longer than usual to reach Riverdale. I checked my watch again. Nearly three o'clock; I was running late. An automated voice over the loudspeaker informed us that we were being held in the station by the dispatcher and asked, repeatedly and too cheerfully, for patience.

Never without a book in my bag, I tried to concentrate on reading. But with the doors held open at yet another stop, the cold air blew in from above ground, and I shivered in spite of my thick wool coat.

I was also shivering, I realized, because of what happened the night before. I had returned home from work in the late afternoon on Friday, a rare occurrence for me. Because the museum was a Jewish organization, it always closed early on weekends so that we could get home by sundown for the Sabbath. Most people, whether religiously observant or not, rushed out the door as soon as the last visitor had departed.

I stopped on the way home from work to buy a *challah*, a bottle of wine, and a pair of pristine white candles. At the gourmet market in my neighborhood, I carefully selected a small roast chicken, honey-roasted carrots, and chicken soup with noodles, along with fresh berries, sorbet and biscotti for dessert.

Opening the door to our apartment, I dropped my work bag in the hallway, took off my coat, and quickly put the groceries away. From the top shelf of one of the kitchen cabinets I took my silver Kiddush cup and candlesticks, wrapped in crisp tissue paper. My parents had given them to me just before they moved.

I figured Michael wouldn't be home for a while. When we left for work that morning, he mentioned a meeting he expected to run late. Still, I thought I would surprise him with a lovely dinner. Hopefully, this would partially make up for the fact that I would be spending Saturday with my grandmother, and not with him at our friend's party.

As the sun dipped low in the sky and purple light filled the darkness of the apartment, I unwrapped the candlesticks and softly brushed away the one or two tiny chips of wax that had adhered to their bases. I cleared the mail and newspapers from the kitchen table and set the candlesticks down in front of me. The *challah* sat on a silver platter, covered with a clean white linen napkin. Finally, I uncorked the wine bottle and poured a small amount into the cup. Everything was ready. I unfurled a long, antique lace scarf, yellowed at the edges like old parchment, I held it lightly in one hand and reached up to loosen my ponytail, so my straight, dark hair fell upon my shoulders.

As I draped the scarf over my head, it felt as light as a whisper, as impermanent as a breeze, as if someone had brushed their fingertips over my hair. The striking of the match sounded like a door opening, and as I touched the tiny flame to each wick it felt as if some distant presence joined me in the room.

I blew out the match with a quick sharp breath, carefully encircled the candlelight with my hands and felt my heart beating as my eyes closed. I thought about my mother and my grandmother, about how their faces had changed from young to middle-aged to elderly as with these very same gestures they had ushered in each Friday night of my childhood and young adulthood.

The blessing moved from within me like a breath and softly I whispered the words. *"Baruch atah Adonai, Eloheinu melech ha-olam, asher kid'shanu b'mitzvotav, vitzivanu l'hadlik ner shel Shabbat."*

After a moment, I opened my eyes and took my hands from my face. When I looked up from the candle flames, I saw Michael leaning against the doorway, his tie loosened, his suit jacket slung over his shoulder. His deep brown eyes looked soft in the warm darkness. I was startled and felt a sudden blush creep into my face along with the sense of something – panic, perhaps, or maybe shame - flooding into my body. I felt as embarrassed as if he had caught me in bed with a lover. There was a brief silence before he spoke.

"Good *shabbos*," he said.

I watched his eyes taking in the scene before him.

"Good *shabbos*." I walked over to where he stood and kissed him. I waited for him to embrace me, but he didn't.

"Why didn't you wait for me?" he asked.

"You said this morning that you had a meeting. I thought you'd be late," I answered. "And you know sunset doesn't wait for anyone."

"The meeting got cancelled," he said quietly. "But if you had told me what you planned to do tonight, I would have made sure to be here, even if it meant leaving early. I could have gotten some other Gentile to cover for me." His tone was light, but I could hear the hurt in his voice.

"Michael, honestly, I didn't know I'd be doing this tonight. It was just a spur of the moment thing. It's not like I planned it and didn't tell you."

"Well, don't let me interrupt you," he said, gesturing towards the bread and the wine. "I can go into the bedroom until you're done."

"Michael, please don't be like that."

"Be like what?" He draped the jacket over a kitchen chair. "Excluded?"

"I didn't do this to exclude you," I told him. "I just thought you'd be coming home later."

"Well, I'm here now. What do you want me to do?"

"What do you want to do?" I replied, turning the question on him.

"I'd like to be here when you say the blessings. I want to welcome the Sabbath with you." He spoke with a quiet dignity. "But only if you are comfortable with it."

The old lace scarf began to slide towards the back of my head. He walked over to where I stood in the candlelight, looked down into my eyes, and gently slipped the lace forward over my hair. Then he drew his hands away from my head and waited.

I took the silver cup in my hand and closed my eyes as I began to softly sing the ancient, familiar melody. *"Baruch atah Adonai, Eloheinu melech ha-olam, borei p'ri hagafen."*

"Amen," Michael sang.

Then I translated the blessing into English so that Michael would understand it, saying "Blessed art Thou, Lord our God, Ruler of the Universe, who creates the fruit of the vine."

I debated singing the rest of the Kiddush, but it was long, and I didn't want the moment to feel any more awkward than it already felt. He seemed to wait for me to continue, but I didn't. Then, in his rich, resonant voice, I heard him go on with the melody of the prayer.

"Baruch atah Adonai, Eloheinu melech ha-olam, asher kid'shanu bemitzvotav v'ratzavanu l'Shabbat kod'sho b'ahava u'vratzon hinchilanu." Blessed art Thou, O Lord our God, Ruler of the Universe, who sanctifies us with the commandments, and has been pleased with us. You have lovingly and willingly given us your holy Sabbath as an inheritance in memory of creation.

I was shocked. He took the silver cup from where I had placed it on the table and raised it slightly as he continued singing, *"Zikaron l'maasei v'rei-sheet."*

I found my voice and joined in the melody with him. Together we sang the rest of the blessing, concluding with the final line, *"Baruch atah Adonai, m'kadeish ha-Shabbat."* Blessed art Thou, O Lord our God, Ruler of the Universe, who sanctifies the Sabbath.

I looked at Michael. His dark eyes twinkled.

"Where did you learn to do that?"

"You can find the most amazing things on the Internet these days," he said, laughing. "I've been waiting for the chance to show off. It wasn't that hard to learn." He paused before continuing. "It's weird, but it was almost as if I knew it."

"That's amazing. It took forever for me to learn when I had to sing it at my Bat Mitzvah. After that, I could never unlearn it."

He uncovered the bread, carefully folding the napkin and placing it on the table. *"Baruch atah Adonai, Eloheinu melech ha-olam, ha-Motzi lechem min ha'aretz."* And then he said the same blessing in English, this time looking at me as if the translation was for my benefit. "Blessed art Thou, O Lord our God, Ruler of the Universe, who brings forth bread from the earth."

"Amen," I intoned. "Wow. Wonders will never cease."

"You impress easily," he said. "I have a sneaking suspicion that a bar mitzvah isn't nearly as tough as the bar exam."

"Don't underestimate yourself."

"So," he asked playfully, "does this make me kosher enough for your family?"

I didn't know how to answer, so I busied myself in the kitchen, taking the scarf from my head and laying it carefully over a chair. I started getting plates down from the cabinet. After a minute or two I decided to try turning it into a joke. "More kosher than this chicken, certainly," I said, punching him lightly on the shoulder as I passed by.

"Jill," he said, "you can't keep dodging this."

"I know. But can't we just have a nice dinner tonight?"

"That's fine." He picked up his jacket from the chair. "We don't have to talk about anything." He walked into the bedroom, turned on the computer and closed the door, leaving me alone in the kitchen. I set the table and waited for him, but I couldn't find it in my voice to call his name to let him know dinner was ready, and I couldn't find it in my steps to walk into the bedroom to find him.

After about half an hour, he opened the bedroom door and walked into the living room. I turned on the television, brought out the plates and bowls and glasses, and we ate dinner in silence. Later on, I did the dishes while he sat on the couch and flipped through channels. When, I joined him on the couch to read my book, he returned to the bedroom and silently closed the door behind him.

We went to bed around midnight without exchanging another word.

7

My grandmother was standing at the door of her apartment open when I emerged, breathless, from the confines of the tiny elevator.

"Come in, my darling, come in."

I walked down the hallway, slowly catching my breath after the uphill walk from the subway station. The long corridor, lined with blue painted doors, smelled the same to me as it always had, like a combination of roasted onions and fresh bread, courtesy of the bagel store down the block.

She stood just outside the door, smiling broadly, in her usual outfit – a long-sleeved blouse, tailored black slacks, and thick-heeled black shoes. Her curly gray hair was pulled back from her face with a burgundy velvet headband, one that I had given to her about twenty years ago when she'd admired mine as I set off for a junior high school dance.

I wondered how long she'd been waiting there and glanced at my watch, noting that I was about twenty minutes late. I fervently hoped she hadn't been standing there the whole time, waiting for me.

"*Omi*," I said, using her favorite term of endearment – the German expression for "grandma" - as I stooped to kiss her on the cheek, "I'm so glad to see you."

As I followed her into her apartment, she touched the worn mezuzah on the doorpost with her fingertips, kissed them, and then shut the door behind me, carefully locking it before she joined me in the living room. "Of course it's been too long since you last visited. But I know how busy you are. Like all you young people, work, work, work, all the time." She gestured toward the couch. "Sit down, darling. Let me get you some tea."

I walked into the room, took off my coat and dropped my bag onto the floor. Then I lowered myself onto the familiar old couch. All around the room I saw same familiar objects, the books and the little glass ornaments. I looked over at the family photographs on her console and noticed a new one – my parents at the front door of their new home in Charleston.

My mother hadn't wanted to go, and had only agreed to leave New York after my father and I had assured her that I would keep an eye on my grandmother. I knew that he had been far more enthusiastic about the move than she was. But it had been something of an economic necessity. My dad was a retired high school teacher, and even though they were fairly comfortable financially thanks to his pension, the fluctuating stock market had done a number on their retirement fund. Once I was out of school, they had been driven south by the bad weather, the high taxes, and the costly expense of maintaining the modest house that I had grown up in.

I settled back onto the couch cushions and looked at the table, set for tea. *Omi* had already set out two small plates, one of *lebküchen* – my favorite German spice cookies – and on the other she had placed slices of her homemade nut torte. I could hear her rattling cups and plates in the tiny kitchen. "*Omi*, do you need some help?" I called out, knowing that she would tell me to stay put.

"No, not at all. I'll be right in."

I looked around the apartment again while I waited for her. My grandmother's hobbies were in evidence everywhere: needlepoint cushions nestled in the corners of the couch and in the matching chairs; a basket of brightly hued crocheted blanket squares lay next to the easy chair, with a skein of wool and needles sticking out at an awkward angle.

There were book-lined shelves on every wall. My grandfather had been an inveterate reader of Jewish and military history, but considering our family's history, I often wondered how it felt for them to live with titles like *The Rise and Fall of the Third Reich* and *Minister of Death: The Adolf Eichmann Story* surrounding them all the time. A small upright piano, its dark walnut wood shining in the pale winter sunlight, held court against the far wall of the living room, although I was sure that no one had played it in years.

I stood up and walked over to the console to inspect the photographs of my relatives. The small table was crowded with frames of all different colors and sizes, and every single image was familiar to me. There was one small black and white photograph of my grandmother's mother and father on their wedding day. This photograph had arrived in the mail some years after her arrival in America, sent by a cousin of hers who had fled to Brazil during the late 1930s. The same cousin – responding to the joyous news that there was another relative who had made it out of Germany - also sent her a slightly larger portrait photograph of three little girls in frilled white dresses and enormous cream-colored bows in their identically cut, straight brown hair: my grandmother and her two younger sisters, Hilda and Rachel. These were the only existing photographs of her parents and siblings. Only my grandmother had survived the war.

There were others – a wedding snapshot of my grandparents, taken in an Italian Displaced Persons camp – my grandmother, black-haired and slender in a borrowed white cotton dress, my grandfather with his dark hair hidden under a yarmulke, both of them smiling warily, their arms tight around one another's waists. Years ago, before my grandfather died, there had been other photographs of the two of them displayed here, but now these were lovingly kept on the bureau in her bedroom.

Next to the old wedding picture there was a portrait of my mother and father on their wedding day. They stood together on the royal-blue carpeted steps of our temple's sanctuary, my mother's small, slight figure encased in a white tailored gown, a round, lace-edged bouquet of pink roses in her hands, a pillbox hat and veil affixed to her bouffant. My dad was tall, thin, dressed in a tuxedo, with a white satin yarmulke on his head and a matching pink rose boutonniere pinned to his wide black lapel. His dark, curling hair and long sideburns made him look like a rock star.

Their faces were serious and determined, as if once they departed the temple, they were heading off to lead an anti-war demonstration, which, in retrospect, they probably were. When I was a teenager, whenever I had encountered this photograph, always proudly displayed at my grandmother's house, I used to wince at the sight of their unfashionable hairstyles and clothes. And if they happened to be in the room, I'd routinely sing a couple of bars of "Age of Aquarius." But now, looking at their picture, I wondered how these two young strangers had turned into the parents I now knew – how they had gone from two young people trying to change the world to a middle-aged suburban couple, full of their own demons and prejudices.

And, of course, there were pictures of me. Baby pictures, graduation portraits, a backyard snapshot taken at my third birthday party with me wearing a red and orange jumper patterned with the letters of the alphabet, looking like I had stepped right out of an episode of *The Electric Company*. My bat mitzvah portrait, taken ten years later, all peach-colored lace, shiny silver braces and frizzy dark hair.

And finally, the family picture from almost ten years ago, when I received my graduate degree. In it, my mother and father and I stood with my grandmother on the steps of a stone-pillared university building, my black gown and red hood and golden tassel blowing in the light breeze, all of us wearing proud, spring morning smiles.

To look at the collection of photographs, it seemed as if my life ended the day I graduated. But I knew that somewhere in this apartment, she had a special frame - probably silver or crystal - set aside for what she prayed would be my wedding picture. I sighed. At moments like this, I wished I had a sibling with whom I could share the pressure.

My grandmother emerged carrying a tray with a small china teapot, a sugar bowl, a small cream pitcher and two cups and saucers. "Every time you come over, the first thing you do is look at the pictures," she said. "That hasn't changed since you were a little girl."

She set the tray down. I crossed the small space to join her on the couch. She poured two cups of tea and then leaned back against the cushions.

"So how have you been, *Omi*?"

I scanned her face anxiously for signs of change. I was always worried that her health was beginning to deteriorate. Apart from the fact that her headband looked a little threadworn, she looked the same as always, bright-eyed and energetic. I noticed, a little reluctantly, that her hair looked a little thinner than the last time I had seen her, and her hands were slightly more gnarled.

"A little tired. But very busy, you know, volunteering at the senior center, getting out and about, going to my exercise class, going to concerts. My friend Mitzi and I bought tickets for a wonderful chamber music series in the city this winter. The only problem, of course, is that it's in the city, in the winter."

I laughed with her, as always marveling at the busy, active life she still led. She and a loyal coterie of elderly friends filled their days with activity, which made me feel slightly less guilty about my infrequent visits. I also realized - as I helped myself somewhat gloomily to the irresistible nut torte - that my grandmother probably got to the gym more often than I did.

"That sounds great," I said, surveying the tea tray with a critical eye. "You don't have any Equal, do you?"

"Of course I don't, darling. I don't believe in fake sugar."

"I should have guessed."

"Besides, you're eating nut torte and you're worried about a smidgen of sugar in your tea? You're as bad as your mother."

"Come on. I'm not that bad."

My mother's weight obsession was a well-known fact in our family. Since retiring from her job as a professor, which had kept her running around a college campus and on her feet teaching several hours a day, she had become horrified at the idea of a potential weight gain. Now, anything she ate was immediately exercised away playing outdoor tennis with my father four times a week. Throughout my childhood, she had nagged me incessantly about exercising with her, and constantly policed my consumption of the delicious homemade treats my grandmother would always bring to our house. If she could have seen me with both a slice of torte *and* the cookies on my plate, she would have killed me.

"Have you heard from Mom and Dad?" I asked. "I haven't talked to them in a couple of days."

"I talked to your mother last night," she said. "She called to tell me they're off on a cruise. The Greek Isles, I think."

"Right, I knew about that. I have to call them before they go. Did she say when they were leaving?"

"Sometime next week. She said your father was getting bored again."

"If I lived in the south, I'd be bored, too."

"I'm with you," she laughed. Living in the city, no matter what sort of mess the climate threw at us, was one thing we always agreed upon. "So tell me, how are things by you? How's work?"

"It's okay," I said, through a mouthful of cookie. "A little crazy at the moment. Aviva is about to go out on maternity leave, so I'll be managing a lot of the department's work while she's gone."

"Aviva is the Orthodox girl, right?"

"Yes. I went to her wedding last year, remember?"

"Of course. And she's having a baby, already." Her voice sounded wistful. I knew what it meant, and what she was thinking. The cookie crumbs suddenly felt like wet sand in my mouth. I felt like a transparently guilty suspect on a bad cop show; in my mind, I saw myself being hauled in by the Jewish Continuity Police, being charged with Failure to Marry.

"Well, I think it's kind of soon," I said brightly. "But you know, that's the way it is in her community." I tried to make myself sound sophisticated and worldly, but I knew exactly what was coming next.

"And how about you, my darling? Any dates? Any boyfriends?"

I took a sip of my tea. "Not so much. You know," I hated myself for lying, "with my schedule, it's so hard to meet people."

I thought guiltily about Michael, and what my real answer should have been. *Yes, Omi – I have met the man of my dreams, and we live together so happily. His name is Michael. His parents are from here, they're American. No, he's not Jewish, Omi. But that's irrelevant. I love him. He loves me. We love one another so much. And the fact that he isn't Jewish has made me so afraid to tell you about him. He makes me happy, Omi, and he wants you to like him. I want you to like him. He*

even learned how to chant the Kiddush for me, Omi. You'd love him.
No, I don't know if he would be willing to convert. Please don't be like
this. I wish you'd just give him a chance.

She nodded sadly. "Maybe you shouldn't work so hard, then."

"Right," I replied, using my classic fall-back excuse, "except that
there's the tiny question of paying the rent."

"With the right man you wouldn't have to worry about paying the
rent anymore. A beautiful girl like you should have someone to take
care of her. Besides, I just know the right person is out there, waiting
for you."

"*Omi*, it's not the 1950s. Women make their own way now. I don't
mind paying my own rent." Inside, I was cringing at the sheer scope of
my lies. There was no way I could have afforded the rent in our
apartment if Michael and I didn't live together. With both of our not-
for-profit jobs, money was always an issue. "Besides, even if I were
married, I'd still probably have to work so I could afford to live here in
the city. That's the whole point of having a career I really like.
Everyone works. No one minds."

"You should mind," she said, shaking her head. "As far as I'm
concerned, your mother's generation ruined it for all of you. Now you
don't even have the freedom to choose whether or not you want to have
a career."

"Everyone I know has a career," I argued. "Otherwise, what was all
that education for?"

"Ai, I'm not saying you shouldn't have had an education. I'm just
telling you that a few decades ago, women like you had more choices.
In my day, even in your mother's day you stayed home with the
children. Now, you young women hand off your babies after three
months," she waved a careless hand in the air. "It's all over when
maternity leave ends, and you go back to work and leave your children
with strangers. I see these women from Jamaica and West Africa and
Haiti wheeling double strollers with little blond babies. Babies whom
they pay no attention to while they're busy gossiping in the park. All
because there are no choices nowadays."

61

I attempted to fill my voice with the pretense of infinite patience, "I think it might be a little premature to worry about whether or not I'll be staying home with my kids."

"That's true," she said sadly. "No point in worrying about great-grandchildren that I don't even have yet."

"Oy," I sighed, shaking my head. And then I realized that I never, ever said things like "oy" anywhere but here, no matter how stressed out I got at work or at home. My grandmother, however, always managed to provoke some sort of Yiddish response code hidden deep within my psyche.

In the ensuing silence, I nibbled on a piece of nut torte. It had been a while since my last visit, and on my way uptown I had wondered why I stayed away for so long. Now, I realized, it was to avoid conversations just like this one. Then I realized that I was avoiding conversations with Michael, with my grandmother, with my mother, of course, and probably, if I really gave it some thought, even with Aviva.

Thinking of her reminded me about the manuscript that I had reluctantly stopped reading on Friday afternoon.

"I received a very interesting artifact donation this week," I said brightly, changing the subject. "It's a very old manuscript, possibly about four hundred years old. Aviva isn't sure that it's the real thing, but I think it is."

I could see the glimmer of interest in her eyes. I knew she loved when I told her about life at the museum, no matter how much she may have objected to my life choices in general. "That old?" she asked. "How can you tell?"

"The date says 1536. We've been looking at it – well, actually, I've been looking at it. Part of me thinks that Aviva doesn't want to look at it, doesn't want me to get my hopes up, in case it's a fake. But in a way, she's right."

"Right about what?" She settled back on to the couch cushions, holding the cup and saucer in her hands.

"She thinks it could be part of someone's religious or political agenda. But I don't think that's the case. I suppose it could be a hoax of some sort."

"How can you prove that it's the real thing?"

"We would send it to a lab. They have the equipment and technology to determine the age of the paper. And it's in very delicate condition, almost falling apart. I'm almost afraid of what might happen to it at the lab. Not that the one we use isn't a good one, I'm just afraid that it would come back in even worse condition. Right now, I still think with enough conservation, it could go on display. But if the condition degrades further, it becomes a problem."

"And if it gets too damaged, then it can't be displayed?"

"Exactly. Of course, there are amazing labs out there, but at the best ones, the process is very costly. For something that might not relate to our period of history, it might be tough to ask for that much budget money in order to send it someplace that would handle it the way it needs to be handled."

I placed my cup and plate on the table, and wiped my mouth with a napkin. "It's a bit of a catch-22," I continued. "Without authentication, we won't display it, and if we authenticate it through less costly channels, it might become too damaged to display."

"Do you know where it came from?"

"That's just the problem," I replied. "We're not sure who sent it to us. It came as an anonymous donation. The thing is, the package came to me, with a letter from the person who said she – or he - had met me, and had donated other items to the museum. But I have no idea who it could be."

"And until you figure out who it came from," my grandmother reasoned, "you can't tell whether this is the real thing or not?"

"It's either that or the lab."

"Could you go back through your records? Figure it out that way? After all, this person said they made other donations."

"I could," I considered. "But there are more than four hundred potential donors. And I don't have that kind of time. Especially since Aviva is leaving soon." I hated to bring Aviva back into the conversation – I didn't want to bring up the marriage-and-baby tangent again

– but my grandmother was far more interested in asking questions about the mystery artifact.

"What do you know about the person who sent it?"

"Not a lot," I said. "But it looks as if she's a survivor."

At that word, my grandmother flinched slightly, and automatically, swiftly, pulled down the sleeve on her left arm. She had done that for as long as I could remember, in order to make sure that the tattooed numbers were hidden from view. For that reason, I had never seen her wearing short sleeves, not even on the hottest summer days. I had only seen the number on her arm twice in my life, and both times she had been in the hospital.

I was ten years old the first time, and as soon as she caught me wordlessly staring at it, she quietly asked the nurse to cover it with a bandage. The second time was only a couple of years ago, when I had gone to see her after a gall bladder operation. She was asleep when I arrived, and there was time enough for me to stare, unseen, at the unfaded bruise of blue ink on her forearm.

That number seared itself on my mind: 462735. For days, I thought of it as a code for the subways – *East Side Express - East Side Local - West Side Express - Queens and Crosstown – Brooklyn - East Side Express*. How strange, I later found myself thinking, that I would associate trains with her number, when that was exactly the method by which she had been taken away from her home, her family, her life.

"Well," she sighed, "that does narrow it down a bit. Not many of us left."

"Don't say that, *Omi*. There are plenty of survivors still alive."

"Not really, my darling. Just because you spend your days listening to survivors doesn't mean that there are that many of us left to tell the tale. Every year, more of us fade away. And of those of us still here, many have begun to forget." She made a small gesture, motioning to her head with her hand. "Feeble in body, feeble in mind."

"Some of the survivors I work with are the most vibrant people I know," I told her. "And look at you. At your age, still leading a happy, full life. Still active, no matter what the weather. Still gorgeous, too," I said, smiling.

"You should have seen me in 1936," she laughed. "No one could hold a candle to me." She sighed. "The war. It changed everything. Wearing that uniform. Day after day, watching the bones of my ribs protruding from my middle, seeing my skin turning gray from the years of cold, of hunger. Sometimes, I thank God we didn't have mirrors in the camps. Because the first time I saw my own face after the war, I thought I was looking out a window at some other woman instead of at my own face in the mirror. Once you have seen yourself that way, you can never be beautiful again. Nothing, except maybe your children, and your children's children," she smiled as she patted my cheek with her hand, "can ever be beautiful again."

"*Omi*," I said, "of course you were still beautiful after the war."

"Maybe," she said, her voice sounding resigned. "I remember how my father used to call us each by our own special name. Hilda was his little bird, Rachel was his little cat, and I was his little rose. 'Anna,' he used to tell me, 'all of my girls are beautiful but you are my little rose.'"

She sighed. "He never imagined. He never knew what would happen – that his little bird would die in a cage, and that his little cat died only just a kitten." Her voice sounded tired and far away. "And that his little rose would wilt, but not die." She sighed. "And only thorns would be left."

It was almost too much, except that I had heard this story before, and even more than how upset and powerless I felt at hearing her talk about her family, it always made me nervous when she repeated things that she had told me, because it made me wonder if her mind was slowing down. I placed my hand over hers, and we sat in silence for a moment.

Abruptly, she changed the subject, as if she had returned to the present. "So, there is no good way for you to find out who sent this thing to you? Can't you get someone to help you do the research?"

"I suppose I could. I don't think there's an easy way to figure out whether or not this book is authentic."

"Well, my darling, you know that sometimes the things most worth having come because of the time and energy you have to put into getting them."

"How pithy. Have you been subscribing to *Reader's Digest* again?"

"Very funny. I'm just saying, if you put the same time and energy into finding a husband that you put into figuring out the history of this artifact, maybe you'd be getting married soon." She smiled at me in a self-satisfied way, her face looking a lot like my mother's after she had won an argument.

I laughed. "I can't win with you, *Omi*. You're just too clever."

"Absolutely right. Now come with me into the kitchen," she said, as she rose from the couch. "Your mother would be very upset with me if I only fed you sweets today. Let's go see what we'll have for dinner."

8

Returning home from my grandmother's, I was laden with plastic bags which held containers full of homemade mushroom barley soup, potato kugel, and brisket. She also packed half a loaf of challah from the wonderful Jewish deli on her block, and of course, more cookies. I fumbled with the bags and my keys, and opened the door to the apartment.

It was dark and quiet inside. "Michael?" I called, assuming he'd be in the bedroom, typing away on the computer, or maybe on the couch in our tiny living room, watching a basketball or hockey game.

There was no answer. I turned on the hall light and glanced at the wall clock – it was 10:00. He must still be out at the party, I thought.

I checked the answering machine. The light was blinking so I pressed the Message button. The authoritative voice of my mother immediately filled the room.

"Jill, this is your mother." I sighed. She said the same thing every time she called. I had no idea why felt she needed to identify herself, as if I didn't recognize her professor's voice, the one that tolerated no misbehavior in her lecture hall. "Where are you? It's been days since wo heard from you. We're leaving on that cruise next week, so I want to touch base before we leave. If you get this message before 10 tonight, give us a call. If not, call us after tennis tomorrow morning. We'll be back around 11. Bye."

The machine rewound itself with a whirr and click. I deleted the message, not wanting Michael to hear it. Even though my parents knew we lived together, they barely acknowledged his existence.

Before they moved away, when it was still mandatory for me to go home for Friday night Shabbat dinner, I made the mistake of bringing Michael with me to meet them one Friday, just a couple of weeks before Passover. I hoped that they would invite him to the family Seder.

We prepared ourselves – and one another – for what might happen. He got a nod and a brief handshake from my dad, and the evening

proceeded cordially enough, but during dinner, my
mention of a Christian evangelist, recently in the
better than Hitler" and other comments that made
invitation to the Seder had been forthcoming.

"We already have too many people coming,"
when I had questioned her about it. "I'm sure he's
won't know what to do at a Seder."

"He could learn," I had argued.

"I'm sure he could, Jill, but that's not the point
very uncomfortable for everyone. Besides, if you
you were seeing him, it would be too much for he
enough. This would kill her."

I wanted to argue with her, but it was their ho
And at the time, I thought my mother had a goo
mother knew about Michael, it would be one more
life filled with tragedy and loss. It was easier
protect someone who had already lost so much.

But from that moment on, my relationship with
deteriorate. I got the sense that my family's disapp
all coming from her, and my dad was just going a
me more than once that he tried to talk to her about
as he brought up our relationship, my mother told
way he could understand, because his parents had
Holocaust.

Even though I was sad to see my parents move
because I no longer had to worry about spendin
them. When they flew up to New York on their
always had dinner at my grandmother's. Michael,
not invited.

We tried inviting them to our apartment, but
called with a polite excuse – theater tickets, a co
with friends. Once or twice, when the plan was fo
a restaurant, just the three of us without my grand
come along, but the meals were so tense and quiet

tries to bring them together, I ended up going alone.

I realized that even though my mother knew it was serious, she was going to do everything in her power to communicate clearly that she didn't want Michael to be part of our lives. And I was even more surprised that my dad seemed to feel that he had to take her side. Even though it was something I had kind of expected, it still shocked me. I had naively believed that once they met Michael, they'd find a way to accept him, or at least make peace with the situation. In the past, my boyfriends had always been received warmly, had always been made to feel welcome. But before Michael, they had always been Jewish.

I sighed again, remembering, then put the food away and walked into the bedroom and turned on the light. For a moment, I thought about calling Michael on his cell phone, and seeing if the party was still going on, and if I could still stop by. But I was tired; visiting my grandmother always left me feeling emotionally exhausted, so instead I changed into pajamas and got into bed. I turned the television on for background noise and picked up my current paperback.

The next thing I heard was a key turning in the lock and the front door opening and closing. I opened my eyes and lifted my head from the pillow as Michael walked into the bedroom.

"Hi," I said.

"Hey." His voice was quiet, unenthusiastic. Not at all like his usual warmth toward me. Clearly, I was not yet forgiven for what had happened last night.

"How was your day?"

"It was all right." I watched him as he toed off his shoes, and unbuttoned his shirt. "Were you asleep?"

"I guess." I took off my glasses, which had been pressing into the bridge of my nose while I slept, and rubbed my eyes. "What time is it?"

"Twelve-thirty."

"How was the party?"

"Okay," Michael said, without looking at me. "How's your grandmother?"

"She's fine. And there's a bunch of stuff in the fridge if you're hungry. There's kugel, some brisket that she made for dinner. It was really good. And of course, she sent a ton of it home with me."

"Even though she thinks you live alone?" He stood on his side of the bed and unbuttoned his cuffs. I didn't like the sarcasm in his voice. "I'm glad she's looking out for you. You know, making sure you keep all the right culinary traditions."

"What's with you? Have you been drinking?"

"No, I haven't been drinking. But I've been doing a lot of thinking this afternoon and tonight." He sat on the edge of the bed. "I've been thinking that maybe I should move out for a while."

"What?" I sat up in the bed. "Why would you even think about doing that?"

"Because this isn't working." He leaned away from me, looked at the window to where our curtains fluttered in the breeze. "All day long, here without you, getting ready to go to this party – again, without you — I was thinking that you were going up to see your grandmother alone, with no chance of me being included in your family, and how being with me forces you to live a double life – the one you live with your family, where you're always feeling pressured and sad, and the one you live with me, where we're happy. And yet you still can't choose.

"If you were prepared to stand up to your parents, instead of letting them lead you down some path where I'm not included in your family life – and maybe you're okay with that, but I'm not – or thinking you can manage their expectations with silences and lies – which will probably end with us breaking up — or even if you would just tell your grandmother about us, it would be one thing. But the fact is that I think you don't even feel strongly enough about me to face whatever real or imagined wrath you think your parents and your grandmother will rain down on you if you tell them that we want to get married, and that we want to be together no matter what their opinion is. And I don't think you're going to change your mind about that anytime soon."

"I can't believe you're saying this," I cried. "For one thing, why is this such a big deal to you? My family has no bearing on our life together."

"That's not true. They've made it perfectly clear that they don't like this relationship. And your grandmother doesn't even know that I exist. I mean, Jill, we've been living together for years, and you're still telling me not to pick up the phone when she calls —"

"But that has nothing to do with you," I protested. "It would be the same for any person I lived with, but wasn't married to. She doesn't approve of that sort of thing."

"Come on, Jill. You're thirty-two years old. When are you going to start acting like an adult? Most people don't give a damn what their parents think of them, never mind their grandparents. But I think this problem you have is bigger than just wanting your family's approval." His eyes flashed. "I think you're the person who is uncomfortable with our relationship. Maybe you're the person who thinks you should marry a Jewish guy. And you're putting it all on them."

"That is so not fair. You have no idea how I feel. No idea at all." I felt the burning rush of tears behind my eyes, but I swallowed hard, hoping to keep them in check. "Today I was so close – *so close*, Michael – to telling her about you. And the fact is that in my heart, I don't really care what she thinks. Just as I don't give a damn about what my parents think. But then she gets to talking about everything, everyone she's lost, and I just can't do anything else to her. Nothing in her life turned out the way she expected. How can I let her down again?"

He took my hand in his. "Jill, here's what I think. You don't see it, but the fact is the same prejudice that caused your grandmother to suffer in a concentration camp is the same prejudice that your family has against me. As you said a couple of nights ago, I'm the other, and for them, the other is the enemy. But the way they think is so destructive. It's a terrible way to live, and I see it tearing you to pieces. And deep down, I think there's something in you – and I'm not judging you, because you know I can't speak to the experiences that have shaped your family and your life – but whether you know it or not, part of you has internalized your family's prejudice. And I don't know if I want to stay with someone who has those feelings inside them."

I stared at him, shocked.

"Jill, whatever feelings you have, I don't know if you love me enough to overcome the messages you've heard your whole life. But you either have to overcome them, and find a way to stand up to your family – to be honest with them, honest with yourself - or this relationship has to end. You're either going to let your family down, or you're going to let me down. It's one or the other. And it's a choice you have to make."

"When did you start thinking about this?" I asked.

"Last night, I guess." He looked away. "I thought that after I proved to you that I didn't just have to stand by and watch your traditions, that I was willing and available to participate, to learn, to share these things with you – that you would have a totally different reaction. I guess I fooled myself into thinking I had a chance at being accepted, not only by your family, but by you, Jill. But after last night, I started thinking maybe I was wrong about all of it. And maybe I've been wrong about us, too."

"No, don't say that." I held his hand more tightly in my own. "It meant the world to me that you learned the blessings, and that you wanted to share Shabbat with me. I'm just horrible at expressing it, Michael. That's all."

"I don't know." His face was sad, doubtful. "I think it might be better if we took some time off from one another."

I hated myself for how badly my family had treated him, and how badly I had hurt him by not standing up for myself and for him. "I don't want you to move out," I told him. "I know that we can find a way to figure this out. We can get through this."

"How?" he asked. "You won't talk about it with me, and I know that you won't talk about it with them. And it's not so much that we have to find a way to work this out – it's that you have to find a way to face up to what is happening here. No matter what you do, someone is going to get hurt. I don't want you to disappoint your family, but it seems as if the only way for them to be happy is if you keep lying to them. And I don't want you to do that. I don't want to be part of that."

"What do you want?" I asked quietly.

"You know the answer. I want us to get married, and I don't want it to put us in the middle of some ridiculous shitstorm with your family. I just want us to love one another. In a home where we can pick up our telephone, where we can celebrate Shabbat together if that's what you want to do, and where we don't have to worry about living up to some outmoded rules about religion and tribalism." His face was flushed, his voice filled with sadness. "I want us to have a life together, but not like this. Not when I have to be hidden away from people you love because you're ashamed of who I am."

I held up a hand to stop him from talking further, but he clasped it in his own as he went on. "Okay, so maybe you're not ashamed of me, Jill. But that's how it feels. And even if you're not, I want you to stop being so defined by what happened in your grandmother's past that you're willing to sacrifice our future." He let go of my hand.

I thought about the afternoon at my grandmother's, about how her father had called her his little rose, about her two sisters, my great-aunts, whom I only knew through a single image, as two small girls with hair tied up in creamy white bows. I thought about how she made sure her sleeve was covering her tattooed arm, and about how there was sadness beneath every expression of her sweetness. And I thought about my parents, who were off on another of their fabulous trips, this time to Greece, a warm place, full of heat and bright sunlight. My family seemed so normal on the outside, and even though I had listened to their remarks about "the *goyim*" all throughout my childhood and adulthood, sometimes even I was shocked by the hate and mistrust that seemed to live under the surface of their skin. Perhaps, I thought suddenly, that was the reason they traveled so much. Not so much because of the cold and the snow, but because they were trying to deal with the darkness and the shadows trapped inside them.

"Please don't do this, Michael." I leaned forward and touched his arm. "I hear what you are saying. And you're right. I need to find a way to talk to them. I need to find a way to tell them you are part of my life. No, that's wrong. I need to tell them that you *are* my life."

73

Some of the anger left his face as I looked at him.

"All right," he relented. "I won't move out. But I think we should set a time limit on this. I'm willing to give you a month, Jill. If you haven't told them by then, you never will."

He got up from where he had been sitting on my side of the bed. I picked up my book from where it had fallen after I fell asleep. Then I took off my glasses and laid them on the night table. I watched him as he got ready for bed. I sat silently while he went into the bathroom, and I listened while he brushed his teeth. All the familiar sounds of the night that I had learned to live with, had learned to love.

He walked back into the bedroom and I heard the quiet sound of his breathing as he set the alarm clock.

"I'm not ashamed of this." I said softly. "And I'm not ashamed of you."

"Then act like it," he said curtly, and then he turned out the light.

9

It was Sunday morning around 10:30, and I was headed into the office. Not so much because I had work to do. I did, of course, but because I wanted some uninterrupted time to think – about work, about my family, and about exactly what had taken place between me and Michael the night before.

He had woken up early and gone out for a run and to pick up the paper, and then he'd come back briefly for his gear before he headed across town for his usual morning indoor tennis game with some guys from his office. He left a note for me saying that he'd be back in the early afternoon.

I debated with myself for about ten minutes over whether to stay inside, curled up with a cup of tea and the Sunday *Times*, versus heading out into the cold and going to the office for a couple of hours. Finally, I decided to throw on jeans and a sweater and head downtown.

After the fight – I couldn't call it anything else – with Michael last night, I didn't want to hang out in the apartment, with all of the signs and symbols of our relationship around me. I knew that if I didn't somehow find the courage to talk to my family about him, we wouldn't be sharing this space for much longer.

I called his cell phone and left a message that I was going in to work, which I knew he would pick up as soon as they were off the court. I figured he was coming home after his game for our traditional Sunday morning bagels and coffee, so I told him not to bother getting me my usual hazelnut coffee and toasted onion bagel with butter. I didn't want to pretend it was a typical Sunday morning, because it wasn't.

Now, with the cold morning drizzle threatening to turn into sleet, I made my way along my usual commuting route, except today my hair was slung into a ponytail and I wore no makeup. The harbor sky was full of smoky clouds, the water below a dirty dark gray, and the Statue of Liberty was barely visible from the edge of Wagner Park.

The museum entrance was full of visitors going through Security. I waited my turn on the line and finally flashed my ID to the weekend guards. I then waved to the box office staff, all of whom looked cheerfully harried by the crowds, before taking the elevator upstairs to my office.

Although light streamed from a couple of offices down the hall – meaning that the education staff was already here, preparing for the day of kids' activities, it was too quiet. I turned on an overhead light and switched on the radio in the conservation area, which was tuned to the pop station of choice for most of the junior curators. I hastily changed it to the classic rock station, and turned it up loud enough to drown out the sounds from downstairs.

I looked at the clock: it was 11:30. I wasn't in the mood to call my parents, especially since things were so rocky with Michael, but I knew I had to get it over with. They would surely be back from tennis by now, so I picked up the phone and dialed their number.

"Hello?"

"Hi, Dad."

"Hey, sweetheart, how are you?" I could hear the smile in my dad's voice. "We hadn't heard from you in a few days. Everything okay up there? We wanted to make sure we talked to you before we left on vacation."

"Vacation from retirement? Lucky dog."

"It's nice work if you can get it, certainly," my dad chuckled. "But tell me how you're doing."

"Everything's fine here. Just busy. You know how it is. I've had to put in a lot of late nights at work. We're mounting a new exhibition, which is crazy enough, but one of my colleagues is also going out on maternity leave. So I have a lot on my plate right now. How are you doing? How was tennis this morning?"

"Same as always. My backhand needs work. And your mother is the first one to tell me. But we won't talk about that. Everything here is fine, it's sunny and 70 degrees outside. How could it not be fine here, unless you're used to experiencing actual seasons?"

I laughed. "Hey, it's cold and raining here. So you're not missing much."

"Between the crap that passes for pizza and the fact that I can only get bagels in the freezer case, I'm missing enough about New York, believe me. Your mom's right here, I know she really wants to talk to you. But listen, don't let the work stuff stress you out. It'll get done."

"Easy for you to say, considering you're retired."

"And believe me, Jilly, there are days I wish I wasn't. It's so boring down here. I'd rather face a classroom full of historically-challenged eleventh graders any day! That's why we're going on this cruise. I'm going bananas down here in the Southland. Not a hint of smog in the air, not an oldies station to be found. If things don't get better, I'm either going to have to go back to work or take up golf."

I laughed. "Get satellite radio. And make sure your swing doesn't mess up your backhand."

"It might even improve it, who knows? Hold on a second, let me get Mom for you."

"OK, Dad. Thanks."

"Bye, sweetheart. Love you."

I waited, thinking about how much I missed my dad. Talking with him always made things seem so much less complicated. I wished I could talk with him about Michael, but I knew his response would be something like *a breakup might be all for the best, sweetheart.* I knew that in his heart he wasn't sure if my mother was right, but he knew he had to go along with her, if for nothing else than the sake of peace in the house. I also knew he wanted us to start getting along again.

"Jill?"

"Hi, Mom. How's it going?"

"Did you get my message last night?"

"Yes, but I got home too late to call back. Are you excited about your trip?"

I felt like I had to divert her to talk about something that made her happy in order to avoid a conversation that would just end up annoying me.

77

"Yes, we're very excited. But is everything okay there? We haven't heard from you in days."

"I called on Wednesday, Mom."

"But today's Sunday. My neighbor's daughter calls her every day. You know how worried we get, especially with you in the city. We're so worried that there's going to be another terror attack. You know, I read the Metro section online every day, just to find out what's going on up there."

This was fairly typical of our conversations. It started out innocently enough, but I always ended up feeling that it was easy to see that with my mother and grandmother, the apple didn't fall far from the tree, and that the harvest of guilt had originally been planted in my grandmother's orchard.

"Everything's fine up here, Mom. Nothing to worry about."

"That's good. Listen, I'm going to email you all of our travel information. Just in case. Should I send it to your home or work email address?"

"Whatever's easier. I check them both a couple of times a day."

"Then I'll send it to both. I don't want you to get in trouble for receiving personal email at work. And I just want to make sure you can get in touch with us in case anything happens."

Even though I had lived with her for so many years, I was still always annoyed at how my mother always seemed to be waiting for something bad to happen. I knew it had a lot to do with what her parents had gone through, but it drove me crazy nonetheless. It didn't matter what real life threw at her; it was always a waiting game to see when and how the other shoe would drop.

"Nothing's going to happen, Mom," I said, irritated. "And you don't have to check *The New York Times*. You know that if something happened to me, Michael would call you."

I could practically hear her neck stiffening over the phone. "Well, be that as it may, I was also thinking about your grandmother. Have you spoken with her?"

"I went to see her yesterday."

At least I had this much to report, so that she couldn't accuse me of neglecting her mother, the Holocaust survivor. "She's feeling good and she looks great." I fished around for something to say that would reassure my mother that my grandmother was doing just fine. "She's got tickets for a chamber music series this winter."

"I wish she wouldn't venture out in all that snow and ice at her age. Why can't she stay home and listen to WQXR? Anyway, I'll send everything to you this afternoon or tonight. We're flying out on Wednesday and we meet the ship on Saturday."

"How long is your cruise?"

"Two weeks, but we're going to stay overseas longer. Once the cruise is over we're going to Tunisia and then to London for a few days. We're flying home through Heathrow. You'll see. It's all in the itinerary."

"Great, I'll look at it when I get it."

"I'll call you on Tuesday night, before we leave, okay? Will you be home?"

"Hopefully. But leave me a message if I'm not there, and I'll call you back if I don't get home too late. I was telling Dad, there's been a lot of late nights these days. We have a lot going on at work. I'm actually here in the office right now."

"Well, that's good, honey." I could hear the hope in her voice and I knew what she was thinking. *Good, she's not home spending the weekend with that goyische young man.* "Maybe it'll lead to a promotion."

"I wouldn't count on it," I told her. "Anyway, I should get to work. I'll talk to you before you leave, OK?"

"All right. Take good care, honey. We love you."

"Love you too," I said, and I could feel a little knot in my throat. True, she pissed me off constantly these days, and she was negative and paranoid. Not to mention the fact that she obviously hated my boyfriend. But she was still my mother.

"Bye, Mom," I said, and hung up the phone.

I sat back in my chair for a few minutes and looked out of the window at the gray sky over the park. The rain was lashing against the windows. I got up from my desk, turned on some more lights, and found the white gloves in my desk drawer. Then I entered the code to open the vault and drew out the manuscript, wrapped in its acid-free paper, from where I had hidden it in the back. I brought it over to the counter, and sat down to read further.

> Attend me not, false suitor; let me be.
> The stone is not yet cast, no fate is sealed.
> In favor false was his intent revealed.
> Why should this serpent make a wife of me?
> This scholar, with insidious mastery -
> Affection for one sister is concealed
> And to a father's nobler faith appealed
> Whilst downcast eyes doth mock his charity.
> His bold intentions writhe with serpent's shame
> About me, wise beneath his knowing smiles.
> And God shall find me faithless, should he prove
> To be the heir of one who prized our name
> And now makes me the prize of cunning wiles.
> I look upon his face, and know no love.

It was all at once that I knew of William's intention; to have me for his wife, to steal the loving scholarship of my hands, and to replace me in my father's esteem as the heir to his noble teachings.

It was clear to see that he admired my sister Cecily; for as it is told, she was the fairest of the three More sisters. For I, in my face and features, did bear the likeness of my dear mother; tho' by God's grace I was of like wit to my father. Yet it was whispered by our friends that William had been instructed by my noble father to court me, with the intent to make me his wife. These rumours did cause much sadness and strife in the once happy hours that my family shared.

Soon in the night my sister Cecily stole to my chamber; there in the moonlight did I see her fair countenance blemished with tears. At once I knew that the bitter music of her sorrow had been composed by William, and most gently I said unto her - Weep not, dear sister, for what trouble brings thee to me at this late hour? She said to me, Meg, thou art a traitor to us all, for it is thy grace that separates me from my heart's dearest.

I am amused even now, to recall how I silently laughed, for I could no more imagine such a man as anyone's heart's dearest than I could imagine taking a pig to my bosom, and nursing it as a child of my own flesh. It was then I recognized that it was the truth that she spoke, in her genuine care for this unworthy soul. How can it be told, for Holy God made my sister a heart less cynical than my own, and perhaps she could see a goodness in him that had eluded my eye.

Nonetheless, I feared for her happiness with him. Though he did love her, virtuously and wisely, in my presence and in the presence of others, I sensed duplicity in his intentions towards her. His demeanor in secret, however, though he tried to keep it from me, did pervade the odour of lust in her company, and I feared for her sweet innocence. She was a mere girl, and he a man of the world. Who knew in what trickery he could dissuade her from her virtuous life?

In her tears, I assured her that I did not love him, and had no intent to be his wife, then or ever. I spoke to her of my joy of learning, and how I would forsake that joy for no mortal man, save to vouchsafe the wishes of our dearest father. Yet I spoke not of my fears for her, for it is told that the wise shall keep their fears silent, lest they should prove the speakers of truth.

She held me to her, her face alight with joy, as I swore unto her that I would no more hurt her than I would take a torch to my books. Yet the motto warns: Swear not, lest ye be foresworn! Would that I had taken those words to heart, for as the palest of sunlight touches a rose in the next morning, I was summoned to my father's side, and it was told to me, as my heart bled for my fair sister, how I was betrothed.

I must tell you, reader, that for the first moment of my life all defiance filled me, and I lashed out in dire anger at that noblest of men. I wailed, I screamed, I said that I would have none of William, and bemoaned my fate like a chastened child. In that moment a gentle smile curled my father's lip, as he said unto me, For it is so, that even my wisest child is, at her heart's core, a mere woman.

Do not suffer unduly, child, he said, for it is my wish to see thee thus espoused, and cared for after my death. Thou can no longer live a child in thy father's name; soon thou shalt have a name of thine own – you shall share his, for it is good, and it is my wish that thou mayest be, perhaps, even more than More.

I wept without consolation, even as he sought to cheer me with his wit and his clever turn of the jest, at the thought of bearing any name *but* my own, but there was little to be done. My father, so unselfish in his love for me and for his God, had made his wish; there was nothing for me to do but grant it. And would I, his docile servant, his obedient child, hasten to defy his word? Never, was my answer. But in that hour, when I wept for the final time as my father's child, I told that man of Cecily's plight; how she had declared her love for William only a short time before, and of my imminent betrayal of my word to her.

It was then that my father told me his deepest secret: of the years he spent apprenticed to his master John Colt, and how he fell rapturously and singularly in love with his younger daughter. But his master, in fairness, espoused him to the elder, as it would tarnish the honor of the house to have the younger daughter marry before the elder one. He said unto me, - Meg, it is a far nobler thing to wed before Cecily; other suitors shall attend her, but before she can be espoused to a man of honor, thou must first be wed. This was the wisdom of my master; from this I shall not be deterred.

- And as thou hast witnessed, I am the happiest of men, for that eldest daughter was thy dearest mother Jane, who rewarded me with four delightful children, for whom I would gladly give my life and heart. Do not despair, little Meg, for it is not in thy nature to seek gladness when thy wit would fain choose reason. This is the most reasonable course, and God will grant thee safety and peace. -

Though in word I did consent to this; in my heart I was sinful, rebellious and disobedient. I left my father in his chamber no longer as a child, but as a woman who swore eternal hatred unto her betrothed for his dishonor to my fair sister.

Without uttering a word of consolation to her, William attended me a few hours later in the sitting-room, and said these words to me: Margaret, we are to wed soon; and in truth it is long past time for thee to give up the things of childhood – thy books, thy papers, must all be in my keeping, for it is thy duty as my wife to be commended only unto me, to be subject to my will and wisdom, and I wish for thee to quit all things except those in keeping with my affairs.

I turned upon him and said - Quiet, foul Serpent; for my soul belongs no more to thee than to the body in which it dwells; I am commended to my Self and my God and my noble father, so there will be no more of thy words. Make thyself of use, and commend thyself to the misery of my dearest Cecily; for in truth thou hast made a mockery of her innocent heart, and there will be sorrow in this house of thy creation. Wisdom indeed! There was no thought in thee but to use her ill, and to espouse me. Thus thou hast dividest me from those I love, and usurp my words for thine own evil work.

His cheek then did turn pale, and he countenanced me as a guilty man, and said, If thou shouldst reveal any of my doings to thy father, I shall honor my allegiance to him no more. There are changes yet to come, there are storms that are coming to damage the fields of our fair land, and thy father should have a care to see that his harvest is acceptable to the King.

It was in that moment that I found all of my suspicions alight, for I believed William to be in the most dishonorable employ of that evil Monarch, heretofore my father's friend and confidante. It was William who hath enticed him into that royal Web with no thought but for himself and his own comfort. Many men knew of my father's wisdom; should William not reap this praise for himself?

Perhaps my father's greatest sin was a trusting heart; for if ever it brought him to a more cruel end, he was loath to look upon his betrayer, and in faith, linked the name and soul of his most favored child to the evil usurper who sought to gain his fame.

My cell phone rang, startling me out of the pages that lay beneath my gloved fingertips. I picked up absently.

"Hello?"

"Hey," Michael's voice strained to be heard over the echoing sounds trapped inside the tennis bubble. "I just got your message. Are you still at work?"

"Yeah," I said. "How was your game?"

"Good today, for once. Are you going to be much longer?"

I looked down at the beautifully formed letters on the page that I had just finished reading, and made a swift decision. "Probably," I said, pushing the hair out of my eyes. "I have a couple of things I want to catch up on this afternoon, while I have some quiet time. It's going to be a crazy week."

"Not a problem. I have some work to catch up on, too." His voice sounded relieved. I guessed he didn't want to keep fighting with me, either.

"OK. I'll be home for dinner. Maybe we can go out. I'm in the mood for pizza."

"That would be great," he said. "I'll see you later."

"Bye." I pushed a button on my phone and ended the call. I realized in a single empty moment that neither of us had ended the call by saying that we loved one another, but maybe, I thought, it was something I'd need to get used to from now on.

I gingerly turned the page and to my surprise, the paper on which the words were written was a different consistency – deeper in color and stronger and thicker in texture. I touched the sheet carefully between my thumb and forefinger. I looked down and saw that the ink seemed sharper, bolder, although the handwriting was the same, the words seemed to be more hastily composed.

I stood by, pale as a milk-colored rose, as Cecily was ushered into my father's study. Next to me, with his terrible hand on my sleeve, stood William, with his mouth curled into a smile as insidious as that of the serpent of Eden.

When I heard her distraught cry, I broke from William's cruel mastery, and hearing the terrible sound of my own name like discordant music on his tongue, I ran from him, following my sister out of the door of my father's house. I cried out after her, but she refused to turn back. I decided to leave her to her grief, and hastened down the long lane and out the gates. I walked, endlessly, for what seemed like days but could not have been more than hours.

Along the road I wept without consolation, raging against Holy God, crying out with my own heartbreak and that of my sister, knowing that for all of her days Cecily would gaze upon me with bitterness and distrust.

I walked on, not seeing the dust rise where my footsteps lingered in the road behind me, not smelling the perfume of the blossomèd air, not even noticing how the wild dark eyes of the roadside's children hunted my shadow as I walked, unaccompanied, unescorted, a highly improper woman, eyes blinded by grief and my hands twisting with the useless will to defy my father and his apprentice.

I stopped for a moment and looked at my hands, seeing the tips of my fingers stained with ink, and the scarlet mark of an old candle burn on my upturned palm. I thought of the certainty with which my selfsame hands had consoled my sister in the night, offering comfort as if it was a crop of sweet and mellow fruit waiting to be harvested, when, oh, without the protection of the night, without the duplicity of the shadows in which her love for William had been sown, how in the merciless sight of the morning, only blight and loss and seasons of insatiable hunger would be revealed to her.

I wondered how my father could have failed to protect his daughters from William, and yet I knew in my soul that my father, when it came to reading the character of those whom he wanted to trust – as opposed to those who had earned the merit of his felicity - was an unholy fool. Although he was gifted with a mind that could unravel the most intricate workings of the law, and a soul and heart that knew the true name of justice, he also possessed a false wisdom borne by ambition that in his mind turned warning signs to jests, and believed that the peace of laughter and a phrase of holy writ could turn enemy into friend, warrior into lover, snake into archangel.

Even now, I thought, my father knew me – his own dearest Margaret – as one who sought to live out his teachings, his noblest spirit, but that since I had been born as a woman, he did not, and would not, know my heart.

I had first thought that it was my tears that had soaked the ruffled collar of the new gown – unbeknownst to me, a bethrothal gown – that I had most unwillingly donned at William's – and my father's - behest, but when I looked at the darkening sky I felt the spatters of cold rain upon my pale cheeks, and so I gathered my courage and made my hastening way through the marketplace, amidst the cries of the sellers and the shocked looks of the women hawking their wares. Although I was not a courtier, my smoothèd hair beneath the angular lines of my hood and the well-cut lines of my gown betrayed me as a woman of good family, especially among those women with dusty curls beneath their caps, and skirt hems stained with mud.

To escape the shrill cries of the men and the pitiless glances of their women, I ducked my head beneath the low lintel of a roadside shop, and heard the tiny silver music of bells over my head as I opened the door.

I stood in the doorway, my gown and hood soaked with rain, the taunts of the sellers still echoing in my ears, and a heart sickened by my father's foolish betrayal of my sister and myself. At once, a young man emerged from a darkened back room, hastily smoothing his curls back from his forehead with a deft hand.

-Yes, Madam? he asked, and there was a tone of scholarly civility in those two words that reminded me of my father's gentle voice.

I did not know how to respond. I looked around at the walls crammed with texts and papers; I smelled the glorious scent of what was perhaps an ocean of ink. Though it did not become my wit to ask, I did just that, of the man who stood expectantly before me.

-What shop is this? I asked, trying to put the quiet command of my father's voice into my own shaking one.

-This is a bookseller's, he answered perplexèdly, as if I were slow of mind and speech, and I could hear in his words the inflection and accent of a distant land.

I felt a flash of anger in my eyes at the impertinence of his reply. -I am aware of that, I said impatiently. -I am asking: who is the bookseller?

There was an amusement in his face as he said, as he somewhat dismissively bowed before me, -It is my shop, milady.

He then turned away as if he would deal with me no more. I was disgusted – to be taunted by common vendors outside of this door, and then to find such disdain amidst the shelter within.

-Who art thou? I asked, with a threat in my tone. I intended to tell my father of this man's ill-treatment of me, and realized, just as the words left my mouth, that the world's treatment of me was no longer a care of my father's, but of William's. I shivered with the indignity of this truth.

He turned, and there was a smile in his deep brown eyes. - My name is Daniel.

I fixed a cold gaze upon him. -What is thy family name? I demanded.

He did not seem to become flustered at my scrutiny. -Daniel will do, he replied quietly. -And now, my lady, is there some way that I may be of service to thee?

At the bottom of the page was scrawled a note in another person's handwriting. A bold, black line and an arrow pointed to this area in the text. The words read as follows:

S. dijo: Fije un rato fijo para su estudio ..- ....; diga poco y lega mucho, y salude siempre a cada persona con una sonrisa alegre (A: 1:15)

My high school Spanish was rusty, at best, and I could only make out a few of the words – *estudio, poco, mucho, siempre* – *study, little, much, always.*

I got up from the counter and walked down the hall to the museum's library, in search of a Spanish dictionary, but when I reached the doors, they were locked. Frustrated, I returned to my desk. I knew better than to try to use one of the Internet's online translation programs. Once, years ago, as a lowly exhibition assistant working on a translation for an exhibition of children's drawings on concentration camps in Poland, the subtleties of the words in Polish that I had attempted to translate online came out completely incorrect – and, of course, made no sense in context – which I did not realize until my boss, Larry, who spoke fluent Polish, kindly pointed it out to me. By then, the labels had already been done, and I spent a very long night recreating them.

Picking up a pen, I wrote down the sentence and made a note on the pad by the side of the counter to ask someone on staff to help me translate it. I then returned to the first set of handwriting and continued along to the next page.

I straightened my shoulders at his rudeness and spoke with a shadow of warning in my voice. – Thou shouldst remember courtesy, I said, drawing myself up to my full height with a deep breath.

-I have no need of such, Daniel replied, for I am not at court.

-It is not only courtiers who require courtesy, I answered quickly, desirous of wounding him with a quick small arrow of my wit. – Like thee, I am not at court, but I am the daughter of –

-I know who thou art, he said. -Thou art Mistress Margaret More.

I was startled by his recognition of me, this young man whom I had never before seen, with his voice full of a distant music and his eyes alight with a silent defiance I had not before countenanced in any man.

He spoke again. –Among those who tell of thee, it is said that thou art called the daughter of justice.

I stood back, greatly surprized by his words and the respect in his voice. A faint blush warmed my cheeks and I was stricken by an unfamiliar sensation of disquiet. No man had ever provoked such a response in me, and so I wrapp'd my discomfort in a cloak of wit as I answered:

-And should a daughter of justice be treated so unjustly? I smiled triumphantly, as if my conquest of his ill-temper was assured.

He bowed his head slightly and then raised it to me once again, and the smile in his eyes was genuine. –Forgive me, Mistress More, he said. –Thou art correct, there is no need for such ill-behaviour. I can only beg pardon by saying that I was at study, and did not wish to be interrupted.

- Thou art of scholarly mind? I asked him. I could not help myself, for I was most intrigued by one in whose likeness I saw my own desire for knowledge.

–Yes, he said briefly. He looked at the door behind me and was silent. –Now is there something in which I may interest thee? I can only guess that perhaps thou might wish to find a text for thy father, without letting others know of thy errand, since thou hast come unaccompanied and in great haste.

I was stunned at his measure of my motives. -I am sure there was, I told him humbly, but I have forgotten.

He smiled graciously with but a drop of mischief in his eyes. –Then thou must be compelled to return, Mistress More, when thou hast remembered why thou hast come.

-I shall do that, I said, with all of the dignity I could falsely muster, and I swept out of the shop to the mockery of the silver bell over my head. I emerged into the rain, and hastened back along the road to where my father and betrothed waited to accuse me of rebellion, and where my sister waited to accuse me of treachery and falsehood. I sighed as I walked, and upon my return I slipped quietly in the doorway and trod, unheard and light of foot, the steps to my chamber.

Were William to find me, reader, or to look upon these words, I would surely be a bride disgraced, with no hope of the respect and esteem my father craves on my sorrowful behalf. Now, it is only the grace of darkness that lends me its fair self to conceal this story from his eyes. It is late, and my eyes grow dim with fatigue and distress.

Pray for me.

10

I returned home from the museum late that afternoon, with my mind still so focused on the words of the manuscript that I barely noticed what train I was taking, and almost boarded a rerouted weekend express instead of a local. Only the weather woke me from the manuscript's trance. As I emerged from the station a couple of blocks from our apartment, I noticed the cold had finally forced the rain to surrender to an icy mix of snow and sleet, and the pavements were wet and slippery as I made my way back home and up our front steps.

Even Michael noticed how preoccupied I was. At first, he didn't ask any questions. He probably assumed that I was still upset about our argument. After a while, he walked into the bedroom, where I was intently reading every Web document on Margaret More that I could scare up.

"Did something happen at work?" he asked. "You seem distracted."

"I am," I replied, rubbing my eyes. "I don't even think I've had a chance to tell you about this artifact."

"The one you mentioned the other night? From the mystery donor?"

"That's the one. It's a diary of some sort." I stood, stretched, and took from the printer the sheet of papers I had printed out. "Anyway, I've been reading it – carefully, since it's in really bad shape. And if the authorship really is what it appears to be, it was written by the daughter of Thomas More, one of King Henry VIII's advisors who was executed for treason and eventually was named a saint by the Church. I'm trying to find out what I can about her, so I might be able to have some clue as to whether or not it's authentic."

He seemed intrigued. "I know who Thomas More is. He was one of the greatest – maybe the greatest - legal mind of the Tudor period. What have you been able to find?"

"Not a whole lot." We walked slowly down the hall and into the living room, and sat down together on the sofa. "There doesn't seem to be a lot of information available about her, and what there is only relates to the fact that she was her father's daughter, more than anything else. There is one fact that I find very interesting, however, from a scholar named Richard Marius, which I found quoted in an online biography of Thomas More. Listen to this." I read from the paper in my hand. "Once, as Thomas More was conversing with the Bishop of Exeter, he accidentally took a letter from his daughter, Margaret, out of his pocket. The bishop took it and looked at it and saw that it was written by a woman. After reading it, he declared he would not have believed it possible for a woman to write such a thing, unless More himself had assured him that it was so.'"

I put down the paper and looked at Michael. "In some way, that statement goes along with what she writes – if she actually wrote it, that is — in this book. She talks about being a scholar, and a writer, and the fact that her father wanted her to marry a man that she didn't like or trust at all. And then, another interesting thing surfaced today while I was reading." I walked over to where I had left my work bag by the door, and removed the note I had out of from the manuscript from the inner pocket. I walked back into the living room and handed it to Michael. "How's your Spanish?"

Michael took the note and peered at it. "Sorry," he said, shaking his head. "I took Latin in high school.

"You're no help," I told him affectionately. "But what I wrote down here is what suddenly turned up, in what appears to be another person's handwriting, in the margins of the story."

"Is it some sort of note about the text?"

"I'm not sure, because I don't know what it says. But tomorrow I'll ask someone at work to translate." I leaned back on the couch. "I'd just love to know whether or not I'm dealing with the something authentic. I know we should send it out to the lab, but it's so expensive to send it to the better ones. And I'd hate for anything to happen to it."

"Can't you tell how old it is by comparing it to another artifact?" he asked.

"Maybe. I mean, we use all sorts of techniques to date things from the early part of the century, even some nineteenth century documents a few years back. But figuring out the age of a piece of paper is always the worst. The process is rigorous, and best left to the scientists. We know that they can tell from the elements of the paper's content – the amounts of linen, fiber, cotton, or even tree pulp - approximately how old an object is. But there are a few different kinds of paper in this book – there's one that is really thin, almost falling apart, and another, which I just discovered today, that's in somewhat better shape, but still, not anything I would want to subject to the rigors of light or heat or acid.

"And the endpaper," I continued, "looks Italian, even though the text says the writer is writing from somewhere in London. When we were looking at it the other day, Aviva said she thinks the endpaper is hand-painted, which means we might be dealing with a piece that is, in part, more fine art than artifact."

He seemed to be thinking for a moment, and then asked, "Can you take the manuscript to another museum – maybe an art museum - and see if they have some sort of experience with this kind of object? Surely they've seen things like it before?"

I sighed. "You'd be surprised. If it's something significant, I don't want to tip our hand. So many institutions are looking to get their hands on big-ticket items."

"But who would be nasty enough to lay claim to an artifact that would take the spotlight away from a Holocaust museum?"

"Oh, just about any institution trying to increase their attendance numbers. Not to mention contributions and financial support from members, board members, et cetera. The more attention you get in the press, the better it looks for the board members whose names are on the letterhead. It's like they say in Development: prestige empties pockets. Or maybe it's 'prestige opens purses.' Something like that."

He grinned. "I see your point."

"I suppose there are people around whom we could trust to take a look at it," I said thoughtfully. "But honestly, only Aviva and I have seen it so far. We haven't even shown it to anyone in the department, or even to our boss. Before I do anything, I really need to talk about it with Aviva, and see if she has any ideas about what our next steps should be."

"What has she said about it?"

"She's very cautious. Overly cautious, if you ask me. For some reason, she seems convinced that it's a hoax. That someone associated with the 'religious right' might be trying to pull a fast one on us."

"Well, Thomas More is a Catholic saint," Michael reasoned, "in spite of the fact that he was an attorney." I grinned at him. "Aviva might be right."

"I don't know," I looked at Michael, and laid a hand on the soft fabric of his blue-jeaned knee. "She does have a good point, however, which is that I sure can't figure out how this artifact has any sort of relationship to Judaism or Jewish heritage."

"And the Spanish doesn't exactly point you in that direction," he agreed. "Still, as you said, it came from a survivor. And something that old is pretty cool."

I nodded. "So much of what we deal with only relates to the war years. It's interesting to be focused on a different era of history."

"I think that's great," he said, placing his hand over mine. "Imagine all the new ideas, and new history for you to learn about. A great, big, beautiful world just might be out there, waiting for you to emerge from the sadness."

"All right, let's settle down, people," I said, as I walked into the conference room and raised my voice to be heard over the voices of seven junior registrars and curators who, as usual on a Monday morning, were busy relating stories of the various forms of mischief they had gotten themselves into over the weekend.

I was late for work that morning as the result of a train delay, even though I left the house early, after realizing right around midnight that I had totally neglected my usual preparations for the morning staff meeting during the time I had been in the office on Sunday.

Having been so preoccupied with the manuscript, I forgot that today was my day to lead the meeting. And then, when I arrived, there was no sign of Aviva, and when I checked my voicemail she had left a message saying that she was going to a doctor's appointment. It was already twenty after nine, and so I gathered my notes and the assignment charts from my desk, hurriedly grabbed my half-full coffee cup, and walked down the hall to the conference room. I was definitely cranky and I felt unprepared, but I was determined not to let them see me sweat. From my pocket, I took the piece of paper on which I had scrawled the Spanish words, and unfolded it and tucked it into my notebook.

"Sorry I'm late. I hope everyone had a good weekend," I said, putting my cup down on the table and taking my seat at the front of the room. "I know we're getting started a little late this morning, but before you give me your rotation status reports, and before I give out the catalog database assignments, which I know you are so very eager to receive on this early Monday morning —" there was a little laughter "— here's a quick question. Who here speaks Spanish?"

Fern, the youngest and most earnest of the curators, raised her hand. "I studied abroad for a year in Spain."

There was a distinct murmur of scorn from two of the less motivated staff members. "Josh and Meredith, settle down," I said. "Fern, thank you for volunteering. I need this translated, please."

I opened the notebook and passed the paper down to her, and watched as she unfolded it and looked at it.

"'S. dijo,'" she read aloud. "'Fije un rato fijo para su estudio ...diga poco y haga mucho, y salude siempre a cada persona con una sonrisa alegre'." Easy. The translation would be "'S. – whoever that is – says: set a fixed time for studying' – and then there seems to be a word missing here. The rest of it is 'say little and do much, and greet every person with a glad smile.' I don't know what the letter A and these numbers – 1:15 - mean. But it looks like a citation of some kind."

"Set a fixed time for study?" Robert asked, looking up suddenly from the status report he had been reading. "I recognize that. It's from *Pirke Avot* – Ethics of the Fathers. Hang on a second."

As he pulled a Blackberry out of his pocket, I watched his hand brush against the fringes of his *talit katan* – the garment that marked him as religiously observant - which he wore every day. "Don't laugh, but I've got the online Encyclopedia Judaica stored in here."

I smiled. I liked Robert, who was older than most of the others. He was extremely well-versed in Jewish studies, and definitely the person I hoped would be taking over some aspects of the upcoming new exhibition in Aviva's stead while she was out on maternity leave.

Robert had trained as a historian, but since we already had a senior historian on staff, who definitely wasn't going anywhere for a long time, he willingly learned how to be a registrar. He had been an exhibition assistant on a team that I led the year before, and during some of the late nights during installation, he told me a little about himself. I had assumed he was born into a religious family because of the way he dressed, wearing *tzitzit* and a *kipah* every day. But I was wrong; his father was Jewish, and his mother was not, and he had converted to Judaism about ten years earlier.

"Here it is," he said. "Chapter one, verse fifteen. 'Shammai said: Set a fixed time for the study of Torah; say little and do much, and always greet every person with a cheerful smile.'"

"That's what it says?" I was mystified.

"According to what this paper says, and what Fern translated," Robert told me, looking over the paper she had handed to him, "the 'S' stands for Shammai, one of the great rabbinic sages, to whom the comment is attributed, and the word 'Torah' is the one that's missing from the rest of the quote." He looked puzzled. "You found this written somewhere in Spanish? What's it from?"

I hesitated for a moment, wondering if I should tell them about the manuscript. I knew how excited it would make them, and also thought about the time and research they would put into helping me to authenticate it. But they all had a lot of work to do for the new exhibition, and I realized I wanted to talk to Aviva about first informing Larry about this artifact. I decided to say nothing to them, for now.

"It's nothing. Just some research I've been doing. But you guys have so many hidden talents," I said with a broad smile. "It would be a shame to let them go to waste. Now, let's get started with the status reports. Fern, will you go first?"

11

"Aviva, guess what? There's a Jewish connection in the manuscript," I said jubilantly, when I saw her sitting at her desk after the meeting. She didn't respond. I touched her shoulder. "Aviva?" She turned to face me, her face swollen, her eyes red. I stepped back. "Oh, my God," I said. "What happened? Is it the baby? What did the doctor say?" She shook her head and pointed to the door of the conference room. "Are they done? Can we go in there?"

"Of course." I hurried back down the hall to the empty room. She followed behind me at a slower pace. It seemed as if all her energy was gone.

We walked in and I closed the door. I sat down and watched as she carefully lowered herself into the chair next to me. I grabbed a tissue from the box on the table and handed it to her.

She wiped her eyes. "It's not the baby," she said. "Don't worry. Everything is all right with the baby."

"Thank God." I breathed. "What is it, then?"

"It's Jacob." She looked down at her hands, and started twisting the gold ring on her swollen finger.

"What's wrong? Is he upset about the baby?" I tried to think of words to console her, wondering, after being married for less than a year, and having only known each other for a couple of months, how ready they were to become parents. "Listen, he wouldn't be the only first-time father who was worried about a new baby. It's a huge change. He'll adjust, believe me." I patted her hand.

"It's not that. He's been cheating on me."

I stared at her, stunned into silence.

"And I wasn't at the doctor this morning. I went to see our rabbi. I went to talk to him, to ask him what I should do."

I let out a long breath before I spoke. "What did he say?"

"Nothing helpful." I could see a glint of anger behind the sadness in her eyes. "Apparently Jacob had a girlfriend, all along, before I ever knew him. From outside the community, of course. That's why the matchmaker was in such a hurry to marry him off. They – his family, the rabbi - wanted to get him away from 'bad influences.' But it didn't work. He never gave her up."

"Aviva, are you sure?" I reached out and touched her arm. "How do you know? Could it just be a rumor?"

"Her name is Angela," she recited in a bitter, matter-of-fact way. "She's twenty-eight. They met at work. I heard all about it over the weekend." Her face was flushed as she absently stroked her belly. "I didn't want to say anything to anyone, but I was suspicious. All the late nights in the office. All the times he ducked out of the house right after dinner, saying he was going to study. And then I ran into my friend Sari on the subway last week. She asked how Jacob was, and said her husband Isaac never saw him at *shul* anymore. She said we must be busy getting ready for the baby."

She took a deep breath before continuing. "I asked him about it after Shabbos. He didn't say anything at first. He just sat there, looking guilty, stroking his stupid goatee, saying it was hard to explain. And then he said he was in love with her. That he had been in love with her for years. They had actually talked about getting married. And then, a little more than a year ago, he brought her home to meet his parents. They knew about her. They *knew*."

I could hear the anger in her voice. "Of course, everything fell apart after that. He brought her to the house, and right in front of her, his father threatened to disown him. And then, right after that, the rabbi paid a visit to the family and came down on him like a ton of bricks. Everyone got involved. They made him promise to give her up. But he didn't."

I didn't say anything. There didn't seem to be anything to say. She wiped her eyes again. "The rabbi and his family rushed him to the matchmaker. They said they wanted to get him married immediately. Everyone convinced him it was the right thing to do. He should settle down with a nice girl, an Orthodox girl, and live the life he was supposed to live. No more lies. No more deception. Except of course, for the lies they told me and my family. That I was exactly what he was looking for. And this was the kind of marriage he wanted."

The door to the conference room suddenly opened. "Oh, sorry," a voice said, and the door closed again. We sat for a few moments in silence.

"So what happens now?" I asked.

"Nothing," Aviva said. "After I spoke to the rabbi, he said that he'd be willing to talk to Jacob again, and ask him to stop seeing her. He said he would encourage Jacob to find another job, to lessen the contact they have because of working together. But beyond that, there was nothing that he could do. And for the sake of our baby, we had to find a way to work things out."

"Is he willing to work with you," I chose my words carefully, "you know, in terms of some sort of counseling?"

She nodded. "But I don't know that it's going to change anything. I don't know if he'll want to give her up now, any more than he wanted to then. He said she knows about the baby, and it doesn't bother her that he's married. He said she understands he had to marry a Jewish girl, and that he's expected to have a family with me. In fact, she was at our wedding, sitting with the other women from his office."

I could feel my eyes widening in shock, and she nodded. "Oh yes, apparently, somewhere mixed in with those four hundred people who came to celebrate our *simcha* was my husband's whore."

In all of the years that we had worked together, I couldn't remember ever hearing her say anything unkind or derogatory about anyone, and the fact that she would use such a word showed me just how distraught she was.

"And, as I'm sure you're aware, according to the terms of our *ketubah*, our marriage contract," she said bitterly, "only Jacob can decide whether or not we can get divorced."

I looked at her, horrified. Before I could speak again, she put up a hand to silence me. "The rabbi was very clear about that. If Jacob wants to give me a *get*, then he can. But if he wants to stay married, we stay married. And besides, with the baby on the way, I don't have a lot of options."

"You can stay with us," I said, the words coming automatically. "You know that, no matter what."

She sighed and shook her head. "Jill, you know I can't do that. If I left him, I could never go back. I'd be ostracized, a runaway wife. Even my parents said so. The other morning, when you came in early, I was on the phone with them. I told my father I was suspicious, that I thought something was going on. I asked him if I found out that Jacob was being unfaithful, could I come back home. But he told me no, I was a married woman now, my place was with my husband.

"He told me I was a wife now, and I could never be a daughter again. He said it made him angry, angry enough for him to want me to come home, but he knew it would be wrong. Then my mother got on the phone and told me I had to turn a blind eye, that if I wanted to keep my home, my marriage, my place in the community," she seemed to almost spit the last word from her mouth, "I would ignore it, if there was anything to ignore.

"And now, it might not even remain a secret. Now that I know about this woman he doesn't have to pretend with me anymore, and he can do whatever he wants, just so long as he's discreet, and he doesn't flaunt it they way he did before we were married. And everyone else in our families is willing – happy, even – to pretend it isn't happening. And they think I should pretend it isn't happening, either. Because it looks right from the outside. We have a proper Jewish home, he has a proper Jewish wife, we're about to have a child, and the community has total control of our lives.

"And Jacob has total control over our marriage. There's even a word for women like me – *agunot* – the anchored ones. And worst of all, if I were to leave him now, my baby," she seemed to choke on the word, "my baby could never marry anyone within the community, because the child of a runaway wife would never be accepted."

Awkwardly, I patted her arm, and the gesture felt totally inadequate. Like Aviva, I felt powerless. I knew there was nothing I could do or say to help her fight against the injustice that had been committed against her, all in the name of love.

But perhaps, I thought, it wasn't really about love. Aviva was not a modern young woman. She had probably been in love with Jacob, the way that my friends and I had been in love dozens of times with guys that we dated. But even if she hadn't been pregnant, there was too much at stake – the least of which was love. And even if she didn't love him anymore, I knew she couldn't throw off the relationship, even if it was only a year old, the way that my friends and I could.

She had married Jacob, she had staked her life on a system of laws and traditions that had ensured her community's survival for generations, and all at once, in her trusting eyes, I saw why. She would probably never have the courage to walk away from the life and the laws of the Orthodox community that had defined her since birth. And no matter how liberating I thought it would be for her, I knew that if she woke up tomorrow morning in my life, she'd be lost.

"Anyway," she sighed, "I wanted to tell you what was going on, since you'll probably be hearing pieces of these conversations for the next couple of weeks. But I'll try not to fight with him on the phone when you're around."

"No, no," I soothed her. "Don't worry about it. The only important thing is that you take care of yourself, especially now."

"I know." She took another tissue from the box and touched it to her eyes before she crumpled it into a ball in her hand. "But I'm scared. I'm so afraid that I'm going to go through all this alone."

"You won't be alone," I reassured her. "Even if I have to learn Lamaze in the next ten days."

A ghost of a smile brightened her face. "You're a good friend." She sighed again. "I just don't know what I'm going to do. What will people say?"

"No one here will know, unless you say something to them." I stood, and put a hand on her shoulder. "I'll make sure you're covered. If you need me to do anything, if you need to be out of the office, whatever, just let me know."

She smiled gratefully as she gripped the arms of the chair and heaved herself to her feet. "I know. It's not this group of people I'm worried about, though."

I nodded. She walked ahead of me and opened the door. "I'm just going to the ladies' room, okay? I want to wash my face, try to put myself back together. And then I need to find some time to talk to Larry about my maternity leave. So I'll probably be upstairs, in case anyone is looking for me."

"Whatever you need," I told her, and I watched her make her way down the hall. I knew it would be a while before I could talk to her about what I had found in the manuscript, and I wondered, in light of what was happening in her life, if she'd even be interested in hearing about it.

Then I walked back to my desk. I sat down, unlocked and opened my desk drawer, and took out my purse. Inside my wallet was a small black and white picture that Michael and I had taken in one of those old fashioned photo booths on the boardwalk at the Jersey shore, on a bright autumn day not long after we had met.

In the photograph, we both wore ratty old sweatshirts and jeans. We sat in the tiny booth with our arms wrapped around one another. My hair was shorter then, only down to my chin, and my sunglasses were pushed up on to the top of my head. I was smiling at the camera. Michael's hair was a riot of windblown curls, his eyes were crinkled at their corners, and he was laughing.

I looked at the picture, and then looked over the wall at Aviva's cubicle, where the wedding portrait of her and Jacob held pride of place by her telephone. He stood with his arm firmly encircling her waist; her hand lay against his chest. Aviva had told me afterward that when the photographer posed them for the picture, it was the first time she and Jacob had ever touched one another. I looked at it for a long moment, and then I put my wallet away.

That afternoon, I found another typed envelope addressed to me in my office mailbox. Even before I reached my desk, I slit the top of it open with my thumbnail. Inside there were several sheets of paper, maybe seven or eight of them, folded into thirds. I looked at the pages as I walked slowly down the hall back to my office.

Unlike the other letters, there was no address or salutation, only the same inconsistently ink-patterned, typed words, seeming to pour out in a torrent on the pages.

In the winter of 1941, things began to change. We believed - foolishly - that we would be safe, because we were German citizens first, and Jews second, and that the true war - Austria's war, Poland's war — would not come to us. But suddenly we began to feel its cold hands reaching further into our lives. We knew, soon enough, that we were Jews. We discovered new things about being Jewish every single day. We learned how to swallow our tears when we saw the children lined up for school in their dark blue coats, with their yellow stars shining upon them like a tiny universe.

We learned how not to notice the German women who yelled the words "Filthy Jew" at us in the streets. We learned how to cover our noses and mouths to protect us from the smoke when the torches were put to our shops. And then soon, we learned how to be hungry. The merchants were forbidden to sell anything to us. It became more difficult every day to keep the family fed and clothed. Soon the Jewish children in our town were sent home from school and not allowed to return. One day the doctor and his family disappeared. Their door swung on a broken hinge, like a mouth trying to speak. The priest who had once been so cordial to us was now silent when we passed him in the streets. We heard whispers. But we did not want to believe them.

The morning came when all of the men in the town were taken. Aron read a story to Minna, and together we watched her fall asleep, and then when he came to our bed I fell asleep in his arms for the last time. He went to the square before dawn, long before I awakened. He never told me he knew he would be taken away that morning, but I am certain that he knew it was the last time he would ever say good night to me. Knowing how I loved him, he hid the truth from me.

I pushed open the door to our office. Aviva was nowhere to be found, but her sweater was still draped over the back of her chair, so I knew she had not left for the day.

I sat at my desk and looked at the paper again. Aron and Minna. I wrote the names on my notepad. Finally, I thought, some clues for the donor database. If I, or Aviva, or another curator had taken enough notes on this person's past artifact donations, the information we had on file might be detailed enough. By looking up the names of family members, I might be able to figure out who sent the manuscript.

I opened up the database program, typed in the names and waited for the results. There was a flash of lettering on my screen:

296 ENTRIES FOUND

I paged through the names. Some of them were familiar. Becker, Dumas, Fairstein, Lilienthal, Sutton, Weingast. I clicked on the entry for one donor – Mimi Fairstein – whom I remembered visiting about two years ago:

FAIRSTEIN, MIMI: Wedding Ketubah, circa 1890, Vilna, Poland. Listed on document are donor's grandparents'names: Aaron Kelberg and Minna Gratz.

No luck, I thought. Aron and Minna clearly had not been the writer's grandparents. I sighed. I didn't expect to find the source on my first try, but with 295 entries to go, I was going to need a little help with the research. The only question was who could I trust enough to ask.

I picked up the typewritten sheets and continued to read.

I was tired in those days, exhausted, underfed. That morning, I slept so deeply and never heard the trucks come into the square. I never heard the voices of the soldiers crying Sieg Heil, never heard the echo of the gunshots as they shot the men who refused to join the ranks. I never heard the exhaust of the engines as they drove away with our husbands and fathers and brothers like so many animals, crowded onto the transports. It was only later, when Aron did not return from work, that I found out he was gone.

Minna was only three, and she would ask me in her voice like a little silver bell, Where is Papa? Where did he go?

Some of the other mothers, knowing the men would never return, told their children that their fathers had gone to Heaven, to visit G-d. But I told my daughter the truth. I don't know where Papa is, I said. But I am certain that he is not with G-d.

A few weeks later, on that spring morning, the

transports came for us. People asked me, years later, if you knew they were coming, why did you not run away? But we had heard the rumors for weeks, of other towns and villages where people had fled under the cover of night, only to be captured in the forest.

Before Aron was taken away, he had received letters from some who found hiding places in the homes of people they trusted. They sent letters written in code, in Yiddish, in French, in any language that would not betray their whereabouts, letters smuggled inside bills and lists and meaningless bits of newspaper. They came from those who had hidden in attics and under floors, in barns and byres and stables, and they told us how the ones who went to the square that morning were taken away in trucks, to labor in camps.

The others, the ones who were unfit for work, or religious, or rebellious, or simply because of a whim, were taken to the forest and lined up and shot, one by one, the men, the women and the little children. And then their bodies were desecrated by lime and acid, left to rot, sometimes buried, sometimes left exposed, naked and dead in the burial pits, for all to see as a warning. These were Jews, the letters whispered. This is what will happen to you if you are a Jew.

Sometimes I would awaken in the night, thinking I heard their cries, but it was my own child, crying for her father, from hunger, from fear. I would go to her, hold her hand and sing lullabies, but she would not be comforted. How could she? For I had nothing but my false bravery to give her.

Once Aron was taken I knew there was not much time. I knew that there were not many mornings left in which Minna and I could dwell in safety. But I did not know where to go.

After Aron left we moved back in with my parents. My mother loved being with her granddaughter during the daytime, but as soon as Minna's voice disappeared up the stairs to her nursery each night, my mother's eyes would fill with powerless tears, knowing our fate could be determined at any moment. It was only a matter of days before they came for us.

One morning, on the first hot day in a spring when there had been little rain, I woke early as I always did. My mother and daughter and sisters were not yet awake. But a hummingbird fluttered outside my window, and the summer breeze made the branches of the trees tap against the glass. The sunlight and blossom made me feel as if I still lived in the world that G-d had created for us. And I

The words abruptly ended. I turned to the next page and saw that only one word was typed on it, in the center of the paper:

Chava

I looked at the pages that followed. On every page was the same word, sometimes typed just once, and sometimes over and over again.

Chava Chava Chava Chava Chava Chava

I went through the pages again, feeling a knot tighten in my stomach. Although it was warm in the office, I shivered. There was something strange and terribly unsettling about it all.

Then I remembered: Chava was my Hebrew name.

12

My office phone rang. I picked it up with a shaking hand. "Hi, this is Jill," I said, trying to make my voice sound calm and professional.

"Jill, it's Larry." I looked over at the caller ID display and saw that it was, in fact, my boss. "I've got Aviva up here in the office. Do you have a couple of minutes to talk about the plan for when she goes out on leave?"

"Sure. I'll be right there," I told him. I hung up the phone, smoothed a hand over my hair, and picked up a notepad and pen.

With a swift attempt to shake off the sense of trepidation that the typewritten words had evoked, I walked down the hall, opened the door to the stairwell, and climbed the steps up to the fourth floor. Larry's office was in a suite with the other department heads, whose offices overlooked the harbor. I had worked for him for seven years, moving up from exhibition assistant to junior curator to my current position, all on his watch.

Dr. Larry Grossman held a Ph.D. in Jewish studies and archeology. He was responsible for the creation and maintenance of the museum's collection and for planning and executing the special exhibitions we developed with scholars and historians from around the world. He had been with the museum for more than fifteen years – even before we had a permanent building. Aviva, who had joined the staff the year before me, had been there for eight.

Over the course of the past seven years, the three of us had spent a great deal of time together, especially during the long, hectic days of exhibition installations. After sharing late night dinners, conversations, and a couple of installation crises, we all liked, and, perhaps more important, trusted one another.

These days, the usual craziness of our department, coupled with Larry's intense travel schedule, often meant we used email as our primary form of communication. He had just returned from a two-week trip to Israel, where he had been meeting with surviving members of the

Haganah — soldiers who had smuggled Holocaust survivors into Israel immediately after the Second World War. It was important to record their testimonies for an exhibition that was still more than three years away.

Even when he was on the opposite side of the world, he remained in constant contact with the office, and so during his absences I frequently received emails sent from Tel Aviv or Haifa, composed long after I was asleep in New York. When Larry wasn't traveling, Aviva and I usually managed to meet with him at least a couple of times a week, and also during our regular monthly department meetings.

Larry's assistant, Mira, looked up from the exhibition blueprints on her desk as I entered the suite. "Hi, Jill," she smiled at me. "You can go in."

"Thanks," I said. I knocked lightly on the door and pushed it open. Inside, Larry sat at his desk, and Aviva in one of the two chairs directly across from him.

"Come on in, Jill," he said. "Have a seat."

I took the chair next to Aviva and looked over at her. Her eyes still looked a little red, but it wasn't obvious that she had been crying. I wondered if she had revealed anything to Larry about what she had told me this morning, and then figured, judging from the fact that she looked as if she were keeping it together somewhat cheerfully, that she probably had not.

"So, as you know, Aviva is going out on leave in a few weeks," Larry began. "And as you also know, we have a special exhibition opening this summer." He smiled at us both. "I know I hardly need to even say it given all the hard work you've been doing with the team, dealing with the catalog updates and rotations in the rest of the collection. At least we won't have as much to do while the exhibition is being installed."

"The rotation schedules are done through April," I said. "Aviva and I have gotten those out of the way."

"That's great," he said. "That will definitely help matters along. So here's the plan. I'm sure you also know we are going to need to make some changes in the department, so that we'll be covered until Aviva comes back to us in June."

We both nodded.

"Aviva tells me you've talked about it, and you both agree that from among the junior staff, Robert Goldstein would be most up to the task of taking on some of the senior registrar's responsibilities."

"Definitely," I said. "He'd be my pick. He's smart, he puts in the hours, and he doesn't only get the work done. He asks great questions and seems to learn a lot from the process."

Larry leaned back in his chair. "Sounds just like the two of you, when you first started here," he said fondly.

Aviva and I both smiled. "Fern Dixon is good, too," Aviva said, "but I don't think she's been here long enough."

"She's been here almost a year?" Larry asked. We nodded again. "You're right. I don't think that's long enough. But that she's good, is good to know. Now," he continued. "Jill, you were at the planning meetings last week with Aviva. So you know where we are in the process. You'll be coordinating the de-installation of the current exhibition after the closing date on May 15th, and getting the space prepared for the fabricators before Aviva goes out on leave. I want you and Robert to pick your team – you'll need two exhibition assistants, one registrar and one curator - so that she can advise you about who should get the fabricators and the painters on board and coordinated. Also, Jill," he looked at the calendar on his desk, "I'd like for you to put off making house calls for a few weeks. While we're working through this transition, I really need you here in the office."

"Okay," I made some notes on the pad. "I can do that."

"And you'll let Robert know today? I'd like to make the announcement at Friday's staff meeting."

"Sure," I said, looking at Aviva. "We can let him know this afternoon."

"Good," Larry said. "I want the team to be prepared."

"We'll be fine," Aviva said confidently. "We're ready."

I watched as she absently brushed the bangs of her wig from her eyes, marveling at her resilience, considering how distraught she had been earlier in the day.

"So," Larry continued, sounding more conversational. "Has anything interesting been going on since I've been out of the office?"

Aviva and I glanced at one another, and I nodded slightly, almost imperceptibly.

"Actually," she said, "we have something interesting to tell you. Jill received an anonymous donation last week."

"When you say 'anonymous donation,'" Larry asked, "do you mean that it came from someone who doesn't want to be acknowledged, or that it came from someone who didn't disclose their identity?"

"The latter," I answered.

"My favorite kind of donation," he said sarcastically. "What's the story?"

"We're not sure yet," I told him. "It's a manuscript. Very weathered looking on the outside. Inside, there are a couple of different kinds of parchment. It's been bound by hand, and it looks as if the endpapers are hand painted." Aviva nodded in agreement. "The date on the first page is 1536."

I watched Larry's face for a reaction, but he only nodded and leaned forward in his chair. "Okay," he said. "Go on."

"There was a letter inside, addressed to me. Whoever wrote it said that they had met me, and had donated other items to us in the past. But there wasn't enough information in the letter to even get started searching the database."

"Then Jill got another letter," Aviva continued. "But there still wasn't much to go on. We know – or it appears – that the donor is a woman who was born in Germany and says she's a Holocaust survivor."

Larry nodded. "But nothing specific?"

"Not really," I said. "No place or year of birth – she only says that she comes from 'a small town outside Berlin.' She says she was married in 1937, and that the manuscript had been in her family for some time. But there's nothing specific – no city, no town, no dates of birth, no last names."

"That's a shame," Larry said. "The Gestapo rounded up German

Jews based on census information. If we had an address or a date of birth we could consult the Bad Arolsen Archives and do a little detective work."

"Well, today I got a third letter," I said. "And it's not like the others. It's not as," I paused as I searched for the right word, "—structured as the other ones. The text reads as if recounting her survivor experience is starting to take its toll on her. The good news is that it includes some specific information – the first names of her husband and her daughter – but there's something strange about the way it's written."

"How so?" Larry asked.

"Well, at first," I said, "it appeared that she was trying to tell me the story of how she obtained the manuscript, and how she managed to hold on to it through the war. But this last letter is more about her experiences of the time before the war – there's nothing at all about the manuscript in it. The other letters were formally structured. They began with my name, the museum's address, – salutation, date, the whole bit. This one was just typewritten pages that began without any introduction, as if she was picking up the story in progress. And the last few pages made no sense at all. They didn't even have any of the story on them, just the name 'Chava' typed over and over again."

"Do you think that could be her name?" Aviva asked me.

"I don't know," I said, "but it's a thought." I didn't tell them that I had been so focused on my own Hebrew name that I hadn't even considered the possibility.

"But anyway," I continued, "I've been reading the manuscript, whenever I've had a spare moment or two."

"Not that we've had many of those," Aviva laughed.

"And from what I've read," I said, "it looks as if this manuscript was written by the daughter of St. Thomas More."

"You mean the Thomas More who served at the court of King Henry VIII?" Larry asked. "He disagreed with the king about the legitimacy of the Church of England, if I'm not mistaken. And wasn't he beheaded?"

"You saw *A Man for All Seasons*, too." Aviva smiled.

Larry took off his glasses and rubbed his eyes, and then put them back on. "And this manuscript is written by his daughter, allegedly."

"His daughter Margaret," I said. "About whom there is precious little biographical information available."

"What sort of condition is the manuscript in?"

"Not great," I said. "It looks as if it sustained some water damage at some point. And the binding is going to pieces. I can't remember ever needing to be so careful with an artifact. I can't tell what sort of conditions it was kept in over the years, maybe in a box or a closet. There's a lot of dust, but I can't tell if it's recent. Aviva and I also saw some dirt in the binding, but again, we're not sure of the date. We would need a lab for sure to date any trace minerals, not to mention the paper. It's very brittle. It worries me to think of it under some sort of light, or exposed to chemicals."

"It would worry me, as well," Larry said. "But to authenticate it, we don't really have much of a choice. We'd need to find some budget money, that's for sure." His brow furrowed. "But aside from authenticity, of course, my only question is, aside from the fact that this came – potentially - from a survivor, what does this have to do with Jewish heritage?"

"My question exactly," Aviva said.

"Well, this morning, something turned up." I turned to Aviva apologetically. "I didn't have time to tell you. Over the weekend, I came into the office to read further, and I found a note on the text, in what appears to be another person's handwriting. It's in Spanish, which I don't happen to speak, so Fern and Robert translated it for me this morning in the meeting. I can't remember the exact wording, but as it turns out, the citation matches up with Pirke Avot, chapter 1, verse 15."

"'Shammai says, set a fixed time for study, say little and do much, and greet everyone with a cheerful smile,'" Larry quoted immediately. "Which follows immediately after the more famous Hillel quote, 'If I am not for myself, then who will be for me? If I am only for myself, then what am I? And if not now, when?'"

"Is this the Jewish connection you were talking about this morning?"

Aviva asked me. "After the meeting?"

I was surprised that she even remembered what I had said, given everything else that was going on. "Yes," I answered. "But so far, even though it's in Spanish, that's the only Jewish thing about it."

"Does it have anything to do with the text?"

I thought about it for a moment. "Actually, I think it might. The notation is drawn between the quote and a moment in the story during which one person greets another. However, it certainly wasn't with a cheerful smile."

"It could have a further significance," Larry said. "Hillel and Shammai were the founders of two major schools of rabbinic thought – Bet Hillel and Bet Shammai – the house of Hillel and the house of Shammai. These schools differed in their views of how holiness should best be expressed by the Jewish people. Essentially, Bet Hillel believed in community – that Jews should live among others in order to fulfill the commandment to be 'a light unto the nations.' Bet Shammai, whose members refused to bend to the rule of other nation's laws, to the contrary felt that the Jews had to be separate – away from outside influences, living in a self-contained society, in order to achieve a better relationship with holiness. It's speculative, but it makes me wonder if this quotation is invoking Bet Shammai. Is the author a person who is making a statement of separation from the larger community?"

"But to think that, you have to assume the writer is Jewish," Aviva ventured. "Or someone who knew *Pirke Avot*, which at that time would have been a forbidden text in England, under the reign of Henry VIII and Katherine of Aragon."

"But if it's in Spanish," I said, "it might have belonged to a *converso*."

We looked at Larry, who was silent for a moment. "Let me get this straight. What we've got, supposedly, is an artifact that was sent directly to you, Jill, which appears to be a manuscript that dates back to Tudor England. This manuscript was allegedly written by a Catholic woman. It contains a single Jewish inscription, written in Spanish, and you think it might have come from a Spanish Jew secretly living in

England. And this supposed secret Jew, this *converso*, may have had some sort of contact with one of the preeminent Catholic families of that time in order to obtain, and comment on, this story."

He picked up a pen and made some notes on the paper in front of him. "And this came from a donor who appears to be a Holocaust survivor, about whom we have little or no information to go on."

"Right. Except in the letter I received today, she mentions being married to a man named Aron – one A – and that she has a daughter named Minna. I did a database search using the two names, but the search returned nearly 300 records."

"That's exactly what I was afraid of," Larry said. "And right now, unfortunately, with everything else going on, you don't have the time to go through 300 records."

We nodded.

"I have to say, I'm intrigued," he said. "If this came from a legit-imate source, I'd be delighted. But I can't spare either of you to go chasing after a donor's name. If you want to research the database, I'll have to ask you to do that on your own time, but I don't see how you'll even have the time until after the installation is completed."

"I understand," I said to Larry. "That's why I came in on Sunday."

"Does anyone else know about it?"

I shook my head. "Only the two of us," I said, indicating Aviva.

"I'd like to keep it that way, for now." He looked at us both. "But this is certainly intriguing. In the meantime," he said, rising from his desk, "I have a quick phone call or two to make, but I'd appreciate it if you'd meet me in the conservation area in about ten minutes. I'd like to have a look at the manuscript."

"Okay," I said, "we'll meet you downstairs."

Aviva and I both stood and walked out of the office. I followed her past Mira's desk and out to the elevators. She punched the Down button with some force. "I know it's only one floor," she said, "but I hate waddling down the stairs."

As we waited, we glanced out of the wide windows at the gray sky and the winter afternoon beginning its descent into evening. The elevator arrived, we walked inside and the doors slid closed. "You know, Jill, I know you don't like to do this, but I think you should take the manuscript home with you. You can't keep coming in on Sundays." She looked at me meaningfully. "I mean, you have a life outside of here."

I decided to ignore the implication that I was using work to avoid figuring out things with Michael. "I know, but with this weather, I'm a little nervous about taking it outside."

"Don't be worried," she reassured me. "Let's clear it with Larry when he comes downstairs. After he looks at it, we'll wrap it up and put it in one of the big cases. And bring some acid-free paper for your table. Take it home, get through it, and bring it back in a couple of days." The doors opened. "You know what to do. Just be careful with it, and it'll be fine."

"Excellent," Michael said, as I opened the door and lugged the heavy steel case in from the hallway. "I'll inform the authorities that you've located Jimmy Hoffa."

"Shut up and give me a hand," I said breathlessly. "I had to carry this all the way from the subway."

"And then you had to schlep it up four flights of stairs," Michael added. "Here, let me help you." He took it from me as I shut the door. "Jill, this is really heavy. You should have called me from the station. I would have come down and given you a hand."

"It's not so bad. Just bulky," I said, and gave him a kiss.

"So what's inside?"

"The mystery artifact," I said. "And a load of packing material."

"You actually brought it home? That's great," Michael's eyes were warm with excitement. "Can we take it out now?"

"Not a chance," I told him breezily. "First, we have dinner. Then we clean off the table, and then we clean off the cleaner that we used to clean the table, and then we make sure that there are absolutely no beverages, no liquid substances, no dust, and no dirt of any kind in the room. Then we lower the heat and get the room down to a reasonable temperature. And then," I said, taking the roll out of my bag with a flourish, "we cover the table with this paper."

He raised an eyebrow at me. "And then?"

"Then, and only then, do I risk my job and my professional reputation by taking the manuscript out of its case." I brushed my hair out of my eyes. "I hate bringing artifacts home, as you know, but I'm even more paranoid than usual about this one."

"So that means if I spill coffee on it, I have to represent you in the lawsuit."

"No, that means if you spill coffee on it, I will find a way to have you disbarred and possibly killed. Because then, and only then, will we be even."

"Well, all righty then," he grinned. "Let's have dinner. I can't wait to take a look."

After going through all of the preparations, Michael and I finally opened the case and laid the manuscript out on the table. "It definitely looks old," he said, as I set the book squarely in the middle of the paper.

"It does. But as Larry pointed out today, the difference between an object that looks four or five hundred years old and one which is actually only one hundred years old – but looks older - is negotiable. We just don't know what we're dealing with yet. Still, he said he would make some calls – discreet calls – to people in the field who might be able to help us date it."

I handed Michael a spare set of gloves and watched as he put them on. "Good idea," he said, "bringing these home."

I was glad I had remembered the second pair. The last thing I wanted, I thought, was for Michael to feel excluded from any other part of my life.

I carefully opened the book, and together we peered at the pages. Michael squinted at the elaborate writing, and I watched his face as he read the poem on the first page.

He read in silence, and then he looked at me. "It's a sonnet," he said.

I looked at the poem, and then at him. "You're right. I was so focused on the story that the form of the poems hadn't even occurred to me."

"This has all the elements," he said. "Check it out. Fourteen lines, the right amount of syllables, and it's written in iambic pentameter, which, if I remember correctly, is ten beats per line."

"Yes," I said. "And it follows the right format in terms of stresses on the particular syllables."

"And the rhyme scheme is Petrarchan," he pointed to the last few lines of the text.

"You're right," I said, smiling. "How cool is it to find out that I'm not the only person in this relationship who studied poetry?"

He grinned. "Pre-law, art history, English literature. It's all humanities."

"God bless the liberal arts degree," I said wryly. "And here we thought it was all useless knowledge."

We smiled at one another. Finally, Michael spoke. "Let's keep reading."

I sat at the table and watched him as he read the manuscript, carefully turning the pages. He seemed to be concentrating deeply on the words before him. Only once did he look up, after he saw the Spanish notation.

"This is what you were talking about, right?" he asked.

I nodded as he looked at it. "Did you find out what it says?" he asked me.

"I asked someone at work to translate it. It's from an ancient Jewish text, which is, so far, the only Jewish thing about this book. It's a kind of proverb, which tells the reader to set time aside for studying Torah, to say little and do much, and to greet others with a cheerful smile. But I think," I hesitated for a moment, "that it might have something to do with what's going on in the author's story. You know, how she first meets this person Daniel? He certainly didn't greet her with a cheerful smile."

"Well, she interrupted him," Michael said. "He was busy. He said he was studying."

"The way she describes it, his manner is just so odd," I said. "There's something more going on here."

"Well, do you think she interrupted the time he set aside for studying Torah?" Michael asked. "With this notation in the text, there might be something Jewish taking place here."

I didn't say anything for a moment. "I don't know how likely that is," I said to Michael. "There were supposedly no Jews in England at that time. Following the Spanish Inquisition, most of the nations of Europe denied citizenship to Jews. In fact, most countries followed the example of Spain and persecuted any Jews who remained among them. So the study of Torah probably would have been an offense punishable by death."

"What about the Jews who left Spain after the Inquisition? Would any of them have fled to England?"

"If they did," I said, "they'd be *conversos* – Jews who lived as Christians, and practiced Judaism in secret. That's the direction that we started talking about in our meeting today, when we tried to figure out what the Spanish notation might indicate."

"Maybe that's who this Daniel is," Michael said. "A *converso*."

"Could be," I said. "Let's keep reading."

As he turned the next couple of pages, I stood from my chair and went around to his side of the table. "This is where I left off," I said, as we turned the page together.

My heart is pierced by one who does forsake
The mind my father loved. This evil one
Who preens himself as More my father's son
Than his own child. This garden snake
Supplanted my own Eden, and did wake
The clouds of doubt. But it is done.
This prideful husband, silenced wife, and none
Is wiser. Father, how I long to shake
The blinders from your eyes. Excellent man!
Do not believe the son you love is true

To your sweet word. He binds me in this cage
Of dire philosophy, that woman's plan
Is but to serve, and not to think. And you -
And you, who taught me all, taught me not rage.

There was no peace upon the House of More after the storm of my unwanted and unwilling betrothal broke over us all.

In private, in what should have been the most tender time between a man and woman promised to one another in marriage, William, like some vengeful and angry God, poured out his wrath at what he deemed to be my faithless and willful heart. But in the depths of his empty soul, I knew the pleasure he took in seeing me bend to his will and my father's. I, who had been brought up to increase and apply the knowledge of my own mind, was suddenly forced to surrender to the impending dread of my bridal day, when my wisdom and learning would be relegated to a dark place where it would wither and die.

My dearest sister Cecily was inconsolable. No word would she hear from me in my own defense; even as I humbly bowed my head in the presence of her heartbreak, and as my own soul shattered to know that her sweetness towards me would be no more, and that her dear innocent heart would be forever bruised and broken. She would not look at me; it was as if she had no elder sister. No name would she call me; no plea from my father softened her heart; and when we sat in the same space together I remained unacknowledged and unseen by her dear familiar eyes.

And when I watched her eyes, so frequently veiled with tears, I saw them filled with love and affection for William; though he betrayed her by falsely delighting in me while in her presence – as if to pronounce his own cruel sentence upon us both. My father, believing William's feigned affection for me, was reassured that my future would be sealed in joy; he did not see Cecily's despondence, or if he did, he did not take her pain upon his conscience the way I did. Because I had been the cause of her suffering, I did not want to shield my father from it; but as I prepared for my bridal day, my father made no time for us to be alone, and because William was always at my side, the justice I wished to pursue in Cecily's name remained trapped, blind and silenced, in my heart.

I was determined, before I wed, to tell Cecily of my pain at having destroyed her hope of a life and love with William, and that had there been any choice given me, I would have gladly stepped aside and spared her this heartbreak.

I thought to write these words in a letter to my dear sister, since she wouldst not look upon me, nor listen to me if I tried speaking with her. And thus, in search of the parchment and quills that my husband-to-be now forbid me, I returned to the bookseller Daniel in whose shop I had retreated from the grim London rain.

In the middle of the afternoon I stole from the house, whilst William and my father attended to matters of law, and as the sun journeyed through a sky the colour of bluebells at daybreak, I made my way back into the city. This time, I had dressed carefully, plainly gowned in dark grey with my face was shrouded in a thick veil, so that I would pass, mostly unnoticed, along the city streets.

Indeed, without my father's care and Cecily's affection, I felt the abandonment of a widowed heart, and as I covered my face before setting out on my journey, I wished that I could someday be freed from my terrible future with William by a widow's veil, instead of donning the bride's veil that would bind me to him until death.

Upon my entering the shop I heard the silver bell over my head, and waited for him to appear. He looked less fearful than he had the first time.

-Mistress More, he said, with a slight bow and less condescension than I expected in his dark eyes. Thou art returnèd.

-I have, I said, also bowing slightly to match his gesture. I am in need of paper and quills.

-I have both, he said, and also some words for thee.

-What words are these, I asked.

-Words of penitence, he said, and there was warmth in his eyes as he spoke. I am afraid that my manner upon our first meeting was most inappropriate. Thou hast been right; courtesy is not merely required of courtiers.

-Thou art forgiven, I said quickly. And yet, there was doubt in my soul, for perhaps he believed I would make a better purchase, if indeed he was kind to me as he had not been before.

-I thank thee, he said simply. And then, he seemed to examine me closely. Why dost thou clothe yourself in the garments of mourning? he asked me. Has there been illness or death among those dwelling in thy house?

There was genuine concern and civility in his tone. -I thank thee, I said. But in truth, neither has come to us. In fact, I am to be wed.

He gazed upon me with eyes that seemed to see the truth. –So I have heard. And yet, he said quietly, there seems to be no joy within thee.

I did not know what to say to him. I watched his eyes upon me, and knew that I would fain keep silent than to insult him with a lie.

-Thou has spoken in truth, I said, for my betrothal brings not joy. It has brought only sadness and despair to my house, and troubles my heart with fear.

-All women fear marriage, he said. But – he checked himself – from what is said of thee and thy wit, thy learning and thy grasp of ideas, thou art not like other women. Yet with thy great learning, what is it that thou dost fear? Daniel asked of me.

I wondered how Daniel had come by his knowledge of my learning, and then I thought of William, and his determination to divide me from it, and from all that I held dear, my books and my papers, my knowledge and my sacred study. – I know not, I said to Daniel. –Perhaps it is only the loss of my own courage. For I have never known such fear.

My words seemed to trouble him. The darkness of his eyes and the uprightness of his posture seemed suddenly weighted by sadness.

-Have I spoken out of turn? I asked hastily, for a sadness has settled upon thee.

He looked at me for a long moment, as if he could know my very soul, before he spoke, and his quietness of his voice filled the silence like a soft melody.

- I know fear, he said to me. It is my dearest friend and companion for these many years.

"Look at this," Michael said.

On the bottom of the page, at the edge of the paper, next to these lines, there was another notation, this time in Hebrew.

אִישׁ חַרְבּוֹ עָלַיְרֵכוֹ, מִפַּחַד בַּלֵּילוֹת

"Another note," Michael said. "Is it the same handwriting?"

"It looks that way," I said. "But thankfully, it's not in Spanish. After all of these years at the museum, Hebrew I can manage."

I looked at the letters. "This says *Ish harbo el-y'recho, mipchad baleilot.* I know this text. It means, 'Every man has his sword upon his thigh because of fear in the night.' Well, that makes sense. He's talking about being afraid of something."

"If Daniel was a *converso*," Michael added, "he had a lot to be afraid of."

I looked at Michael. "Actually, this SS348 is a citation I recognize – it's verse three, line forty-eight, from the Song of Songs, which is one of the most beautiful love poems ever written."

Michael looked impressed. "How did you know that?"

"From studying poetry, of course," I joked. And then I blushed. "And also, because when I met you," I said softly, "I re-read it."

We smiled at one another, and then he reached out and caressed my face with a gloved fingertip. We looked at one another for a long moment without saying anything more. Then we continued reading.

I turned the page. Another verse of poetry unfolded before our eyes. "Is this from the Song of Songs, too?" Michael asked me.

"No, it's another sonnet," I said. "And it's in Margaret's handwriting."

13

Upon my lips shall fate's kiss place her seal.
My maidenhood coerced, by birthright sold
And still, a mystery doth yet unfold
As letters on the sacred page reveal.
Two souls entwined by separate ordeal —
Upon my troth another's plight is told
Of Summer's journey fair to distant cold
And how Spring's veil of rain thy faith conceal.
Though tossed by tempest cruel of fear and loss
Haply the sun of thy sweet eyes hath gazed
Upon my loveless countenance in Hell.
This new redeemer bears not wounds nor cross,
Tho' with the light of truth, thine eyes have blazed
With fire in which my soul desires to dwell.

"I can't believe I didn't notice these were sonnets," I said to Michael.

"This one is certainly different," he remarked. "The others are so angry. Or they're about scholarship. This one seems to be a love poem."

"Which was the original purpose of the form," I concluded. "Almost every sonnet I've ever read was a love poem."

"I think there's more evidence here that he's Jewish, if in fact she is talking about Daniel," Michael said. 'This new redeemer bears not wounds nor cross. That's powerful imagery. And in the last line, there's the image of her soul desiring to dwell in fire. There's already a direct reference to Hell a couple of lines before that; do you think she meant that she was attracted to him enough to turn her back on her own faith?"

"It could be," I said. I didn't really want to go down the road of this conversation, so I pointed to the lines above the end. "This certainly points to a *converso's* journey from Spain to England – 'summer's journey fair to distant cold, and how spring's veil of rain thy faith conceal.'"

Michael nodded. I noticed that he turned the page as carefully as I would have.

As I have stated: I did not know what it was I feared, for I did not know my fate; but it was a bright summer's day that my fear was realized. On that bright morning, the Holy God turned his face from me, and imprisoned my soul in a holy bond with the apprentice William.

Some weeks before the marriage I was forced to the Church to plight our troth, to head the banns read aloud. My dearest Cecily was there, her hands bearing blossoms even as her fair countenance bore sadness and despair; my sisters and brother attended me as well; seeming pleased with my fate so firmly and inextricably sealed for all time. And of course, my foolish father, that trusting soul, alight with God's grace as he heard the sacred decree that would seal my soul in despair forever.

I had taken my leave of Daniel the day before, with quills and scrolls of paper newly purchased, with which I hoped I could write not only to my fairest sister, but also to my father. I wished to tell him of William's incivility, of his desire to defraud and defame my father of his years of noble service, and to take all that my father had earned for his own. And of course, I wished to confess most humbly to Cecily – to beg pardon for the unintentional sin of her distress that had led to the strife that now severed the bonds of our family like an unholy blade.

I had continued my conversation with the bookseller Daniel most civilly, for after I inquired of the source of his fear he made no answer, only with brusque cheer did he then direct my attention to the items I had come to purchase from him. And yet, an uncertainty in his eyes belied the careful dignity in his manner.

As I took my leave of him, he gazed upon me most kindly, and said – Fear not, daughter of justice, for in thy marriage I shall pray that no harm comes to thee. And should you ever be afraid, know that thou hast true friends among those who seek wisdom.

I paused, moved by his kindness and yet alarmed by the way his soul seemed to know mine. – I shall remember, Daniel, I said softly, and left him alone, again, to the sound of the tiny peal of the silver bell.

Soon after the passage of these most blessed hours in the presence of my friend, I found myself listening to the dreaded sound of the church bell that signified my bond before God with William – a peal that was rung over my head on that terrible morning during which we were wed, I remembered Daniel's words as I prayed that no harm would come to me. And yet, beneath my serene countenance my soul raged once more against God, for forcing me to honor my dear father's wish, even as I knew that it would be my undoing.

Of the marriage day itself I can only say these things; I was loath to be led up that strange aisle, with the last moments of my father's noble name clinging to me. As the priest turned his face to me and decreed that in purity I was given to this man, I knew the truth: that in charity I deferred to my father's wishes, and within the depths of my most secret heart, I cast all doubt upon God, and turned my faith only unto my wits; that with my desire to the seek knowledge whose presence blessed me with hope, I should find some way to escape the inescapable woe that this marriage visited upon me.

But it was not to be; this holy bond, for me, was nothing more than servitude to an evil and deceitful master, and nothing less than the complete subjugation of my womanhood and my identity as the daughter my beloved father had raised me to become. And within moments of the priest's pronouncement, I knew the first stirrings of the trap in which I had become ensnared; that I was bound in duty for all time to a man for whom I cultivated an ever-burgeoning hatred; yet in my love for my father I could not forsake my duty to my husband; and in the wit and learning that had been so long prized among those who loved me, there was real danger to my self and my eternal soul.

In the same moment that I took the most holy vows; I was a deliberate sinner outside of His grace, with no hope ever of redemption. And yet in those moments as I falsely spoke eternal fidelity unto the monstrous man I hated, I knew in my heart that I could not displease my father. I looked into his face of sweet humility and there saw Christ; and I could not harden my heart against either of them, neither my father nor my Saviour.

Thus I spent that day, my wedding day, garbed in white, as if to profess mourning for my own soul, clad in a gown in the same hue as a funeral shroud; and bedecked with roses and lilies. I was forced to smile as if I truly possessed love's radiance. My sisters' laughter came to me upon the morning breeze, for with my marriage, they were now secure in their marriage prospects. All except for Cecily, whose pain was evident as if marked upon her very soul. I thought of my dear noble mother Jane, dead after four births; I watched my father's new wife Alice, with her young daughter. I let my gaze fall upon woman after woman, seeing the restless servility of those who were espoused, and the modest flirtations of those who were not.

And my wit struggled with the logic of the marriage bond; for what is it within us as women that seeks to dwell with another? Surely it is arbitrary as the grass which grows beneath our feet! I ask, would the grass grow in the knowledge that it is to be trampled? Or is its growth within its nature, and without reason? Then I ask, why would a woman, born with the capacity of reason, seek to be bound to another in a life of servitude?

Surely wisdom does not forsake the fairer sex, yet the fairer sex is taught to forsake knowledge; it is not a mutual abandonment. A woman is taught that the greatest of all sins is to neglect her child; but a woman who neglects her true value - her wit, her intellect - also neglects her child, and all children born from that child, and so forth through time; these children are only given half-measures of knowledge.

It was with thoughts of my future child that night, when William first came to me in our chamber, I submitted as I was instructed, all the while praying that God would let me conceive right away, and thus put an end to my humiliation. But I knew the Holy teachings about the matters between husband and wife; this was my duty. At any time he could take his pleasure; he could force the sin of his lustful perversion upon me.

That very night, William entered my chambers and destroyed, with all of the proud ferocity of a husband, all of my texts and my papers; I was not present, having been delayed in bidding the king farewell from my wedding feast. When I came upon William in my chamber, his face flushed with drink and with rage, he flew at me with accusations of infidelity of the mind and of the soul.

I paled at his anger towards me until I saw its source - he had read the letters I had written to my father and my sister, in which I told them my fears and suspicions of William's ill character, and pleaded once more for the liberty of my soul, and for Cecily's forgiveness. He clutched the unfinished letters in his fists, and swore unto me that no word of his duplicity should ever reach them. And wasting no time, he thrust my papers and quills, and copy-books into the fire.

I cried out with rage and loss, knowing that the words of my heart could never be recovered from the flame, for fire kindled in the rage of destruction is all consuming, and ashes are mute. He turned on me with hate in his eyes. – Never again shalt thou speak of me thusly, he thundered. Thou art mine to rule and mine to bid, and as long as thou hath been bid to carry my name thou shalt do as I say, or else risk banishment, for even your father cannot save you should I decide that you are better sent away, far from the realm of the works of man and God. Thou wilt speak of me with honor and thou wilt bear thyself with silent dignity, for I will not have a wife who shames me by her knowledge, or her unwomanly mastery of thoughts.

All at once I was sure. He married me only because of what the house of More brought to him, and for what my father had promised to him in my name: the rich legacy of his business dealings bringing gold to his purse. I feared most, however, that with William fluttering between my father and the king like a terrible wingèd beast, that my father's words and deeds in the name of Holy God would cost him his proximity to the throne of England. Even though William appeared to stand his son and friend, to me, he was a declared enemy.

I then thought, as William smiled with a serpent's knowledge, that perhaps my father did not love me as I once believed. If he had, would he not have granted me my heart's desire? I would hath lived a spinster's life of books and study, and my sister Cecily would have been a wife, instead of the ruined woman that I believed William hath made of her.

My countenance, heretofore as strong as stone in the presence of his anger, suddenly shattered into tears. He took me, then, my virgin body cowering underneath the brutality of his fiendish hands. He conquered me by force as an enemy, with every thrust as a sword that runs through the despised. He took me as a king destroys a traitor – with pleasure in the act, with knowledge that his enemy is conquered and defeated. And after the blood, and the bruises, and the pain inflicted by his hands, his teeth, his clenched fingers that held my wrists behind my back as he took his pleasure, he smiled with cruel satisfaction, and upon hearing my muted tears, laughed softly and sleepily to himself, as sated as a glutted serpent.

After he fell asleep, I silently, tearfully cleaned the blood from between my thighs. My body was bruised and blackened as if I had been harmed by a criminal in the night. I could barely move with the pain that throbbed in my shoulders, my limbs; my pale skin was marked with evidence of his victory. I knew myself to be his hostage; I knew myself to be damned.

I knew then that I would never be redeemed in love, that anger and sadness and silence, where there had once been love and peace and wisdom, would guide my footsteps and grieve my heart for all of the days of my life.

After that night – in which he destroyed the sanctity of my body and the work of my hands and soul with brutality beyond the imaginings of my worst fears, he set about locking me in his rooms, unbeknownst to my father and my sisters, with nothing more than my needle-work for a companion. He would not have me study my books any longer; rather, he would have me taught only the housewifely arts. I wished desperately for a way to escape his imprisonment, and thought again of Daniel's words – that I had true friends among those who sought wisdom.

Yet it felt as if those friends were lost to me. My dearest sister refused to meet my countance, in spite of my pleas for forgiveness. My mother was dead; my stepmother a stranger to me. My books were forbidden companions; and even my Lord and Saviour seemed as far away as the stars that shone above the oceans at the very end of the earth. And worst of all, my father had abandoned me to the cruel will of his apprentice. I was without justice. I was friendless indeed.

Yet I had to believe in my heart: had my father known of the punishments which William inflicted upon me in the time leading from our betrothal to our marriage, he would have defended me, for even after I was told of my duty to William, in my heart I knew my father still wanted me to learn.

My father spoke often of the sweet intellect and forethought which endeared me to his heart. Indeed, my father believed that my learning was more valuable to me than if I had my mother's fair beauty or the riches of the king's very throne. William was not, as my father believed, of like mind. In spite of William's foolish pandering to my father's face, behind his back, William spoke of him as weak-willed and insidiously charmed where his daughters were concerned.

William spoke all of these things to me before our marriage, during which time he would know that I was powerless to deny my father's wishes for my marriage; he strode about the corridors of our house as if it was his own, as if he was already the son and heir to my father's fortunes. And perhaps worst of all, he flaunted his feigned affection for me in the presence of dearest Cecily, taking my arm as we went in to table; ignoring her if she addressed him; and flouting the false conventions of our courtship to her sick and bewildered heart.

But it was for my father that I had an even greater fear. With this evidence of William's falsehood, his deceit and deliberate cruelty, I feared that when such time comes as the breeze of the

Monarch's whim blew my father with a puff from his pedestal of righteousness, William would be present to collect the windfall, undisputed heir to his house and his servants, his gold and his books of law. And I, as his servant, could only look on as blindly and stupidly as any wife.

I let out a long breath as we came to the end of the page. "I seriously hate this guy," I said to Michael.

He nodded. "I imagine her story isn't so uncommon, being under the rule of a terrible husband with economic ulterior motives. And of course, there was no divorce in England at that time, especially for Thomas More's daughter. Think about it: Thomas More was the very person who prevented the divorce between Katherine of Aragon and Henry VIII. If he could prevent a king from divorcing, he certainly would never have let his daughter dissolve her own marriage. He was so much a man of the Church that there was no way out for her."

"But her husband raped her!" I said, indignant. "Couldn't she have told someone? Her father? The king? Her priest? Wouldn't that have gotten her out of this horrible situation?"

"Come on, you know better than that. They were married, her husband was within his rights to do whatever he wanted with her."

"I don't know." I shook my head. "It just doesn't seem right that she had to suffer like this without there being some sort of recourse for her to get out of the marriage. After all, there was such a thing as dissolving a marriage – I mean, that's what the rift between the king and Thomas More was all about." I frowned, puzzled. "And if that's what was uppermost in the minds of William and Thomas More at that time, then isn't it even more ironic that the dissolution of Henry VIII's marriage to Katherine of Aragon might have paved the way for Margaret's independence, even though it cost her father's life? And of course, the even greater irony is that her father was the very man who prevented a solution for Margaret from coming to pass."

"Yes and no," Michael said. "For one thing, Henry VIII was a monarch making the rules, and of course, he was a man. He had appointed scholars, cardinals, all kinds of legal and religious thinkers to evaluate the validity of his marriage to Katherine. When the law of the Catholic Church proved to be indissoluble, he simply decided to disregard it and create his own sovereign church. He had that sort of power."

"The power to keep women tied to abusive husbands," I snorted. "Some power."

"I know. You'd think that the queen would have been able to fight him on the grounds that their marriage vow was unbreakable. But I don't think Katherine of Aragon had any rights in the matter, and she was – second only to her mother, Isabella of Spain - probably the most powerful woman of her day. Poor Margaret wouldn't have had any rights at all, and fewer still since her father was so intimately linked with the Catholic Church. But the question of divorce is beside the point anyway, since we're talking about annulment, not divorce."

"Right," I said. "But Judaism had divorce. The concept existed. The sages had already been considering this question for hundreds of years."

"That may be true," he answered, "but think about it. Even though the legal system – where divorce was concerned – may have been descended from Judaism, once a marriage was solemnized according to Christian doctrine, divorce didn't really exist as a possibility for any nation under the sovereign rule of the Church."

"Oh, man, I feel like I'm back in Western Civilization 101." I yawned and looked at my watch. It was nearly one in the morning. "It's really late."

"You're right." He stood and stretched. "We should get some sleep. Even though I want to keep reading."

"There's always tomorrow night," I said. "Let's get it packed up, so we can avoid potential coffee disasters in the morning."

Because Michael had a meeting downtown at Foley Square, we rode the subway to work together the next morning. I kissed him goodbye at Chambers Street and then spent the next few stops thinking about what we had read the night before.

Rather than take all the risks of hauling the manuscript back and forth between my apartment and the office, I had left it at home in its case. Even though I considered all the disasters – fire, flood, overheating – that could happen to it while I was gone during the day, I decided to put those unlikely possibilities out of my mind before I drove myself crazy.

When I arrived in the office, Aviva wasn't in yet. I figured I would be running the meeting again, even though it wasn't my turn. I searched the computer files that Aviva and I shared for her notes on the catalog assignments, and printed them out while getting my own notes ready to go.

Just before the staff meeting, there was a knock on my cubicle wall, and when I turned around, Robert was standing by my desk.

"Good morning," he said shyly. "I just wanted to say thank you again for the great news about the promotion yesterday. I'm really looking forward to learning more from you."

"You're welcome," I said, absently running a hand through my hair. "I think it's going to be an intense couple of months, with Aviva gone, but we both think you're up to standing in for her. And I'm glad you got here a little early today," I continued. "You can help me run the meeting, if you like."

"Sure," he smiled. "What should I do?"

"Well, to begin with you can make nine copies of this report," I handed it to him with a smile. "Not glamorous, but necessary. I'd like to hand the status report section of the meeting off to you – what you'll need to do is make notes, type them up afterward – there's a form in the shared drive that we use. It shouldn't take you more than twenty minutes or so to write it up. Just show me the report when you're done, and then once I check it over, you can email it to Aviva, Larry and me."

He nodded. "I can do that."

"Then later today, we can talk about choosing our exhibition assistants for the summer schedule. Larry wants us to get our team in place before Aviva goes on leave, so the sooner we can take care of it, the better."

"Sounds good," he said. "Let me get this copied. I'll be right back." Just as he was about to walk away, the office door opened and Aviva walked in, her work bag slung over her shoulder and her cheeks pink from the cold. "Sorry I'm late," she said briefly. "I'll be ready for the meeting."

"It's under control," I told her. "Don't worry."

She took off her coat and put her bag into a desk drawer. Robert stood wordlessly with the paper in his hands, looking at her *sheitl*.

"What?" she snapped. "What are you looking at?"

"Nothing. I'm sorry," he said hastily. "Let me go make these copies."

I spoke as soon as he was out of earshot. "What was that all about?" I asked her. "Did you really need to snap at him?"

"I hate when people stare at my hair. I just want to say, 'Yes, it's a wig' and be done with it. Besides, he shouldn't be staring in the first place." She glared down the hallway in the direction of the copier. "He knows better. He knows that I'm a married woman."

"Sure," I said, "but that doesn't mean you're not a woman."

"Don't start that feminist crap with me this morning. I'm not in the mood."

"I didn't mean it as a feminist statement, but whatever. I'm sorry."

"Besides, why would anyone notice my hair when the only thing anyone ever sees anymore is this enormous pregnant belly in front of me all the time?" She looked as if she were about to burst into tears. "I'm going to get a cup of tea."

I watched as she stalked off towards the break room. Nothing she had said made sense, but Aviva was certainly under an enormous amount of stress. I followed her to where she stood with her back to the door.

"Aviva, listen, don't worry about the meeting. I asked Robert to help out and — "

"Jacob left me last night."

She turned and looked at me. I was horrified. She nodded, as if she were acknowledging the shock in my eyes. "I don't know if it's permanent. He said he was going to go away for a few days, and he needed to think about things. But I'm pretty sure," she said hollowly, "that he's staying with her."

"But what about you? You really shouldn't be alone right now."

For a moment I thought about walking out of the building, catching a train, and going uptown to Jacob's office and having a very serious – and potentially violent – talk with him – and Angela, too. But I didn't think it would do the department any good if one senior staff member was out on maternity leave, and the other was in jail for assault.

"My sister Devorah came over. She's going to stay with me while he's 'thinking about things.'"

"Okay," I breathed. "I'm glad she's there with you."

"Me too. My mother didn't want her to – as she put it – 'get involved' – but Devorah told her to buzz off."

"Good for her," I said.

"Yeah, at least someone's on my side in this," she smiled grimly. "Anyway, I'm sorry I've been so snippy this morning."

"Snippy? Please – you're entitled," I reassured her. "I can't even believe you came in today."

"It's the only thing keeping me sane right now," she said. "Coming in here every day, if you can believe that. I don't want to be at home, especially right now. And it's not like I can get the nursery ready, you know."

"Oh, that's right," I said, having forgotten the Orthodox tradition – or perhaps superstition - of not preparing the baby's space until the baby actually arrived. "Well, listen, the offer stands. The meeting's under control, so why don't you just sit in? We should probably both keep an eye on Robert anyway, so we can give him a hand if the others give him a hard time."

"Good idea," she said. "If he went running just because I snapped at him, he might need some help."

"Are you kidding? You're pretty fierce for an Orthodox girl."

She smiled a little. "Listen, modest doesn't necessarily mean demure," she said, glancing at her watch. "It's almost nine thirty. We'd better get the meeting underway."

We were a few minutes into the status reports – Robert was doing a pretty good job of moderating the conversation – when the intercom buzzed on the phone in the conference room. Josh went over to pick it up.

"For you," he said, nodding at me. "It's Mira."

I got out of my chair and walked across the room. Josh handed me the receiver. "What's up?" I asked.

Mira's voice was barely above a whisper. "Hi, Jill. Larry needs you to come upstairs."

"Okay." I eyed the junior staffers, who were starting to talk amongst themselves during the delay. "Can it wait until after the meeting?"

"I don't think so," she said. She lowered her voice into an urgent whisper.

"Two men in black suits and priest collars just showed up here, and now they're in the office with Larry. Schiffman is in there, too."

Schiffman, otherwise known as Dr. Steven Schiffman, was our executive director. This didn't sound promising.

"But they've got the door closed, so I don't know what's going on," Mira continued. "Larry just stuck his head out a couple of minutes ago and said, 'Get Jill up here.' He sounded stressed out."

"Shit," I muttered under my breath. "Okay, I'll be up in a second."

I hung up the phone. "Meeting's delayed, folks," I announced. "I have to go upstairs. I'll email you when I'm done and we'll figure out a time to reconvene." Aviva looked at me quizzically. "No idea," I said, and hurried out of the conference room and up the stairs to the fourth floor.

14

"Jill, thanks for joining us." Dr. Schiffman smiled calmly and gestured to the sole remaining chair in the office as I knocked softly and pushed the door open. "Have a seat."

"Thanks," I said, and looked around. Larry was sitting at his desk. Dr. Schiffman returned to his usual perch by the window, where he stood with his arms folded.

The other chairs were, just as Mira had reported, occupied by two priests.

I glanced from one to the other. The younger one was dark-haired and green-eyed, almost handsome. The other was white haired and stern-looking, with many more gold insignia on the lapels of his somber black jacket.

"Gentlemen, this is Jill Levin, our museum's senior curator. Jill, I'd like you to meet Father Jameson and Monsignor Tully," Larry said. "They're from the Cardinal's office at the Archdiocese of New York."

"Hi," I said. They both smiled at me, but neither one returned the greeting.

"Well, to get right to the point," Dr. Schiffman said, "these two gentlemen stopped by this morning because they have some questions for us."

"That's right," Father Jameson said. "Dr. Schiffman and Dr. Grossman very kindly agreed to see us unannounced. It's our understanding that you may have received a recent artifact donation of some interest to us."

Larry nodded at me as if giving me permission to answer. "I'm not sure what you mean, sir." I said. "Do you mean the manuscript we're currently investigating?"

The priest nodded. "We received word about it late yesterday, after Dr. Grossman spoke with some of his contacts in the field of antiquities. Our office received a call from a colleague wanting some information about whether such a document might exist. And as you might expect, we are extremely interested in anything that might relate to the life of Saint Thomas More, whom as you may or may not know, is one of our Church's most honored martyrs."

Larry spoke up. "We haven't been in possession of this artifact for very long. The authentication process is certainly underway, but we have no definitive answers yet. That's one of the reasons why I put some calls out into the field."

The two priests looked at one another. "If it would be of any help to you and the Museum, we would be happy to take over the process," Father Jameson said smoothly. "We have people in Rome who would be able to authenticate it very quickly."

"That's very kind," Dr. Schiffman said drily, "but how would it affect the provenance? And could we be sure of getting it back?"

I watched as Larry put his head in his hands.

The monsignor smiled. "How can there be a question of provenance? If the document is what we think it is, we cannot think of how it could possibly relate to your museum. After all," he said silkily, "it has no bearing on your institution's mission."

"Can you tell us, Monsignor Tully," Larry asked. "if there's any record of it among your archives? Obviously, if it were stolen, we would be obligated to return it to the Archdiocese."

Father Jameson sighed before he answered the question. "We don't know of any records. We only know that there was a rumor that such a document existed."

I saw the monsignor look at him sharply.

"For decades, there has been talk that Margaret Roper made a full accounting of her sins to her confessor, just before she died. As you might imagine, there was not as much interest in her life over the years, since she was not a candidate for sainthood, nor was she under consideration to be honored by the Church." Father Jameson looked at me almost apologetically. "We were not as interested, in the old days, in hearing from the woman's point of view."

I nodded.

"We were, however, concerned about how certain aspects of

Margaret Roper's life might reflect on her father's standing in the Church, if any of these stories were indeed true. The rumor I mentioned was one that came down through the centuries, passed from seminarian to seminarian, and scholar to scholar. There was talk that she had kept a diary. But no one could ever locate it."

The elderly man interrupted. "All of this is, of course, just speculation. After all, this is based on nothing but gossip and rumor and apocryphal stories that have been passed down through the centuries. No one can be sure, since the confidence between a confessor and penitent is held as a sacred trust. We may never know if Margaret Roper actually said such things. This artifact could very well be a hoax." He looked at me and smiled, as if he had noticed me for the first time. "As you can imagine, we are very interested in seeing it."

Dr. Schiffman seemed to be considering something, and then he turned to me. "Jill, can you tell us the circumstances of the donation?"

"It came to me in the mail," I said. I could sense Larry telling me not to reveal too much. "It was addressed to me personally. But there was no return address on the package. A series of letters have arrived from the donor, who appears to be a Holocaust survivor. Since we received the book, we've been discussing ways to authenticate it. But it's in very fragile condition, so we're being as careful as possible."

"I see," Dr. Schiffman said. "Gentlemen, as far as I can determine, from your side, your interest in this artifact is based on a rumor which remains unsubstantiated. From our side, this object arrived addressed personally to our senior curator from a Holocaust survivor, which does constitute a connection to our museum. I think, then, it would be most fitting for us to continue the authentication process here. However, we would be pleased to share the results with you as soon as we can determine them. And if you would like to schedule a time to come in and look at this artifact with Dr. Grossman and myself, we would be happy to accommodate you."

"So there is no way," the younger priest said, "that we could look at it now?"

I spoke up, my voice shaking a little as I thought about the artifact in its case, safely stored away in my apartment.

"It's not actually here at the moment."

Dr. Schiffman looked at Larry, puzzled. I could see Larry trying to come up with a fast one. "At the lab," he murmured. Dr. Schiffman nodded.

"Then I guess there's no way we can persuade you," Father Jameson said. "I trust, however, that if you discover anything – shall we say, inflammatory – you will let us know first?"

"Certainly," Dr. Schiffman said pleasantly.

"You understand, of course, that the Church is in something of a public relations crisis at the moment. Between *The DaVinci Code*, and the unpleasantness with the removal of certain clergy due to lawsuits in some of our parishes, we have a lot of work to do. As colleagues in religion," Monsignor Tully smiled chillily, "we hope that you will be sensitive to that."

"Of course. We certainly mean the Archdiocese no harm," Larry said. "We just want to see how this relates to the content and mission of our museum."

"Indeed." The two priests stood, as if on cue. "We'll report back to His Eminence, the Cardinal and will be in touch shortly with his statement," Father Jameson said.

"Statement?" Larry asked.

"His Eminence is quite concerned about this document becoming public, even if it does turn out to be a forgery. Should this have no connection to your museum except having been in the possession of a survivor of the concentration camps, we will expect you to return the manuscript to the Church, where it will become part of the Saint Thomas More archive at the Vatican. We trust that you will comply," the monsignor concluded serenely, "since we do not want to have to take this any higher."

I stared at the two of them, the priest who had smiled at me, and the monsignor. I had never seen religious figures playing good cop / bad cop, but I realized that I was seeing it now.

"Understood," Dr. Schiffman said, and then moved to shake hands with them both. "We'll cross that bridge when we come to it. Thank you for coming in, gentlemen."

The two priests shook hands with Dr. Schiffman, nodded at Larry and me, and then left. As soon as they were out of earshot, Larry got up from his desk and shut his office door.

"That was an interesting start to the day," Dr. Schiffman said wryly. "I wish I had known what the hell we were talking about."

"I'm sorry that we didn't have the chance to brief you, Steven," Larry said apologetically. "I just found out about this artifact yesterday. And I only put the calls out yesterday afternoon."

"I guess that's how they found out about it," I said.

Larry sighed. "I need to find out which one of my contacts made that call to the Archdiocese."

"Guess he's off the holiday party list," Dr. Schiffman supplied, grinning.

"And Jill, what do you mean, the artifact isn't here," Larry asked me. "Where the hell is it?"

"At my apartment," I said contritely, expecting to be reprimanded for removing an artifact from the premises. "I've been looking it over at night, after work. I'm just too busy to look at it during the day."

"Thank God," Larry breathed, to my surprise. "I was worried that they were going to find some way to take it with them."

"Well, I'd love to discuss this further, but I need to get back upstairs for a 10AM meeting with the Chairman and the marketing committee," Dr. Schiffman said, "but I trust that the two of you will brief me on this later? I'll have Ariel call you when I'm available."

"We'll wait to hear from her. Thanks, Steven," Larry said, and we watched Dr. Schiffman walk out the door and across the hall to his office.

"What do you want to do?" I asked Larry.

"Keep it safe at home for now," he said. "I don't want to tangle with the church over this. It could be a PR nightmare, for them and for us. The last thing we need is for some reporter to get hold of the story of how the Jews and Catholics are wrangling over some piece of antiquity.

The spin machine would be out of control, heaven knows what sort of problems it could provoke. It could undo all the work of Pope John Paul II and Cardinal O'Connor. It could possibly even set interfaith relations back dozens of years."

"From what they said," I remarked, "it sounds as if there's reason to believe we're dealing with an authentic document."

"But we need to figure out the connection," he said urgently. "As soon as possible." We both stood, and I turned to walk out the door.

"Jill," he said, and I turned. "Not a word about this visit. You can tell Aviva, but don't tell anyone else. Okay?"

"Will do," I said, and headed back down to my office.

"I've been thinking a lot," Robert said, "about the Spanish quote from *Pirke Avot* that you mentioned in the meeting the other day."

We were meeting to discuss our choices for the exhibition team. Just before, I'd had only a few minutes to tell Aviva about what happened with the two priests from the Archdiocese, and she was as shocked as I.

I was trying not to show the combination of stress and shock and curiosity that was now conspiring with a lack of caffeine to give me a massive headache. Instead, I was distracting myself with my meeting with Robert, while sipping from a cup of sweet tea at my desk.

Robert was wedged into the one extra chair normally located at the edge of my cubicle. He had pushed it over to where we had laid out the plans for the de-installation over my desk.

Earlier, we went through the meeting write-up and I was pleased with the way it turned out. I'd had to make very few corrections. He had an instinctive sense of how to express things diplomatically, such as when a team member had fallen behind in their assignments, had not used their time effectively, or even, unbelievably, didn't have enough to do.

"Have you mentioned the quote to Aviva?" he asked me. "She knows so much about sacred texts from her time in yeshiva. And, you know, I have a Masters in Jewish studies."

He blushed a little, and I liked him for being proud of his studies while not wanting to seem as if he was showing off, which was, in my experience, atypical of most Jewish studies scholars. "I'm sure that between us, we would be able to help you with your research."

I grinned at him. "Stop fishing for information, Robert. Besides, Aviva's just over the wall," I indicated the cubicle behind me. "And we're not allowed to tell you what it's about."

He grinned back at me. "Okay," he said. "I get it. But let me ask you this: Does the fact that you're not allowed to tell me now imply that you may be allowed to tell me at some point?"

"Maybe," I said. "It's something that I have to discuss with Aviva and Larry."

"Yes, it's something she has to discuss with Aviva and Larry," I heard Aviva's voice echo from behind the wall.

We laughed. "All right," Robert said. "I get it. But listen, if there's anything I can do to help, I hope you'll keep me posted."

"Oh, don't worry," I heard Aviva's voice again. "You're going to be so busy within the next few weeks that I can promise you won't be asking for extra work."

"Anyway," I said, "we should get back to figuring out the team. I think Fern and Josh are good choices for the assistants," I told him. "For the junior curator spot, do you think Meredith or Sandy would be better?"

He debated for a moment. "I think we should give Sandy a shot. We were both assistants on the Yiddish Theater exhibition, and I think she did a great job."

I nodded. "Sure. I think she's good, too." I wrote the names down on the pad by my desk. "So that's the team."

"Great," he said, as my phone rang. "Give me one second," I said, as I picked up the receiver. "Hello?"

"Is this Jill Levin?" A female voice, elderly, that I didn't recognize. "Yes it is."

"Jill, this is Mitzi Feldman. I don't know if you remember me, but I'm a friend of your grandmother's. I live next door."

"Oh, sure…Mitzi," I said, feeling my stomach sink in dread. "Is everything all right?"

"Well, I remembered that she told me you work at the museum, and I just thought I should call to let you know that your grandmother is fine, but she had a little fall last night on our way home from a concert."

"Oh, my God, is she okay? Is she in the hospital?"

Out of the corner of my eye I saw Robert's look of concern and the top of Aviva's head as she peered over the cubicle wall.

"She's fine, and she's home now," Mitzi said. "She got checked over last night. They didn't need to admit her or anything. We got home at about two this morning. I was with her the whole time."

"That was good of you to look after her," I said. "I wish I had known. I would have come right to the hospital. She should have called me."

"I knew she wouldn't call you," Mitzi said, and I was grateful that there wasn't any accusation or blame in her voice. "She wouldn't want you to worry about her. And actually, the doctor said it's just a stress fracture, thank God. You know, at our age, a fall can be a disaster."

"I know. What happened exactly?"

"Well," she said, "we were coming back from the chamber music series at Lincoln Center last night. She got out of the cab first, and I guess she slipped on some ice. You know with this crazy weather we're having, raining one minute and freezing the next. In the dark you can't even tell which is the ice and which is the concrete. She lost her balance and, well, down she went."

"Oh, God," I said, running a hand through my hair.

"But the cab driver was very nice. He got out and helped her right back in and took us to the emergency room at Columbia. And he didn't even charge us." Mitzi said, sounding pleased.

"So she had X-rays and everything?" I asked.

"Yes, of course. I knew that as soon as she went right over on that ankle, that she had fractured it. But thankfully, it was just a little fracture, nothing too serious. But the doctor said she should stay off her feet for a week or two, because with our old bones it's easier to make

149

it worse if you keep walking around on it. They put her in an air-cast, you know, the kind you can take off at night. And she has a cane, but she doesn't want to use it, of course."

"Did he give her anything for pain?"

"Oh, sure. The pharmacy brought it over first thing this morning. Thank God they still deliver."

"Good," I said. "I don't want her to be in pain."

"She's going to be fine. You know her. And listen," Mitzi's voice was philosophical, "she was lucky it wasn't a hip."

"I guess," I said absently, as I watched Robert and Aviva exchange glances.

"I thought you would want to know," Mitzi said. "You know how independent she is. I knew she wouldn't call you. But I did remember that she said you worked at the museum, so I looked up the phone number. I think maybe," and Mitzi sounded hesitant, "you might want to pay her a visit. A fall is a shock to the system, and I know it would make her feel better if she could see you."

"Oh, of course. Of course I will," I said hastily.

"Especially since your mother is out of the country," she reminded me.

"That's right," I said. "They're on a cruise."

"Well," she sighed, "my son and daughter-in-law are right up in Scarsdale. But from the amount of visiting they do, they may as well be on a boat in the middle of the ocean."

"I'll come up tonight, Mitzi, right after work."

"Good. When you come, just knock on my door first. I have a key. And I don't want her to have to get up to answer the door."

"What does she need? What should I bring?"

"Oh, nothing, nothing. You know, there's a whole bunch of us in the building, we order from FreshDirect. Both me and Sadie Goldenstein in 5B have computers. We all get together, at her place or mine, to do an online order once a week, and then we split the delivery charge and the tip when it comes."

I couldn't help laughing a little, since Michael and I also ordered our groceries from FreshDirect, and we considered ourselves at the forefront of technology.

"I'll come after work, around six."

"All right, darling. Just ring my bell and I'll let you in."

"I will. And thank you for letting me know, Mitzi."

I hung up the phone.

"What happened?" Aviva asked immediately.

"My grandmother fell and fractured her ankle," I said simply. "She's all right, but I'm going up to see her later."

"I'm so sorry," Robert said. "Is there anything I can do to help?"

"No, I don't think so. But maybe we'd better finish this up tomorrow," I indicated the plans on my desk. "I have to get up there. And before I go, I have a couple of calls to make."

"Not a problem," he said. "Let me get these out of your way." He folded up the papers and tucked them into a folder, and gave me a quick wave and a smile as he left the office.

Aviva came around to my side of the wall. "Are you calling your parents?"

"They're somewhere in the Aegean right now. But maybe I can send them an e-mail," I said absently. "It would be easier than trying to track them down on the ship, and probably having to leave a message with a ship-to-shore operator. And I'm pretty sure that their cell phone won't work overseas." I paused. "Maybe I should wait until after I see her. I don't want to alarm them."

"But you're calling Michael, right"

I nodded.

"What do you think he'll say?"

"He'll want to go with me. But I don't know if that's a good idea, especially if she's hurt." I sighed. "I just don't know."

"Oh, dear God," I heard the immediate concern in Michael's voice. "What happened?"

"She fell," I said. "Fractured her ankle."

"Is she okay?"

"Her neighbor Mitzi says she is." I rubbed my eyes. "But she also asked me to come up to see her tonight after work."

"Of course," I could hear the click of his computer mouse in the background. "Let me see. I've got a six o'clock conference call – the L.A. office again, but I can move that...oh, no, I can't. But I can get Daphne to cover for me." I heard more clicks. "Oh, crap. Except that she's out of the office."

I found myself feeling almost moved to tears by his concern. I swallowed a lump in my throat, and thought, for just a moment, that I really wanted him to find a way to go with me. And then my concern was replaced with a sudden sense of panic. There was no way he could go with me. It wasn't fair, I thought, for him to use this as a way to finally meet her face to face.

"Look, it's OK," I heard myself say. "I can go on my own. Really, I know that you'd go with me if you could."

I held my breath, waiting for his response. And the more I thought about the possibility of them finally meeting, the more scared I became.

"Are you sure?" he asked.

I hated, *hated* myself for feeling relieved that there might be a way out of this. Heaven knew that my grandmother would probably be feeling pretty ornery about having to be off her feet, and I didn't want to give her anything else to be upset about.

"Because it doesn't look good here," he continued. "It's a crazy day. I'm so sorry. I don't think I can get away."

"It's okay. I'll be fine on my own," I said. "But I'll let you know how she is, okay?"

"Sure," he said. "I'm just so sorry I can't go with you." His voice sounded disappointed.

"I know. But listen, it's only a stress fracture. She'll be fine, I'm sure."

"Just call me if you need anything."

"I will," I said. "Love you."

"Love you, too," he said, and I hung up the phone.

After a discreet moment or two of silence, I heard Aviva's voice from behind the wall. "Are you leaving?"

"I probably should," I sighed. "It's already five-thirty."

I opened the drawer of my desk and took out my purse. Then I gathered up my coat and scarf from the rack on the back of the office door. I carried everything with me to the elevator and pressed the button for the second floor, because I wanted to stop at the café to pick up some treats to bring with me.

Mentally calculating my walk to the subway, I also figured I should stop at a bodega and pick up some roses for her. And, I thought, I should also pick up some for Mitzi, since she was nice enough to call.

I put on my coat and waited for the elevator to arrive. I was worried about my grandmother, worried that Mitzi had kept something from me, and worried that Michael had thought everything was all right, that had he not had the convenient excuse of his meeting, tonight would have been the night when he would have insisted on meeting her. As moved as I was by his concern for her – a woman he had never met - I knew in my heart that I hadn't wanted him to go, not really, and that my grandmother, already vulnerable, would not necessarily have appreciated his presence, or have even seen the genuine kindness and concern for her in his intentions.

Except, I thought, she would have appreciated his presence if Michael were Jewish. The elevator doors opened and I stepped inside, and felt the slow heavy push of the car's downward weight as it lowered me closer to the ground.

15

Mitzi knocked lightly on my grandmother's door just before she turned the key in the lock. I stood behind her. "It's me, Anna," she said, as she opened up the door. "And look who I brought with me."

I watched as my grandmother turned her head toward the door, and saw her face light up with pleasure as I walked in.

"*Omi*," I said, putting my bag down on the floor in her hallway, "what happened to you?"

She was reclining on the couch, wearing a dark blue velour outfit that appeared more comfortable than the clothes I usually saw her wear; yet her hair looked perfectly styled. The television at the far end of the room, which was rarely on when I came to visit, was tuned to the nightly news.

From a distance, she did not look like a woman who had been in the emergency room until 2AM. But as I anxiously searched her face for any sign of discomfort, I saw that she looked pleased to see me, but that her eyes looked tired. Her left foot was bound in a plastic cast, and she sat with it propped up on pillows.

She laid her paperback on the coffee table as I approached with the bouquet of pink roses nestled in the crook of my arm.

"My darling, what a wonderful surprise!" she said, extending her arms in a wide embrace. I stooped to gently kiss her cheek, inhaling her familiar scent of hairspray and *L'Heure Bleue*. I smiled as I handed her the bouquet.

"These are for you," I said.

"Oh, you shouldn't have," she said, as she took them in her arms. "They're beautiful. And I have the perfect vase for them on the kitchen shelf. You'll go put them in water, right? Because," and she raised an eyebrow as she handed the bouquet back to me, "I have to have words with my friend Mitzi here, who had no business bothering my granddaughter with this." There was a twinkle in her eyes as she spoke that softened the harshness of her words.

Mitzi shook her head and raised her hand as if to stop her from talking. "Just doing what I can to make you feel better."

"And I'm glad you did," she said, as she reached out to touch Mitzi's hand. "It was good of you to call her."

I smiled at the two women, thinking that it was a wonderful thing that they had one another to rely on. They were both widows, and both on their own, and I loved how they had filled their lives and activities with each other's company, and the company of other neighbors in their building and their community. And I was also certain that it was no accident that Mitzi knew I worked at the museum. I figured they shared information with one another about their children and grandchildren's lives specifically because they knew what was inevitable at their age.

It occurred to me that it must be a terrible, and yet courageous job to choose the person who you'd want to tell your family if something suddenly went wrong in your life. I tried to imagine whom I'd want to tell my family if something happened to me, and realized that I hadn't been lying to my mother when I said it was Michael.

I tried to put the thought out of my mind as I touched my grandmother's shoulder. "Are you all right, *Omi*? I wish you had called to let me know this happened."

"Oh, this," she said, waving a hand towards the air cast. "Just a little fracture, nothing too bad. I'm still planning to go to my book group on Friday, as long as there's no ice on the ground."

"Mitzi said that the doctor told you to stay off it," I said, a little sternly.

"Listen, I'll see how I feel," she said dismissively. "I can't stay in the house all day every day."

"Just be careful," I warned her. "I don't want to have to call Mom."

"Listen," she said, "at least she can't blame this on butter and sugar the way she blamed them for my gall bladder attacks."

I laughed in spite of myself. "Speaking of butter and sugar, I brought you some cookies from the museum café."

She turned to Mitzi. "What do you say? Should we have some?"

Mitzi nodded. "Sounds good to me."

"I'll be right back, then," I told them. As I retrieved the bags from the front hallway, Mitzi sat down in the chair across from my grandmother. I walked into the kitchen with the bags and the flowers. I could hear their lively voices trading information, gossip, criticism of the chamber music group they had seen the night before and the incredible youth of the doctor whom they had met in the emergency room.

I found the vase on the shelf in the kitchen, filled it with water, cut the stems, and arranged the roses. I unpacked the bags I had brought with me; placed two containers of soup, a platter of Asian chicken salad, and some knishes in the refrigerator. Then I cut the string on the box of café cookies and laid out some plastic forks and spoons on the counter, along with some napkins and paper plates, so that she wouldn't have to worry about washing dishes for a couple of days.

I took some cookies out of the box, arranged them on a blue china plate I found in the dish rack. With the vase in one hand and the plate and some napkins in the other, I walked back out into the living room.

"Just set those beautiful flowers down right there," my grandmother said, pointing to the center of the coffee table. "I want to be able to enjoy them." She smiled up at me from the couch. "Thank you again, my darling."

"You know, your good girl brought roses for me, too." Mitzi said. "You're blessed with your family, Anna."

My grandmother patted me proudly on the arm as I passed by her to set the vase and the plate of cookies on the table.

"These cookies aren't as good as yours, *Omi*," I said, "but they're pretty good. Now," I stood and straightened my back, "do either of you need anything? Some tea? Juice? Ice water?"

Mitzi laughed. "Such a little hostess, just like your grandmother."

"I'm fine," my grandmother said. "How about you, Mitzi?"

"Nothing for me," she said. "Come sit down."

I took a cookie from the plate and a napkin and sat down in the chair across from Mitzi. "There are lots of goodies in the fridge, *Omi*, so you don't have to worry about cooking for a couple of days. I brought you some things from the café. And it's all kosher," I said, as I bit into the cookie.

"You didn't need to do that," my grandmother protested. "I have plenty of food in the house."

"I wanted to," I told her. "You're always feeding me."

"Well, I'm a Jewish grandmother," she said wryly. "That's my job." We all laughed. "Anyway," I said, "there's broccoli and mushroom knishes, and a really delicious chicken salad with Asian noodles, and some chicken soup with asparagus and wild rice."

"Sounds delicious," my grandmother said.

"In my day," Mitzi said, "no one thought of that as Jewish food. It was brisket, potatoes, and anything made with a ton of eggs and oil. Thank God for Lipitor." She reached out to take a cookie from the plate and then settled back in her chair. "So," she said, nodding at me, "your grandmother tells me that you don't have a boyfriend."

I shot a look at my grandmother, who shrugged her shoulders with nonchalant grace. "Oh, does she?" I replied.

"We tried to get the phone number of that young doctor - Dr. Nathanson - in the emergency room. Anna here told him that she has a very pretty, single granddaughter. But it turned out that he was already married."

"He was very nice," my grandmother said, shaking her head sadly.

"So I was thinking," Mitzi continued, "maybe you'd like to meet my sister's grandson. He's such a nice boy. Just about your age. His name is Sam; well, his name was Sam, but now he calls himself by his Hebrew name, Shmuel. Lives in Brooklyn. He's one of those – what do you call it – those young people who have become religious again."

"Ba'al teshuvah," I supplied easily.

"That's right," Mitzi said. "He's a very nice boy, and very smart, just like you, for all that I don't understand why he's living the way he does. Grew up in New Jersey, hated going to Hebrew school like every other kid on the block. At one point my sister didn't even think he was going to become bar mitzvah. At thirteen he had some notions about Marxism and how organized religion was the opium of the masses." She sighed.

157

"But Sam – Shmuel, I mean – always has notions of one kind or another."

Choking back a laugh, I imagined the first date - a bearded, badly dressed guy going on and on about Kabbalah and Talmud, or worse, disapproving of my failure to keep the laws of *kashrut*, not to mention the laws regarding female modesty.

My grandmother nodded her encouragement. "What do you say, Jill? Do you want to meet him?"

I stared at her in disbelief. Was this really the kind of guy my grandmother wanted to set me up with? I could understand her wanting me to marry someone Jewish, I thought, but the idea of being set up with a person who sounded so patently wrong for me made me resent, even more than usual, the religious blinders that apparently shielded my grandmother from seeing me for who I was.

I managed a smile and turned to Mitzi. "That's very kind of you to think of me," I said, "but I don't think I'd be religious enough for him."

She shook her head sadly. "That's just the thing. My sister and I would love for him to meet a girl who's maybe not so religious. Maybe then he'd come back to his senses. Right now he won't even eat at his parents' house anymore. He says they're not kosher enough for him."

I smirked a little, having confirmed my suspicions. "Then I'm definitely not kosher enough for him."

My grandmother and Mitzi exchanged worried glances. I could see on their faces they were afraid their plans were about to backfire.

"Well, you know, my darling," my grandmother said, "a date is a date. And it sounds to me like you haven't been on too many dates recently. Just meet him. No one is saying you have to marry him."

My head started to hurt again. I thought about all of the times when I had been in this apartment, and how, especially in recent years, all of the conversations seemed to lead to one place: the goal of seeing me married to a nice Jewish boy.

I looked at my grandmother's expectant face. I had a feeling that she, in her way, believed I was playing hard to get. She probably thought I was lonely, and maybe even desperate to meet someone, but that I had my pride. So she expected me to sigh, or roll my eyes, but I also knew she thought I would give in, that I would ultimately relent and say, "Sure, yes, I'll meet him. It couldn't hurt." And I would see her face – and Mitzi's – light up with hope, that the two wayward grandchildren would finally start living the lives they were supposed to be living, and that everything would turn out happily ever after.

"Actually," I said, not quite believing that the words were coming out of my mouth, "I've met someone."

My grandmother looked astonished. "You have?"

I nodded. The words were out there. I'd said it and there was no turning back. And I figured, great: now I'm in for it. I breathed a silent prayer of thanks that Mitzi had stayed. Maybe it would be easier with someone else in the room.

"So? Who is he? What does he do?"

I swallowed. "His name is Michael. He's my age. He's a lawyer."

My grandmother nodded and smiled delightedly at Mitzi. "A lawyer," she said. "How about that?"

"So…you just met?" Mitzi asked. "When did you start dating?"

Here it was. I knew I could lie to them. And of course, I knew I was capable of lying because I had been lying for so long. I could fictionalize everything: when we had met, who he was, and who we were together. But I was tired of it, and I knew our truth had a deadline. Michael had given me thirty days to tell her about us, and it seemed as if the time had finally come.

"We didn't just meet," I said quietly. "We met a long time ago."

"So it's someone you've known for a while, and you just started dating?" My grandmother looked puzzled. "That sounds very nice."

"*Omi,*" I said gently, "I've been dating him for a couple of years."

Her face grew confused, and then upset. "And you didn't tell me? Why not?"

Mitzi rose awkwardly from her seat. "I should be going," she said hastily. "I'll see you later, Anna."

I saw my grandmother try to smile. "Thank you again for everything, Mitzi," she said quietly. "Jill will see you out."

When Mitzi and I reached the door, she reached up and patted my cheek. "I know you don't want to upset her," she murmured. "She's been through a lot in the past couple of days."

"I know."

I closed the door after her and went back into the living room. *Omi* looked at me with eyes that seemed to hover between anger and sadness. "So," she said, "you've been keeping secrets."

I nodded guiltily.

"From your mother and father, too, or just me?"

"From everyone," I lied. "Not just you."

"But why? Why didn't you want to tell me that you had a young man in your life? Is there something so wrong, so terrible that you had to keep him a secret? Now I can only imagine that maybe he's not a good person, or that you think we'd disapprove of him. What is it that you're hiding?"

"*Omi*," I said miserably, "he's not Jewish."

I watched her in silence. She pressed her lips together and looked down at her hands. I saw her fingers tug at the blue velour sleeve that covered the numbers on her arm. I could hear the murmur of the television and the soft tick of the clock on the wall, and the sounds of the city streets outside her window. After a moment she looked back up at me.

"I see," she said.

"*Omi*," I began, and then my voice trailed off into nothingness. I wanted to tell her I was sorry, but I knew it wouldn't make any difference, because I wasn't sorry.

After a few moments she spoke again. "With your job," she said. "I thought in that place you wouldn't meet anyone who wasn't Jewish."

There didn't seem to be any point to telling her that there weren't only Jews working for the museum. "I didn't meet him through work," I told her.

"I feel like I should ask you about him," she said. "If he's a good person, if he's good to you. But now I'm afraid to."

"Why?" I felt so guilty I could barely manage the word.

"Because I don't know how you could do this. How you could turn your back on your family, your faith, your heritage. But maybe I don't know you anymore. If you lied to me about this, how am I supposed to know what's a lie and what's the truth. You kept him a secret," her voice sounded empty, "and who knows what else you could be keeping from me?"

"I'm not keeping anything else from you, Omi," I said fiercely. "What else do you think I'm hiding?"

"I don't know," she said sadly. "Maybe you're not going to be Jewish anymore? Is that what's going on?"

"How could you even think that?" I asked. "What does that have to do with anything?"

"Well, obviously you don't care about our heritage. About who we are. About our history. Otherwise, this would be a very different conversation, wouldn't it? I'm sure that if he was going to convert, I would have met him already. So I can only imagine that it's going to be the other way around, that you're going to go his way. You're going to become one of them. And how is that supposed to make me feel?" I saw the color rising in her face, heard the anger in her voice. "After everything I went through?"

I felt a burning in the back of my eyes. I didn't know how to answer, so I didn't. Instead, I looked down at my fingernails. After a few more minutes, she sighed and turned her face toward the television.

I watched the news with her in silence for a little while longer, and then when I had finally had my limit of trials and terrorism and murders and missing children, I stood up and gathered up my coat and my bag. Before I left, I kissed her on the cheek, and she put her hand over mine for a moment before she shook her head and waved me away. And then I walked out the door and went home to Michael.

Miss Jill Levin
Museum of Jewish Heritage
New York

Dear Miss Levin:

I know you will forgive my last letter. As I said to you, I am growing frail as the days pass, and sometimes it is hard for me to express myself clearly. I wish to tell you about how I managed to survive the camps. But first, I must tell you about those who did not.

Signs were posted in the shops, in the streets, even on the trunks of trees along the road to the country villages – everyone was to report to the square in the center of town. It gave the date, and the time. It was like the voice of a judge pronouncing a death sentence. All of a sudden, a town that was once full of life, of friends, of the sound of children playing, was now silent and full of fear. No one could weep. No one could pray. We heard that the church was hiding mothers and children, that there might be a chance to save ourselves. And then someone's sister in a neighboring town told us that if the priest agreed to take you, the church would create a false death certificate in your name, saying that you had died in the typhus outbreak the year before.

The week before we were rounded up, I went to the convent. I remember the face of the nun who opened the heavy door. She had merry eyes, and cheeks like ripening berries. Inside the church there were ghostly white statues with suffering faces, and the strange and suffused light from the Sacred Heart lamps. There were candles burning at the feet of the statues – not like our yahrzeit candles, the remembrances of light – but tiny, isolated flames in red and blue glass that cast strange colored shadows in the dim corridor.

She led me down that long dark hallway, to a room where the priest sat at the head of a big carved wooden table, like a king awaiting the offerings of his subjects. A fire crackled in the fireplace, not for comfort, but seemingly as a reminder of the hell they believed in - a hell to which we were about to be condemned.

I did not say a word. I waited for him to acknowledge me. I thought how he had once been our friend. I thought about how I wanted to save my mother, my sisters, and how once, not so long ago, he would have greeted each of us warmly as we passed by one another in the town. But now, things had changed and he was someone to be feared. So I knew that I could not ask him for very much. Even though I wanted to save my mother's and sisters' lives, I knew that I could only ask for the life of my daughter. I would not jeopardize her existence by expressing how I wished for them to be spared as well.

I know why you are here, he said to me. I watched his face as it changed in the flickering light. One moment he appeared almost kind, almost wise. In the next moment, the light would change, and a frightening darkness crept into his features. I thought of how G-d asked Abraham to sacrifice his son, and how I was about to ask this man of G-d for my child to be spared. I did not have

Abraham's courage or trust in G-d. I could not obey the signs that said my child was to be taken away in a convoy. I had to take the chance that she would be rescued by an angel. I could not allow her to die.

My Minna is strong, I said to the priest. She will help any way she can. She is a good learner, and she is a trustworthy girl. You have seen her in the street, I said. You know she is an obedient child, with a good temper and a pleasant disposition.

She is a very pleasant child, the priest said, as if he were choosing a sweet roll from a box in the bakery.

I did not want to beg him for my own life but I felt the words rushing out in spite of myself. If you were to take both of us, I said, I could help in the school, I could teach the children to play piano.

He stood, his firelit shadow looming over me, his black cassock making him appear like a large dark bird, a vulture. I imagined us trapped in his claws, soaring above the earth, far, far away from our home, our town, to be – what? Dropped to the ground? Consumed by animal mouths, our picked corpses left to rot and wither? I thought I knew this man, so long ago, before everything changed, but now he was transformed, as everyone seemed to be, by hate and fear.

A long moment passed, and then he finally said, "We will take the child. There is still time to save her soul."

The letter ended abruptly. I shifted a little in my chair, looked out the window at the gray skies over Battery Park, and laid the delicate sheets of typing paper on my desk and closed my eyes for a moment. The night before, I hadn't slept much. After I left my grandmother's apartment, I walked to the subway and waited for the train to arrive. The ride passed in a blur of stations and passengers getting on and off, absorbed in their books, their music, their conversations. I thought about how lucky they were, how lucky we all were, to be able to get on and off trains as we pleased, to go where we wanted to go. As the train pulled into a station a couple of stops before mine, I rose from the plastic seat and walked out the open doors and up the stairs to the street.

It had been raining lightly and the garish reds and pinks of the neon signs were reflected like spilled paint on the wet streets. I walked for a while, past the apartment building where I lived with Michael.

After a while, I found myself at Washington Square Park, standing by the arch and looking toward downtown, where my view was of a place where the Twin Towers no longer stood. I thought about that cool September morning, how I had believed I would never again be as afraid, or as disoriented, as I had felt during those terrible moments when I fled uptown, my clothes and hair covered with ashes and pulverized concrete and ground glass, covering my nose and mouth with my hands, my eyes so full of pain and dust that I could barely see the street in front of me.

After a little while, I turned around and walked back home. When I walked in, Michael, alarmed by my tears, had thought at first that my grandmother had been more seriously injured. But once I managed to tell him I had finally told her about us, and about her cold and silent response, he led me to the couch and held me, stroking my hair, not saying anything, letting me cry.

We didn't look at the manuscript that night. We sat together on the couch and I told him the whole story – not that there was much to tell. As I spoke, I watched the emotions change in his eyes. He looked sad and angry and confused and hurt and then angry again.

When I finished telling him what had happened, we sat holding one another. I could hear his heart beating beneath the familiar soft red cotton of the t-shirt that he slept in, and I breathed in the comforting scent of his skin and the fresh smell of detergent. After a few minutes he stood and held out his hand. I took it in my own and we went into the bedroom. He removed my clothes as if I were a child he was putting to sleep, and handed me my favorite old blue flannel nightgown. I put it on, feeling its warm, worn softness draping itself over my body. Then we lay down next to one another, and he gently traced my features with his fingertips until I fell asleep.

I looked down at the letter again, and then turned the pages over. There was nothing on the other side. I put the papers down on my desk and leaned back in my chair. Outside the windows, the clouds had given way to a pale February afternoon sunset that looked as if it were about to surrender to the advancing clouds of another icy night. A fierce wind shook the lacy branches of the trees that lined the harbor walk, and the water below chopped and churned against the sea wall.

It was getting late. Exhausted by another day of meetings and by a series of mild Braxton-Hicks contractions, Aviva had already left. The office was quiet. In a few moments, I knew I would hear the announcement that the museum was closed for the day, and then I would pack up my gear and head home.

I had found the letter in my mailbox late in the afternoon, during a bathroom break between exhibition planning team meetings, but only now had I gotten the chance to read it. I wanted there to be more information about Chava – whoever she was. But now that it looked as if Minna had possibly lived, as what was known in survivor circles as a "hidden child," maybe that would be another angle to search for the family's identity.

"Hey, Jill. You doing okay?"

I turned to see Robert standing at the edge of my cubicle. "Oh, I'm fine, Robert. Thanks."

"How's your grandmother doing?" He shifted the pile of books he was carrying to the crook of his other arm.

"She's doing well. Thanks for asking."

"No problem. I was worried yesterday." He craned his head to look over my cubicle wall. "I was looking for Aviva. I saw her in the library taking out these books but I told her she shouldn't be carrying them around."

"That was sweet of you," I told him. "She's gone for the day."

"Do you think it's okay to leave them on her desk?"

"I'm sure it's fine to leave them." I looked at the titles. "I highly doubt that anyone is going to be interested in stealing a copy of Talmud commentaries."

He pulled a couple of slim volumes out from the pile. "*Tractate Gittin, Talmudic Tales of Virtue and Vice,*" he said, reading the titles. "I think you're right about nobody wanting to steal them, although these sound a little intriguing."

"I don't think too many of our colleagues can read Aramaic," I said.

"But Aviva can read Aramaic." There was a real admiration in his eyes. "Although that worries me a bit."

"Why?"

"Because Tractate Gittin explains the laws regarding divorce."

I didn't say anything for a moment. "I'm sure it's just research," I lied quickly. "Anyway, speaking of research," I made a quick decision, "there's something I'd like you to look into for me."

"Sure."

"I'd like you to look into the artifact database and see if you can match up any donors with people who were hidden children. I'm specifically looking for information about a woman named Minna, or anything that sounds like an Americanized version of Minna. She would be the daughter of a survivor, and her date of birth would be sometime around 1938 or 1939. Do you think you can do that for me?"

"Absolutely. When do you need the information?"

"As soon as you can, really. But I don't want it to interfere with your other assignments. If you have some time to run the search, that would be great."

I wearily turned my key in the lock. When I walked in, Michael had the table set for dinner, with lit candles and flowers and our good wineglasses and plates. The smell of porcini risotto – one of Michael's many specialties – filled the apartment.

"Hey," he said, walking into the hall from the kitchen while wiping his hands on a dishtowel. "I'm glad you're home."

"Me, too," I said. "What's all this for?"

"Two things," he grinned. "First, I want us to get through dinner because we still have quite a ways to go in the manuscript." He put a hand on my shoulder. "And, second, to cheer you up."

"I'm okay," I said softly. "You didn't need to do anything."

"I know you're okay. But you haven't had the best couple of days, between everything at work with Aviva – I know a lot of the burden is falling on you. And last night," he trailed off, not finishing his sentence. "Anyway, I want you to relax. We'll have a great dinner, and then we'll see what happens next with Margaret and her horrible husband, who probably never once cooked porcini risotto for her in his whole life."

"Probably not," I agreed, as I put my arms around him gratefully. "He doesn't strike me as the domestic type."

We cleared the dishes off the table and went through the same ritual of cleaning and laying out of paper that we had two nights earlier. When everything was ready, we put on our white gloves and took the manuscript from its case. Michael watched as I carefully turned each page until we reached the part where we had left off.

But what appeared before us was unlike what we had already seen. For one thing, the paper looked as if it had been folded, and then smoothed out by the process of having been bound into the rest of the book. The lines of the folds were still faintly in evidence, and there were fewer words on the page than on the others. The handwriting of the diary still looked familiar, though, and so did that of the commentary in the margins.

Tonight as I walked to my chamber I heard the voices of my father and William joined in hushed and urgent conversation. The heavy wooden door was only slightly ajar and I hid in the shadows beneath the lintel. I hoped that my father was counseling William about the cruelty toward me and Cecily, which I had no doubt he had witnessed. But instead, I heard a different subject entirely, one that bound my heart up in narrow ropes of fear:

I heard my father's low murmur, the confident tones of his voice sounding dismal and burdened by sadness, and William's voice cool, strident, even as his words slithered easily through my father's despair. I could not hear my father's exact words, but I did hear some: he spoke of the Monarch's decision to put aside his wife, that he in good conscience could not support his friend the King, that his loyalty as a subject could not lead him to traduce the will of Holy God.

Their voices dissolved into whispers. Then I heard my father say that only the new scholar appointed by Henry could help keep the King within the bonds of the Holy Church; that this scholar could deduce the ancient Hebraic laws pertaining to the marriage of one's dead brother's wife; that as the wife of Prince Arthur, surely Katherine's marriage to Henry, even if valid in a court of Hebrews, would be considered unsound for a Christian king.

I heard my father say that if it could be proved that Henry had made a marriage according to Jewish law, he could still be pardoned within the realm of the Holy Church; that the marriage to Katherine would be annulled, and the soul of the King would be preserved. I heard William's voice answer the sound of my father's hope; he said, The Bookseller — the Jew — will do what is required.

Then I heard the sound of William's boots as they crossed the floor, and I fled to my chamber before he could see that I had listened at the doorway.

I am troubled at the thought of what will be required of the Bookseller, for I know in my heart, that the man that William has spoken of is Daniel. So he is a Jew. This is the cause for his fear, and rightly so.

This is why he recognizes the fear in my eyes, for although I believe in the True Saviour, Lord Jesus Christ, I know He hath abandoned me. And this, perhaps, leaves only my belief in Daniel's God, the wrathful and jealous God who metes out punishment such as I have merited for the sin of my pride and my unworthy desire to seek knowledge that is only for those who have been set above me by Holy Writ.

And yet, Daniel hath affirmed my desire to seek knowledge. Who is this Jew who encourages my defiance! He knows of me as the daughter of justice; I wonder only whether he knows that I have become the wife of evil and despair?

In the margins next to the final section were scrawled two notes, which were familiar to me, after years of Hebrew school:

הִגִּיד לְךָ אָדָם, מַה־טּוֹב וּמָה־יְהוָה דּוֹרֵשׁ מִמְּךָ, כִּי אִם־עֲשׂוֹת מִשְׁפָּט וְאַהֲבַת חֶסֶד, וְהַצְנֵעַ לֶכֶת, עִם־אֱלֹהֶיךָ

It hath been told thee, O Man, what is good and what the Lord doth require of thee: only to do justice, to love mercy, and to walk humbly with thy God.

and

בַּת צֶדֶק צֶדֶק, תִּרְדֹּוֹף

Daughter) Justice, justice, shalt thou pursue.

16

"So Daniel was Jewish," I said to Michael. "We were right."

"But as a scholar at the court of Henry VIII?" He shook his head. "That must have been really uncomfortable, to say the least. From what I can understand of her words, it sounds as if he was there to try to make a case that the levirate marriage made between Henry and Katherine was invalid."

"Perhaps," I said sarcastically, "you could define levirate marriage for those of us who didn't go to law school?"

"It's a standard marriage regulation rooted in ancient biblical law," he said. "When a woman is widowed, and she hasn't had any children, by law, she is supposed to marry the brother of her dead husband."

"What if the brother was already married?" I asked, puzzled.

"Well, we're talking about a time when men had more than one wife, before the notions of traditional marriage were invented. This law is definitely pre-Church, and pre-monogamy."

I rolled my eyes. "That figures. I suppose it was to keep her dowry in the man's family," I frowned. "So much for the old biblical saw of 'pleading for the widow.'"

"Well, right, it did have a lot to do with the dowry, but it was more about the children, and the ability to maintain inheritance through the line of the firstborn. This way, even though the widow was in the brother's care, the arrangement guaranteed that her children would inherit."

"I thought she didn't have any children. Isn't that the point?"

"Yes. The right of inheritance applies to the children that the widow would have with her dead husband's brother. Any children she had with him would inherit before any children he had with other wives, because children of a levirate marriage were considered to be the descendents of the woman's original husband, who was usually an older brother. So, the law of levirate marriage reinforced the inheritance through firstborn sons."

"And this is relevant because Katherine of Aragon was married to Henry's older brother," I finished. "And there were no heirs from that marriage."

"Exactly," Michael said. "And she failed to provide a male heir during her marriage to Henry – though she did have a girl, Mary, who became queen, as did Mary's half-sister, Elizabeth, who was Anne Boleyn's daughter."

"Ah, yes. Anne Boleyn – the second of his wives, and the first to be beheaded."

"Right," Michael said. "The whole reason that Anne became Henry's wife was because the line of male succession was at risk. Katherine of Aragon was put aside, and the Church of Rome along with her."

I shuddered, remembering our visit from the two priests. "I don't even want to think about the Church of Rome right now."

Michael smiled sympathetically. "I don't blame you. So that's what happened to Katherine of Aragon. After that, it was one wife after another. The next one was Anne Boleyn, who was also put aside, though rather more dramatically than Katherine."

"I'll say."

"Even though the line of succession through the firstborn male was fulfilled by Edward VI," he continued, "who was the son of Jane Seymour, both Mary and Elizabeth outlived Edward, and both succeeded him on the throne of England."

I shook my head. "I don't know how you remember all of this history."

"Listen, you think about history all the time. It's just that you're more focused on the twentieth century variety."

"So you're thinking that Daniel was there to provide some sort of information about the laws concerning levirate marriage?"

"That's what it sounds like to me," he said. "I'm guessing that the question at stake here is whether a marital contract based upon an ancient Jewish law could be upheld by the Catholic Church. The problem is that biblical law was always evolving depending on who was making the rules, and what was in their agenda."

"What do you mean?"

"Well, there are actually two arguments regarding the actual statute. The levirate law said that a man was entitled to marry his dead brother's wife to keep the inheritance in the family. But an earlier law says something quite different. I'm referring to a precept in Leviticus, in the Hebrew bible – we studied this in law school – that predated levirate marriage. It was part of the so-called Holiness Code – and it said that marrying one's brother's wife was punishable by death. And I'm guessing that Thomas More and William Roper, were looking to Daniel's knowledge of the Hebrew bible and Talmudic commentaries on both laws in order to ultimately come to the response that Henry wanted."

"I'm still completely baffled as to how they would have even found Daniel," I said. "Jews might have managed to live in London after the Inquisition, but they and their practices must have been very carefully hidden."

"What do you know about the Jews of England in the Tudor period?"

"Just that there weren't a lot of them." I thought about it for a moment. "But Robert or Aviva would probably know more. They're the trained folk. I'm a conservator and an art historian – they're the scholars."

"Can you ask them? I'm really interested in the backstory here."

I was delighted by the curiosity in his eyes. "I'll do that," I replied. "Because the manuscript doesn't tell us."

We looked at the page again. "I'm intrigued by these notations," I said, pointing to the first one, "especially if they are in response to William talking about what is required. Daniel is quoting from the book of the prophet Micah, chapter six, verse eight, which is one of the most famous biblical writings. I can translate, actually, because this was the inscription above the door of my synagogue. It reads, 'It hath been told thee, what is good and what the Lord doth require of thee: to do justice, to love mercy, and to walk humbly with thy God.'"

"It makes it sound as if Daniel was his own person. That he was serving God, not the king."

"And the other one is also very famous, from the Book of Deuteronomy – '*Tzedek, tzedek, tirdof'* — 'Justice, justice, shall you pursue,' except that he has written the word 'bat' in front of it, which means 'daughter,' as you probably know."

"And Daniel referred to Margaret as the 'daughter of justice.' So he's talking about pursuing the daughter of justice?" Michael raised his eyebrows. "Who was married to her father's apprentice."

I considered it for a moment. "Maybe he thought he could save her."

"Although I'm not sure if pursuit meant then what it means now. What we see here might not mean he wanted her for himself; it might mean instead that he was taking the course of action he thought she herself - or even her father - would take. But there's not enough here to know one way or the other."

"That makes the possibility of his pursuing her even more intriguing," I said. "If Daniel was able to get the marriage ruled in favor of an annulment, it would make Thomas More happy. And then, perhaps, he'd gain access to Margaret."

"As a Jew? With Margaret the daughter of one of the most prominent Catholics in England?" Michael shook his head. "Keep dreaming."

"Well, if he was a *converso*, he was living as a Christian, right?"

"He might have been practicing the Jewish rituals in secret. And obviously, More and Roper knew he was Jewish."

"But they brought him to the court nonetheless," I pointed out. "They may have only been hiding his Judaism from the other courtiers."

"They certainly would have had to hide him from the queen," Michael said. "And any of her supporters. A Jew ruling on the marriage of Ferdinand and Isabella's daughter would definitely be putting his life in danger."

"From whom?" I asked. "Other than the queen's supporters?"

"Catholic clergy, anyone who knew that Jews had been banished from England centuries earlier, anyone who thought the Spanish Inquisition was a good idea. And who knows who else?" Michael said.

"And perhaps even Henry himself. Obviously, he was trying to prove that his marriage was invalid, and he was the sort of monarch who didn't really care whether the means justified the end. I remember in my class on the evolution of biblical law —"

"Ah, now I understand how you know so much about this," I interrupted.

He blushed a little. "It's true. This is a classic case study. Anyway, in order to marry Katherine, Henry received a dispensation from the Pope, so that it was legal for him to marry his dead brother's wife. Normally, he would have been prevented from marrying her on the grounds that she was intimate with his brother – a law of the Church that hearkened back to the original statute in Leviticus."

"I see," I said. "So because the Pope gave Henry this dispensation, the marriage was considered valid. So the law of inheritance would apply."

"That's right. But I get the sense that by finding a way around the Papal dispensation, and declaring the marriage to Katherine as invalid, More was trying to find a way to annul the marriage without Henry having to leave the Church," Michael said. "And More would have been gravely concerned about this turn of events. Henry was his childhood friend. But it's likely that he feared not only for Henry's soul, but for the souls of the English people if the Church of Rome was abandoned by their sovereign ruler. Which, of course, it eventually was."

I nodded. "Thomas More was executed because he didn't believe that Henry could be the supreme head of any church. And Henry thought that was treason."

"More wasn't alone. There was also a bishop – his name was Fisher – who blatantly sided with Katherine of Aragon, and wanted to retain the sovereignty of the Holy Roman Church in England – and he was also executed for treason. After Henry was excommunicated by the Pope, the king declared his own religious sovereignty, created his own church, brought in his own people." Michael smiled a little. "I mean, it's weird, but it sounds a little like the sort of behavior you see every day on Wall Street. Hostile takeovers, mergers and acquisitions."

"Except that people's lives and souls aren't at stake."

"Oh, that's right. On Wall Street no one needs to worry about having a soul."

I laughed. "In twenty years, when you're in private practice doing corporate litigation, I'm going to remind you of this conversation."

"God, if it comes to that, I want you to shoot me."

I laughed. How easy it was to imagine still being together in twenty years, I thought.

"Anyway," I said, "there's one connection to the museum. And today, I think I finally got some information from the donor that I can use."

"Another letter?"

I nodded. "It seemed a little clearer than the last one, which was really strange. But it says that she hid her daughter in a convent, or anyway, that the priest there agreed to take her. So I've asked Robert – you know, the guy I told you about, who's helping me while Aviva is out on leave – to do a little research based on the girl's name and her birth year. In the database we have a category flag for people who were hidden children, or who knew of hidden children, because, unfortunately, some of these children never went back – or were never returned - to their parents."

"Why?" Michael asked.

"Well, because no one expected the parents to survive or return, hidden children were sometimes adopted by Christian families in Poland and Germany, and some of them were so young that they had no memory of their birth parents, so that even if their parents were lucky enough to survive, their children didn't remember them, and didn't want to go back with them." I sighed. "So, I'm hoping to figure out who this donor is, thinking she would have told us about her daughter, even if she didn't get her back after the war. At least," I said, "it's some specific information to go on."

Michael nodded. "That's good. I really hope you can find out who sent this to you. I'd like to know more about how she managed to hold on to this book."

"Well, at least we know a little more now about why it's important to the museum. The connection to Judaism, through Daniel, is there."

"At least Aviva's mind will be at rest about that," Michael agreed.

"I don't see Aviva being at rest about too many things at the moment." I had told Michael the night before about what was going on with Jacob and Angela. "Especially with the baby about to arrive."

"Is she going to work right up to the end?"

"I think so. I don't think that's what she intended, but she told me she can't stand being at home right now. She's scared."

"Understandable. What do you think is going to happen with him?"

"I don't know. Aviva said that their rabbi was going to put some pressure on him to get a new job, to stay away from Angela. But I don't know if that's realistic. I'd like to think she'd be strong enough to ask him to give her a divorce."

"But he's really in control of that, isn't he?" Michael asked.

"Yeah. What a system." I frowned. "Ancient times, modern times," I waved a hand above the manuscript, "when it comes to marriage, women get the worst of it."

"That's only true for some women," Michael said, looking at me. "When two people love each other, it doesn't have to be that way."

I considered his words for a moment. My mind went immediately to the two wedding photographs on the table in my grandmother's apartment – the small one of her and my grandfather taken in the Displaced Persons camp, and the other, the portrait of my parents, on the steps of the *bimah* in the synagogue. And I thought about how no one opposed those marriages – in the case of my parents, there was nothing to oppose – my father was a nice Jewish boy. And in the case of my grandparents, there was no one left in either of their families to judge them one way or the other.

I looked at Michael again. I wanted to think that he was right, but I didn't know how I could live with my family's disapproval. I wondered if my grandmother had managed the news on her own, or if she had left a message for my parents via the ship-to-shore operator. I could just imagine it. "Call me immediately," it would say. "Your daughter is dating a *shaygetz*."

"You might be right," I said. "Anyway, let's read a couple more pages, and then get this packed up. I think I should take it back to the office tomorrow."

Michael looked disappointed. "I was hoping we could get through it together before you bring it back."

"I know," I said, "but I'm going to ask Larry if I can let Robert have a look at it. He knows a lot about Jewish history in the medieval period. And since he's doing the research – even though he doesn't realize what it is – it seems only fair."

I could tell what Michael was thinking; how much we were both enjoying poring over the manuscript together, even how much fun we were having getting the apartment ready to take it out of the case. And, I thought, we hadn't fought in days.

"Listen," I said, "I'll let him take a look at it, and then I'll bring it back in a couple of days. Okay?"

"Sure," Michael said, his tone full of understanding. "But I'll miss looking at it with you. You know, watching TV just won't be the same now."

"I hear you," I smiled. "Why watch Law and Order, when you can live it?"

I had not been able to return to Daniel since that last day before my marriage, having become newly occupied – at William's direction- with the trivialities of my life; my dresses and my hair, tending my needle-work and growing the flowers that pleased William, and bearing the merry visitations of the courtiers who came to see us, all the while pining for a child and for my books, one as much as the other.

One day, some time after my wedding, I found the opportunity to sneak away from the house, with my father and William again occupied with matters of the monarchy, to leave our home and visit the Bookseller's again. I had hoped and planned and looked forward to my visit there, and though he was a Jew, according to my father and William, I felt that I did not have cause to fear him. Indeed, he was, I believed, the only person who could help me – my only friend among those who sought knowledge.

And also, Daniel seemed unlike the People of the Tribe about whom I had been told; he did not wear the trappings of his faith – at least, not in my presence – no fringes dangled from his waist and no covering lay upon his head.

When I entered the shop he smiled as if happy to see me. –How now, Mistress Roper, he asked, with a small bow and a smile.

–I am well, I answered him. But the sadness of my eyes betrayed me.

–I hear thou hath been married, he said.

–Yes, I answered.

–I wish thee much joy of thy marriage, he said politely.

– And I thank thee for thy good wishes, I rejoined civilly.

He peered at me again. – I do wish only joy for thee. Yet in the manner in which thou speakest, without smiling, without joy in thy voice, I fear that thou art unhappy. When I think, Mistress Roper, that a newly wed bride should be as the lark in the spring sky, and yet in thy dress and demeanor, thou art as shrouded in darkness as a stone in a churchyard.

I looked upon him, wondering if it was the cunning Jew within him that could know the secrets of my heart without the words ever coming to my lips. –Hush, I told him, for who are you to ask me of such matters?

-I am none but your friend, he said.

-You cannot be my friend, I told him, for I have no friends. Once, my father was my best and sweetest friend, but he hath sold me as one would sell a plot of land or a field of grass. He spent years feeding and tending and cultivating my soul only to put it into the keeping of one who would let it lay fallow.

Daniel sighed gently, almost as a lover might. –Thy father is still thy friend, he said tenderly. -I know this for he hath been a friend to me; in a friendship borne of the love for learning. Thomas More hath stood before me, in this very space in which you stand, and it is in thine eyes that I see his love of learning and justice. For thy father is a just man, and he hath spoken of thee in constancy and love.

-He hath put thee into the care of one who will keepest thou safe, Daniel said, his voice growing more quiet as if burdened by its very secrets. He hath placed thee in the hands of one who shall never himself be at risk because the reins of power are not within his reach. William Roper is of little importance to the monarch. Thy father is wise to make you the wife of such a man, for he wishes to protect thee from the monarch's whims.

I stared at Daniel. –So it is true. Thou art the Jewish bookseller of whom they hath spoken.

The unmasking of his secret was apparent in his eyes.

-And thou art acquainted with my father, I said. Then thou must also be acquainted with my husband.

-I am, he said, and there was sympathy in his voice. William Roper is not the same sort of man as thy father, but because he is such as he is, Roper shall keep thee safe. Though he tries to curry favour with the king, he is only tolerated because of the monarch's love for thy father. But he hath no power, nor will he, among the churchmen and councilors who surround the throne.

As I looked upon Daniel, I realized then that I had betrayed my eavesdropping and that it was dangerous for me to know of my father's business.

-Thou must never let them know that I know of these matters, I pleaded. If thou art my true friend, thou must never reveal to my father or to William that we have spoken of such things.

-My lady, he said, it is I who must ask secrecy and discretion from thee, as I have obtained it from thy father and which he graciously bestows upon me in silent approbation, he said humbly. But I must ask thee not to speak of me to thy father, or to thy husband, for it is dangerous for thee to know that I am acquainted with such men, and the purposes for which we seek knowledge of the affairs of the throne. Should things not come right with these matters, I shall hath more to fear than thou shalt ever know.

I knew that he spoke of his Jewish faith, his misplaced and misguided belief that there was no Saviour, that for him there was no redemption nor hope of heaven, that he still toiled and waited in vain for a false messiah – a hope that was nothing more than a lie. I knew that I should recoil from him, for tho' he was going about my father's business, and the work of preserving the Holy throne, he was not one of us. I told myself that I should leave his shop, that the tiny bell over the door would ring over me in mockery of the True Faith, and yet the warmth in his eyes compelled me to be still.

I felt his glance become one with mine, his eyes as sweet and pure and dark as honey. At that moment the terrible tense breath of doubt left my body, and I felt that he was, indeed, my friend.

After that moment we talked easily. I leaned upon the table before him as he shewed me texts and books of study and I admired and breathed and drank them in as one whose thirst could never be satisfied.

And as the hour wore onwards we spoke of other things, and while I could not bring myself to tell him of the marriage that felt to me like the walls of a prison, I confessed to him my other great sadness: my fear that my sister Cecily could never be restored to me.

It was then he told me the story of his own sister, the only other member of his family who had escaped the tortures of Spain. His mother and father had been taken from their home in the night, never to be seen again.

There was grief in his eyes when he spoke of them; he said someone whispered to him that they had died upon the racks and in the fiery furnaces of the Inquisition, refusing to accept the faith of Christ.

I bristled slightly when he said that; he saw and laid a gentle hand upon mine.

– Do not be distressed, Miss Margaret, he said, by our faith. For it is not an imperfect faith in an imperfect God that causes such destruction; it is the injustice born when faith is used as a weapon to divide nations from one another. And thou shouldst be most distressed by this injustice, rather than concerned about the state of my people's souls, which have survived undimmed by doubt for thousands of years.

I nodded with something that resembled understanding and gestured that he should continue telling me the story of his family. He and his sister, by the grace of God, had been staying in another city in the home of his teacher, and when word reached them that their parents had been murdered, his teacher had fearfully placed them on a boat that was bound for England, hidden beneath the deck by a sailor bribed to take them.

On the journey his sister had taken chill in the damp quarters. She died the day before they reached England. Her body had been given to the sea. There was not even a grave where he could place a stone in her memory.

My heart ached with his loss, and I was more determined than ever to bring peace between Cecily and myself. He told me to find her in a silent moment, one that would not be witnessed by my father or by William, and he told me that in the next weeks there would be moments when they would be concerned with matters more urgent than my marriage.

I blushed when he said that word, and felt the heat of his eyes upon my face. It was then that I gathered up my shawl and my parcels, and told him that I must return home. There was an unbearable sweetness in our parting, for after our silence had been broken, I faced the emptiness of my return to a house in which the monster William lived. But at the last moment before we parted, Daniel had given unto me a parchment to study, with assurances of his continued friendship, and I carried the tiny scroll against my breast like a shield, and felt strengthened by the comfort of his nearness.

When I stole to my chamber that night I unrolled the scroll that he had given to me and to my surprise there lay on the page the words of a poem, written in his fine and precise hand:

Draw me, we will run after thee; the king hath brought me into his chambers; we will be glad and rejoice in thee, we will find thy love more fragrant than wine! sincerely do they love thee.

I am dark, but comely, O ye daughters of Jerusalem, as the tents of Kedar, as the curtains of Solomon.

Look not upon me, that I am swarthy, that the sun hath tanned me; my mother's sons were incensed against me, they made me keeper of the vineyards; but mine own vineyard have I not kept.

Tell me, O thou whom my soul loveth, where thou feedest, where thou makest thy flock to rest at noon; for why should I be as one that veileth herself beside the flocks of thy companions?

If thou know not, O thou fairest among women, go thy way forth by the footsteps of the flock and feed thy kids, beside the shepherds' tents.

Behold, thou art fair, my love; behold, thou art fair; thine eyes are as doves.

Behind thy veil; thy hair is as a flock of goats, that trail down from Gilead.

Thy teeth are like a flock of ewes all shaped alike, which are come up from the washing; whereof all are paired, and none faileth among them.

Thy lips are like a thread of scarlet, and thy mouth is comely; thy temples are like a pomegranate split open behind thy veil.

Thy neck is like the tower of David builded with turrets, whereon there hang a thousand shields, all the armour of the mighty men.

Thy two breasts are like two fawns that are twins of a gazelle, which feed among the lilies.

Until the day ends, and the shadows flee away, I will get me to the mountain of myrrh, and to the hill of frankincense.

Thou art all fair, my love; and there is no spot in thee.

Come with me from Lebanon, my bride, with me from Lebanon; look from the top of Amana, from the top of Senir and Hermon, from the lions' dens, from the mountains of the leopards.

Thou hast ravished my heart, my sister, my bride; thou hast ravished my heart with one of thine eyes, with one bead of thy necklace.

I clasped the unrolled paper to my heart, and felt it beating against the inscribed words. I knew the text – it was the Song of Solomon – but surely this bookseller – this man – this son of Abraham, Isaac and Jacob – this dearest friend — could not have meant the words for me. I rushed to the looking-glass and saw my own pale countenance. But there were no doves in my eyes, no jeweled thread upon my lips, and the same plain scholar's face looked back at me as always.

Hearing the footsteps of my husband approaching, I quickly rolled up the parchment and hid it away, imagining only that Daniel the bookseller had meant this poem as a token of luck for my well-being as a newly wed bride. With my own foolish imaginings safely disposed, I extinguished my candle before William's steps reached my chamber, and prayed that he would not trouble me with his obscene lust and cruelty that night. But he did not enter my chamber, and I soon fell asleep.

In the night, I dreamed of Daniel's eyes, his curling hair entwined in my fingertips, his sweet voice nourishing my hunger for music and words. But when I woke up in the morning, and saw William's head bent next to my father's at their desk, deep in some discussion of law, his sparse blond hair barely covering his scalp, I dismissed my dreams as fanciful, and went to find Cecily in the garden.

I feared at first that she would not listen, for I was loath to explain to my sister how our father had wittingly usurped her beloved, and promised me to him; but after I had confided in the bookseller about the sadness that lay between my sister and myself, I took Daniel's counsel on the matter. For even though I was not able to speak with my father out of William's presence, the bookseller encouraged me to find Cecily among the gardens where she wept in quiet solitude.

Thus, I was finally able to console my sister. I had begged her to turn to me for comfort in her darkest hours of spurned despair, and - thank God for the goodness of her pure and clear heart - she finally understood that we had both been wronged. It was only thus that allowed her to conceive of true honor in those she loved; she spoke of both myself and my father as blameless for her own misfortune.

And so I was able to free my conscience of this unwitting sin; with my beloved sister's forgiveness I could turn my mind towards other thoughts that had begun to occupy me. The time of my bleeding had been and passed, and I was clean; my linen was clean in the mornings, and within me I felt a new stirring. I wondered if the miracle could be happening - if I could have taken with child - if I would now be spared the humiliation of my husband's brutality. I prayed to the Lord that it would be so; that I could do my wifely duty, and perhaps even be relieved of the burden of my mortal life while delivering him of a child.

Such would be the sweetest wish granted, I told myself – to be released from the bonds of this life, where there was no joy for me but that which I could steal, away from my home and hearth, away from the man into whose my hands my soul had been given.

And then I thought of Daniel and wondered if my wish was not a selfish one, for while my friend lived and breathed, and while we couldst share our love for knowledge, couldst there not be hope for me?

17

I decided to take a cab downtown early the next morning; taking the
bulky artifact case home after a late night at work was one thing, but
lugging it through crowded rush hour subways was entirely another. For
the twenty minutes it took to get downtown – a miracle considering the
hour – I luxuriated in the rare treat of a car ride.

After paying the driver, I got out of the cab, shouldered my work
bag, and carefully extricated the case from the back seat. I then walked
into the museum, passed through Security and took the elevator up to
my office.

I took off my coat, put down my bag and the case, and turned on my
computer. A new email from Robert came up almost immediately. It was
timed from 10:36 the night before:

To: Jill Levin <jlevin@mjh.org>
From: Robert Goldstein <RGoldstein@mjh.org>
Date: February 6, 10:36 PM
Subject: Hidden Child Research

Hi, Jill:
I took a look at the database and ran a search using the information you gave me. The closest thing I could find was a record
for a Marnie Berkson, who went by the name of Minna as a child.
Her mother, father, and two brothers died at Belsen. She was the
only survivor of her family, due to the fact that she was hidden by
a Polish family outside of Lodz –

It's not her, I thought, disappointed.

and gave several artifacts to the museum before her death in
2002. Not sure if this is who you are looking for. Another avenue
I can look into is the Hidden Child Foundation which is a branch

of the ADL. They have pretty detailed records of where and how children were hidden during the war. I know some people there who might be able to help, but as for artifact donors, I don't think there's much more I can do to refine the search. Let me know if you have any more information or if you'd like me to contact the HCF for you.
See you tomorrow.

Robert

Before I could reply to Robert, I opened up a new window and started composing an email to Larry. He was traveling again – this time to Berlin, and I hoped he would be able to get to his email within a reasonable amount of time.

To: Larry Grossman <lgrossman@mjh.org>
From: Jill Levin <jlevin@mjh.org>
Date: February 7, 8:39 AM
Subject: Manuscript

Good morning, Larry,
I would like to let Robert take a look at the manuscript that we discussed before you left. I think he could be helpful in terms of figuring out the significance of some of the Hebrew notations; there are a couple more that have surfaced. Let me know if that's OK with you – I know you wanted us to check in with you before we let anyone else know that it exists. Have you heard at all from the Archdiocese? Hope all is well in Berlin. See you soon.
— Jill

I got up from my chair and went to the break room, and returned with a cup of coffee. Then I started getting my notes ready for the meeting, and read a memo about the exhibition de-installation that Aviva had left on my desk. Within a couple of minutes, I heard my e-mail notification alarm go off.

To: Jill Levin
From: Larry Grossman
Date: February 7, 8:53 AM
Subject: Re: Manuscript

JL:
MS OK to show RG but keep under wraps otherwise.
No word from ArchD of NY – yet.
All well in Berlin.
See you Tues.

LG

I grinned. Larry's emails never fail to get right to the point, I thought.
And then I opened up the email from Robert and hit the reply button.

"This," Robert said quietly, "is amazing."

I watched his face as he pored over the pages one by one. The three
of us – Robert, Aviva, and I - stood at the counter in the conservation
area, looking at the manuscript.

With Larry out of the office, Aviva and I had decided that we could
afford to take the hour that we normally used to meet with him about
rotations and schedules, and use it to look at our mystery artifact. And
so, after the staff meeting, and after making sure that the other staff
members were safely occupied with assignments elsewhere in the
museum – mostly in the Core building, away from the offices. Robert
came up to the conservation area, as I asked him in my email earlier that
morning.

I carried the case over to the other side of the room while Aviva
placed a sign on the door that said "In Conference – Do Not Disturb,"
and forwarded our phones upstairs to Mira's desk.

After a few moments of standing at the counter, I could see that

Aviva was getting uncomfortable, so I dragged a chair over and motioned for her to sit. She did, lowering herself carefully into the seat. Neither of us wanted to disturb Robert, and we were intrigued by the rapt expression of concentration on his face.

When we reached the point where Michael and I had left off the night before, I touched his gloved hand with my own and said, "This page is as far as I've gotten."

"I'm surprised," Aviva said. "I figured you'd have finished reading it by now."

"Lots going on at home," I reminded her.

At lunch the day before, I had told her, briefly, about the conversation that had transpired during the visit to my grandmother.

"I understand," she said quietly.

I saw Robert raise a quizzical eyebrow. "Is everything all right with you?" he asked her.

"Fine," Aviva said curtly.

I looked at Robert, and imagined he had some suspicions about Aviva's personal life, based on what he had asked me about the Talmud volumes he had left on her desk.

"So," I asked, indicating the manuscript, partially because I wanted to know what he was thinking, and partially because I wanted to distract him, "What do you think?"

"I can see why Larry was being careful about whom he wanted you to tell about this," he said. "I mean, the Archdiocese is one thing, but actually there are a number of Jewish institutions and archives who would love to get a look at a book like this. There's so little Jewish scholarship in evidence – or evidence of Jewish scholars, for that matter - from England in the Tudor period."

"I'm surprised there's anything at all," I said.

"There's not much," Robert said, "but some interesting information from this period does exist. Some of it may be apocryphal, some not. But Jews were definitely expelled from England during the reign of Edward I in 1290. Some, however, managed to remain. Either they converted, or pretended to convert, or they hid their religious identity and practiced their Jewish customs underground – in some cases, literally underground, in basements, or in secret back rooms. We know they existed, because after the expulsion from Spain and Portugal in 1492, some of the Jews who were living secretly in England provided safe passage and refuge for those who had to flee. And I know for a fact that late in the reign of Henry VIII, there was a revival of Hebraic studies in England. As a result, he endowed a professorship in Hebrew at Cambridge University, which is still in existence today."

"I didn't know that," Aviva said, puzzled. "I thought that Henry was opposed to the Jews being part of English society because he was married to Katherine of Aragon, a strict Catholic in the mold of her parents, Ferdinand and Isabella – two of the greatest enemies the Jews have ever known."

"Well, it's true that Henry was Catholic in his early reign," Robert nodded. "But in his later years, when England was firmly established as a Protestant country, he extended some tolerance – though not a lot – to other faiths. The revival in Hebraic studies, however, was rooted more in the conflict between the Catholic Church and the Church of England – not for the sake of Judaism itself, certainly."

"A few years ago, I read an article in the *Jewish Week* about a collector who unearthed an edition of the Talmud that dated back to the Tudor court," Aviva said. "It was supposed to have been used in evidence for the annulment of his marriage to Katherine."

"Sure," Robert said, "because all of the laws pertaining to marriage and divorce were based on the Talmudic commentaries on Leviticus." I saw a look of recognition come into his eyes, and he looked at Aviva expectantly. "Wait, I think I get it now. Was this why you were looking for Tractate Gittin?"

I looked at her. She swallowed. I knew she didn't want to tell a lie, but I also knew she wouldn't tell him what was going on, and that she would be just fine letting him believe this version of events.

After a moment she answered, avoiding his eyes. "Sort of," she said uncomfortably.

"The Talmudic angle would go along with the direction I was

thinking about," I said quickly, "which would make sense, given that this person Daniel is a bookseller. Even if he was a scholar in secret, he would still have access to the texts through his profession."

"If it was a secret," Robert said, "it might have been more of an open secret than you'd think. There's actually documentation in the archives of several British museums pertaining to the trial of Katherine of Aragon which implies – though not overtly - that Henry VIII had Jewish scholars at court during the years leading up to the dissolution of his first marriage. Daniel could have been one of them."

"I was wondering, because I couldn't imagine that someone like Daniel could have lived openly," I said. "I didn't think that there were any Jews in England at that time."

Aviva smiled. "I could see why you'd think that. But history gets written by the winners. We all know that. The fact is, even though they were unwelcome, and even when they had to live in secret, even when their lives were at risk, Jews lived among Christians all throughout the medieval period, and every period of history before and after. I mean, when you think about it, when the Renaissance finally happened, and the Enlightenment, all of the Jews who were suddenly 'tolerated' didn't come from nowhere, right?"

"Unlike this manuscript," Robert said, "which seems to have appeared out of thin air. You say you don't know where it came from?"

"I've been getting letters," I told him. "From a survivor. Little by little she's been telling me her story. And it has something to do with this book. Yesterday's letter said that she managed to hide her daughter, Minna," Robert nodded, and I acknowledged the recognition in his eyes, "in a convent in Germany. So I was hoping we'd be able to trace the donor that way, which is why I asked you to run that search in the database."

He shook his head. "No such luck. But I can still get in touch with the Hidden Child Foundation if you think it will help."

Aviva looked from him to me. "Listen, if we had that information from the donor – that she had hidden her child – it would be in her record."

"Unless," I said glumly, "her child didn't come back to her. She could have died, or she could have been adopted, or she could have refused to go back with her mother after the war. You know that was the reality for a lot of hidden children."

They both nodded.

"Anyway, the letters, for some reason, seem to be coming thick and fast these days," I told them. "It seems as if I get one every day, or every other day. Hopefully, I'll have more information soon." I pointed to the manuscript. "But she hasn't talked about this in a while. It seems as if she's intent on telling her story. That seems to be the priority."

"Maybe she hasn't been able to tell it to anyone," Aviva suggested, "which could be why we have never heard of Minna."

"But why would she tell it to Jill?" Robert asked. "No disrespect intended, but it seems strange to me that she would direct her story to you."

I smiled. "No offense taken."

"Well, this person has met Jill," Aviva said defensively. "She mentioned in the first letter that Jill told her that she was the granddaughter of survivors. Obviously this person feels a connection to her."

I looked at Aviva, trying to conceal my delight at the sense that she was finally thinking about the manuscript, and its donor, in a legitimate way.

"I just wish I had a way to ask her about this book," I said. "Not that her story isn't important, and of course, it's vital that she tells it, but I'd really like to know that what we're dealing with is the real thing."

Aviva looked at her watch. "The hour's up," she said. "I'll get Mira to transfer the phones back down here."

"Do we have to?" Robert asked. "I'd much rather stay here and keep reading."

"You know better than anyone that we have to get back to work," I told him cheerfully. "So help me get this packed up. And hopefully, we'll get another letter today."

18

"See what a good girlfriend I am?" I said, as I put the artifact case down in the hallway. "I brought it back, just like I said I would." "Thank God," Michael quipped. "There's nothing on TV tonight." "We could always watch *Law and Order* reruns on the DVR," I reminded him. "Maybe we could get a few tips from Briscoe and Green on how to figure out where this manuscript came from."

He grinned and shook his head. "You've already seen them all," he said, as he pulled me roughly into his arms and kissed the top of my head. "I'll be so glad when February is over and I can watch sports on a regular basis again."

"That's the problem with this month, sports nut. Football's over, baseball hasn't started yet, and March Madness is still a couple of weeks away."

"There's always SportsCenter," he reminded me. "And ESPN Classic."

I made a face. "Anything but ESPN Classic."

He laughed as he took my coat from me and hung it on the rack. "Did you find out any more information about the manuscript today?" he asked.

I nodded. "Larry said it was okay for Robert to take a look at it, so I showed it to him and Aviva today. Of course, Robert knew all about Jewish history in Tudor England. I didn't even know that there *was* any Jewish history in Tudor England."

"Neither did I. So what did you find out?"

I grinned at him. "Dinner first," I said. "Then we'll read a little more. And then, I'll fill you in on today's installment."

"Oh, come on," he said, as he followed me into the kitchen. "That's totally playing unfair."

"You're a lawyer," I said playfully. "What do you know about fair?"

What is this force dividing dark from light
Infusing dawn with day and cloud with rain?
For surely this Divine pow'r doth explain
The ancient poet's music of delight.
Alas! My vow hath kept thee from my sight.
My cagèd heart transcribes thy code of pain.
And yet, the verse of thy song's sweet refrain
Hath caused a rose to blossom in the night.
Thy words hath bound my heart with clasp unseen
As tenderly as the encircling vine
Protects both branch and flow'r from savage sun.
How lovingly I prize these tendrils green!
As still I wait for that moment divine —
Thy love prevails; our words shall be as one.

It was nearly eighteen months of marriage before the Lord saw fit to bless me with my most darling child Thomas, named for my dear father. But within days of having borne him, my heart's darling was taken from me, and sent to be with his nurse. We bided under the same roof, but my baby was kept from me, in a locked room to which only William and the nurse had the key. He was brought to me for only a few moments, once a week, at the whim of my husband. I held my baby tenderly for those few precious moments after Mass each Sunday, when my husband consented for me to see our child. It was because – as he said – I was in a state of holy grace following Communion, and thus it was the only time when my child could not be hurt by my presence.

It was said by my husband that any child would be infected by the learning which I had so long cherished, and that his son should have better than a half-mother, as he called me. He said that my father had nurtured only the quizzical, difficult aspects of my temper and had thus killed the mothering instinct within me. I would hold my child until William insisted he be taken away again, and I would descend into sadness so dark and endless that it was like death without death's release.

It was then that my sad-sickness and decline began; bereft of my books and my child, I had nothing to live for. My father was busy with the duties of his public life; I was left in the company of my foul master, and it was not long before, having given birth and having returned to the Church after the forty days that followed, that I longed to see my friend Daniel again, and feared for his safety in the turning tide of the Monarch's terrible sea.

After more than two years in the prison that masqueraded as my marriage, after giving birth to my son, after hours and days and months of cruelly enforced ignorance and drudgery, as commanded by my husband, the hour arrived when I was at last able to steal away, in those tense and terrible days while my father toiled in vain at court and William, ever-present by his side, nodded like a jester at his every plea to the King.

The good Catholic Queen Katherine, that most honorable woman, daughter of the esteemed Isabella of Spain, had been put aside in all but name; the Boleyn girl, Anne, had returned from France as adept at archery as she was at deceit; she had taken the arrows of youth and beauty from her quiver and loosed them towards the heart of the throne of England. Her aim was true; the King was by her side at all times, having forsaken his true-wedded wife, and Anne Boleyn, it was plain for all to see, with her prettiness, power, and sly ambition had taken Henry from his God.

It was strange – I remembered how the young Henry, my father's childhood friend, had played with me long ago, his countenance as bright as the sun, his manner full of delight and cheer, lifting me high in the air and swinging me in his arms when I was merely a child and he was merely the second son of a King.

He had been my father's dearest friend. I remembered how his quiet and shy elder brother Arthur had been a doomed monarch-to-be, newly-wed to Katherine, the flower of Spain, when he died in that sad and sodden wintertide, far away at Ludlow; and how young Henry suddenly took his brother's place as the Prince of Wales, burdened with an ill-fitting crown that he was ill-prepared to wear.

And now that self-same Prince Henry was both our king and as a stranger to us; with the darkest of clouds forming in the sky above his glorious throne. Surely, his inability to produce an heir with his Queen was a sign of God's displeasure with Holy England; and I feared that the king's meddling with nature was sure to induce a storm against our country, and surely, my father would be lost in the tempest to come.

But one bright spring morning, I told the nurse and servants that I was going to town to market for herbs and medicinal plants, so that the physicians could make a posset of herbs for the nurse to give to my baby. I feared that he would have to endure one of the spring illnesses that were invading the wet countryside.

Silently, in the hope that no one would try to stop me, I ran, light-footed, to the town. The road beneath my feet felt deliciously familiar. Blossom perfumed the morning air, and the breeze blew lightly upon my face. I felt safe; that even if William were to find out that I had gone to town, surely even the servants could make him see that I did so only in service to him for the health of our child.

Upon reaching the city I rushed through the streets like a girl;

though the years had burdened my soul and I was certain that the unrelenting hours of sadness now showed in my face. My heart beat faster as I approached the familiar door; I prayed that he would still be there.

The bell sounded familiarly like the voice of an old friend. And, alerted by its sound, all at once he appeared from the rear of the shop as he had on the day we first met. Upon my first glance I was struck at the change in him. His appearance had been altered dramatically – the dark curls were tinged with dusty grey and the sweetness in his honeyed eyes had dimmed.

He looked warily upon my face as if I was a stranger, and then his smile emerged as the sunlight after a storm. He bowed before me, and called me by the name that I had not heard for more than a year.

-Mistress More, I had not thought to see you again.

How my heart ached at hearing my cherished name upon his lips. I bowed to him, a mirror of his own sweet gesture. – You are correct, friend, for it is not Mistress More you see before you.

-You are right to correct me, he said. For you are Mistress Roper. But I cannot help but think of you as your father's daughter.

I nodded, still shocked at the way the months had touched his countenance; time had not been a friend to him. It showed in the stoop of his shoulders, in the wariness of his expression. But his smile was the same, and my heart raced at the familiar music in his voice.

- I am still his daughter though a wife, I replied dutifully.

- I hear also, he said with a warm smile, that you are a mother. And I, too, smiled at the thought of my baby. – Yes, I said, I have a little boy, named for his grandfather.

- His grandfather often speaks of him, Daniel said. He is very proud. And motherhood suits you as sunlight suits summer roses.

I blushed like the very rose of which he spoke. – I see you have learned the courtier's ways, my friend.

He nodded. – When one is bid to dance, he said, one must know the steps.

I smiled at him most ruefully. – Indeed, these are not easy days at court.

He looked around him as if there was someone present to hear, and then he said, - It is better for us to say no more about it.

We were silent, and suddenly it was as if the months that had passed had built a wall of time between us. He spoke first, saying:

- My lady, how did you enjoy the poem I gave you?

I cast my eyes to the floor. – I liked it very much, I said, in a low, trembling voice. I have studied it often these past long months.

- Thou hast? he said, and there was tenderness in his voice. – I had hoped thou wouldst.

- Yes, I said, and to hastily cover my discomposure I added, - It is always good to study the Holy Word.

He looked as if he was making a decision, and then he pulled aside the curtain that separated the back of the shop from the front. – Come with me, he said most urgently. – Come here.

I thought of all of the nights I had read the text - nay, the verses of love - that he had given me. How I had looked upon each holy, and yet unholy word, with hope in my heart and desire beating in my blood at the thought of my friend's eyes, as they had watched me in those last moments before I became William's bride. And as I looked at Daniel, my eyes widened in disbelief; he could not have been asking the thing that I had hoped and dreamed…and knew was a sin against Holy God, against my vows, against my eternal soul.

- I cannot, I said, and in my dismay and confusion I said, – I am a married woman.

Then his cheeks reddened, and he said, - I only ask thee to come with me because there is something I must show thee.

I wanted to die. I had given myself, my desires away; I wished to be dead and buried beneath the floorboards and I could not look at him. But when I met his eye again he was gazing intently at my face. My husband had never looked at me in such a way. To cover my embarrassment I stammered, - Please forgive me.

- There is nothing to forgive except for my own poor way with words. Only, do come with me, he said.

I followed him into the back of the shop. A single candle burned, illuminating the darkness. There was the sweet, sharp smell of ink, and I inhaled deeply of its richness. A large press stood sentry in the corner of the room. In the center was a long table, crowded with papers and parchments and leather and binding cord. But on one side of the table, away from all of the work materials, there lay on a smooth, uncluttered surface, a long sheet of parchment, a scroll wound upon two smooth cylinders of wood. Upon the parchment were symbols I had never seen before. I bent low to examine it, and all at once, I knew what it must be.

- This is the Holy Word, Daniel said. The Word of my people. I have waited so long to show this to thee. This is the text I was studying that night; when thou came in here first and I was so disdainful of thee.

- Yes, I said, with the smile of that precious memory softly curving the corners of my mouth. - I remember.

- I hate to be interrupted at study, he said. - Even by one as important as Thomas More's daughter. Before I met thee, I had hoped to find thee - a woman of grace and learning, a woman unafraid of truth. The more I heard about thee, the more afraid I became. I heard of thy wisdom; I heard of thy wit, thy countenance alight with the bright intellect of a scholar but with the beauty of a princess. And I imagined thee to be arrogant, proud, an unknowable lady, from what I had heard of thee. But now - he said softly - I know thee.

I stood in shock at his words; for no man had ever spoken of me in a way that made me feel as if he knew and understood the depths of my soul, the most secret hopes of my heart.

He beckoned me to draw closer to the scroll. I did not - could not - touch the parchment. I knew it was a text forbidden to me, as a woman, as a believer in the True Saviour. But the Hebrew symbols filled my eyes as if they were the notes to some strange and lovely melody, and I could not look away from them.

I felt Daniel's presence next to me. I could hear his heart beating as though it were my own.

- It is dangerous to have this in the open, I said quietly. - If anyone were to find it I could not bear the thought of what might happen.

- My lady, he said with a smile - Thou must not trouble thyself with imaginings. Nothing shall happen to me.

- Dost thou not treat me as if I were a child! I said. I do know, Daniel, that there are dangers in such things, and I fear for thee. Thou hast said that fear hast been thy closest companion these many years. Dost thou not forget thy parents? Thy sister? The journey of fear from the realm of the Spanish Queen?

He held up a hand to silence me, and I ceased speaking at his gesture, knowing that I had wounded him, and ashamed that my words had been the sources of the sadness that had come into his eyes.

And then I spoke more softly: Daniel, I fear for thy safety. Even if thou art under the protection of the King, he is a king of whims, ruled by his own desires. No one is safe. Not even those dearest to him. And if anything should happen to thee, I - and I suddenly stopped speaking.

- If anything happened to me, he said tenderly, thou wouldst go back to thy husband. As thou wilt today. As thou hast done on that last day we met, all those months ago.

I was silent. - But I would not go willingly, I said, my voice near to a whisper. I did not go willingly then. And I shall not go willingly today.

We looked at one another. I could see the candle-flame reflected in the darkness of his eyes. I was frightened; I knew that my soul was plunged deep into sin; and yet I could not look away from his face any more than he could look away from mine.

His hand reached out for mine; at once it guided my fingertips towards one of the wooden cylinders upon which the parchment scroll was wound. He laid his hand atop mine as he spoke:

-By this holy Word, he whispered softly, I am thine, Margaret. My soul is bound to thee; thou art my beloved.

I felt the smooth wood beneath the skin of my fingers, the heat of his hand above. In the candlelit darkness I felt the presence of his body as he moved towards me; and though I knew the sin that I was inflicting upon my mortal soul, I could not help it. I saw his tenderness, felt the touch of his hand on mine, sensed his other hand as it caressed my shoulder. My body leaned into his; at once we let go of the scroll and our fingers were entwined. He turned my body toward him and lifted my face towards his own. I knew his mouth; my lips opened for his kiss. My kiss was my vow; his was his promise. My soul belonged to him alone.

He unpinned the hood upon my head and laid it aside; his hands felt like flowers in my hair. And yet I could not utter the words that would shatter my marriage to William; Daniel did not force them from me. Instead he guided me towards the room beyond the shop, beyond a heavy curtain through a doorway that led to another, smaller, chamber; he unlaced the laces of my heavy gown without taking his eyes from my face; and all along our kisses burned as one. I who had never known the depth of a caress; had never known a touch that did not come as a bruise; had never known a kiss that did not come with a savage bite; I hardly recognized love in the sweetness of his touch.

As he removed my gown, my laces, my linen; I wanted to feel shame, but did not; instead I felt desire; yet I felt virgin to him – I warmed to the touch of his hands on my skin, on the curves of my breasts and hips.

William had never touched me in such a way, had never looked at me with anything other than disgust, had only used my body as a means to satisfy his own evil desires. But this was different; this was the truth of marriage that had been hidden from me.

Daniel and I lay together, gently, upon the feathered cushions of his narrow bed. My trembling fingers pushed at the buttons of his shirt until they were undone; and we were naked together, as beloved and bride. Only the candlelight bore witness to our love as we moved together in that moment of sacred bliss that was above even the highest and holiest places in our souls.

I became one with him in a way that I was not with any other man; in a way that I had never known nor would ever know with William; beyond wife, beyond daughter to the place where I was simply woman, a soul created in the image of God, a soul that knew finally that divine love that gives light to creation itself; that highest form of love which is God's gift to his most beloved children. Daniel and I created this together; it was ours.

We lay together silently after, our love had calmed and soothed us, and without windows our chamber felt as if we were the only beings in an eternal night.

At once the tiny bell sounded from the other side of the curtain.
– Wait here, he said quietly, hastily buttoning his shirt and lacing his trousers, and fastening his dark velvet cloak around his wrinkled clothes.

I hastened to a dark corner of the back room as he went out into the shop. With trembling fingers I smoothed my hair and took up my linen and laces, even though I had never dressed without the help of my maid. I struggled with the heavy folds of my rich gown as silently as I could. From outside, I could hear the low rumble and hiss of male voices from the other side of the curtain as I pinned my hood back on to my hair, and after some moments I heard the bell again and then Daniel returned to me.

- Thou must depart, he said roughly. Thou must go at once.

I looked at him with a heart full of fear.

- Margaret, he said, and my fear lessened just enough to hear how sweet my name sounded upon his tongue. – I know thou art afraid but I cannot tell thee anything more. Only believe me when I say that thou must return home at once.

He pulled the curtain aside and looked at me in silence for a moment. – I shall be thinking of thee; try not to fear.

I put out a hand to him before I left the room. – And I shall be thinking of thee.

His fingertips touched mine lightly at first, and then our fingers entwined, and then our hands were firmly clasped; as a bride and a bridegroom in the moment of first bliss, so too did we embrace in the only way we could.

I felt myself withdraw from him, and then I turned my back and left. I hastened down the city road, and all around me there were the sounds of terror and fear.

- He has been taken, I heard the voices say; the King has jailed his

206

dearest friend in the Tower. More has been taken.

My heart beat with fear; the fear for my father, the fear of my own sin.

I ran all the way back to our home; and there I found William and my sisters and my brother and stepmother waiting for me.

They cried to see me; clearly they believed I had been made a prisoner as well. When I could get my breath, I listened and wept to hear their terrible story. William spoke of how my father had been taken without warning to the Tower; how Henry's face had been like stone, and how the Boleyn girl had silently assented to my father's imprisonment, even though her own father had been one of my father's dearest friends.

I knew the truth that I did not wish to know: the most horrible of betrayals had befallen my father; he had been betrayed by his friends, by his King – and perhaps even by his God.

I was overcome by grief at the news of my dear father's imprisonment and begged to retire to my chamber. I wanted nothing more than to be alone; to consider what I could do to appeal to the King on my father's behalf; to wonder if perhaps there was something Daniel could do to intercede on my father's behalf. Daniel, I thought, and my face burned with desire, and I knew that I must be alone.

As I left the room, William bid me a cruel smile. – Wife, he asked me slyly, where is the posset for our child?

I looked up from the manuscript and shook my head. "This is very intense."

Michael nodded. "Does any of it fit in with what Robert was able to tell you today?"

"Even more so now than it did this morning," I said. "The fact is that Daniel's existence isn't as much of a surprise as I thought it would be. Apparently Henry VIII had some Jewish scholars at court trying to prove that his marriage was invalid. So the fact that Daniel was Jewish might have been more of an open secret in terms of who knew at court, but given the religious climate in England, it would have to be a secret kept from the common folk, who were eager to please the monarchy by rooting out, and probably killing, unbelievers in their midst."

Michael nodded. "Sure, that makes sense. The courtiers kept silent when it was in the best interests of the court, but he would have had a lot to fear from townspeople, especially in terms of his ability to make a living while still concealing his identity."

"Also, Robert mentioned something about Henry obtaining a version of the Talmud, because he was interested in the laws regarding marriage, particularly as they applied to his marriage to Katherine of Aragon."

"And it sounds, in this, as if he had a Torah as well as a Talmud," Michael said, "So you think we may be on the right track?"

"It's possible," I said. "But I'm still really troubled by the fact that we haven't found a way to authenticate this manuscript." I walked into the living room and sank on to the couch, and Michael sat down next to me. "I keep coming back to that."

"No new letter today?"

"Nothing," I said. "I was really hoping that another one would come today. And I guess I'm a little worried, because she said in her first letter that she was ill. I keep worrying that she's going to be too sick to write, or that she might even die, before we know the whole story."

Michael grimaced. "That's pretty harsh."

"I know. It's a terrible way to have to think about this. But nothing panned out in terms of the research that Robert did. He's going to try to get some information from the Hidden Child Foundation, but we're talking about thousands of records, with no guarantees. We don't even know who we're looking for."

"It's really frustrating," Michael said. "I hope you can find something. But it's more than that, isn't it?" He peered closely at my face. "I can tell there's something bothering you."

I didn't speak for a moment. "I don't know. At first, I wanted it to be real for the museum, so we would have something that no one else had, a story that no one else could tell. But now, I feel like this story is meant to tell me something. Something about her, maybe even something about Margaret. Not just because the manuscript and the letters have come to me, but because whoever she is, she's telling me her story. The fact that we don't have a record of her daughter as a hidden child, and that we can't seem to get a read on who she is tells me that she may not have shared this information before. And for some reason, she's chosen me to hear it."

"I don't want to say this," Michael spoke gently, "but you know, you have to think about what Aviva said in the very beginning. This might be authentic, and it might not. You have to keep all of the possibilities in mind. But she might have 'chosen you,' as you say, because as the granddaughter of someone who went through this experience, you would be the most vulnerable to hearing the story."

I sighed. "You might be right. I just don't want to think that this is something dishonest. I'd be so disappointed to find out Robert, and Aviva and I, and now, you – got taken in."

"I know that." He put his arm around me and drew me close. "But if turns out that we all got taken in, it's no different for us than it is for you. In some way, we get taken in because we allow ourselves to be."

19

The letter arrived the next afternoon. Even before I opened it, I brought it over to Aviva's side of the cubicle. "Another letter," I said, as I showed her the envelope with its uneven type and lack of return address.

"Good," she said. "I was hoping for another one today. I don't know how much longer I can keep up this schedule."

I noticed that she looked even more tired than she had yesterday as she shifted, uncomfortably, in her chair.

"Should we call Robert?" I asked her. "He'll want to know." She looked reluctant. "Has he read the others?"

"Not yet."

"Then let's read it first," she said. "Then we can decide."

"Fair enough," I told her, as I reached for the letter opener on my desk. I glanced at the first page and it looked as if it were simply a continuation of the letter than had come before it.

I wept to know that I had so little time left with Minna, and yet, my heart was at peace knowing that the convent had agreed to take her, since we did not know then what deportation meant – only that it was safer for our children to be sheltered while we went off to face whatever the future would bring.

And then the postman brought us a letter the next day, addressed to my mother, from my cousin Rivka in Warsaw. She wrote mainly in code. She was part of a group called Oyneg Shabbes, an underground society of young people, writers and artists and teachers mostly, who were making a record of life in the ghetto where the Jews were now forced to live. She told me that they thought the end would come soon; there was much sickness in the ghetto, and every day more and more innocent people were being taken away for 'relocation' as they called it.

She wrote to us to say that if we had anything precious, anything we needed to save that was too big to bring with us, that we should bury it in the ground.

She said that she had heard that we should take our jewelry, that if we needed to sell it for money, or trade it for our freedom, we should have it with us. But she said that anything else we treasured should go in the ground, in secret, that we should not trust anyone to keep our possessions for us, and that when it was all over we could always come back for them.

She told us that Oyneg Shabbes was collecting the documents of the ghetto, the memorial books, the holy texts, the schoolbooks, and saving them in milk cans and burying them underground. She told us that they didn't have much time, and from what she had heard, neither did we.

The night before I was to take Minna to the convent, I packed my daughter's things in her little case, and then I tried to sleep. It was still dark outside when I awoke, knowing what I had to do. I watched my Minna sleep for a little while, and then I had to awaken her, to bring her there under the cover of darkness.

We left the house as silently as we could. On the way, Minna was quiet. The only words she uttered were when she picked a little white rose from a bush along the path, and held it out to me with a serious little face, saying, "Ist fur Sie, Mama."

I brought Minna to the door of the convent. The smiling nun opened the door, and with a kind gesture, she quietly slipped me an envelope from within the folds of her sleeve. This, I knew, would be the death certificate. I could not look at it, could not check to see if it was correct, or even if the forgery would pass inspection. I could not look at my child's name on that paper.

The nun had a young, pretty face. I watched as she laid a hand on Minna's head. "Do not worry," she said quietly. "We will care for her. She will be safe here until you come back." Then the nun reached out and took my hand in hers. "May G-d bless you and keep you," she said. "May He guard you and your child and may He guide your steps." My heart softened as I heard the words of her blessing. "May you depart in peace, and may you return in peace."

I bit my tears back as I crouched down to look into my daughter's eyes. I told Minna to be good, that it would only be for a little while, that I loved her very much. I kissed her and let the nun lead her inside. She took the nun's hand so trustingly. Before the door closed, Minna turned back and looked at me with eyes that seemed to know the future. I saw her trying to be brave for me, and then, she waved goodbye.

Oh, my dearest child, my firstborn, with her doll's face, her questioning eyes. I lost her that morning as surely as I lost my Aron.

I stumbled home with her rose clutched in my hand. I went into the house and took the book that my mother had given to me, and I wrapped it an oilcloth that we used to protect the wooden table in our dining room. I placed it in an old metal box that had once held bread. Before I put the lid on, I kissed the rose that Minna had given to me, and laid it between the pages.

And then, as the sun rose hot and bright in the sky, I carried the box out of the house and down the lane, to where the road leveled out into a wheat field at the edge of the woods.

I had brought a shovel with me. As the sun grew brighter and hotter in the sky, I dug a hole in the field of wheat, and as I was digging I suddenly heard the trucks. I heard the trucks, and the German officers, and their voices as they ordered the Jewish prisoners out of the trucks. I heard them as they ordered the prisoners to dig the burial pits, and I heard them as they laughed at the men and women as they stripped naked, waiting to die.

And then I heard the gunshots, and the screams, and the crying of children, and the prayers of old men and the pleas of young mothers, and the only answers to them were more gunshots, until there was nothing but silence. And when it was over, the Nazi soldiers poured lime and acid on the bodies so that they would decompose faster, and then they filled in the pits with dirt. I don't know if anyone was left alive. It would not have mattered if they were.

I stayed in the field, hidden by the stalks of wheat, until I heard the last truck drive away. It was only then that I was able to put down the box in my arms, the box that contained the only thing I had left to give to my daughter, if we both somehow managed to survive. I finished digging the hole, and buried the box within. Then I went back to the house and waited.

And then the next morning came, bringing with it the convoy that would deport us. As I stood with my mother and my sisters, and the soldiers lined us up in rows before loading us on to the trucks that would take us to the cattle cars, which would take us to Dachau, I held fast to the one hope I had – what I had told no one – that I was four months pregnant.

I passed each page to Aviva as I finished reading them, but when I reached the final sentence, I held on to the paper.

She looked up from the second to last page when she was done reading. "Aren't you done with that one yet?" she asked.

"Yeah," I said reluctantly. "But I'm not sure..." my voice trailed off.

"Come on," she said firmly, holding out her hand for the paper. "Whatever it is, believe me, I can handle it."

I reluctantly passed it over to her, and watched her face as she reached the final line. I watched her eyes as she looked at the sentence, and then looked at me.

"I'm sorry," I said. "That was the last thing I wanted you to read. It's a mother's story — having to hide her child, then finding out that she was pregnant."

"It's all right," she said tiredly. "Listen, if nothing else, it puts things into perspective."

I rubbed my eyes. "I've been waiting for this letter. I had been hoping for more information about the manuscript," I said softly. "I said that to Michael last night."

Aviva nodded. "Jill, I don't have a good feeling about this," I said. "Based on everything I've ever read about Dachau, this doesn't end well"

"You're right," I said. "And it's not about the manuscript anymore, is it?"

20

Aviva and I sat for a long time without speaking. She held the last page of the letter in her hand, and the other pages of the letter sat, face-down, on her desk.

Finally she spoke. "Have you found the rose inside the book?"

I shook my head. "Not so far. But I haven't finished reading it yet. I'll look for it tonight, though, when I get home. I hope it hasn't fallen out or anything. Now I'm worried that somehow, during all of the times I've taken the book out and put it back, I might have lost it."

"If you find it," she asked, "will you call me at home tonight and let me know?"

I nodded.

She stood, placing a hand against the small of her back as she stretched. "I'm going home," she said. "If that's okay with you. I've had enough for today."

"Of course. It's almost five-thirty anyway."

"Since when have we ever left at five-thirty?"

"True," I said. "Although I left at five-twenty-five last night."

"Bad girl," she grinned. "Don't stay too late. I really want to know if that flower turns up."

"I do, too," I said. "As sad as this story is turning out to be."

She placed a hand on my shoulder. "Jill," she said gently, "we deal with stories like this one every day. I don't have to tell you that."

"I know," I said. "But somehow this story feels different. It makes me wonder how, for all of these years, I've managed to maintain a distance between myself and the things we hear and see every day."

She considered my words for a moment. "I wonder about that sometimes, too. Sometimes I think I'm a terrible person because I don't get emotionally involved with the artifact donors, that I've helped to create all of these guidelines to make the interview process run smoothly – you know, only ask for the facts, don't engage a survivor or their family in discussions about how they feel about their artifact, don't linger when you say goodbye. But if we got emotionally involved – if we bore the burden of every story, every name, every face, every piece of testimony that we hear – how could we possibly do what we do?"

I nodded. "No, you're right."

She continued. "Remember how bad it was here after the Towers were destroyed? You'd think it was bad enough that we were here, we watched it happen, we saw those buildings explode, heard the impact of the planes, the sound of the engines so low overhead, and then seeing those poor people jumping from the upper floors. Maybe we thought that because of working in a Holocaust museum, we'd never see anything as bad as what we've already encountered in preserving this history.

"But we were wrong. Seeing three thousand people murdered right before our eyes on a beautiful summer morning was as bad as anything I've ever seen in our archives. People don't often realize it, but history protects us. Those black and white photographs of the Holocaust, of what happened in the camps – they're separate, part of the past. We can draw a line between ourselves and what happened then, because it didn't happen to us. What this woman went through, the one who sent us the manuscript – remember, for her, these memories are real. She can see them in color, she can touch their surfaces. We know what that feels like now.

"Remember how, after September 11, when the victims' names and obituaries were being published, we sent out *The New York Times'* *Portraits of Grief* as an email to the entire staff every single day, because we felt it was another way to bear witness to what we had watched that morning? That was a perfect example of not being able to separate ourselves from what had happened. And after I saw the toll that it took on us, on our staff, on how we were able to function as custodians of history, it was never more apparent to me that we need to know how to draw that line."

"I know that," I said. "But the problem is that this manuscript has become personal. There's something about getting these letters, about the sense of responsibility. Knowing, for some reason, that this person wants me to hear her story."

"And that's entirely possible. But you don't know why she chose you. It could be because you shared some of your own family's story; it could be because she had your business card in her wallet. You don't know. But you can't let it completely define your relationship to this artifact, which, for better or for worse, has to remain professional. I know you know this, but sometimes I think you are so committed to your job that you lose sight of the boundaries that make you so good at it."

"Thanks," I mumbled. "And you're right – I've let this get to me, way beyond the normal professional boundaries."

"That's understandable. Because of your family's history – and listen, I could say the very same thing – because of my family's history — we chose this line of work because we wanted to be curators *and* we wanted to bear witness to the Holocaust, which is a good thing, and obviously you've done that with the best of intentions. Bearing witness is one of the most sacred obligations of Jewish life.

"But Jill, what kind of witnesses will we be if we're blind to the rest of the world around us? The whole point of this museum is that there was life before the Holocaust, and life after the Holocaust, and even – when you consider how hard people fought to survive, and to maintain their identity - life *during* the Holocaust. And what it comes down to is the fact that both you and I are here because life went on. So, you can't beat yourself up for maintaining a respectful distance from these stories. You've chosen to hear them, but hearing them also means you have to survive, too."

"Thanks, Aviva." I told her. "You've given me a lot to think about."

She smiled as she reached for her bag. "I'm glad," she said. "Don't forget to call me if you find anything."

"I won't," I said. "See you tomorrow."

After she left I picked up my phone and dialed Michael's cell phone number. I heard the voice mail pick up immediately, which meant that he was probably still in a meeting.

"Hey," I said. "It's Jill. Listen, there's something going on with the manuscript. Something may be hidden in it that we haven't found yet. I'm leaving now, but I don't want to do this without you. I'll have my cell phone on, so leave me a message and let me know when you'll be home, okay? Love you. Bye."

I had the manuscript out when Michael turned his key in the door.

"Hey," he said, "did you get my message?" He put his briefcase down and shut the door behind him.

"Yeah, I did," I told him. "I was on the subway when you called."

"I figured." He took off his coat and came over to kiss me. "How are you doing?" he said, as he tousled my hair. "You sounded stressed in your message."

"Rough day," I said.

"Sounded like it. I see you have everything ready to go." He indicated the manuscript, already laid out on the paper that covered the dining table. "What's going on? You mentioned that something might be hidden in the manuscript?"

"I got another letter today," I told him. "And it's not that I expected it to be a happy story, but what I read today was just...very sad."

I felt Michael's eyes on me. "What did it say?"

I motioned for him to sit with me on the sofa. I told him about the story of how the little girl Minna was taken to the convent to be hidden, how this person had experienced the horror of listening to a mass murder in the woods where she had buried the manuscript in an old metal box, and finally, about she was deported to Dachau knowing that she was pregnant.

"I see," he said sadly, "but you still haven't told me what you think might be hidden in there."

"The letter said that while they were on the way to the convent, Minna picked a white rose and gave it to her mother. Just before she buried the manuscript, she put the flower inside." I looked at him. He touched my hand without saying anything. "It might still be there," I said. "And I didn't want to look for it without you."

Together we walked to the table and put on our gloves. I carefully turned to the page that we had finished reading the night before, and I saw that there were still quite a few more pages left in Margaret's story.

I delicately turned the remaining parchment pages that lay beyond where we had stopped reading. There were only two pages left, when, tucked between them, I spied the brittle stem, the tiny dark leaves and pressed yellowed petals, as fine and fragile as the paper itself.

Michael and I looked at one another wordlessly. I made no attempt to remove it from the book, and neither did he. There didn't seem to be anything to say, so we sat, silently, looking at the small dead flower.

"I have to call Aviva," I said finally. "I told her I'd let her know if we found it."

Michael went into the bedroom and returned with the cordless phone and handed it to me without speaking. I dialed her number.

A man's voice answered. "Hello?"

Surprised, I took the phone from my ear and checked the digital display to make sure that I had dialed the right number.

"Um, hello," I said, putting the receiver back to my ear. "Is Aviva there?"

"Yes, but she can't come to the phone right now."

I recognized Jacob's voice. Aviva hadn't told me that he had returned. I wondered if I had interrupted a fight, or an attempt at reconciliation.

"Okay," I said awkwardly. "Could you give her a message for me?'

"Sure."

"Could you please tell her that Jill from work called? And could you tell her," I chose my words with some care, "that I found what we were looking for?"

"I'll tell her," he said curtly. "Bye."

I heard the click of the phone as he hung up. I hoped he would give her the message, but more than that, I hoped she was all right.

"Jacob was there," I told Michael. "She never told me that he came back."

"Maybe he didn't come back until tonight," he reasoned. "How did he sound?"

"Like he always does. Cold. As if he doesn't want her talking to anyone."

"And you're basing this on the two or three one-minute phone conversations you've had with him," Michael reasoned. "Or the fact that you don't like what he's doing to her?"

"Both," I admitted. "I really don't want her to take him back."

"It's hard to say what she'll do, considering all of the pressure she's under to conform to her community's standards," Michael said.

"But Aviva's not like that," I said. "She's not like some brainless little girl who got married at eighteen and lets her husband take over where her parents left off. Aviva doesn't take any crap from anyone."

"But when it comes to keeping what she has – her home, her life, even, perhaps, her baby," Michael pointed out, "she might be willing to compromise."

"I think she's making a huge mistake, if that's what she's doing."

"Listen, I agree with you, and I've never really talked to the guy. Then again, I suppose that I've never met William Roper, except through Margaret's side of the story," he nodded towards the manuscript, "and I don't like him, either."

"You never know," I said. "He could redeem himself in the last couple of pages."

Michael smiled. "My eternal optimist," he said gently, and we turned back to the page where we had left off.

Regard the apple crush'd beneath the foot
Of Eden's curse. A new hell waits -
A father bows his head to force and fate -
A daughter's slender neck below the boot.
The blossoms have been severed at the root.
I wander'd through that garden of delight
Finding that serpent clothed in garments white -
A father found a son; a daughter mute.
This woman's bridal slippers walked the path
Where learnèd feet have trod. The answers sigh

In futures which shall relive Eden's glory.
O cursèd trap - O autumn aftermath
The vines are twined and tethered as they lie -
In paradise false; thus ends Margaret's story.

It is with sorrow that I relate the final chapter of my dear father's life, for I know nothing of it as it should have been, or indeed the way it was; I know only the evil fate which befell him at the hands of that false king clothed in the robes of Judas.

With my father departed, imprisoned in that Tower which has interred the souls of so many innocents, William had unchallenged rule of the house; of the servants, of my stepmother and sisters, and of me. When he was at home, he barely looked at me; I was nothing to him but a contemptuous woman, and now that he had a son, he no longer sought me out for the satisfaction of his physical desires.

This was not surprising; and I certainly did not miss him when he was away. I welcomed his rise at court, for it meant that he was frequently in the company of that evil and corrupt Monarch, where I hoped against hope that he could in intercede on my father's behalf.

But it did not appear that he would, for he was too engrossed in the rise of his own fortunes to worry about the man who had sheltered him for most of his life. Instead, William ignored my father's case, curried favor with Henry and set about reaping the fortunes of his own traitorous dealings. At court William had fine rooms; he was intimate with the king and courtiers, and it was said that he had a mistress with whom he spent long nights when he did not come home.

I knew that William went daily to the Tower, and there he saw my father and relayed messages from him, but to me it was as if he went merely to taunt my father with the notion of freedom. On the rare occasions when I saw William at home, I would ask if my father had sent any word to me, a smile would play on his lips, and then he would tell me that he had not.

As I awaited word from my father, I, too, inhabited a silent prison. In the looking-glass I no longer saw a scholar; I saw a woman who had been made whole by love, even as the grief of my father's imprisonment stole the joy from my eyes and the hope from my heart. In those terrible months of silent waiting, I observed how the seasons began to unfold within me like so many petals, blooming one by one among the sweetness of the summertime gardens. I knew my own secret, Daniel's secret; for the secret we had made together was growing within me.

When my father's sentence of death was declared, when my father was found guilty of treason, when God turned his face from the man who had served him in love and faith for his whole life, and who had taught his children to faithfully keep the commandments, it was then, and only then, that William granted me one final audience with my father.

I dressed carefully that morning, seeing that the rich and heavy brocade gown I wore hid the burgeoning curves of my body. Finally, William came for me and I was permitted to go to the Tower to see my father. As we made our way through the London streets, to board the boat that would take us to the prison's gate, William's hand firmly clutched my elbow as if I were a sack of gold that he had stolen. My footsteps were heavy, laden with the weight of my silent secret, with the weight of the final goodbye yet to come.

We arrived at the gate beneath the dark portcullis, its spiked fence reaching into the air like the lances of so many soldiers. Guards surrounded us, searched us for illicit books and papers. By some good fortune, because of the Monarch's fear of spies and of collusion, the guard bid me to enter the cell alone, and it was there that I observed the ruin that had been the father I had loved.

That my father had long lost the grace of the foul Monarch I am sadly sure; for no other crime, other than the loss of my father's friendship owing to the Boleyn matter, merited my father's imprisonment as a traitor to the crown. I was loath to discover the cruelty with which my father had been suffering in his last hours. He did not speak when he saw me. He only smiled slightly; yet holy grace was in his eyes. I could see from his wasted condition that he was denied every liberty; his books and papers had been taken from him by the henchmen of the evil Monarch.

In the grace of learning, in the light of wisdom did my father flourish; and when that sun was cast down from the sky by the King's careless hand, so did my father cease to live; as the grass beneath the chill of the first frost is denied breath and light, so was my father without his texts and papers. There is no more cruel a fate than could have befallen him, and it is thus that I see the true death of my father; rather than at the hands of the executioner.

For all of the years I had waited to be alone with my father, so that I could tell him of my own unhappiness, of my own heartbreak - so that I could question his wisdom in choosing such an unsuitable husband for me - at that last, terrible moment, I could not speak. His own despair told me that there would be no answer. I could only sit quietly with him, his hand in mine, with the hope of life and liberty now fled as a bird from the nest.

A fist crashed upon the heavy wooden door, to tell me that my time was ended, that I must do as I was bid. I hastened to my knees to utter a brief prayer, when I felt my father's hand upon my head and I heard his dry lips murmur a final blessing. I stood, and took his hands in mine, as the guard banged his fist on the door again. I watched my father's eyes look into mine for a final time. And then, all at once the door opened and the guard entered, and roughly pushed me out of the cell.

I fled into the hall where William waited, my eyes blind with tears and anger. I told him that I must leave, I must get out, I could not breathe. He peered at me with suspicion in his eyes.

- I must leave this place, William. I beg thee, I said.

- Very well, Wife, he said. But I bid thee go directly home and wait there for me in thy chamber.

- Yes, husband, I said demurely.

I fled the stone-flagged floors and stairways of the tower and out into the courtyard. I had not been in London for so long that it was almost as if I did not know where I was. The streets, however, were suddenly familiar, and I ran through them, careless of the hem of my gown trailing through the muddy streets, and my hair underneath my hood and veil as it was loosed by the wind.

I prayed that my beloved, my friend was still there, safe in his shop. And as I reached the door my hand went forward to open it – then all at once another hand arrested mine. It was a very young manservant in green and white colours of the Monarch's livery.

- How now, Mistress Roper? he said with a sly look. – You have come seeking forbidden texts for thy father?

- Take thy hands from me, I cried. I come seeking nothing but my own purposes.

- Thou art suspect, Madam, the young man said. – Thou hast been followed from the Tower. And having seen thy father, thou must realize that there is no hope for Thomas More; he is a traitor to the crown, the enemy of England.

- Why dost thou suspect me? I cried again. I only hath seen my father once since his imprisonment, this very morning. I have just come from the Tower where my father is a broken man. Even if I were to bring him a forbidden book, as thou hast called it, I said daringly, he wouldst not read it. The loss of his liberty has all but blinded and crippled him; he is none but a shell.

- Thou art suspect, Madam, he said again, because of the letters which he hath sent to thee. Did he think that his letters would not be read and intercepted? He laughed. A trusting man is thy father; he is betrayed by none but his own words.

- His letters? I asked, in a shocked voice. I know of none.

- Come now, Madam, he said teasingly. Do not play with me. He hath sent dozens of letters to thee. And every one of them hath been read by the King.

I stood, stunned. By now the commotion outside his door had alerted my beloved; I heard the tiny silver bell as the door opened, and he emerged from under the lintel.

- Unhand this woman, said Daniel to the King's man.

- I shall not, he replied. I shall bring her home to her husband, where she belongs. She shall have no truck with thee, bookseller. Do not try to profess her innocence for the sake of the silver in her pocket.

I watched Daniel's face flush with anger. - I told thee to unhand her, he said quietly, and I shall not tell thee again.

The King's man said nothing, but instead twisted my arm behind my back. I cried out with pain. And all at once Daniel was upon him, pushing him aside and prying my wrist from his brutal grip.

Freed, I shouted - Daniel, no! as the two men struggled. Then with a decisive fist, Daniel hit the young man, who stumbled and fell to the ground with threads of blood trickling down his face.

I watched in silent horror. Daniel sank to the ground and examined the man, and helped him to his feet. - Young man, go now, return to the castle, he said quietly. I shall see that this woman makes no forbidden purchases. And then she shall go home to her husband.

The young man staggered to his feet and shamefully began his journey back to the palace. When he was out of earshot, Daniel drew me into the sheltered walls at the side of his bookseller's shop, and spoke to me. - If thou art all right, dearest Margaret, then go, Daniel uttered quietly. I will take care of this. Only thou must reach thy home before this story does.

I nodded. - Yes, I said, thou art right. I must go, only -

- He looked at me with tenderness and sympathy. - I know all about thy father, dearest Margaret. I wish I could have made things go more safely for him. But thou must know that I did my very best.

I could not speak for fear that tears would choke the breath from my words.

- Dost thou know of my matters at court? he asked quietly.

I shook my head. - Nay but one conversation I hath overheard, years ago.

- Then I shall tell thee quickly, he said.

- I was known to thy father, first as a bookseller, when I first arrived in England. And then, we grew to trust one another, as one scholar to another. I told him of my past. I was a scholar of Talmud in Spain, pursuing my studies and practicing the rituals of my people in secret, and when this was discovered, as I told you, I was forced to leave. That is when I first came here, to make my living as a seller of texts. Thy father was one of my first and most loyal visitors. Through our talks, I learned of thy father's liberal nature, his fairness, his genuine love and respect for all faiths. Thus I revealed to him that I was versed in the ancient holy texts of the Jews. He was intrigued; he told me that I could be of some assistance to the King.

- I was admitted into the most secret chambers at court. I was known to the bishops and the Cardinal. They were wary of me; they suspected me of my people's alleged cunning. But soon, no doubt because of your father's influence, his knowledge of law and his devotion to your Church, they began to trust me. Soon they revealed their aims to me. It was well known that the King sought to annul his marriage to the Queen. As I have told thee, Katherine of Aragon was no friend to me or to mine; her parents,

Ferdinand and Isabella, sent many of my kin – including my parents - to their deaths on the rack and in the heretics' fire. And they are also responsible for the loss of my sister in the depths of the sea.

-And so the courtiers and advisors – thy father chief among them - asked for my help. They sought to build a case, upon the foundation of Talmudic law, stating that Henry's marriage to Katherine was illegal. And because of this, they wanted to state that the Pope never had standing to grant the dispensation to make their marriage legal; because the law of the Jews had no valid standing or legality among the servants of the Church.

- I was to help them create the statement to the Pope, he said, based upon my knowledge of Talmud, of Torah, of Jewish law. I was to state for them that no law binding upon my People could be applied to a Christian prince.

- And now it has all backfired, he said. It has gone awry and thy father is the man who will pay the price. It was Henry who came to him when all other options were exhausted, Henry who begged him not to resign, not to come out against him. When thy father knew that our case before the Pope would only serve to divide the Church from England, he knew that he could not uphold it. And yet, he thought that by resigning, he would have a better chance of holding influence over the Pope, once it was seen by Rome that he was no longer under the rule of the English throne. But Henry would not understand this. Henry only thought of how it made him look – a weakened sovereign abandoned by his most trusted advisor.

- It was then that the King ordered his arrest; and ever since, thy father has been imprisoned in the Tower and meanwhile, he has tried from his cell to sway the Pope's ruling, using the evidence that we have gathered for him. But the Pope will not be swayed, Daniel said. Thy father did not know it would inflame the Pope's wrath to be told he had authorized - and solemnized - what Henry refers to as a Jewish marriage.

- I do not believe that there is Jewish marriage any more than there is Christian marriage, Daniel said. I only believe that there is love and there is hate. There was love, once, between Henry and his Katherine. And there is the hate that he now feels for her, the same hate that I feel for her mother and father, the same hate that drove me to serve the King.

- But now I know that there is love as well. I know that the King loved thy father, once. For I have loved thy father as well; he is an honorable man who shall die for a noble purpose. It is my only wish that he had been as nobly served by others as he himself served the Monarch. But there is a love beyond that, the love that will survive thy father's death, the love that will survive though we may never see one another again. There is the love that I have for you, my dearest Margaret, and that is the only love I will ever know, ever feel, ever remember.

I felt the tears upon my face. - My beloved, I said, thou hast served my father well, I said, to console him, for I could not bear the misery and grief in his eyes.

- I wouldst hath done so for his own sake, Daniel told me. - But I hath done so for thy sake as well, for the sake of thy beauty, thy wit, thy soul - even for the sake of thy God.

I bent my head to hide my tears. I could not speak.

- And for the sake of thy God, dearest Margaret, and the God of thy father, I shall pray for him. It is all that we can do for him now.

- There is more, I said. For our love need not die with him. I can only pray that I will care for our child with the same love thou hast show to me and mine.

At once I saw the joy in his eyes. For a moment he could not speak. Our eyes met and held; we shared in the moment of our creation.

- Are you well cared for? he asked. – Doth William know?

I shook my head. – He cannot know, I said, for he would know at once that the child was not his.

Daniel nodded, understanding in his eyes. – I will do what I can to protect thee, he said. With what little influence I may have left, I will try to keep thee safe. And I will pray for thee, and for our child, my beloved.

- And I shall pray for thee as well, I said.

There was a clattering of steps near the door as the King's soldiers made their way through the streets, and at once I turned my back and hurried back towards the dock where the boatmen waited to bring me back home. I heard the tiny echo of the bell as Daniel went back into the shop, and the terrible sound of the door as it closed behind him.

There was another handwritten note under Margaret's words, in Spanish:

No me impulse dejarle, o dar vuelta detrás y no seguirle. Para dondequiera que usted vaya, iré; dondequiera que usted se aloje, me alojaré; su gente será mi gente, y su dios mi dios.

"We should just get a Spanish dictionary and be done with it," Michael said, as he took off his gloves to rub his eyes.

"Wait a second, though – '*y su dios mi dios*' – that's easy – 'and your God my God.' That's from the Book of Ruth."

"I don't know that one." He put his gloves back on. "Is it in the bible?"

I nodded. "In the Hebrew bible, it's part of the *Ketuvim* – the writings. There are three sections total – the five books of the Torah, the books of the Prophets, and the last section, which is what this is from. You've probably heard some of the Book of Ruth – in fact, I suspect this is it, here, in Spanish. 'Entreat me not to leave you, or to not follow after you, for wherever you go, I will go, wherever you lodge, I will lodge; your people shall be my people, and your God my God.'"

"Oh, sure, I've heard that."

"What's interesting, though," I said. "is that it's very commonly read as a conversion text. Ruth was a Moabite woman married to the son of a Judean woman, Naomi."

"Does 'Judean' mean that she was Jewish?" Michael asked.

"Well, insofar as they had Jews back then," I chuckled. "At any rate, Naomi and her family certainly would have been considered Children of Israel."

"Interfaith marriage, back then?" Michael grinned. "Ooh, scandalous. Better not tell your grandmother, she'd be so disappointed."

"I'm ignoring that remark," I said sarcastically. I really didn't want to get into a discussion of our own problems.

"Anyway," I continued, "Ruth and her sister-in-law Orpah were married to Naomi's sons, after they had come to Moab to escape famine in Judea. After Naomi's husband and her sons died, she decided to return home. Orpah stayed in Moab, and went home to her own people, but Ruth decided to go to Judea with Naomi, even though Naomi told her not to come. That's where this quotation comes from – which is Ruth's response to Naomi – that Ruth would remain loyal to her, because they were bonded by their grief. Ruth did not want her to be alone, even if it meant giving up her own home and her own faith."

"That's very powerful," Michael said, "especially when you think about it in this context. I wonder if it means that Daniel was willing to convert."

"Or," I ventured, "I wonder if it means that they were willing to see beyond one another's beliefs, that in the end it didn't matter how they interpreted God. They were also bonded by grief – the loss of Margaret's father, the loss of his parents and sister. Maybe they felt they had already suffered enough."

"They had to live with reality, though," Michael pointed out. "No matter that she was pregnant, obviously, or why he was at the court – and it sounds as if we were on the right track – or what they felt about one another, the political climate was too much for them to set their faith aside and be together. And besides, she was married. And in spite of whatever innovations in marital law that Daniel – or Henry – or the Pope, for that matter, was responsible for bringing about, there was no possibility for Margaret to get out of her marriage."

"You're right," I said quietly. I looked thoughtfully at the manuscript. "I guess I just wish it could have been different, that she could have walked away from her marriage and been happy, with her books and her writing and their child." I took off my gloves. "She was independent enough to have managed on her own. She didn't have to be ruled by some outmoded system of religious beliefs. She was too smart for this, too intelligent to be trapped into an eternity with someone who treated her so badly."

"You're thinking of Aviva," Michael said gently.

"Yes," I admitted. "I am. I can't stop worrying about her. I worry that she'll go back to Jacob, and that he and her family and her rabbi will somehow blame her for everything that's going on with him."

"Do you think that will happen?"

"Sure I do. The only authority she has to go on is religious authority. I don't see her as being able to overcome that. And I'm afraid that they'll convince her to leave her job, and that somehow she'll start believing that she's a bad wife for not wanting to stay home and have more kids while he runs around on her. And as smart and feisty as she is, there's just so much pressure on her."

"You have to hope for the best. I know it's a bad situation, but she'll do what's right for her and the baby. Besides, it's not like this for her." He pointed to the text.

"I'm not so sure about that," I sighed. "In a way, it is."

21

The fact that our office was unlocked the next morning when I arrived meant that Aviva was already at her desk. I dropped my bag on the floor next to my chair and peered around the cubicle wall.

"Hey," I said. "How's it going?"

She turned in her chair to face me. Her eyes were tired, and her normally rosy complexion was pale, with even darker shadows under her eyes. "I'm so sorry, Jill," she said. "I just couldn't bring myself to tell anyone."

I walked around the wall and took a seat in the guest chair. "Tell anyone what?"

"That I took him back."

I shook my head. "That's your business, Aviva. You shouldn't have to feel like you owe anyone an explanation."

"I know," she said, "but I told you what was going on. I guess I was just scared of your reaction. I know you're probably disappointed, that you think I should have stood up for myself." Her voice sounded angry. "But that's not what it's about. This is about my family, my baby. I have to do what's right for them." She sounded like she was reciting words from a script.

"Aviva," I said, "I trust you. You know how to make tough decisions. I've seen you make difficult decisions every day, and you've never let anyone down. What I think isn't important. I know you would do anything for your baby, you'd learn to live with anything if it meant you were doing what you thought best."

She looked at me. I could see the suspicion in her eyes. "Come off it, Jill," she said angrily. "You know you don't mean that. Don't give me platitudes about doing what's best for my baby when you think I should leave him."

"Hey, listen," I said, finally getting annoyed. "Don't get all over me just because you're upset about what's going on. Take him back, kick him out, whatever – just be true to yourself, and what you want – or pretend that you're doing what you want; it doesn't really matter – you're the one who has to live with the consequences. And if you can live with them, that's fine. But you're the one who's saying that you have to do what's right for your family. If you don't really feel that way, I can understand that - but don't take it out on me."

She looked at me, miserable. "I'm sorry," she said. "You're right. I shouldn't be taking this out on you. Last night was," she stopped speaking for a moment, "very difficult."

"I can't even imagine. I'm so sorry that I called and interrupted you."

"Don't feel bad. I asked you to call. I didn't think he'd be back so soon. I figured it would be another day or two."

"Well, with the baby coming any day now," I said, "I can understand that he'd want to be back before it happens."

She nodded. "That's what the rabbi said he should do."

"At least he listens to someone," I said.

"It's ironic. He thinks I should be listening to the rabbi as well. And the rabbi says I would be a better wife if I didn't spend my days here, with people who aren't religious. In fact, Jacob gave me a very hard time about you calling me last night. He thinks all of my 'secular' friends, as he calls them, are urging me to ask him for a divorce."

"What about his secular friend?" I asked, sarcasm in my voice.

"The rabbi spoke with him about her, too," she replied. "Somehow he managed to convince Jacob that no matter how he may feel about her, leaving your nine-months-pregnant wife is a really bad thing. Scared him with hellfire and brimstone, probably."

"I thought we didn't believe in hellfire and brimstone."

"Well, there's the whole concept of sin and atonement, which can be pretty effective. Especially coming from Jacob's rabbi. The guy is like ninety years old, long white beard. Pretty much what you'd imagine God to look like. Even his eyebrows are judgmental."

"Go figure," I said.

"Anyway, the rabbi convinced him to come home, and then he told both of us that we needed to give this another try. But I don't know," she said. "I don't know what I want to do."

I looked at her tired face, and softened my tone. "Aviva, you'll get through this. Get through having the baby, and then decide what you want to do."

"Just like a Jewish Scarlett O'Hara," she said. "'I'll think about it tomorrow.'"

"'Because after all,'" I finished, "'tomorrow is another day.'"

She chuckled a little. "Anyway, I did get the message last night. He told me that you found what we were looking for."

"We did," I said. "The rose was there. Very old, very fragile. I didn't even try to take it out of the book. I was afraid that it would disintegrate."

"Better to wait until you bring it back here. We can take it out with tweezers, get it into a case, make sure we have someplace climate controlled to store it."

"Good idea," I said. I glanced up at the clock. "It's getting late. We'd better get ready for the meeting."

She sighed. "One thing I have to tell you," she said. "I didn't make it easy for Jacob when he came back, in spite of the rabbi's entreaties to me to create an atmosphere of *shalom bayit* – peace in the home. My husband's raging affair is no match for my raging anger – or raging hormones, for that matter."

I laughed. "I don't know how you can joke about this."

"You know how it is," Aviva said, as we gathered our notes and headed for the conference room. "If you didn't know how to laugh, you'd do nothing but cry."

It was another long day at work.

Around noon, Robert, Aviva and I received an email from Larry in Berlin. Although he was scheduled to be back within the next few days, he wanted to let us know as soon as possible that some of the new exhibition's artifacts would be arriving ahead of schedule. But the worse news was the exhibition's original curator, who hailed from one of our counterpart museums in Europe, had informed Larry that we needed to change the schedule, so everything would be moving up by a week.

Thus, the team was scrambling to make sure we had the new installation plans ready to go when Larry got back. This meant making sure we had our bids done for outside vendors and consultants, and that the painters and fabricators were booked for new dates and times. We also had to make sure our vaults were ready to receive the artifacts that would be coming to us on loan from other institutions.

All of this, with the added pressure of a new schedule, meant that Aviva, Robert and I had no time to discuss the manuscript any further. I managed to find a minute during the day to check my mailbox for another letter, but nothing had arrived. Around three thirty, I called Michael to let him know I would be home even later than usual. A few minutes later, I heard Aviva's voice from behind the wall of the cubicle, arguing in hushed tones with Jacob about when she'd be leaving.

We assembled the team late in the afternoon, after we confirmed new dates with the painters and fabricators. Together, we started to build the models and lay the blueprints and sample labels out in the conference room, so that everything would be ready for the presentation when Larry returned. The assistant registrars were working frantically, making sure that the artifacts from our own collection were already catalogued and slated for positioning in the new exhibition. This would enable us to clear the decks for the new items arriving from Europe over the course of the next couple of weeks.

Aviva left, exhausted, at six. The two exhibition assistants, Fern and Sandy, and Robert and I ordered in pizza and kept on working until nine thirty. Finally, having decided that we could do no more until the next morning, we put on our coats, walked across Battery Place to the Ritz-Carlton, hailed a couple of cabs, and headed home.

Because of traffic on the West Side – we hit the West Forties right around the same time the Knicks game was letting out of the Garden - I didn't get home until after ten. I trudged up the stairs to our apartment and unlocked the door.

"Where's my dinner?" I shouted as I walked in.

Michael called out from the bedroom. "You going Roper on me?"

I laughed. "What's going on? How was your day?"

"Shitty," he said, walking into the hall. "Rough day today. More budget cuts coming down. We had to let four people go."

"I'm so sorry. That can't have been fun."

"It wasn't."

He looked upset, as he stood in the hallway wearing a dark blue t-shirt and jeans. I took off my coat and hung it up. Then I walked over to him and put my arms around him, and he lowered his face into my hair. We held each other for a moment or two longer than we usually did.

"I know people usually expect the not-for-profit world to be a kinder, gentler place. But it's not."

"No, it isn't," he agreed. "Not where the bottom line is concerned."

"What happens now?"

"You know, the usual. Everyone takes on more work. The development staff gets reshuffled. New strategic planning process takes place. Hopefully, they raise more money next fiscal year. Same old song and dance. Life goes on."

"Sounds familiar," I said. "Like every other non-profit I know."

He followed me into the kitchen and watched as I opened the fridge and rummaged around, looking for a snack that I could eat this late that wouldn't give me total indigestion.

"Did you have dinner?" I asked him.

"Yeah, I brought home pizza," he said. "There's a couple of slices in there for you."

"Already had pizza," I said. "We ordered in."

He grinned. "Great minds think alike."

"This'll work," I said, as I took a container of cherry-vanilla yogurt from the shelf and closed the refrigerator door. Then I pulled a drawer open and took out a spoon.

I walked into the living room and settled myself on the couch, taking a pillow from the middle of the cushions and wedging it under my arm.

239

"How was your day?" he said, sitting down next to me.

"Crap-tastic," I answered cheerfully, stirring my yogurt. "Started out getting attacked by Aviva and ended with an unfinished presentation."

He looked puzzled. "What's up with Aviva?"

"Pretty much what I imagined. Worst case scenario."

"She took him back?"

I nodded. "And he's blaming her job for their problems. I overheard them fighting today about what time she'd be home from work."

"Maybe he's got a point," Michael said. "She's about to have a baby. And it seems to me as if we've just seen so much bad husband stuff going on in the manuscript that you're expecting life to imitate art."

"Ah," I smiled, "but you forget, that manuscript is supposedly non-fiction. So I'd say it was more like life imitating life."

"Maybe so," he said. "By the way, your grandmother left a message earlier."

"She did?" I said. "Perhaps détente is going into effect, then."

"Maybe," he said cautiously. "Should I play it for you?"

"Sure."

He walked over to the machine and pressed the button. "Hello, Jill," the familiar voice said. "I'm sure you're very busy, but please call me when you have a moment. I don't want to bother you at work." There was a pause. "And whoever you are, Jill's boyfriend, if you're listening to this message – well, hello to you, too."

I wondered exactly what she meant as the message clicked off. "It's too late to call her back," I said.

"Hey," Michael said, "at least she acknowledged that I exist."

"I wouldn't think it's necessarily a good thing. It's just another thing for her to complain about, another item for the guilt trip. I mean, just listen to her. 'I don't want to bother you at work. I know you're busy.'"

"Maybe she really doesn't want to bother you at work. Listen, sometimes *I* don't want to bother you at work."

"I know," I said. "but I'm still angry at her."

"Listen, there's no point in you being angry." Michael said. "She's the way she is, she's probably not going to change. That much we know.

But the fact that she even acknowledged that we're together, you have to think of it as a step in the right direction. Besides, we both had bad days at work, we're both affected by this thing with your grandmother. But you might want to think about things differently – maybe she's coming around."

"Please, Michael. I don't need a lecture tonight." I spooned the last of the yogurt out of the container. "I just want to watch TV and go to bed."

"What about the manuscript?" he asked.

"What about it?"

"We don't have too much further to go," Michael said. "I know you're tired, but I was wondering if you wanted to finish it tonight."

His voice sounded hopeful. And he was right. I was exhausted. I was worried about Aviva, worried about work, and all I really felt like doing was going to bed, reading for five minutes, and falling asleep.

But Michael had such a bad day, I thought. And it wasn't his fault I got home so late. Besides, I thought, I couldn't keep the manuscript at home forever. It was time for me to bring it back to the museum. I looked at him and tried to smile. I didn't have the heart to tell him no.

We prepared the apartment carefully. It was almost as if we knew it was the last night, the last time that we would have the manuscript in our possession. We laid the paper over the table, and put on our gloves in silence. Then Michael unlocked the case, opened it, and removed the manuscript from the packing materials.

He laid the book on the table before me as tenderly as if he were placing a sleeping infant into a crib. I adjusted my glasses, pushing them up on to the bridge of my nose with my fingertip. Then I opened the book, gingerly touching the thick brown binding, softly turning each delicate parchment page.

When we got to the pages where we had left off, it appeared as if the texture of the paper changed once again. The words looked as if they had been scrawled in haste, the black ink flying like a flock of startled birds across the paper. I looked at the pages in some surprise.

"It's different," I said to Michael. "It's Margaret's handwriting, but it doesn't look like a diary entry. It looks like a letter."

My dearest Daniel ~
I hath sent this to thee to be delivered by my sister, Cecily. I know that I cannot come to see thee myself, ever again.

When I arrived at home after seeing thee, William took me roughly by the arm and dragged me as a punished dog to my chamber. He closed the door behind us and in a sudden fury, struck me across the face. I fell to the floor with a cry.

- I hath long suspected thee of treachery, he shouted. Thou art a sinful woman, a disobedient wife.

I pulled myself up from the floor, and all at once the door opened. It was my sister Cecily, her face glowing with fury like an angel. She hurried into the room, and helped me up and onto a stool, and then with her handkerchief dabbed the blood from the cut at the corner of my eye, where William's fist had struck me. Then she crossed the floor to where William stood. - Thou hath done enough, she said in a voice low with menace. Now leave.

- Thou shalt not come between husband and wife, William growled at her. This is not a matter for thy interference.

- If thou strikest my sister again, Cecily said, and if thou doth not leave us in peace, I shall reveal thy doings to whoever shall listen. I shall bring shame and loathing upon thee, William Roper. For I will relate thy penchant for false seduction; I will tell of how thou hast ruined me, how thou hath tempted me with wine and false promises, and how unbeknownst to me, and against my judgment, thou hath taken my maidenhood from me. I have no shame any longer; I seek only thy destruction, and I shall bring it about.

His face paled like a child confronted by an angry mother. And then, in a moment, he recovered his composure. – Then all of the world shall know thee as a ruined slut, he said tauntingly.

– They shall not, she rejoined. – For I shall name thee to the King and his authorities as the man that hath raped me.

He paled again, this time looking defeated. – I shall leave thee alone now, he said. But think carefully of the shame thou shalt bring upon thy house if thou wouldst bring shame on me. The charge of rape shall stick to thee as well, Cecily, for no man would have thee if he knew. Thou mayest tell of my doings, he said, but thou wouldst also destroy the house of More; thy father's name would rot in the gutter along with thine, he said, with a treacherous smile.

–And as for thee, Wife, he said with a sneer. I know of thy doings as well. I know that thou hast consorted with the Jew, and only God Himself will see fit to bring thy punishment upon thee. Already I see the signs of the curse that holds thee in its grip, he said, pointing to my pale skin and fatigued eyes, now bruised and bloody with the signs of William's brutality.

–But they friend the Jew is not long for this world, William said. –The King suspects him of treachery, of helping thy father undermine the throne by supplying him with the texts for his treasonous study.

– My father has no texts, I shouted at William. It is all a falsehood, concocted by thee in order to gain my father's worldly goods and his power among righteous men.

-Thy father hath no power, William laughed bitterly. – He hath been blinded by his love of God, like thy friend the Jew. And now thy father will die of his folly, William said, and thy friend as well.

I felt my face lose its composure, and Cecily's hand gripped mine. – Get out, she said bravely. Leave this chamber at once.

He turned to leave. But before he did, he fired one last malicious phrase at us both. – I thank God for making me not a woman, said he, for thou art worthless creatures, good only for carrying the seed of men. Would that God hath been clever enough to find a way to people the world without thee.

He slammed the door shut behind him, and Cecily and I cradled each another in our arms for a few moments.

In the light of the tower window my sister did regard me, and said unto me - -Thou art ill, Margaret, and it is long since the grace of humour has lighted thy countenance. Thou art not the sister that I know, for where I once knew wit and gentleness, there is sadness within thee and a dulled tongue.

I replied, - Alas, little one, that thou hast been spared this fate; where once thou knew envy, I only know despair. Marriage hath brought nothing to me but a long and merciful wait for Death. My dearest Cecily, gentle sister, I would not have had thee suffer this fate, for thou must know that it is my husband who denies me all pleasures, and hath replaced wit with bitterness, and gentleness with rage.

-But I shall reveal a truth to thee, my dearest sister, and that is that I hath found love, even though the priest may say that this love is a sin of the gravest kind; and that yes, I may even be condemned to the fires of hell for it. William, for once, is not lying; I hath consorted with my friend, and he is a Jew.

-But I am sure of one thing only, Cecily, and that is should I be forced to endure an eternity of hell for having loved my friend, my beloved, my dearest one, and if the demons should rage against me for giving birth to his child, then I shall endure it. For my soul belongs to him, our souls belong to one another, and God Himself is the One who hath united them in this holy bond.

Cecily gasped as I revealed the swelling curve of my belly beneath the heavy folds of my gown.

- O my sister, she said frantically, thou must conceal this from William. He will kill thee shouldst he come to know of this.

- I know, I said, but William is busy at court; he will not come back before the hour of my deliverance is at hand.

-But what if he doth, she cried.

-He hath not returned to me out of desire since the birth of our son, I said. -And now it is said that he stayeth at court in the company of his mistress. I am no fool. Should he come back to his rooms here, he will not see me.

-You cannot be sure of that, Cecily wept. -For with this new transgression he may wish to control thee even more. What if he doth imprison you as he hath imprisoned our father? And a woman who hath borne a child out of wedlock couldst be punished unto her death for such a sin.

-I smiled serenely at my sister's fair countenance. -Would that it were so! For I am not strong, and when my hour of deliverance is near, then I shall pray for God to take me from this earthly place, and God shall find a way for Daniel to care for our child.

Cecily seemed loath to speak and her silence best became her. She looked around my stone chamber, perhaps for the first time understanding all of my cloistered years of silence, and she said unto me, - Margaret, it is long since I have held thee in my confidence, for it is long since I hath cast my sin of envy upon thee. Not only because of thy marriage but also because our dearest father held thee in his highest regard; he confided in thee his love of learning; he made a marriage in thy name but was arrested before he could get me and our other sisters to husbands. It was for many years that I believed, it is Margaret who is our father's heart's dearest, and Cecily only the pale shadow reflecting her light. But it is only now, dear sister, that I see the ghostly years of anguish, that I see the prison of thy pain; and that is why I hath come to you today, with these –

Then, from within the sleeve of her gown, she brought forth the letters which my father wrote to me in his last hours.

And she thrust forth the parchments written in my father's familiar hand. It had been so long since any of his words had come to me, that I leapt upon them, reading and weeping and again weeping, that his words had come to me so late upon his death. Cecily said nothing for a moment; she did not embrace me in my wretched sorrow, nor did she explain the words of our father's hand.

She said, after a silence – Thou must read them, dear Margaret, for these words were meant for thee. William had received these missives in thy name, and bid me to conceal them from thee.

– I thought perhaps that he might seek to destroy them, she said, and so I hath told him that I would hide them, that I would not tell thee of their existence. But when he said that after our father's death, these letters may bring us wealth – I knew that William truly was the serpent you described, and I knew that the time had come to show these letters to thee.

And it is thus with wretchedness and anger that I knew William kept my father's words from me.

It is with such sadness and loathing that I longed to say to my imprisoned father: I too, know of the loss of liberty and the loss of learning; how God's grace beckons from that noble place of the mind, where learning is mingled with duty and so bestowed in the service of the Lord, and how that grace is denied me; how I am kept apart from my work; how I must record these hours in secret, away from the traitorous eyes of my lord and husband. O father, I too hath known brutality at the hands of a traitor!

The letters made ample mention of the grace in which he died, but he was filled with sadness at the parting of our family, and bid me to bide the time usefully before we should meet again in Heaven. I read the missives in which he wished me grace and the protection of the Lord to guard my footsteps always, and for the blessings of God to befall me, and my dearest child Thomas, and any future child. He closed his last letter by saying that he did not wish for me to give birth to a daughter unless she was brought forth into the world with her mother's grace of learning; for such a girl he would prefer to all the glory of Heaven.

It was then I wept without solace, for unbeknownst to my father, because I knew in my heart that such a girl was about be born, and indeed, the mother of that child had been denied all grace and learning.

But without thy love, my Daniel, it is my wish indeed that God would spare me any future births, for I could not bear to be without thee; our parting will most certainly end my life.

When my tears ceased, my sister looked at me with tenderness and pity.

-I shall do what I can, Cecily said, to protect you and your child. Even if it means putting myself in William's way.

I reached a hand out to her. – The birth is but ten weeks away, I told her. But I cannot let you cast your own soul into sin for me.

-My soul hath already been ruined, she said sadly. I can only hope to find love, as thou hast, and weather the fires of hell should it ever come to me as it has come to thee. But thou hast given me hope, Margaret, that love can still be born out of the depths of the most broken soul. And when your hour is come, I will bring the child to your beloved.

I embraced her then, and for ten long weeks, she was true to her word, mortally endangering the holy purity of her soul by giving herself over to William's evil desires.

And then the night came when I cried out with the pains of birth, and she came to me and held my hand, held the roped sheet that I pulled upon as I waited for our child.

And then she was born, our daughter, in the quiet dawn of the morning. William was at court, he had not been home for weeks, after becoming exhausted and contemptuous of my sister. Together Cecily and I held the child and washed her and cared for her, and made ready for her to be brought to thee.

And so my hour hath come, my beloved, my friend, and I am not strong. I have given life to our girl, our daughter, my love, and Cecily hath vowed to deliver her unto thee with this letter.

I bid thee to name her according to the laws of thy People, for she shall be with you and yours; she must not be a stranger among them. Thou must name her with a name that will give meaning to her life, and will establish her as our sweetest hope, as the girl who will renew our love as she grows, in God's grace, into womanhood.

It is now, Daniel, that I bid thee to flee. Thou art in danger. William hath said thou art to follow the fate of my father, and I believe it to be so. Thou must wander again, this time with our daughter to console thee. I bid thee, Daniel, go.

Thou it doth grieve me to imagine a world without thee, I know also that I shall never be permitted to venture beyond these walls again. I know the time of sickness is upon me and soon, I shall join my father and knoweth God's grace in the World to Come.

I bid thee, Daniel, to flee with our daughter. I bid thee to teach her the teachings of my father, of your father, of our faith and of our God, and the love that we hath created together. I bid thee to seek me in the next world when, in the words of the poet of thy People, the voice of the turtledove shall be heard in our midst, and the time of singing will be at hand. And in his words, I bid thee to set me as a seal upon thy arm, and as a seal upon thy heart, for love is strong as death.

Into thy keeping and thy protection I give to thee not only our child, but all of these papers, the secrets of my heart, the true and unbidden story of my marriage and my love for thee. I would like to think someday, in safety, thou shalt bind them in a book, and hide them in some secret place, so they may be preserved through our daughter and the daughters that will come after her, and perhaps, at some day, they will tell the truth about me, how I was once a woman of wit, grace and learning, but I was imprisoned by a husband moved only by cruelty and jealousy, who hath used the name of my noble father only for his hateful gain. And though love was late in coming to me, though delight was almost a stranger to my soul, I hath found thee, my beloved, my friend.

Now may I haply go to God and my dear father. I beg thee to commit my words to some noble place, away from the eyes of those who would traduce my name, as my body shall soon be committed to the ground and my soul sanctified unto the Lord.

Daniel, though I hath bid thee to flee, be thy soul at peace. For peace is mine. I am content that through thee, these words will flourish in some uncharted future, like the eternity of nature ever anew; my words shall go with thee to a safe harbor; and they shall rest in the minds of the worthy, safe at shore.

I bid thee depart with our child in safety and love; by the grace of God and Holy Word, I am ever thine own –

Margaret

I leaned back in my chair and sighed deeply. Michael turned over the final page and saw nothing more. Then he closed the book.

"I wonder when she died," Michael said. "You went online for biographical information about her, right?"

"She died about ten years after her father," I said, almost automatically. "That was a long time to be sick, a long time to live after Daniel left."

"Did she ever have any more children?"

I shook my head wordlessly.

Michael sighed. "It doesn't say what happened to Daniel."

"I guess that he got out," I said. "That Cecily got this last letter – and hopefully, their baby to him, and he did as Margaret asked. He created this book."

"But there's still a missing piece," Michael said. "We don't know where it came from. We don't know where Daniel went. We don't know what happened to their child. We don't even know her name."

"Well, I assume that he went to Germany. I know from the last letter that the book was buried there during the war, and somehow it was recovered. But beyond that – in terms of how it got to Germany in the first place, is still a mystery."

"Are you bringing it back to work tomorrow?" Michael asked.

I nodded. "Yes. It's time. Besides, I want to put this in the same room with the letters, look at them all at one time, hoping that somehow, we'll be able to obtain some sort of answer. Or at least, we can speculate." I sighed again. "But we're no closer to authentication than we were a couple of weeks ago."

"No, we're not," he agreed. "But as long as the letters keep coming, you might get some more information."

"That's true." I put a hand on his shoulder. "Come on," I said. "Let's pack this up and get some sleep. We've both had tough days." Michael placed the book back into the case. We tucked the packing materials – the excelsior, the bubble wrap, the soft, acid-free material that we used for wrapping – all around it, as if we were preparing it for a long journey. Then we closed the case and locked it. We rolled up the paper and I watched as Michael opened the door of the hall closet and put in inside. I was about to tell him that there was no need for us to keep it, but I could tell that he didn't want to throw it away. And somehow, neither did I.

He moved the case over to where my work bag lay by the door, and then he shut off the lights in the living room. We went into the bedroom and got ready to go to sleep. In the darkness of the room I waited for him, and when he finally came to bed I watched as the dim light streamed in from the window, illuminating the shadows of his body, and listened to the muted city sounds from outside.

He got into our bed and we reached for one another. I felt the familiar touch of his skin underneath my fingertips, the warmth of his caress on my naked thigh, the softness of his lips upon my mouth.

Afterwards, I lay in his arms and watched his eyelids slowly flutter closed as he fell asleep, and pressed my cheek against his chest so that I could hear his heartbeat. I watched his chest as it rose and fell with each breath.

22

I arrived at work the next morning, lugging the case into the building. Aviva wasn't in yet. The morning meeting had been postponed to the afternoon in an effort to finish up the presentation we had begun assembling the night before.

I locked the manuscript in the vault even before I had my coat off. Then I put my belongings by my desk and went down the hallway to the conference room. It didn't look as if anyone was around yet.

As I passed my mailbox I peered inside. There were two letters there. One had a pink post-it affixed to the front. I lifted it from the envelope and read it:

Jill: Can you please come talk to me about this later? Ariel will find you an appointment. See you then. –SS

I extracted the letter from its heavy cream-colored envelope emblazoned with the gold and burgundy seal and began to read:

Dear Dr. Schiffman:
Since we have received no word from you, nor your staff, regarding the authentication of the Margaret Roper diary, on behalf of His Eminence I must regretfully inform you that we intend to pursue other avenues of viewing the document and determining whether or not it is 1) an authentic representation of Margaret Roper's works and 2) if indeed it should remain the property of your institution.

At the request of the St. Thomas More Vatican College, the archive of our Venerable Most Holy Martyr Saint Thomas More, we are pursuing legal action to take appropriate steps to determine the rightful possession of these documents, which we must assume were once under the rightful ownership of the Holy Church prior to the archive's existence.

We seek to restore these documents to Church ownership without delay.

Our lawyers will be in contact with you within ten business days to determine a time for deposition regarding the authentication process.

In the interim, should you wish to surrender these documents to the Archdiocese, we will gladly cease this action.

Yours very truly, in the Name of Christ our Lord —-
Monsignor James Francis Tully, O.S.F

Oh, dear God, I thought, as I leaned heavily against the wall. I couldn't even think about losing the manuscript, about it being locked away in some dusty archive and never seen again. I couldn't think about Margaret's story being condemned to silence for as long as the Church pleased. I hoped that the other letter would be the answer to the prayer I felt in my heart.

I looked at its face, lettered with the same familiar lettering, no return address. I slit the envelope open with my thumbnail and pulled out a bulky packet of brittle pages. Smoothing them out with my hand, I leaned against the wall and began to read.

```
Miss Jill Levin
Senior Curator
Museum of Jewish Heritage
36 Battery Place
New York, NY 10004
```

```
Dear Miss Levin:
I hope that the last few letters have reached
you, for I realize that I keep needing to look
up the address of your museum. I cannot remember
certain things anymore. Indeed, because my
memories of the Shoah are so powerful, they do
not leave room for much else.

I wrote last to you of how I buried the book at
```

the edge of town, how I left my daughter Minna in the care of the convent, and how I was then deported to Dachau with my mother and sisters.

When we arrived at Dachau, I heard the cries of the mothers as they were taken off the trains, and the children's screams as they were separated from their mothers. Not even the sound of the trains arriving in the depot could block out the sound of all those crying children. The fear was louder than the puffing smoke, louder than the clacking wheels. And then, as we were led away from the depot, we could hear, in the distance, the cracking of gunshots coming from the forest. With every bullet we shuddered and wondered which of our people had died.

They told us that we were the lucky ones. The children, the old people, our mothers and great-aunts, our grandmothers and grandfathers, were not allowed to leave the trains. Their journeys continued on to Auschwitz. My mother was among them. We found out later that they were stripped of their belongings, and, almost immediately, sent to the gas chamber. We, the strong ones, the young women, were to remain at Dachau, where we would spend the next three years, dying slowly.

I was assigned to a work detail with my sisters. Our job was to dig pits in the forest near the camp. They told us that we were digging bomb pits for the soldiers, but we knew otherwise. I had heard otherwise with my own ears, that day in the forest.

But now we were sent to do the work for those who were not strong enough to dig their own graves. Almost every morning, as we walked along the forest path, we tripped over bodies, bones and blood that had been strewn, skulls exploded by bullets. These were the ones who had tried to run. The others lay in the freshly dug craters, sometimes five or six bodies deep.

We worked for seventeen, eighteen hours a day, with almost no food, no sleep. I grew thin, so thin that nothing of my baby showed on my body. Yet I was scared. I knew that if the soldiers found out I was pregnant, I would be killed. Sometimes I wished they would find out, so that I could simply die.

I do not know what it is in me that wanted to live. Some people call this the spirit; or say that it is God's voice, telling us to live. I don't know what to name it. I only know that I wanted it to be silent.

One day I returned to the camp after working from before sunrise. A woman had given birth earlier that day. She was chained to a metal pole in the center of the camp. Just out of reach, lying in a wooden crate, was her baby. One of the women whispered to me that she was being forced to watch her baby die. The soldiers wanted to see how long it would take. They were starving it to death, and taking bets among themselves on how long it would take for it to die. The mother was screaming and screaming. All night we listened to her cries, the pitiful sound keeping us awake. Just before sunrise, we heard the sound of bootsteps going out to her. The screaming stopped, and there was silence. And then, one final, terrible cry. And then — nothing.

The next morning, we saw that the mother had been stabbed over and over again with a bayonet. Her body, still chained to the pole, was slumped to the ground, her threadbare uniform dress soaked in blood. The baby had been stabbed too. You could hardly tell that it had been a human being.

This is what I witnessed. I cannot tell you the thoughts that were going through my head. I dare not tell you the thoughts I had for my own baby, for what our fate would be.

There was not time, as we have now, to wonder about G-d's whereabouts. That is the pretty question that people ask us now, the pretty poem they want the survivors to recite. Where was G-d during the Shoah? But I try not to trouble myself with that question now, since I did not allow myself to think about it then.

But perhaps G-d protected those who were murdered first, because, even though they were lost, perhaps they were spared because their suffering was brief. I do not doubt that G-d breathed life into my soul – I do not doubt that there was even a G-d of Dachau, a G-d of Auschwitz, for even in the midst of death there were people who cared for one another, there was trust, there was hope, and to me, that is G-d.

Because I am not convinced that G-d is life. There are times when the will to live is a curse and not a blessing, and survival is nothing more than a burden - a mere heart and lungs and brain devoid of humanity, functioning only because it is their habit to do so.

Soon I grew too numb to worry about hope, about pain or fear. The world was death, the world was dead. One of my sisters disappeared. Later, we heard that a train took her and some of the others to Sobibor, where they were murdered in the gas chamber. I was sure Aron was dead. I feared in my heart that I had listened to his murder that day in the wheat field, but to stop those sounds in my memory I had convinced myself that he had been gassed long ago, his body burned, or tossed like garbage into one of the mass graves in some faraway place. I prayed that my Minna would not be lost to me, but I also feared that my prayers would be answered for I wondered, after experiencing the hell that was called Dachau, if I really wanted my daughter to live in a world that had permitted this place to exist.

If the Nazis did not discover Minna, and the countless other Jewish children hidden away in the convent, then they would be safe. And when the war was over, I would be able to return to her. Yet I did not know if we could live our lives in peace and freedom. And I feared that Minna would learn to forget any life that existed

before she was hidden behind the walls that
concealed her from a world that did not want her
to live.

I knew that Minna would be all I had left, because
my baby, my new baby, could never be brought into
this world. I had made a plan to spare my baby
from the suffering I had witnessed, a plan so
that I could stay alive to find Minna if I could
ever manage to live long enough.

Early one morning, I began to feel birth pains.
I worked as silently as I could that day, digging
new graves out of the barren ground. That night,
I quietly slipped out of my wooden bunk and
awakened my sister, the one who remained with
me. We went out to the latrines. My sister stayed
with me through that night, muffling my screams,
stroking my hair, my face, easing me with her
soft words, singing quietly to me in the warm,
liquid music of our own language.

After a number of hours, outside, in the cold,
on the frozen ground, amid the piles of human
waste, my child came into the world.

I saw my daughter for only a moment. The cord
linking us was still attached. Her eyes were a
dark, milky blue, the color of the sky just
before dawn. I was not convinced that she could
see out of those eyes; I did not want her to see
me, I did not want her to see the hell into which
she had been born. I wanted to protect her from
her own life.

She was so weak that she could not even cry. My sister cut the cord, and then took my baby from me. I lay on my back, looking up at the sky. My entire body was beyond pain. From behind the haze of the ache inside my eyes, the sky looked crimson, the stars were the color of new blood. My sister wrapped the baby in the remnants of a uniform she had taken from someone's corpse, and then she placed a scrap of an old blanket over her mouth and nose. She crooned softly to the baby in that last moment. It took a very short time for her to die.

In my heart, I named her Chava Lila, the Hebrew word for life, and the Hebrew word for night. I named her for the dark blue color of her eyes, for the night in which she arrived, and for the moment just before morning, in which I gave her back to G-d.

My sister took the body away. I do not know where she buried her. I never found out, for a few days later, my sister, too, disappeared. She was gone before morning. The soldiers found her burned body, still smoldering, upon the ground by the electrified fence. Her mouth was open as if she was silently screaming. She had killed herself.

Some months later, I – we – the ones who were left – did not hear the sound of soldier's voices one morning. We listened, fearful, as the sound of tanks rolled into the camp. Then vehicle after vehicle followed the tanks. The guards and soldiers were nowhere to be found.

From inside the tanks and Jeeps emerged American soldiers. Some of them threw up when they saw us. Some of them took photographs as if they did not believe we were human beings, as if we were some terrible new species they had discovered. They photographed the barracks, the bodies in the ditches, our wasted bodies and faces.

Within the next few hours we were given substantial food – it was the first time in years we had seen anything but the thin gruel and the small slice of bread we were given once or twice a day – if we were fed at all. My stomach contracted with spasms the first time I tried to eat. But one of the American soldiers helped me hold the fresh white bread in my shaking hands, helped me to take slow bites of a potato so that I would not be sick.

After about a month, after the paperwork was done, after they had asked me my name and who my parents were, and I had answered in halting breaths, this same soldier helped me into a Jeep, along with three other women from my town, and took us home.

He went with me along the road to the convent; I was not strong enough to walk there on my own. My heart rejoiced at the thought of seeing my child, my Minna. But as we approached the convent, I saw that it had been burned to the ground. Another woman who had hidden her child there knelt down amidst the ruins and embraced one of the stones, weeping as she cradled it in her arms. I stood watching her. I could not cry.

Another woman told me someone had talked. Someone had told the authorities there were Jewish children being hidden. They were all arrested. The Jewish children had been shot and killed that day, their bodies taken away for burial – no one knew where. The priest, the nuns, and even the little Christian children had been taken away on the last train to leave our town. No one ever returned.

The marble statues of their saints and angels, once so majestic and haughty and cold, were shattered amidst the stone ruins. Nothing remained of anything. I had with me only Minna's forged death certificate, and the small piece of cloth in which Chava Lila had breathed her first and last. All that remained of me were those two things. I was left alone, bereft, clutching at these remnants of death, for they were all I had to prove that once, long ago, my children and I had been alive.

And I knew that somewhere, in a distant field, was the book. The book my mother had given me, the book I had promised to pass on to my daughter. I knew my Minna was gone. I knew I never wanted to see the book again. I knew it would remind me of the life that had gone before, the life that had been murdered.

But I knew that someday, somehow, I would need to find the strength to return to that place, to find the book so that somehow, I could take these remnants with me into whatever life awaited.

I did not know what to do. I did not know whom I could trust. I knew I was not strong enough to find it on my own, I knew that I could not go back to the place where I had first heard what death sounded like, to that field where I thought I could hear the sound of my Aron's voice, my beloved, as he cried out his final prayer to a G-d who was blind and deaf.

Even though I knew I could never forget, even though I knew that I knew I had survived hell, I also knew only death could take these images and memories away from me. But I was not ready to die. I knew that I did not want to die. But I did not yet know that I wanted to live.

"Jill?"

I looked up to see Aviva, standing in the hallway, still wearing her coat and holding her work bag.

"No," I said without thinking, putting the pages behind my book. "There is no way I am letting you see this letter. I don't care what you say."

"Jill, it's not that."

I looked closely at her. She was pale, and her eyes looked fearful.

"What is it?"

"It's the baby," she said. "My water just broke."

23

Aviva and I stared at one another. Her eyes held a mixture of surprise and fear, and I was sure that mine did as well. "Did you feel this happening on your way here?" I asked her.

"Not until I got to the office," she said. "I had some light contractions last night, but this water thing," she looked at her long skirt in dismay, "just happened."

"But if you felt contractions, why didn't you go right to the hospital?" I asked her. "Why did you come to the office?"

"Because," she said simply, "I knew I wouldn't be alone here." Then her face contorted with pain as a new contraction hit. And then, almost as quickly as it had come, it passed. "That felt like the first real one," she said, breathing deeply.

All right, I thought. Now is not the time to panic. "Okay, let's get you sitting down," I said to Aviva, as I put my arm around her, took her bag from her shoulder, and guided her to the conference room, where the elements of the team's presentation lay in various stages of construction. "I'll call the ambulance."

"I don't know if I need to go to the hospital yet," she said, her eyes far away.

"Don't be an idiot," I said. "I'm calling now."

"My cell doesn't work in here."

"Neither does mine."

At that moment, Robert walked into the conference room with a sheaf of papers for the presentation. "Robert," I said quickly, "Aviva's in labor. Do me a favor and stay with her while I call 911."

"Of course," he said, putting the papers on the table and quickly coming to sit by Aviva, who looked at me in some dismay.

"Leave the door open," she said, ever modest, as I went to close it before running down the hall to the closest phone.

"For heaven's sake, Aviva," I said impatiently, "do you really want the whole department in here staring at you?"

"Maybe you're right," she conceded.

"Besides," Robert interjected, "I mean, I know we shouldn't be alone together, but really," he grinned, "this merits special circumstances."

Aviva laughed, and her laugh suddenly turned into a cry of pain. She gripped the sides of her belly tensely, doubling over slightly.

"I'll be right back," I assured her.

I ran down the hall and called 911. I told the operator we had a woman in labor, gave the address, and received her assurance that they'd be on their way immediately. Then I called Security to let them know that Aviva was in labor in the conference room, and that the ambulance was on the way, and to please clear the area where the school groups were waiting to get through the metal detectors.

I hurried back to the conference room to find Aviva sitting in one of the straight-backed conference chairs, trying to breathe through a contraction, with Robert crouched on the floor beside her, singing softly in Hebrew.

"They're on their way," I told them. "What's the timing?"

"About ten minutes from the last one," Robert said.

"What does that mean?" I asked.

"I have no idea," he said resignedly. Then he began singing the strange melody again, in a voice that sounded as if he were singing a lullaby.

"Ya`ankha Adonay beyom'tsara yesag'gebh'cha shem 'elohai ya`akobh,
yishlach-`ez-rekha mi-kodhesh umitzion yis`adecha.
Yizkor kol-minchotekha ve`olath'kha yedhash eneh selah.
Yitten-lekha khil'bhab'hecha vekhol-`atsat'cha ye'allai'."

The Lord answer you in the day of trouble! The name of the God of Jacob protect you!
May he send you help from the sanctuary, and give you support from Zion.

May he remember all your offerings, and regard with favor your burnt sacrifices.

May he grant you your heart's desire, and fulfill all your plans.

I looked at Aviva. She was breathing deeply and calmly, and seemed more at peace than she had all morning. I watched as she carefully took her arms out of her coat sleeves. "It's so hot in here," she said, as Robert continued to sing in Hebrew.

I picked up the papers that Robert had dropped on the table and started to fan her with them. "What's Robert singing?" I asked quietly.

"Psalm 20," she said. "When a woman is in labor, it's traditional for her to hear it twelve times before her baby arrives."

"I hope you have time for twelve renditions," I said anxiously. "Let's hope this baby isn't in a hurry."

"That would be a first for the museum," she giggled. "But don't worry. It's a short psalm."

Robert smiled at us as he sang. I continued to fan Aviva. "Why don't you take that off?" I said, indicating her *sheitl*.

"Are you kidding me?" She glanced at Robert.

"Why not?" I asked. "It's bound to come off in this process anyway."

She leaned towards me and spoke in a low voice. "I know what you're saying, but I —" Then her face suddenly paled again. I could tell there was another contraction starting.

"Where the hell is the ambulance?" I said, checking my watch. "Does Jacob know where to meet you?"

"I'm not sure. He knows that my doctor is at Downtown Hospital, though. That's where they need to bring me," she mumbled, grimacing.

"You called him, right?"

She shook her head. Then she motioned for me to come closer to her. I bent low so that she could whisper in my ear. "He didn't come home last night."

"Do you want me to call him?" I asked, bewildered. I had assumed she had called him from her cell phone as soon as her water broke.

She nodded, breathing in and out rapidly. Robert moved a little closer to her and sang loud enough for her to hear the words over the sounds of her breathing.

I left the conference room and went back to my desk. Aviva had given me Jacob's office and cell phone numbers months ago, just in case something happened at work – or if she happened to go into labor while she was in the office.

I dialed his number at work, and his voice mail picked up immediately. "Jacob," I said, "this is Jill Levin, Aviva's friend from the museum. She's in labor. The ambulance is on the way, and they'll be taking her to Downtown Hospital. So she wanted me to let you know," I said, a little awkwardly. "I'll try your cell in a minute. Okay. Bye."

I pressed the button to disconnect the phone, and then called his cell phone and got the same result – voice mail. I left the same message for him and then went back to the conference room. As I passed the elevator, I could hear it coming up from the ground floor, and I fervently hoped it was the EMTs.

I couldn't hear anything from behind the closed door. I slowly opened it and saw Aviva sitting in the same chair, but now Robert was directly across from her. He held both of her hands tightly in his own, as he continued to sing to her.

After the last repetition of the psalm, Robert leaned over and murmured some words that I could not hear, and I watched as she nodded, her eyes still closed. He loosened their entwined fingers and reached for the box of tissues, and then he handed one to her. She wiped the sweat from her face, and then clenched the tissue in her hand as she tried to muffle another groan of pain. He then leaned towards her again, and placing his fingertips gently on her forehead, he tenderly removed her wig. She tensed at first, and then exhaled deeply as her blonde hair tumbled down over her shoulders in a torrent of curls.

She then opened her eyes and looked up at me. "Did you find him?"

I shook my head. "I left messages on his voice mail at work and his cell phone."

She nodded. And then, with her face filled with pain, she leaned against Robert's shoulder and began to cry.

We watched wordlessly as the ambulance, lights flashing and siren blaring, pulled away from the curb. I waited until it reached the end of Battery Place, shivering in my thin sweater, and then I turned to head back inside. Robert held the door for me as we walked back into the building.

"I feel like this day is already shot to hell," I said. "And it's only ten o'clock."

"I know what you mean." He smiled tiredly. "I feel like I've already put in a full day."

"You have," I told him, touching his shoulder. "It was good of you to stay with her. You made her more comfortable than I ever could have."

"You mean singing the psalm?" he asked. "I'm just glad I could do that for her. I get the sense that things aren't so great with her husband."

I didn't say anything while we waited for the elevator. The doors opened, and I pressed the button for the 3rd floor. As soon as the doors closed, and we were alone, I spoke.

"No, they're not. And that's really all I can tell you. But I hope that you won't talk about it with other people on the staff. I don't want anyone else to know. She doesn't deserve to have the staff gossiping about her, and heaven knows she's got enough going on right now. I'm only acknowledging this at all because, well, it was obvious from what happened this morning. But I'd appreciate it if you'd keep it to yourself."

"Of course," he said firmly. "I would have, anyway."

I softened a little. "Thanks," I said. "And I know Aviva would thank you, too, if she were here."

"I just hope he'll call us to let us know what happens."

"I hope so, too. And I hope he'll call us after the baby is born," I said, "but I don't know if she'll even remember to tell him."

The doors opened and we walked out of the elevator and down the hall to my office. "Listen," I said, "I know we're supposed to be working on this presentation, but I really don't want to be away from the phone right now."

"Doesn't your cell phone work in the conference room?"

"Nope," I said. "No windows."

"Right." He nodded. "So what should we do?"

"I was thinking we could look at the manuscript again while we're waiting to hear about the baby. Besides, I've been thinking that I'd like for you to take a look at some of the other notations. I finished reading it last night at home," I said, "so I brought it back in this morning."

He looked delighted. "Is it in the vault?"

I nodded. "Do you want to get it out? We can meet in the conservation area in five minutes – I just want to send a quick email to Larry to let him know that Aviva went into labor. Oh, and I have to call Ariel and figure out a time to meet with Dr. Schiffman. Seriously, you'd never believe the letter I got this morning. I'll tell you about it when I come back downstairs."

"That sounds good," Robert grinned. "And hey, I guess I've been truly promoted now that Aviva is officially out on maternity leave."

"That's right," I replied with a smile. "Welcome to the team, kiddo."

I found Robert paging through the manuscript when I got back from my desk, having left a message for Dr. Schiffman with Ariel. I also sent an email to Larry, letting him know Aviva was now officially on maternity leave.

While Robert read, I filled him in on the meeting with the two priests from the Archdiocese and the letter that had come to Dr. Schiffman. I also noticed, from the speed of Robert's gloved fingertip along the pages that he was a quick reader, going through the pages at a much faster pace than Michael and I ever had.

"I'm impressed," I said, as I stood behind him looking down at the manuscript. "It took me a while to muddle through some of the Renaissance language."

"I guess I'm just used to old books," he said modestly. "There's a lot of idiomatic language throughout the Hebrew texts that I studied in grad school."

"Idiomatic," I repeated. "Good SAT word."

He chuckled. "I'm full of good SAT words. But listen, I'm very interested in the condition of this manuscript." He closed the book and ran a gloved hand gently over the cover. "Did it come in any sort of storage case, something we could look at for secondary age characteristics?"

"Unfortunately, no," I said. "I thought about that too. One of the letters said that she had buried it in an old metal box during the war. She had a cousin who was part of *Oyneg Shabbes* in the Warsaw Ghetto."

"Emanuel Ringelblum's group," he said. "The ones who buried the ghetto's historical documents in milk cans."

"Exactly," I said. "That's how she got the idea to bury the manuscript."

"That's actually a sign in our favor," I heard a deep, quiet voice behind us say. We turned to see Dr. Schiffman walking towards us. "Not a lot of people know about *Oyneg Shabbes*. Although there was the exhibition at the Washington, DC museum a couple of years back. Still, it's fairly obscure information outside of the Holocaust museum community."

"Dr. Schiffman," I greeted him. "I just left a message for you."

"I got it," he smiled. "And I heard about Aviva. So I figured that I'd come down and check in with you, see how things are going. I hear that you've both had quite a morning," he added sympathetically, nodding at Robert.

"We're okay," Robert said. "Just concerned about Aviva."

"Of course," he replied. "But I'm sure she'll be fine. In the meantime, Jill, I imagine you've read the letter from the good Monsignor?"

I nodded. "What do you think we should do?"

"Well, I don't think we should turn it over to them, that's for sure," Dr. Schiffman said. "Not without a very good reason. I don't take kindly to being threatened with legal action, as if they can bully us into handing it over. There's a better way to talk about things. Anyway, is this it?" he asked, looking down at the counter where we had left the book open.

"Yes," I told him. "This is it."

Dr. Schiffman looked down at the pages, bent down to examine the lettering and the yellowed parchment page more closely. "It certainly looks authentic," he said.

"I finished reading it last night," I volunteered. "If it's real, it's pretty much the Church's worst nightmare. If the authorship is true, this is the diary of Margaret More – the daughter of Saint Thomas More. And it details an extramarital love affair with a very unlikely person – a *converso* from Spain who fled the Inquisition. As a result of the affair, she gave birth to a daughter. But as it turns out, this *converso* was actually a Talmud scholar consulting on the annulment of Henry VIII's marriage to Katherine of Aragon."

Dr. Schiffman's eyes widened. "That's certainly an amazing story," he said. "No wonder they're resorting to such extreme actions. I could understand why they'd want to bury something like this. But it also sounds like there is a legitimate Jewish connection," he continued. "I'm just not sure that it's strong enough for us to maintain that it belongs in a museum that only deals with late nineteenth and twentieth century Jewish history."

"What about the donor?" Robert said. "From what Jill has told me, this came to her from a Holocaust survivor."

"That may be true, but without actual provenance we can't determine how strong or authentic the connection really is. Jill, is there any way to track this person down? I mean, it's easy enough to send this out to the right lab, and someone who would handle it with the care it needs. It would be worth the expense, certainly, if it does turn out to be authentic." He indicated the parchment. "They can determine the age of the paper easily enough. But keeping it here, keeping it safe, that's another story."

"If the Archdiocese can prove that it was stolen from their archives, then we have a problem," I said. "But I think you're right, I think the best thing to do is try to figure out whom this belonged to, and if they really are a survivor."

Dr. Schiffman looked at his watch. "I need to get back upstairs," he said, "but if there's anything I can do, just let me know. I know this is going to take a lot of research, probably looking up most of the old donor records. Maybe you can at least narrow it down by names of who is still alive. I know you have the Berlin presentation to deal with, but we need to get this resolved and it can't wait for Larry."

"Thanks, Dr. Schiffman," I said. "We'll start working on it."

"If you need extra help, send me an email, that's probably the best way to get to me. But hopefully there's something we can do to prove this belongs here."

I smiled. "I know. I just hope it doesn't come down to lawyers."

"Me neither," he said. "But we need to move quickly. The clock is ticking." He walked towards the door. "And call me if you hear anything about Aviva."

Robert and I watched Dr. Schiffman leave. "So it's serious," Robert said. "We could really be in danger of losing this."

"Yeah," I replied. "And I can't bear to think about it. After reading this story, I feel really attached to Margaret and Daniel. And I think they deserve better than to be locked away in some Vatican archive."

"A lot of people would disagree with you," Robert pointed out. "On both sides of the argument. Intermarriage isn't only an issue for Jews, you know. This would create a scandal for the Catholics who want to preserve the image of their saint, and for the Jews who would be angry about the relationship between a great Jewish scholar – potentially a great Jewish scholar who influenced the outcome of one of the most controversial eras of English history – and a Christian woman. There are a lot of people who would probably rather see this go away."

"You're right," I said, "but that doesn't mean it should be locked away just because some people won't like the message."

After a moment, Robert closed the cover of the manuscript, turned it over and gingerly opened the manuscript's back cover. "You know, if this were a Hebrew book, it would read from this direction. This would be its front cover." He looked down at the hand-painted endpaper, with its gold and green swirls and flourishes. "Very pretty," he said, touching the paper, "but very water damaged." He pointed to the where the paper had started to come away from the edges of the binding.

Then he peered more closely at it. "Wait a second." He ran his fingertips over the paper. "This looks as if it's been torn away from the edge. And there's some sort of irregularity underneath the endpaper." He took a magnifying glass and looked at the edge of the book. "Is it in the binding?"

"No," he said. "I think there's something in here."

He took a tiny pair of tweezers from one of the drawers underneath the counter and with a firm gloved hand, lightly drew the torn piece of the endpaper back from the inside cover. As the paper started to come away, we saw a folded piece of parchment tucked inside the space between the endpaper and the binding.

We looked at one another in surprise. "Get another set of tweezers," Robert said, "and we'll see if we can get it out."

I took a second set of tweezers from the drawer. As Robert held up the endpaper, I slowly, delicately, pulled the parchment from the binding. I placed it on the counter and carefully unfolded it, fearing that it would tear if I handled it too roughly. As I unfolded it, we realized there were actually two thin pages of parchment folded together.

Robert replaced the torn end of the paper and closed the book. Together, we looked at the first piece of parchment, with its elaborate, unfaded lettering.

"This looks like Hebrew," I said. "Can you read it?"

"I think so," he said. "But it's not Hebrew. It's Aramaic. Hebrew was only used for holy books in the medieval period. But Hebrew and Aramaic look quite a bit alike. Let me see if I can translate."

He read aloud from the parchment. 'This is the last will and testament of Daniél Solomon de Guedalia, Rabbi of the Rema Synagogue.'"

"Does it say where this congregation was?" I asked.

"Yes, it does," Robert replied. "Right here," he pointed to some letters which I could barely decipher. "Krakow, Poland."

I stared wordlessly at the parchment, wondering how Daniel had made out of England and into Poland.

"Anyway," Robert said, "to continue, it says here, 'To my beloved daughter I leave this manuscript. This will is witnessed and inscribed by Chaim Shimon ben Aharon, *sofer,* ' which means 'scribe,' 'in the name of Rabbi Moses ben Israel Isserles.' It's signed here, at the bottom, and it's the same signature that it says above – Daniel Solomon ben David, and," he peered more closely, "yes, it's right here - the other rabbi's signature. It's dated in Hebrew as well – 17 Iyyar 5322."

"Oh," I said, slightly disappointed. "It doesn't say anything about Margaret. So I guess it doesn't tell us much."

"Are you kidding?" Robert's voice was incredulous. "This is absolutely amazing - an actual document signed by one of the most widely known Talmudic scholars of all time."

"What are you talking about?"

"This is from the Rema synagogue. And the Rema – that's the acronym for Rabbi Moses Isserles – was one of the foremost Talmudic scholars of his time. This synagogue was founded sometime around 1553. But his followers lasted for a couple of hundred years – the site of his grave in the Jewish quarter of Krakow used to attract thousands of people every year on the anniversary of his death. And it looks as if he knew your bookseller – at least well enough to witness his will."

"Well, it did say in the manuscript that Daniel was a Talmudic scholar," I said.

"But Jill, you realize that even without the manuscript, that two signatures of Talmudic scholars on one document – especially one Ashkenaz and one Sephardic – how rare this is?"

I opened up the second piece of parchment. The handwriting was sharp, familiar, and clear. I knew instinctively that it was the same hand that had written the Spanish and Hebrew notations in the manuscript. And yet, the form seemed familiar as well, and I knew all at once, it was another sonnet. But this time, it was not written by Margaret.

Now, death is mine; for thou hast shown the way;
Thy soul hath followed me unto mine end.
We chose a faith no Monarch would defend –
A higher law of love must be obeyed.

The light doth fade upon the close of day
And now may our entwinèd souls ascend —
My love, my jewel, my dove, my sweetest friend
Hath gone before me to a distant grave.
Yet we are bound; I hath preserved thy name
And my heart's loyalty for time to come.
As I hath carried forth thy noble fame
In love which cannot ever be undone.
Thus is my fate. Now Death awaits our song.
Dear Margaret, thou shalt not attend me long.

"Daniel wrote a sonnet to Margaret," I said softly. "This one is his."

"What are you talking about?" Robert asked. "The poems, you mean?"

"Yes. All through the manuscript, she wrote these magnificent sonnets, about her life, about her marriage, and about Daniel. He must have read them all. And then, at the end of his life, he wrote one for her."

I passed the paper to him.

"It's a nice poem," Robert said diplomatically. "I'm still more interested, however, in this other document, with these signatures." He grinned at me. "Which is not to say, of course, that the writing isn't lovely."

I smiled back at him. "I hear you. But to me, this has become a love story, rather than a historical document."

"You curators are such softies," he joked.

I laughed. "You have a point, Robert. We still need to prove that this is the real thing."

"I think that can be done easily," he said. "Especially since these pages are detached from the rest of the manuscript."

"And actually," I said, looking down at the paper, "this parchment is in pretty good shape. This is something we might actually be able to authenticate in the lab, especially since, as you said, it's not bound into the rest of the manuscript. There'll be no danger to the rest of the book."

He carefully turned the pages at the back of the book until he stopped, suddenly, and looked at a thick torrent of Hebraic letters on one of the pages between the end of Margaret's story and the damaged cover.

"Jill, did you see this?" he asked.

"No, I said, surprised at the lettering. "I finished reading Margaret's story and didn't think to go further. I thought there were only blank pages."

"Apparently not," he said. "But this is in Aramaic, too. I'll translate."

He peered at the letters and appeared to be translating as he read. *"This book contains the story of the life of my mother, who was a great scholar, and my father, a great teacher, who loved her dearly. She died as I was being born, far away, in a foreign land. After she died, my father brought me here and he taught me the Law, just as my mother's father taught her, when she was a girl.*

"My father Daniel gave this book to me on my wedding day and so for all generations to come, this story is to be passed on to the firstborn daughter in every generation on the day of her wedding.

"So may all of our daughters find love as sacred as the love my mother and father bore for each other, so may we all cherish and revere and protect this book, for it contains the story of our heritage, and of the great scholars who were our ancestors.

"No matter what should happen in time to come, no matter if your future is under threat or if you are fortunate enough to live in fortunate times, the telling of this story is our family's sacred task. Do not forsake it, for within is the story of a great love that led my father to this place where he lived and served the Holy One of Blessing, just as my mother did, and so did her father before her."

Robert smiled as he read the last words. "Signed Chava bat Daniel Solomon de Guedalia."

I had to sit on one of the stools by the counter. "Oh my God," I said finally. "So their daughter did survive. These are her words." And her name was Chava, too, I thought to myself, though I didn't say it aloud.

Robert looked at me. "And it sounds to me as if she didn't know – or maybe didn't want other people to know – that her parents weren't married – and that her mother was a Gentile."

"She couldn't have known," I said automatically. "Even Margaret said as much. She said that she didn't want her daughter to be a stranger to Daniel's people. Margaret knew what she was doing. She knew her daughter would be raised as a Jew."

"Apparently so," Robert said. "And it sounds as if she started this tradition, of the book being passed down through the generations. This could be the reason that it once belonged to a Holocaust survivor. It belonged to a Jewish family."

"A Jewish family," I concluded, "who never realized that their ancestress was Catholic."

Robert gestured to the parchments that we had extracted from the book's binding. "And these papers are probably not that much older than the manuscript," Robert agreed. "Let me check on the Gregorian year that corresponds to 5322, the year that Daniel died," he said, taking his Blackberry out of his pocket.

"You and that Blackberry," I joked. "You've got all of Jewish history tucked away in there."

"Here it is," he said, tapping a few times on the keypad. "According to my Hebrew date converter, it comes out to May 2, 1562. Not that it's the real date," he said. "There have been a lot of changes to the Gregorian calendar since then. But this is as close as we get."

"I wish I knew when Daniel was born," I said. "He must have been pretty old in 1562. I imagine that he was about Margaret's age, maybe a little older, and he outlived her by nearly twenty years. She was thirty-nine when she died."

"Which made him close to sixty," Robert said. "Or older, which was a long life in those days. Which was a good thing, considering that he was alone in raising his daughter. Besides, we can't even be sure that 1562 was when he died. It might just be when he made his will."

"That's a good point," I said. "Do you have any idea why they would have ended up someplace like Poland?"

I watched his brow furrow as he thought about it for a moment. "Well, at that time, Poland and Czechoslovakia were the only real havens for Jews. Most of Western Europe, with the exception of certain areas in Italy, had expelled their Jewish populations, but the Eastern nations were somewhat less hostile. In fact, ever since the medieval period, many of the major eastern European cities boasted major centers of Jewish learning. Think about places like Warsaw, Prague, even some cities in Germany. And as you know, most of them were wiped out, either by pogroms in the early part of the century, or eventually, by the Nazis."

I nodded. Then the phone rang at my desk. "Could be Jacob," I said, running to answer it.

I picked it up on the third ring. "Hello, this is Jill Levin," I said breathlessly.

"Jill?" The voice was elderly, faded, tired-sounding.

"Yes?" I asked, thinking that perhaps it was Aviva's mother, calling to tell us about the baby. I found myself wondering if Jacob had even shown up at the hospital.

"Jill," the voice said, "it's Mitzi Feldman."

"Mitzi," I said, feeling my stomach lurch. All at once I knew that there was something wrong. "What is it?"

Her voice sounded shaky. "It's your grandmother, Jill," she said. "And it's not good."

I hung up the phone, and Robert, seeing the look on my face, was by my side almost instantly. When I had regained my composure somewhat, we quickly and carefully packed the manuscript away with the parchments tucked inside the back cover. Once it was safely in the vault, I sent a quick e-mail to the team letting them know that I, too, had to leave the office for an emergency. And then, I called Michael.

I took a few minutes to brief Robert on the status of the presentation and the team assignments, and was totally confident he could handle the project for the rest of the day, or even, God forbid, the next couple of days. I didn't leave him any specific instructions about the manuscript, or researching the donor database, but I knew he would know what to do in my absence. I let Mira know that I was going up to New York-Presbyterian, and she could reach me by cell phone if anyone needed me.

While I was upstairs with Mira, Robert had gone to the café, and when I returned to my desk to pick up my coat and bag, I saw he had packed a lunch for me to take along. The pure sweetness of his gesture brought tears to my eyes, but I brushed them away. I had to get uptown.

He put his arm around my shoulder as he walked me to the elevator and then downstairs to the exit. Once outside, he hailed a cab for me on Battery Place, bundled me inside and slammed the door shut. The car lurched forward, headed for the West Side Highway. I checked my bag for my cell phone, made sure it was turned on.

The inside of the cab smelled like cigarettes and a disco station blasted from the tinny speakers. We made the left turn on to West Street, passed by the spot where the World Trade Center once stood. While we waited at the light, I tried not to look out the window. There was nothing to see anyway, except for the green fence lining the perimeter of the site.

I looked around at the other cars, amazed to see that people were looking straight ahead, as if they were stuck at a red light at an ordinary intersection. Only the tourists, snapping pictures from the top of the red double-decker bus, seemed to be taking any notice of where we were.

The cab driver was yelling into his cell phone to be heard over the radio. Finally, he hung up. "Radio's busted," he said apologetically. "Can't turn it down."

The ride uptown seemed to take forever. I checked my cell phone again. I tried to read the book that I always carried with me. I tried to think about the manuscript. But I couldn't focus on anything. I could feel my heart beating in my chest; my hands felt cold. I stared at the unpronounceable name of the cab driver, emblazoned on the medallion license that was posted on the Plexiglas partition behind his head. I tried to figure out how many words I could make out of the letters of his name, and then wondered why I was doing it, for what did it matter how many words I could make? My grandmother, my *Omi*, was unconscious and in the hospital. I didn't know what had happened to her. And worst of all, she had left me a message the night before, and I hadn't called her back.

I tried to tell myself she was okay, she was with people who could help her, she was getting good medical care. Finally, the driver let me out at the entrance to the emergency room. I ran inside and checked in at the desk. They told me my grandmother was in ICU, gave me some brief directions and a visitor's pass.

I found Mitzi in the waiting room. She told me she had left a message for my parents – my grandmother, fortuitously, had told her the name of the cruise ship they were on. She checked her messages using my cell phone, and discovered they would be on the next plane to New York, arriving at 8:00 the next morning.

I checked my messages at home and heard my mother's voice on the answering machine, faded and tinny sounding on the ship-to-shore line. She sounded distraught, unable to contact me on the cell phone, wondering aloud if she would arrive too late.

I looked at my watch. It was 1:30. I closed my eyes for a moment, and when I opened them again, I saw Michael walking down the hall towards us, his briefcase hanging from the strap over his shoulder, his coat folded over his arm. I met him at the doorway. We didn't say anything at all; we just held each other for a couple of minutes. Then we went back inside to where Mitzi was sitting, red-eyed, looking up at the television.

"Any news?" he asked quietly.

I shook my head.

"How about your parents?"

"They're on their way." I rubbed my eyes. "They're taking the first flight they can get, which gets them into JFK early tomorrow morning."

He nodded. "I can rent a car, pick them up."

"Maybe," I said. "I can't think right now."

He was quiet for a moment. Then he took off his coat, put his briefcase down, and sat next to me on the couch. "Do the doctors know what made her collapse?"

"They took her for a CT-scan," I said. "But they haven't told us anything yet. And she hasn't regained consciousness at all. Not since Mitzi found her."

At the sound of her name, Mitzi's attention was drawn from the episode of *Judge Judy* that was blaring from the television high up on the wall.

"Mitzi," I said, "this is my boyfriend, Michael."

"Pleased to meet you," he said, leaning forward to extend his hand towards her. "I'm sorry it has to be under these circumstances."

"Me, too," she said, shaking his hand. "This is terrible." She shook her head. "I still can't believe it. I knocked on her door this morning. We were supposed to go to our exercise class at the senior center at eleven. She didn't answer. I just had a bad feeling about it, so I went back to my apartment to get the key."

Her voice became choked. "I found her in the kitchen. She was in her bathrobe and slippers. There was bread in the toaster. It looked as if she had just poured herself some coffee. The mug was in pieces on the floor. There was coffee everywhere, even in her hair."

Michael bit his lip and held my hand a little tighter. "I'm so sorry you had to find her," he said sympathetically. "It was good of you to let Jill know so quickly."

Mitzi reached for a tissue and wiped her eyes. "Well, you know, when you get to be our age," she said, "you make sure your friends know who to call."

I nodded. "Just like when she fell."

"Right," Mitzi said. "Even though Anna said not to call you, I knew, deep down, she really did want me to let you know."

Michael leaned back on the couch and drew my head to his shoulder. "But we thought the fall wasn't that bad?"

Mitzi shook her head. "It's hard to say. She seemed to be fine. I've been keeping an eye on her this week. But lately, she's been forgetful. At first, it wasn't anything you'd notice. Like she'd ask what time it was and then ask again a couple of minutes later. And then she seemed to have trouble remembering what day it was. I'd say, Anna, now you remember that we have class tomorrow, or that we're volunteering at the community center bake sale on Friday. And she'd say, oh, yes, I remember. But then she'd forget."

I was mystified. "Just in the past couple of days? Since the fall?" Mitzi looked guilty. "Jill, sweetheart," she said. "I know it was wrong not to tell you, but it's actually been a few months since she's been like this, and getting worse. I told her it was worrying me. I kept telling her, Anna, you've got to see a doctor, or at least, let your family know that this is happening. But you know how dismissive she can be. As if she didn't want to admit that anything was happening to her. And then the night that she fell," she looked at me sadly, "she made me promise not to tell you this, but the doctor was very worried. She seemed disoriented by the fall. When we brought her to the hospital, and she was in the emergency room waiting to be brought in for x-rays, she kept asking me to help her in German. And she kept calling me Rachel. I kept saying, no, no, Anna, I'm Mitzi. But she looked right at me and said, 'Rachel, *helfen mir. Bitte, helfen mir.*'"

"Rachel was her sister's name," I said softly. "She died during the war."

"I knew that," Mitzi said. "It's why I've been so worried about her. I was going to tell you about it, the night that you came to see her, but I couldn't. I didn't want to risk upsetting her, because I was afraid she would be angry at me, and she would stop telling me things." Her eyes filled with tears. Michael handed her another tissue, and she paused to wipe her eyes again. "And I really didn't want her to feel like she couldn't ask me for help. It's so hard for her to ask for help as it is. She's so strong, and stubborn." A small smile played on her lips in spite of her tears. "You know how she is."

"She went through a lot as a young person," I said. "It made her strong."

"The war made us all stronger than we ever planned on being," Mitzi said, her voice sounding a little less strained. "In fact," she said with a shrug, "I never used to cry like this."

"She's your friend," Michael said. "Of course it makes sense for you to be upset."

The three of us sat in silence. The room seemed strangely empty. The only sound came from the television, where Judge Judy impatiently banged her gavel.

I heard the sound of high heels tapping down the corridor. In another moment, a beautiful young woman with bright red hair walked into the room and touched Mitzi's shoulder. "I came as soon as I could," she said. "How is she?"

Mitzi shook her head. "Not good," she said sadly. "They took her in for a CT-scan. She was convulsing in the ER. It doesn't look good. She hadn't regained consciousness when they took her for the tests."

The woman placed a sympathetic hand on her shoulder. "I'm glad you called me," she said.

"She would have wanted you to know," Mitzi said. "Beth, this is Anna's granddaughter, Jill, and her boyfriend Michael."

The woman smiled at us sympathetically. "How do you do?" she said, extending her hand. "I'm Beth Zuckerman."

We both stood to shake hands with her, and then we all sat down again, Beth on the couch next to Mitzi.

"How do you know my grandmother?" I asked politely.

"Actually," Beth said, "I'm from her synagogue. I'm her rabbi."

"Really?" I could barely keep my jaw from dropping. "But you're so - "

"Young?" Beth supplied, grinning. "I know. I get that all the time."

"Especially," Mitzi said, "because our congregation is almost entirely, shall we say, getting on in years."

"It's not so much that," Beth remarked. "The regulars, of course, are mostly older. But a lot of young families are moving back into this neighborhood. I took over for a rabbi who retired last year. He was with the congregation for almost forty years. But it's a great place to be. We're talking about starting up a nursery school – something we haven't had for a long time. And your grandmother," she said, "was very excited about it. Some of the older people complain when there are

283

little children running around during services. But it delighted her to see them there."

I smiled, feeling a lump come into my throat.

There was a knock on the door. A man with a stethoscope around his neck looked questioningly at us. "Excuse me. Are you the family," he looked down at his chart, "of Anna Altschul?"

I looked around at the assembled group and realized I was the only family member present. "I'm her granddaughter," I said, as I rose to my feet.

"I'm Dr. Sachs," he said. "May I speak with you out here for a moment?"

I looked back at Michael's concerned face, and then I followed the doctor outside into the hallway. "I'm afraid it's not good news," he said. "Your grandmother is in a very deep coma. And I'm afraid it is, in all likelihood, irreversible."

I swallowed. "Do you know what happened to her?"

He shifted his chart to the other hand. "We just got her CT-scan results back. Apparently," he looked down at the report, "she suffered a significant cerebral hemorrhage. The damage to her brain is extensive. I'm very sorry that I don't have better news for you," he said kindly, as he pushed his glasses up on his nose.

"Is there any chance," I asked, clearing my throat, "she'll come out of it?"

He shook his head. "I don't think so," he said. His voice was calm, and I was grateful for its serenity. "I would hate for you to have any sense of false hope. I had the neurologist take a look at the brain scan, and it's likely that most of her ability to function – movement, speech, even basic human tasks like feeding herself, or going to the bathroom – have been compromised."

I nodded, trying to stay as calm as I could, even though I wanted to scream. "Where is she now?"

He nodded towards the door of the ICU. "She's inside. She's comfortable. We have her on a morphine drip, just in case there's any sort of function left in her brain that would enable her to feel pain. But from the sensory tests we've run," he said, "she doesn't respond to any sort of stimuli."

"What happens now?" I asked.

"You can go in to see her as soon as the nurse says that it's okay," he said. "But it's only a matter of a couple of hours at this point. Her blood pressure is very low. The injury to her brain is not survivable."

"Will she stay alive long enough for my parents to get here?"

"Where are they?"

"On a plane," I said, the tears coming into my eyes. "From Europe."

He handed me a clean, folded tissue from the pocket of his white coat, and then placed a hand on my arm as I wiped my eyes. "I can't really answer that," he said. "Unfortunately, it's not really up to me. We can keep her on the respirator, but her hospital records indicate she signed a Do Not Resuscitate order, and she specifically stated it was for any treatment that she received here, in the care of this hospital. So if she goes," he said, "we have to let her go."

"I understand," I said, even though I didn't want to.

"You should go back to your family now," he said. "I'll have the nurse call you in as soon as they're ready for you to see her."

"Okay," I said. I crumpled the tissue into a little ball in my fist, and watched Dr. Sachs walk back into the ICU. Then I returned to the waiting room.

They all looked at me, their faces expectant. I opened my mouth, but no words came out. I shook my head and lowered myself heavily onto the couch next to Michael. Nobody spoke. It was as if my body had told them the answer to their question.

"I'm sorry," Beth said in a quiet voice. "I'm so sorry."

Michael said nothing. I could feel his hand lightly stroking my back. Mitzi pressed her fingertips to her forehead, as if she could erase the thought from her mind. I felt terrible for her. But all I wanted to do was leave. I wanted to pretend none of it was happening. I wanted to go home, go to sleep, and wake up so I could start today over again.

From my bag, I heard my cell phone ring.

Michael said, "Do you want me to answer that?"

I shook my head. "It might be my mother. She was trying to get through earlier." Then I stood and said to the others, "Will you excuse me for a moment?"

I picked up the phone. The display said "unknown ID." I pressed the talk button as I crossed to the other side of the room. "Hello?"

"Jill? It's Robert."

"Hi," I said. I could barely get the one syllable out.

"How is she?"

"Not so good," I said, in a low voice. I repeated the doctor's words almost mechanically. "It's only a matter of a couple of hours, at this point."

There was silence at the other end of the line. "I'm so sorry, Jill," he said quietly. It occurred to me, all at once, that this was something I was going to have to get used to hearing.

"So I won't be in tomorrow," I said finally.

"Not a problem. It's under control," he said. "I'll let Larry know."

"Thanks," I said.

"And also," he said, "I thought you would want to know that Aviva had a girl."

"She did?" I could feel more tears coming into my eyes. "That's great."

"They're both doing fine," Robert said. "The baby weighs seven pounds, five ounces."

"Right," I said, aware that I could barely contain the emotion in my voice.

"Listen, I don't want to keep you. You have my cell phone, so let me know what's going on." I could sense that he was choosing his words with some care. "I know there are people here who will want to know."

I swallowed again. "I'll do that, Robert. And thanks again."

"Take care, Jill."

"You, too. Bye."

I pressed the End button and went back to where Michael and Mitzi and Beth sat, talking a little to one another.

"Aviva had a girl," I told Michael. And then, by way of explanation,

I said to the others, "She's one of my friends at work. She went into labor this morning at the office."

Mitzi smiled tiredly. "That's good news."

I nodded mutely.

"And it makes perfect sense," Beth added. "Not that it's any comfort, but there's a *midrash*, a tale told by the sages, that says on the day Rabbi Akiba died, Rabbi Judah the Prince was born. And on the day Rabbi Judah died, Rav was born. The point is," she smiled sadly, "that God never takes a righteous soul from the earth until another one is born to replace her."

The nurse knocked on the door. "You can go in and see her now," she nodded at me. "Only one or two at a time."

"Do you want me to go with you?" Beth asked, in a soft voice. "I'd be honored to say some prayers for her."

"It's what she would want," Mitzi said.

I nodded. "Please."

"Why don't I go in with you now?" Beth said, "and then I'll come back and send Michael in to you."

I looked at him. "Would that be all right?"

"Of course," he said. "I'll stay here and keep Mitzi company."

Beth took a small book with Hebrew lettering on the cover from her bag, and I watched as she pinned a black silk *yarmulke* to her beautiful hair.

"Are you ready?" she asked.

I nodded again, unable to speak. She gently took my arm and led me out of the room. She opened the door of the ICU, and I stepped over the threshold. Together, we walked down the long line of cubicles, each with its own sound of machines that were keeping people alive.

"She's in number five," the nurse said.

We approached the bed. I felt one of Beth's hand reach for mine, and together we walked towards my grandmother, who lay in a hospital gown, with a breathing tube stretching from her mouth to the machine next to her bed. Another tube drained blood from her brain. And another was hooked up to an IV in her arm.

Her eyes were closed. There was only the quiet beeping of the respirator, and the shallow sound of her mechanized breaths.

"She looks very peaceful," Beth whispered softly, as she let go of my hand. I looked at my grandmother's face. Beth was right; she looked as if she were asleep.

She opened the prayerbook. "May I say the final confession?"

"Please," I managed to say again.

In a quiet, reverent voice, she began to speak:

Compassionate God, God of my fathers and mothers
God of my ancestors, whose souls have already returned to You
May my prayer reach You in Your infinite mercy
For as You turned Naomi's ear to Ruth's pleas, I entreat You: hear my prayer.

I ask of You, Holy One, please forgive me for the sins
That I sinned before You throughout the days of my life.
I beg You to consider the mitzvot that outshone my evil deeds.
I implore You to understand the things that I have done.

Holy One, my pain and suffering may be sufficient atonement.
But I ask You instead to take my light, the soul that You granted to me in love
As expiation for the wrongs that I have committed.
In Your wisdom, know of my good intentions and my good deeds,
Remember that I tried to bring Your infinite light to this world.
For as You have understood and pardoned the mistakes
And misdeeds of your children, in generations past
May it be Your will, Adonai, my God and God of those I have loved
That I may be pardoned and forgiven.

God of Compassion, liberate me from the darkness of my sin,
Healer of Souls, free me from my illness and suffering.

Source of Blessing, grant a complete healing
To me and to all those who are not fully whole.

I make this accounting before You, Adonai my God,
God of my mothers and fathers,
For I know my life and my death are in Your hands.
May a complete healing from my sin and suffering be Your will.

But if my death be Your will, at this time and in this season,
In Your infinite Love, let both my death and my life atone for all my
wrongdoing.
Grant me protection and shelter beneath the wings of Your divine
presence.
Grant my soul a share in the world to come.

O Compassionate, Merciful, Holy One of Blessing:
Bless my dear ones, those who remain among Your living
With whose light my soul is illuminated,
In whose eyes and hearts and memories shall my light continue to live,
As into Your eternity I commit my soul.
For You have forgiven me, and pardoned me,
And granted me atonement, O God of Infinite Light.

Shema Yisrael, Adonai Eloheinu Adonai Echad.
Hear O Israel, The Lord our God, The Lord is One.
Adonai Hu Ha'Elohim. Adonai Hu Ha'Elohim.
Adonai is God. Adonai is God.

She closed the book. We stood together for a few moments in silence,
listening to the sound of the machines breathing for my grandmother.
Then Beth touched my arm.

"I'll send Michael in to you," she said. "So you can spend a couple
of minutes alone with your grandmother."

I didn't say anything, knowing that Beth understood. She quietly slipped past me, and walked back down the corridor. I could hear the sound of her black shoes on the white linoleum floor.

I looked at my grandmother again, at her hands, her face, her arms, torn between wanting to remember her, and not wanting to remember her like this.

Her skin looked tired and papery, and yet, the numbers on her arm looked sharp and unfaded, as if they had been put there just days before. I took one of her small hands in my own. It shocked me that her hand still felt warm. It was as if I could still feel life in her hands, as if she were about to grasp my hand happily in hers as she always did when I saw her.

I wanted tears to come; I wanted to say something meaningful to her. More than that, I wanted her to open her eyes. I wanted to hear her say one last thing to me. I wanted her to die the way people die in movies, where they come back for one moment, just long enough to impart the moral of the story, and then they slip away, peacefully, as the camera cuts away to a glorious image of the sky.

I leaned over to kiss her cheek. I didn't know what to say, so I didn't say anything at all. I simply kissed her goodbye, and as I did, I noticed that there was still a scent of coffee in her hair.

I heard the familiar sound of Michael's footsteps as he approached. He didn't rush to take me in his arms the way someone would in a movie. Instead, he came to stand at my side. We didn't speak. I watched him as he looked at her with tenderness in his eyes. After a moment he placed his hand on hers.

I put my arm around him. Up until that moment, I had thought of this as my loss only. And I realized, as I brushed my face against his shoulder, that it was his loss, too, because they had never gotten to know one another. I thought about the hate and the history that had been a barrier between them. This was the only contact they would ever have.

We stood together for another couple of minutes, at her bedside, not speaking. Then he put his arm around me. We held each other as we watched her breathe, watched as the numbers on the monitors continued their slow descent. After a while, he took my hand and led me out of the room.

24

She died. At 2:00 in the morning, long after Beth left, long after Michael put Mitzi in a cab for home, and long after he had fallen asleep in the waiting room, the doctor came in to tell us that her blood pressure had finally dropped to the point where her heart stopped functioning. The doctor held my hand when he told me. Then he left me and Michael alone for a few minutes, presumably so we could be alone in that first outpouring of grief. But the outpouring never came. Michael held me close, and I could feel his body with all of his life still surging through it, and as he held me, I wanted to close my eyes and feel something, anything. Instead, my eyes fell on the upholstery of the couch we had been sitting on for more than eleven hours, and I found myself wondering why I was looking at the pattern of the green and purple fabric, studying it as intensely as if I would be tested on it later.

I waited for tears, for grief, for any kind of emotion at all, but I felt frozen, as if I were standing on a stone whose cold, hard surface had suddenly taken over my body, numbing me, shielding me. We stood, holding one another for a couple of minutes, and then the doctor, discreetly, came back into the waiting room.

He asked us if we knew of the funeral home where we wanted her to go. We did; Mitzi had tearfully called my cell phone earlier in the night with the all of phone numbers for the rabbi, the temple, and the funeral home most frequently used by their congregation. The doctor told me someone would need to make the call, to let them know that my grandmother's body was being released to them.

One of the nurses offered to help, but ultimately, Michael made the call, in a low voice, at the other side of the room, while I asked the doctor if my mother could call him when she arrived. I knew that she would want to hear from him exactly what had happened and I wasn't sure that I could explain it to her in a way that she would accept.

The doctor gave me his card, and told me in a kind voice that she could call him anytime. After that, there didn't seem to be anything else to say, so we stood up at the same time and shook hands. I was reminded of work, of how I was not supposed to linger at that final moment of an artifact donation, and I saw traces of my own professional training in his demeanor.

I thanked him for caring for my grandmother, and he nodded briefly, as if he wished it could have turned out differently. Then he turned and walked back into the ICU. Michael finished talking to the funeral home, and we picked up our coats and bags and walked towards the elevator in silence. The elevator took us back down to the main floor, and we walked down the long white corridor and through the glass doors, out into the night.

Our clock radio had gone off at the usual time, six o'clock. Michael reached out a hand to silence it. I had remained awake, watching the sky change from black to gray to pink to blue, hearing the sounds of the city as it awakened.

I finally heard from my parents during a layover in London, at about four in the morning. I gave them the news, and telling them was as terrible as I had feared it would be.

My mother said they would take a cab from the airport and meet me at my grandmother's apartment. I told my mother, a little tentatively, that Michael would be with me. Thankfully, she didn't object, but she didn't sound happy about it, either.

I woke him at around eight. I was already dressed, and had made coffee. I brought it in to him and watched as he sat up in our bed and drank it. He ran a hand through his tousled hair and yawned. I sat on the edge of the bed next to him.

"How are you doing?" he finally asked.

I shrugged. "I didn't sleep."

"Why didn't you wake me up?"

"No need," I said. "I'm glad you were able to sleep." I put my hand over his. "And I'm glad you were there with me last night."

He leaned over and kissed me. "I know."

We didn't say anything for a moment. Michael drank his coffee. "My parents called," I told him.

"So your mom knows? You told her?"

I nodded.

"I'm sorry. That must have been really hard," he said sympathetically.

"Yeah. It was." I swallowed. "We're meeting them up at *Omi's* apartment later on. They're going there straight from the airport. I think they're planning on staying there."

"That makes sense," Michael said. "But are you sure you're okay with me going up there with you? I was thinking that you might want some time with them on your own."

I smiled at him. "The only thing I'm sure of is that I want you with me. I already told my mother that you'd be coming up with me."

"What did she say?" he asked cautiously.

"Not a lot," I told him. "But I don't think she was surprised."

"Are you OK with that?"

"We've been through enough in the past twenty-four hours," I said. "They can think what they want." I shrugged. "Whatever."

We looked at one another, and I watched him smile tiredly.

"What time do you want to head up there?"

I looked at the clock. "Soon," I said. "Mitzi said she'd be there to let us in. And then she was going to the hardware store to get some keys made for us and for my parents."

"You spoke with her already?"

"Don't be silly." I grinned at him. "I emailed her this morning at six-thirty. She gave me her email address last night. And she wrote right back to me."

He chuckled. "She's amazing. Tech savvy at eighty-five."

"These women are full of surprises," I said. "I hope I'm just the same at their age."

Mitzi let us in to the apartment and handed me the keys. "I have another set for your parents. This way, you can all come and go as you need to," she said.

"That's great. I really appreciate it," I told her. "And I think my parents are planning on staying here, so don't be alarmed if there are people coming and going for the next few days."

"Do you know if they're planning to sit *shivah*?" she asked. "Because we could do that here. All of your grandmother's friends live in the neighborhood, so it's good for them to have someplace close by. And then you don't have to have it at your house."

"We wouldn't mind," I said.

Michael nodded his agreement before he said the obvious. "But your mother might."

"Well, that's for you to figure out. But it can be tough, at a time like this, having people you don't know coming to your house. At least, here is familiar, for them and for you. And besides, you know, you don't have to sit for the whole seven days. Nowadays people just sit for two or three. You can talk with Rabbi Beth about it."

"We will," I said. "I don't want to make any plans until my parents get here. I feel like my mother should be the one to decide." I tried my best to sound practical and efficient. "The funeral home said that they needed us to bring them some clothes. So we need to choose what she'll be buried in."

"You know where she keeps her clothes," Mitzi pointed to the bedroom.

"Sure, but do you know if she had a favorite article of clothing? Anything she felt strongly about?"

Mitzi shook her head. "Not really. You know, all she really cared about was the long sleeves. She was funny about that number on her arm. And you know, a lot of the elderly people in this neighborhood have them. Me, I was one of the lucky ones, being born in this country. I would tell Anna, listen, why do you let yourself get overheated in the summer. It's nothing we haven't seen before. But she was very stubborn about it. Well, you know. I thought it was like she wanted to pretend that it never happened."

"Maybe," I said. "But I've known a lot of survivors who feel the same way."

"That's right. You work at the museum. I keep telling myself that I need to get down there one of these days."

I smiled. "If only I had a nickel for every person who said that to me."

"You really should go," Michael said. "It's a great place. Even for someone like me, who isn't Jewish. I've learned a lot from visiting there with Jill."

Mitzi patted his arm. "So you go ahead, pick out a nice outfit. She liked blue. You'll find a lot of blue in there, I'm sure."

"We will," I said. "And if it's okay, I'll knock on your door when I've picked a few things out, if you'd like to help me choose."

"I'd be honored," Mitzi said. "Now let me leave before I get too emotional."

We watched her go. As soon as she closed the door behind her, I turned on the radio. It was tuned to my grandmother's favorite classical station, and the soothing sound of Rachmaninoff soon filled the apartment. Michael walked over to the console table where the photographs were displayed. "These are great," he said. He picked up one of me at sixteen, standing in front of glowing birthday candles. "Wow. You look exactly the same."

"Man, I hope not," I said.

"Please, you should have seen me at that age," he said. "Welcome to Nerdville. Population: Me."

I laughed. I realized it felt familiar to laugh in that apartment, even though *Omi* wasn't there to laugh with me. "I better go find something for her to wear."

"Want some help?"

"I'm okay on my own," I told him. "But I'll call you if I need you."

"Sure," he said. "I want to look at these pictures."

I went into the bedroom. It was a little less tidy than the last time I had seen it. There were clothes strewn across the rocking chair, and a pair of shoes lay by the closet door, as if they had been kicked off just a few hours before.

All the familiar objects were just as I remembered them – the photograph of my grandfather on her bureau, the perfume bottles on her dresser, a double photo frame containing pictures of me and my mother on our first day of school, taken more than twenty years apart.

My grandfather's old roll-top desk stood open, still in the same place, right underneath the window, across from the bed.

I didn't notice the typewriter at first. Then I walked over and examined it. It was an old Royal, one that I hadn't remembered seeing before. It looked fairly old, like it was probably from the 1950s or 60s. The heavy black case was open on the floor next to the desk. An ancient package of Eaton typing paper was inside. The once-vibrant orange cardboard box had faded to a pale peach in the sunlight.

There was paper in the typewriter, and some pages, face down, on the desk next to the machine. I picked them up and peered at the lettering, and suddenly realized that the ink pattern looked familiar.

```
Miss Jill Levin
Senior Curator
Museum of Jewish Heritage
36 Battery Place
New York, New York 10004

Dear Jill:
I hope that you were not too distressed by the
last letter I sent to you. I am sure that it made
you feel sad, and angry, and maybe even helpless.
But it is time that you knew the truth. It is
time that you knew my story, and the story of our
family.

Now you know that your mother had two half
sisters, and that I had two other little girls,
who never had a chance to grow up, or grow old
the way I have, and the way, G-d willing, that
you and your mother will.
```

Now you know whom you are named after. I am the person who begged your mother to give you the Hebrew name Chava. She asked me why at the time, but I wouldn't tell her the answer. I just told her that I liked the name. Nor did I ever tell her that her own Hebrew name, Malka, is in memory of her sister Minna.

Perhaps I am guilty of not telling the truth to you and your mother. Perhaps I am guilty of silence. I never could understand the survivors who so willingly shared their stories, who are comfortable with their memories. Perhaps I am guilty of believing these numbers on my arm would tell you everything you needed to know. Then again, not every survivor is guilty of murder.

For that is what it is. Call it what you wish. Call it a mercy killing, justify it to yourself as I have justified it to myself for all of these years.

I tell myself over and over that I did this to spare my baby an unspeakable fate. Always I remembered the mother and baby murdered just before Chava was born. But I still ask myself, and I ask G-d, if what I did was right? And if I had not done these terrible things, would you or your mother have even been born?

I know now I was right to tell you about every-thing I lost, and everything I endured. Because I realize you have kept the secret of your boyfriend from me, and you did so because you are afraid that I will disapprove of him because he isn't Jewish.

And though it breaks my heart, knowing that I will hurt you by saying so, I cannot deny it. I do not approve. I cannot approve. Because I did not survive all of these long years, with my memories of all those whom I lost, and knowing the terrible suffering of my parents, my husband Aron, my innocent children – so that you could throw away our traditions as if their lives – our lives – meant nothing.

It grieves me, my darling, to know that because you have chosen this man, you will be the broken link in a chain that goes back hundreds of years. This is why I have chosen to give you this book, which I rescued after the war from that terrible place in the middle of the field.

As you probably have read by now, all of the firstborn daughters who inherit this book are commanded to give it to their firstborn daughter on their wedding day. Since Chava's time, it has been passed down in an unbroken chain - l'dor va dor — from generation to generation.

This is what my mother told me, on the day I was married to Aron. And if Minna had lived, it would have come to her on her wedding day. It could not go to your mother because she was not the firstborn, even though she does not know about her sisters. But to pass it on to your mother would have dishonored Minna's memory. Instead I kept it for all of these many years, waiting to pass it on to you.

After the war ended, I did not think I would ever find the strength to return to the place where I buried the book. I did not want to go back there. I was scared that if I dug in the wrong place, if I failed to remember the exact spot where I hid the book, I would instead find the bodies of those I heard murdered that day.

But because I lived, I knew the book had to live on through me. If I had died, the tradition would have died as well. But because I was still alive, it meant there would still be a chance for our traditions to continue.

On the day it was given to me, I could not read anything except for Chava's words at the very beginning of the book, since I only could only read German and Hebrew. And after I came to America, and learned to read in English, I could never bring myself to look at it. Whenever I saw it, in its box on a shelf at the very back of my closet, I could only think of the day I buried it, of what I heard, and the fear I felt, sure that my Aron was among the prisoners, and that I, too, was going to be captured and killed.

My mother and grandmother told me the story of the first Chava, who was given the book by her father, the rabbi Daniel de Guedalia, on her wedding day. It was said that Daniel was a great teacher and scholar of Talmud. When Chava's mother was dying, she asked Daniel to teach the Law to their daughter, just as her father had taught her. And Chava, in turn, grew up to be a great teacher, one whose knowledge was so very respected that it did not matter she was a woman. When she was a young girl, she taught the littlest boys in the yeshiva from behind a curtain. And after she married and had children, she taught the Law to her daughters as well as her sons.

My mother told me how my great-grandmother was the first to save the book from being destroyed. Her husband was the rabbi - like Chava's father- of the Rema synagogue in Poland. As the rabbi, he kept the book in the synagogue as it was thought to be a safe place, where all of the holiest texts were kept.

There were terrible pogroms in my great-grand-father's time, and during one of them, the synagogue was burned. Legend says that the rebbetzin, my great-grandmother, rescued Chava's book at the same time that my great-grandfather, the rabbi, rescued the Torah scrolls. The synagogue itself was saved, but my great-grand-mother believed that it was too dangerous to keep Chava's book there. And she was right; the synagogue was destroyed by the Nazis less than 100 years later.

The book became part of our family library. It passed from my grandmother to my mother, and when they left Poland it came with them to Germany. And then, on the day I married Aron, it came to me.

You come from a long line of strong and faithful people who have kept faith with their traditions no matter the cost. As Chava wrote, our generations of scholars upheld the Law as it was taught to them. We have kept faith with our traditions as we have been commanded.

Like all of the firstborn daughters of our family, I have been commanded to pass this book to you on your wedding day. But the truth is that I do not know if I will live long enough to see that day. Nor do I believe anymore that I want to live long enough to see you married.

You, Jill, will be the broken link in this golden chain. Why you are choosing to break this chain I do not know. Perhaps it is because of what I endured and what we lost. Perhaps you are afraid that there will be another war, and another time when we will be taken away and murdered because we are Jewish.

But Jill, even if you marry this man – even if you think that your safety is guaranteed because you change your name, and change your faith, and you and your children and grandchildren are changed and changed again, it will not matter. There will always be those who hate us, those who want to destroy us, those who believe we do not have the right to exist.

And if they do not come for you in your time, they will come for your children or your children's children. And they will know of the Jewishness that runs in their veins. It is a fact of your blood that you will carry always, no matter what your name or your faith might be.

I only hope that once you read this manuscript – and the story of Chava's mother and father, which I was never able to read, that you will understand who you are and where you come from.

I placed the papers back on the desk, exactly the way I had found them. Then I looked at the typewriter, where the last sheet of paper was still in place, as if unfinished. I carefully released the ancient mechanism and took the paper out of the typewriter. I held it in both hands as I read it.

When you were here a few days ago, you may have thought I was surprised to hear about your boyfriend, but I was not. Somehow I knew in my heart that you were closing yourself off from our traditions, even though you work in a place that tries so hard to preserve them. But working in the museum is not enough. You must preserve our traditions through your family, and through the life you live, not only through the work that you do.

And it occurred to me that if you decided to marry this man, and forsake our family's traditions, it would be as if Hitler was still alive, and still destroying us.

I wanted you to have the manuscript but I did not know of any other way to give it to you. I could not find it in my heart to sit down with you, face to face, or as we used to say in my parents' time – panim al panim – and tell you what was in my heart. I love you and I want you to understand me, I want you to know that you – and our traditions – mean more to me than you can ever know. I think about my parents, my husband, my children – all of whom died for our faith. For so many years, I could not say their names out loud. I did not want you to have a greater burden of the past than the one you already carry.

But there is no choice now; you must carry it, because I am growing old, and soon I will no longer be here to carry it for you.

I sent these letters to you, Jill, because it was the only way that I could tell you my story. I'm sorry you are angry with me. But perhaps now that I have broken my silence, you will understand why you must reconsider. You must end this relationship and cut all ties with this young man.

You are the hope for our family's future. And now that you know what is at stake, I know you will not allow yourself to break the chain of our family's traditions. Remember what we endured and who we are, my Jill, my Chava, and I know that you will understand.

I put the paper down on the desk with the others. Then I sat on the bed. My head was pounding, and my face felt hot.

I heard footsteps from the other room and suddenly felt confused. It was as if she were still there, I thought. I could still smell her perfume; I could still hear the comforting and familiar sounds from her living room.

But I couldn't reconcile the woman who had lived here with the one who had written the letters. I could not think of her as the mysterious stranger who survived the horrors of Dachau, who watched as her sister suffocated a newborn child to save them both from being murdered by the Nazis, who sent me the manuscript without ever having read the story inside.

I sat on my grandmother's bed, unaware that I was gripping the paper in my hand. After another moment I looked up and saw Michael at the doorway.

"Are you all right?" he asked.

"It was her," I said, my voice shaking. "It was her. She sent the letters."

"What letters?" Michael asked, mystified.

"The letters. The manuscript. Daniel and Margaret." I continued to stare at the sheet of paper. "It was from her. Everything came from her."

Michael swiftly came over and put his arm around me. My hands were trembling.

"Let me see the letter," he said.

I shook my head. "No, Michael. Please."

I gripped the paper more tightly in my hand.

"Jill," he said quietly. "Don't do this."

He gently extracted the paper from my clenched fingers, and I watched his face as he read it, waiting in the silence for his reaction.

"My God," he said softly. "Reconsider. Cut all ties. Remember who you are."

I could feel the tears starting to come. Before I knew what I was doing I was really crying, coughing, sobbing, almost unable to breathe. And just when I needed him to hold me and tell me that everything would be okay, he instead took his arm from around my shoulders. I could feel his body withdrawing from mine. I could feel him watching me as I cried.

Finally, he spoke. "So? Is this where it ends? With my love for you being compared to what Hitler did?"

I shook my head. "I can't talk about this right now," I sobbed. "I need time to think. We need time to talk about this."

"Is there really anything left to talk about?" he asked quietly. "This says everything she felt. And you know what you have to do." I could hear the bitterness in his voice. "How can you possibly deny her last request?"

"I need to get out of here," I said, feeling all at once the sense of darkness and claustrophobia that I had always felt here. "I need some air."

He stepped aside as if allowing me to walk out without him. "Where are you going?" he asked.

"I don't know," I said. "Can we just talk later?"

He nodded sadly. "We'll have to talk later," he said. "If nothing else."

Minutes later I found myself on the 9 train, heading downtown. I stared, unseeing, at the other side of the subway car. Every once in a while I felt more tears stream from my eyes and roll down my cheeks, but I didn't try to wipe them away. I could sense people staring at me, but I didn't care. I certainly wasn't the first person to weep on a New York City subway, and I wouldn't be the last.

I finally heard the conductor announce the last stop, Battery Park. The train pulled into the station and I could hear the high shriek of the brakes as they ground to a halt. I stood and walked out of the nearly empty car and up the stairs.

Outside, it was cold and sunny, and a little breeze blew in from the harbor. Without thinking, almost automatically, I walked toward the museum.

I pushed the glass door open and the security guard waved me in with a grin.

"Running late today, Jill?" he asked jovially.

I muttered something unintelligible and dug around in my bag for my ID badge.

"No need," he said. "Come on through."

I walked through the security gate and found myself in the lobby. The afternoon sunlight shone through the wide windows, turning the peach-colored stone walls a rosy pink. Visitors' voices echoed and hummed throughout the room. All around me there were crowds of people – schoolchildren and teachers, teenagers from both public schools and yeshivas who eyed each other with curiosity, groups of visitors led by docents and uniformed guards, standing silent and attentive, surveying the scene.

I didn't see anyone from my department, and realized that they were probably all upstairs working on the Berlin exhibition plans in the third floor conference room.

For a moment I debated going upstairs and putting in an appearance, but I didn't feel like I was up to hearing my colleagues' well-meaning condolences. Instead, I ducked into the long, dark hallway which would take me into what we always referred to as the core building – the heart of the museum itself – the three floors which taught our visitors about the Holocaust from the perspective of those who had lived through it.

I entered the space, thinking about how long it was since I made this journey through the exhibition as a civilian; I had first visited the museum just before my interview with Larry, more than seven years ago. I thought about how moved and inspired I felt after touring the galleries, and how I had known that this was where I wanted to work.

Now, after so many years as a curator, I now only spent time in the core building during rotation or maintenance. I had trained myself only to think about things like the temperature in the galleries, and the duration of time that certain artifacts spent under the lights. And on the occasions I passed through these galleries on my way to meetings or events, I found myself checking for fingerprints on the glass cases, or exhibition labels coming loose from the walls. I had come to see it all as a work project. It had been years, I realized, since I had actually paid attention to the story being told by these objects.

At the first gallery, my fingers brushed over the rough gray textured walls of Jerusalem stone at the entrance. I looked up to see the word engraved above me – *Zachor* – Remember.

I thought about my grandmother, about the numbers tattooed on her arm, about the letter she had left behind. And I knew I couldn't bear to remember just now, not yet.

Walking through the first floor, I looked one by one at the display cases of objects representing Jewish life more than a century ago. I paused by those containing hand-sewn wedding gowns, and ancient, yellowing bris and bar mitzvah and wedding announcements. Another case held two beautifully-illustrated family trees that ended abruptly in the late 1930s. The artists who had drawn them did so having no idea how soon they were to be uprooted.

I gazed at silver Kiddush cups, intricately carved spice boxes, wood-handled *challah* knives that had last been used decades ago. I thought about Friday nights, about my mother and my grandmother, and how her mother and grandmother before her had held objects like these in their hands, how their whispered blessings had been passed from one generation to the next.

I thought about the years of artifact donation visits I had made, how I had heard the stories of nearly every object in every case, and how those objects had once been at home upon someone's shelf, in a glass-fronted wooden cabinet, on a Sabbath table gleaming with pressed white tablecloths and freshly polished silver. So many of these objects had been smuggled out, sent to relatives in America for safekeeping, or buried in the ground. Every one of them represented a story of loss, or of survival, or simply the story that a family like mine had been taught to tell itself about its own heritage.

I continued through the first floor galleries, gazing at Torah scrolls rescued from burning synagogues, from pogroms, from the Inquisition. I wondered if perhaps I was looking at the very scroll that Daniel had shown to Margaret on the day they knew they loved one another.

I closed my eyes for a moment and remembered the touch of Michael's hand on mine, the kindness in his dark eyes, the quiet sound of his breathing as we fell asleep.

Margaret was never able to fall asleep next to the man she loved, I thought. *Because at the very moment they loved each other the most, they had to turn and walk away because they knew what would happen to them if they were discovered. They knew it would cost them their lives.*

And yet, Chava was born. Chava, who had no idea that her mother was a Gentile, who unwittingly told the great lie, the same lie that my grandmother told herself, the lie for which she has asked me to choose a life without Michael. Chava, who in spite of her learning, in spite of her heritage and her community, who according to Jewish law, wasn't actually Jewish.

The thought flashed through my brain. *What does it all mean?* I asked myself. *If Chava wasn't Jewish according to Jewish law, then what about the rest of us? What about my grandmother and everything she went through, everything she lost? Did her suffering mean less because she was – and we are — technically Gentiles?*

What is the true religion of our family? And does it mean we are not really whom we have always believed ourselves to be?

I ascended the escalator to the second floor. All at once, I was assaulted with images of the Nazis coming to power – the blood-colored propaganda posters, the spidery, sinister arms of the swastika, the harsh German words condemning all Jews to death. I could feel the hatred. I felt hated.

Is this what makes me Jewish? I asked myself. *The fact that I feel hated because of these objects? Objects that tell me I am meant to feel hated? That I fear – like my grandmother - that there will always be enemies who rise up against us, and the ones who hate us are always there, lurking in the shadows, waiting to come to power, determined that someday we will no longer exist?*

I walked slowly through galleries of documents that took homes, businesses, and identities away from Jewish citizens all over Europe. I read about laws that denied Jews their basic rights, their livelihood, even their ability to get married. I saw photographs of burning buildings and burning books, of children saying goodbye to anxious, desperate parents at train depots.

I thought about Minna, my aunt, who had been hidden away before dawn one spring morning, and whom my grandmother would never see again. I thought about the little flower that Minna had given her that day, how it had weathered all the years underground, all the decades tucked away inside the book.

I turned a corner and found myself face to face with photographs I could barely manage to look at: photographs I had been looking at for most of my professional life, but not really seeing – or letting myself see. Now I felt their impact as surely and strongly as if I were looking at them for the first time. The emaciated bodies, the threadbare uniforms, the shaved heads, the wasted eyes.

I could hardly think of them as people, yet there they were, looking back at me, each one with a name, a history, a family, a story.

I have thought of them as symbols for so long, I thought guiltily. *I didn't want to feel the connection. I let myself be distanced by history, by the black and white of the photographs, as if this could never happen in my Technicolor world. I let myself think about this only as a professional, as a curator.*

But I never wanted to think about this happening to her. I blinked my eyes to keep the tears from coming again. *To my* Omi.

In the next gallery, I looked into a case containing several tiny objects: an embroidered handkerchief; a wedding ring; a sheet of music, the notes carefully drawn on crooked staffs; a tiny metal brooch on a chain. I didn't need to look at the label to remember how all of these had been created by prisoners in the concentration camps.

Or is this what it means to be Jewish? I wondered. *Is it only about being another link in a golden chain? Or is it about having the will to not merely survive, but also to create beauty in the midst of horror? Is it about possessing the willingness to pledge one's life to another, even when that life may have been nearing its end? Is it about being a person who does not lose hope even after losing everything else?*

I walked on, turned another corner and found myself in the gallery that had always been one of my favorites.

Who saves a single life saves a world entire, the inscription read. The surrounding walls contained six stories of righteous gentiles from all different countries, and all different walks of life, who had willingly saved the lives of Jews.

Not even these stories would have convinced, you, Omi, I said in my mind to my grandmother. *Because you were only able to think of them as enemies, full of hatred, not wanting us to live. It was easier for you to hate them – all of them.*

You refused to accept Michael. You never got to know his kindness and his decency. Because the hate that made the Nazis hate us is the same hate that grew inside your heart for all of those years after the war. And it made you wrong, Omi. Because if only you had read the manuscript – if only you had opened the book – if only you had known Margaret's story, you would know the truth. They are already part of who we are.

By now I was crying once again. I wiped my eyes and kept walking.

At the end of the second floor gallery, old newspapers and film clips showed the war finally ended, and how the joy of the Allies' victory was mixed with the newly-realized horror of the destruction that had befallen the Jews of Europe.

I sat on a hard wooden bench and looked around at the photographs of liberation, of parents reunited with children, of husbands and wives taking marriage vows, of family celebrations, of new babies being born.

For a while, I stared at a photograph of one young survivor couple, a photograph that I had always loved. In it, a tall, fair-haired young man gazed tenderly at his dark-haired bride. She looked up at him with a face full of wonder, and just the tiniest shadow of disbelief, as if she couldn't quite believe that such happiness had come to her, that such joy could ever happen again.

And so it is, I thought, *when hate has nearly destroyed a life. But there is a choice.*

I looked again at the bride and groom; the delight in their faces was like a benediction.

I can heed my grandmother's last words to me; I can let the hate that defined her life define mine. I can allow her legacy to make that choice for me. Or I can trust that even now, after knowing the terror and loss she endured, the murders of her parents, her husband, her children, I must understand that she did not really know the story of her own family, or who she truly was. But Margaret and Daniel have given me the truth of our family. And I know now that I do not have to carry Omi's hatred with me.

I do not have to separate myself from Michael the way Margaret separated herself from Daniel, the way my grandmother separated herself from the world. I can carry the blessings of her story the way that Daniel carried Chava to a new land, to a new life. And because of the manuscript, my grandmother's great gift, I will know who I am, and be who I will become. I can trust that even now, in this moment of losing Omi, even after her wanting me to lose Michael along with her, there can, and will, be joy again.

I stood and looked at the photograph of the bride and groom for another moment, and then took the escalator to the third floor. But instead of walking into the galleries, I nodded to the security guard standing by the exit, and walked across the hallway that bridged the new wing of the museum and the core building.

I pushed open the stairwell door marked "Employees Only" and walked down to the second floor.

Walking through the nearly empty hallway, I opened another heavy glass door and went outside into the Garden of Stones, our museum's garden of remembrance, which had been dedicated just a few years earlier. I remembered how my family had come to the museum for the dedication ceremony, and the planting of eighteen tiny dwarf oak saplings in huge granite boulders, which now stood like sentinels throughout the garden.

It was unsure if the trees could actually survive, but that was part of the artist's intention. The ones that did were expected to break through the rocks someday, the growth and strength of their trunks and leaves and branches proving that life could and did continue, even in the most difficult of circumstances.

We had assembled on that warm, beautiful spring day; our staff, our leadership, and a number of Holocaust survivors, including my grandmother.

I had a picture on my desk, taken by one of my colleagues, of my grandmother's elderly hands, my mother's hands, and my own as we eased the young tree into the black earth inside the stone. Now I walked over to what I always thought of as our family's boulder at the very end of the garden. The tree inside it was little more than a weathered twig, seemingly undecided whether to live or die.

I laid both my hands on the granite boulder, feeling its age, its solidity, its eternity. I thought about its being uprooted from the ground somewhere in New England and transported by truck to New York City, and then being hollowed out to make room for new life.

I stood in the sunshine with my hands on the stone, and turned back to look at the museum and up at the sky. A few years ago, the twin shadows of the towers had fallen over this very space, but now there was nothing. Eventually, in a few years perhaps, something would rise to take their place, but for now I looked up into the sky and its emptiness, as blue and bright as it had been that September morning.

This stone, this sky, this space, I thought, looking around. *It is all part of the story. Margaret's story, my grandmother's story, my story. And in the end, all we have left of one another are the stories we that we tell ourselves.*

I could feel my hands as they touched the rough surface of the granite, the cool harbor wind upon my face, the smell of the ocean, the deep and heavy sound of the river as it flowed into the sea.

I looked up again at the empty sky. *They have already come for me once, the way they came for Daniel, the way they came for my grandmother. And they may come for me again. We have never been safe, perhaps we never will be. But if they do come for us,* I told myself, thinking of Michael, *they will come for us both.*

I did not walk back into the museum. Instead, I walked down the concrete staircase and through the tiny park next to the building. The flowerbeds were a mass of dead brown stalks, the grass dry and withered from the salt-laden air.

I knew that the next few days were going to be hard. My parents would be arriving shortly, and we would have to get through the funeral, and the burial and *shivah*. I would somehow also need to find the time to let Robert and Larry and Aviva know what I had discovered about the manuscript.

But first, I thought, I have something else I need to do. I took out my cell phone and dialed Michael's number as I walked toward the subway.

I heard the click of his phone as he answered.

"Hi," he said.

"Hey," I said. "Where are you?"

"Home."

There was a long silence.

"That's good." I finally said. I knew he could hear the tears in my voice, and I felt a tightness in my throat. But I knew what I had to tell him.

"Are you okay?" he asked, his voice sounding concerned over the crackling line.

"I'm fine," I told him quietly. "I'm coming home."

Epilogue

We gathered at my grandmother's grave a year later, for the unveiling. It was the end of February, and it was cold, but there was no snow on the ground. There had been a few flurries in the past weeks or two, but all in all it had been a mild winter so far.

It was early afternoon, and weak winter sunlight streamed through the bare branches of the cemetery trees. Robert and Aviva were there, solemn in their long dark coats. They stood together, and Aviva's little girl, Hannah, lay asleep in her pink winter coat, with her baby cheek pressed against Robert's shoulder.

Jacob had given Aviva a divorce three months after Hannah was born. He couldn't give Angela up, he said, and he was willing to leave the community to be with her. So he did; he left his family, who disowned him, his *shul*, and his wife and daughter, and he and Angela had moved to the West Coast. Fortunately, however, before they departed, Jacob's rabbi had convinced him to give Aviva a *get*, so she would be able to marry again, and their daughter would not grow up without a father.

She and Robert started dating immediately after the Jewish divorce was final. Now they were waiting for the civil divorce to come through. After that, they said, they would marry quietly in the rabbi's study.

Aviva's mother, naturally, was put out by the fact that her daughter was dating so soon after the breakup of her marriage, and furthermore, dating someone who was not interested in forcing her to cover her hair.

But Aviva wasn't interested in listening to her mother. For the first time in her life, she was with someone because she wanted to be, not because she was fulfilling the expectations of her family and her community.

Now, I looked at her; her expression was sad, befitting the gathering. But she looked happier than I had seen her since she had first been matched with Jacob.

Most people, seeing Aviva and Robert together with Hannah,

assumed he was her father. They never corrected anyone. The baby even looked a little like Robert; they both had blue eyes. But whenever Hannah fussed, or tried to grab at something that didn't belong to her – and Aviva assured me she did, quite often – Aviva always sighed and said, "She's her father's daughter." But then she would smile and say, "And thank God she was a girl. If I'd had a boy, Jacob probably would have stayed."

Robert looked sad but contented also, as he held the sleeping baby. He had proven to be a great colleague and a great friend. In the days following my grandmother's death and Hannah's birth, he single-handedly managed the department. Under his guidance, the exhibition presentation came off without a hitch. He then helped Dr. Schiffman compose the museum's reply to the Archdiocese. It stated that I was the legal heir to the Margaret More manuscript, and it was mine to do as I wished. They closed by telling Monsignor Tully – and His Eminence, for that matter - that if I chose to donate the manuscript to the museum, they were more than welcome to come and see it when it was on exhibit.

Robert and Larry also deflected the inevitable harsh questions from the Archdiocese lawyers and politely informed them that they could discuss the matter with me – and the museum's legal team, after I returned from bereavement leave.

And when everything was finished, and the Archdiocese lawyers had backed down, and the exhibition from Berlin was safely installed, Robert painstakingly researched my grandmother's family history for me, tracing her prisoner record from Dachau back through the Bad Arolsen archives in Germany, where he had some friends who helped him with the research.

We discovered that Anna Blumenfeld, prisoner number 462735, had been interred at Dachau in March of 1942, and had been liberated by the 42nd Infantry Division on April 29, 1945. He had traced, as well, the record of her marriage to Aron Blumenfeld, in June of 1937, and the birth of their daughter, Minna, whose death certificate indicated that she had died of typhus in 1942.

Aron, as it turned out, had not been murdered on that summer day as my grandmother had feared. Instead, he had been shipped from labor camp to labor camp all around Poland and Germany. He became ill in late 1944 after years of starvation and incessant hard labor. Finally, he had been sent to Auschwitz-Birkenau in the final months of the war, where he died in the gas chamber. There was no record of their second child.

Robert, along with Larry and Dr. Schiffman, had also contacted a lab that specialized in dating old papers. The lab examined the two sheets of parchment that Robert and I had removed from underneath the manuscript's endpaper. We thought that sending those two separate pages would be less risky than sending the manuscript itself.

The tests proved conclusively that the papers containing Daniel's will and his sonnet to Margaret did, in fact, date back to the Tudor era. We knew from our own examination of the manuscript that the parchment bound in the book had similar characteristics to the paper we had sent them for testing.

When the lab confirmed the test results of the two parchments, we shared with them our own findings about the manuscript. Although they were not willing to certify the manuscript's authenticity without a thorough examination, they did tell us unofficially that we were, in all likelihood, dealing with the real thing.

The manuscript changed everything. Upon hearing about the story of my grandmother's letters, and upon learning exactly what was in the book itself, my mother's immediate response was to contact an Orthodox rabbi and ask if she should undergo a conversion ceremony so that she could "erase the past."

The rabbi asked her what she meant. She told him about the manuscript and about my grandmother's experiences during the Holocaust. To his credit, he assured her that such a ceremony would not be necessary. She told me he also had encouraged her to come in and talk to him about what was troubling her.

I heard the whole story over the phone during one of our weekly calls. I wasn't sure what to say about it at first. Then I asked her what she meant by her comment about erasing the past.

"You know," she said. "This Margaret More person makes us not authentically Jewish, since now we know our family was descended from a Gentile woman."

I was glad she couldn't see my face. "Why does the past matter so much to you? What about the future? What about your grandchildren? They'll also have a parent who isn't Jewish."

"But you are," she said firmly. "So I'm not going to worry about it. At least I know they'll be Jewish because it comes through the mother. I just want to make sure that I am and that you are. Maybe you should have a conversion ceremony, too."

I sighed. Even though she was pissing me off, as usual, I also felt immensely sorry for her. In her voice I now could hear how this new story, coupled with my grandmother's terrible story of suffering and loss, had hurt her and twisted her ideas about who she really was, and who she was afraid of becoming.

I knew she would probably keep calling rabbis until she found one who would tell her what she wanted to hear. She wanted some religious authority to tell her that she was not kosher because of this previously unknown Gentile foremother. And I was also sure that eventually, she would find herself going through some religious ritual that would have a sense of meaning for her — and no one else.

Ironically, it almost seemed as if she was doing penance for some terrible sin – perhaps for not knowing more about her mother's past, or maybe for not preventing me from marrying a non-Jew. As I listened to her voice over the phone, I smiled a little to myself, thinking about the Catholic ideas about sin and repentance which were now part of our family's heritage. How much easier it might be for her, I thought, if only she had a priest she could confess to.

As she talked on, I closed my wedding planner and put it away. There were some plans that I had wanted to talk about with her, but given her current mood, it seemed like such a discussion was out of the question for now. There were certain things between us, I told myself, which were better left unsaid.

One by one and two by two, more people arrived at the graveside. Friends of my grandmother, friends of my parents, friends of ours. Mitzi Feldman arrived with my parents; they helped her along the narrow gravel path. Mitzi moved slowly and there was less spirit in her voice as she conversed with my mother and father. I saw that she had grown frail in the past year. Losing her closest friend, I thought, had taken some of the life from her, too.

A black satin cloth was draped over my grandmother's headstone. At last, Rabbi Beth took her place at the front of the small crowd. Her beautiful black coat made her look older and more serious than usual, but her red hair glowed in the sunlight, a riot of cheer in the midst of her sober clothing.

I watched as Michael bowed his head reverently, along with the others, as the rabbi began to pray. He wore a small black yarmulke nestled in his curling hair.

After Michael and I had read my grandmother's "anonymous" letters together one night, I watched his face move through anger and sadness as he read the story. I saw his grief for the two little girls who never had a chance to be part of our family.

We knew that the Holocaust was part of the history of the family we would be creating together, but we also knew now that we didn't want to be defined by that history alone. Together, we registered for an Intro to Judaism class, which Rabbi Beth happened to be teaching at the local JCC. She greeted us on the first night like old friends.

Having worked at the museum, I thought I knew enough about Judaism to be able to teach the class. But Michael and Aviva were right; I had been so preoccupied with the Holocaust that I hadn't paid attention to the rest of Jewish history.

Every week, the rabbi taught about all sorts of traditions and prayers and customs that I didn't know about. The after-class conversations with Michael, as we took the subway back home, continued throughout the rest of the week. We started celebrating the Sabbath together, and even once had the rabbi and her husband over for a Shabbat dinner.

Now, I turned my head to look at the rabbi, whose rich, reverent voice sounded like warmth itself in the cold winter afternoon.

I tried to keep my mind focused on the prayers, but I felt uncomfortable every time I looked at the cloth-draped stone. Every time I looked around, I expected to see my grandmother, the way she had been at every family event for the last thirty-four years of my life.

I felt my tears starting as I looked over at my mother. She did not seem able to say the prayers either. I watched as she stood in silence, her lips pressed tightly together.

After I had shared with her the letters containing my grandmother's story, I knew how badly she had taken the deaths of her two half-sisters and two aunts, and she was even angrier at my grandmother for keeping them a secret. And now there was no way for my mother to confront my grandmother, or ask why she had kept her own family's history a secret for so long. She would have to learn to live with it, the same way; I told myself, she would have to learn to live with Michael as a son-in-law.

I watched as my father put a protective arm around my mother's shoulders. His face was grim and sad. I had never even met his parents – they died long before I was born – but I could tell he was thinking of them.

"The sages teach us," Rabbi Beth began, "that when a wedding party and a funeral procession meet at a crossroads, the wedding always has the right of way. This is because life always takes precedence over death, and sorrow must always give way to joy. As we remember the life of Anna Altschul, our mother, our grandmother, our friend, we also look to the future, to the fulfillment of her survival through those that she loved most, and knowing the depth of love for her family, which is without end."

"Miriam," she said to my mother, "as you grieve the loss of your mother, remember how her sense of hope lives on in you and in your daughter. Remember your mother's gifts to you, her joy, her stubbornness, her will to live, and her ability to create a new life in the shadow of her terrible history. Most of all, remember the love that was her eternal and unending gift to you and to the future generations of your family.

"And for you, Jill and Michael," she turned to us with a comforting smile, "as you prepare for your wedding in just a couple of months, may you know that in this place here on earth, which represents the crossroads of your sorrow and your loss, that your love for one another has surely given way to great joy in the World to Come."

Now, Rabbi Beth began to sing the memorial prayer – *El Maleh Rachamim – God full of compassion* - which I remembered from the *shivah* service she conducted at my grandmother's apartment. Its melody felt like a thin steel wire being threaded through my heart.

El malei rachamim
shokhen ba-m'romim
ha-m'tzei m'nuchah n'khonah
tachat kanfei ha-sh'khinah
b'ma'alot k'doshim u't'horim
k'zohar ha-rakiah maz'hirim l'nishmot
yakireinu u'k'dosheinu she-hal'khu l'olamam.
Ana ba'al ha-rachamim ha-s'tirem
b'tzel k'nafekha l'olamim
u-tz'ror bitz'ror ha-chayim et nishmatam.
Adonai hu nachalatam
v'yanuchu b'shalom al mish'kavam
V'nomar: Amen.

God filled with compassion,
dwelling in the heavens' heights,
grant shelter beneath the wings of your *Shechinah*,
amid the ranks of the holy and the pure,
illuminating like the brilliance of the skies
the souls of our beloved and our blameless
who have gone to their eternal place of rest.

May you who are the source of mercy
shelter them beneath your wings eternally,
and bind their souls among the living,
that they may rest in peace.
And let us say: Amen

Rabbi Beth removed the black cloth from the stone. I felt a sudden chill as I saw my grandmother's name carved into the granite. In an instant, I felt Michael's arms around me, and I hid my face in the warm dark wool of his coat. He smoothed my hair with his hands and pressed a kiss on my forehead.

Then I looked at the stone again. It didn't seem as frightening to me as it had a moment ago. It was simply her name - her full name – Anna Blumenfeld Altschul, and the dates of her birth and death.

On the other side of the double stone, my grandfather's name and the dates of his birth and death were just as I remembered them, when I last saw them at ten years old. Only now, with my grandmother's name as companion to his, it did not seem as forlorn as it had before.

I watched as each person placed a memorial stone, which had been given to them by the rabbi when they arrived, on top of my grandmother's gravestone. The small, black ovals looked like rough, uncarved gems on the stone's polished surface. After placing their stone, each person walked away down the gravel path, to where the line of parked cars waited along the narrow cemetery road.

I watched as Robert laid his stone next to Aviva's. He switched Hannah's small body to his other shoulder. She murmured a little in her sleep, and then the three of them made their way back down to their car.

My father and mother, the rabbi, and Michael and I were the last ones left. My parents spent a silent moment staring at the double headstone, their heads bowed.

My mother then turned her head and looked at me, and saw my fingers firmly entwined with Michael's. She placed her stone atop my grandmother's grave. Then she and my father walked away, her head against his shoulder, his arm guiding her down the gravel path.

Finally, Michael removed a tiny artifact case from the breast pocket of his coat and handed it to me. I opened it, and carefully removed the small dead rose that Minna had picked and given to my grandmother more than sixty years earlier.

Michael and I walked toward the gravestone. With his hand over mine, we placed the dead rose next to the small pile of memorial stones as Rabbi Beth watched us in silence. We had explained the rose's significance to her, knowing that there was a Jewish prohibition against flowers at an unveiling; because in the midst of death, there should not be any symbol of life. She had understood completely, knowing that in giving this flower to my grandmother, who had been pregnant with Chava when she took it from Minna's small hand, we knew that we were remembering all three of them.

Rabbi Beth led us away from the grave. My fingers were still entwined with Michael's, and I could feel the warmth of his hand in my own cold one.

I knew that the rose was probably too old and brittle to survive, and that it would not be here the next time we came to this place. But that was all right. It would bear the snow, and the rain, and the sunlight for as long as it could, and then the wind would carry it to some other place, the remnants of its petals merging with the air and the light, as fine and fragile as dust.

AUTHOR'S NOTE

This book is a work of fiction. While some of the characters, such as Margaret and Thomas More and William Roper, and some of the places, such as the Museum of Jewish Heritage – A Living Memorial to the Holocaust, are real, all have been used fictitiously.

Although Margaret More was a scholar and a writer, none of her work, to date, has ever been discovered – despite the fact that her husband, William Roper, went on to publish a definitive biography of Thomas More, even though Roper was not known to be a writer nor a scholar.

And although it is believed that Henry VIII did appoint Jewish scholars to his court to research Talmudic responses with regard to the annulment of his marriage to Katherine of Aragon, all matters pertaining to this research in this book are purely speculative.

All other characters are inventions of the author's imagination. Any resemblance to any persons, living or dead, is purely coincidental.

ACKNOWLEDGEMENTS

Throughout my career as a writer, I have been fortunate to have met and worked with people who believed in my talent, and in this story. I offer infinite thanks to my teachers, Joan Mellen, Jeanne Murray Walker, Sara Horowitz, David Bradley, and the members of Temple University's Class of 1995 Fiction Writing program, especially Frank Lauro (z"l), who first gave me the courage to try writing a novel. I am also grateful to Rosalie Siegel for years of professional help and advice in bringing this story to fruition.

I also offer heartfelt gratitude to my Museum family: to Esther Brumberg and Bonnie Gurewitsch, whose help with research was infinitely valuable; to Dr. David Altshuler, Dr. David Marwell, Ivy Barsky, Dr. Louis Levine, Sharon Steinbach, Tina Kunkin Schweid, Tracy Figueroa, Rachel Woursell, Zahava Mandel, Deborah Tropp, Dr. Jay Eidelman, Dr. Ilana Abramovitch, Elissa Schein, Rabbi Audrey Marcus and Warren Shalewitz, and all those whose deep knowledge, love, and friendship gave me good reason for the homesickness that motivated this story. And no thanks could ever be sufficient to express gratitude to my friend, mentor, and role model Abby Spilka, who hired me for the gig all those years ago.

My thanks also to my Larchmont Temple family, whose constant support is a source of inspiration: Rabbi Jeffrey and Susan Sirkman, Rabbi Mara Nathan, Cantor Fredda Mendelson; cherished friends: Lee Perlman, Rabbi Debra Goldstein, Carolyn Kamlet, Meg Fienberg, Stacey Chervin Sigda, Carol Scharff, Mark and Yvette Goorevitch, Andrew and Marnie Foster Marks, and Selma Bernstein. I also thank the LT Outreach Committee, who helped see this project through to publication, especially Ann Gittelman, Jill Sarkozi and Beth Belisle, all of whom were wonderful readers and friends. Special thanks to Rosel and Arthur Wolf for all of their *menschlikeit*.

The Westchester Writers' Group (SIG) has provided countless years of support, smarts, and sustenance for which I am grateful: Sarah

Bracey White, Elizabeth A. Sachs, Donald Capone, Jack Rosenbluth, Linda Simone, and David Charney (z"l).

Special thanks to Julie L. Cohen for her beautiful photographic eye, and to Howard Levine, whose vision for the cover made this story come to life. I am also grateful to the team at O Books who believed in this story and worked tirelessly to bring it to the reading world. The kind and generous staff of Borders Books and Music in Eastchester, NY, cared for me during the process of writing and always made me welcome at my regular table.

Finally, thanks to my friends and family, who have put up with me, and with this book, for more than fifteen years: Megan Kearney Bailie, Christine Gustafson, Mary Kathleen Karczewski Zeman, Dana Phelan, Bill Edelstein, Ellen Thurmond, Stephanie Ives-Bartow, Danielle Freni, David Lacher, Kira Citron, Dom Cervi, Hayley Kobilinsky, Todd Napolitano, Jennifer Thatcher, my online community of Facebook *Bookseller's* friends and supporters, and the extended Ignelzi clan. My mother, Marie Rosenthal, was the original source for Margaret More, and is the best person I know. Laura McNerney is an unwavering champion and evidence that I totally lucked out on the sibling lottery. Connor and Ryan McNerney give me reasons to believe in love, life and joy every single day.

And finally, inexpressible gratitude for immeasurable generosity: Without Amy Dixon, there would have been no time. Without Jeanine Cotter, there would have been no opportunity. Without Sally Srok Friedes, there would have been no future. And without Richard Leonard, I would never have been a writer.

BOOKS

O is a symbol of the world, of oneness and unity. In different cultures it also means the "eye," symbolizing knowledge and insight. We aim to publish books that are accessible, constructive and that challenge accepted opinion, both that of academia and the "moral majority."

Our books are available in all good English language bookstores worldwide. If you don't see the book on the shelves ask the bookstore to order it for you, quoting the ISBN number and title. Alternatively you can order online (all major online retail sites carry our titles) or contact the distributor in the relevant country, listed on the copyright page.

See our website www.o-books.net for a full list of over 500 titles, growing by 100 a year.

And tune in to myspiritradio.com for our book review radio show, hosted by June-Elleni Laine, where you can listen to the authors discussing their books.

MySpiritRadio